Choosing LOVE

MB PANICHI

BELLA
BOOKS

2017

T0154149

Copyright © 2017 by MB Panichi

Bella Books, Inc.
P.O. Box 10543
Tallahassee, FL 32302

All rights reserved. No part of this book may be reproduced or transmitted in any form or by any means, electronic or mechanical, including photocopying, without permission in writing from the publisher.

This is a work of fiction. Names, characters, businesses, places, events and incidents are either the products of the author's imagination or used in a fictitious manner. Any resemblance to actual persons, living or dead, or actual events is purely coincidental. The publisher does not have any control over and does not assume any responsibility for author or third-party websites or their content.

Printed in the United States of America on acid-free paper.

First Bella Books Edition 2017

Editor: Amanda Jean
Cover Designer: Linda Callaghan

ISBN: 978-1-59493-547-3

PUBLISHER'S NOTE
The scanning, uploading, and distribution of this book via the Internet or via any other means without the permission of the publisher is illegal and punishable by law. Please purchase only authorized electronic editions, and do not participate in or encourage electronic piracy of copyrighted materials. Your support of the author's rights is appreciated.

Other Bella Books by MB Panichi

Running Toward Home
Saving Morgan

Acknowledgments

Choosing Love is my first foray into first person narrative and romance minus the science fiction or adventure. It's been a labor of love and a challenge, and I have a lot of humans to thank this time around. Please forgive me if I've missed anyone!

As always, love, thanks and squishy hugs to my BABA pals, who keep me inspired and encourage me to forge ahead. And to Lori Lake, whose writer's retreats actually allow me to get some work done!! I love all you guys!!! Special thanks to Sheryl Wright, who helped me try to stay true to Takoda's Indigenous culture. I very much hope that I have not made any faux paus with Takoda or her family.

Huge thanks, also, to my editor at Bella, Amanda Jean. Her guidance, suggestions and questions helped me flesh out the manuscript and make it so much better. Many thanks and appreciation to Jessica and Linda and Becky and everyone else at Bella Books, for all the great work they do and for allowing me to share my words with the world at large! You guys are the best!!!!!!

Special hugs and love to my wife, April, for her support when I am distracted by writing, and to my dog, Maci, for sitting on my legs and helping me stay warm while I work (and getting me out of the recliner and away from the laptop for snacks, potty breaks, and play time)! Thanks to my extended family for their unconditional love and support, and to my very good friend Bonnie, who wasn't going to be friends with the office manager thirty years ago!

And, last but never least, thanks to all you fine and wonderful readers!! I couldn't do it without you!! Your support always makes me smile in wonder!!

About the Author

MB Panichi lives in Richfield, Minnesota in a little house on the corner with her wife and their two dogs. She has two previous books with Bella, *Saving Morgan* and its sequel, "*Running Toward Home*," which are both Sci-Fi/Adventure/Romances. In real life, MB holds down a day job as a QA Analyst. She still obsesses about her drums, her "heavy metal" band days and Star Wars.

CHAPTER ONE

Summer sun blazed through the south-facing window in my parents' kitchen. I set a plate of lunch in front of my dad, then joined him at the table.

He studied the ham sandwich, chips and apple slices for a second before folding his newspaper and setting it aside. "Thanks, Amry." I watched while he took a big bite of the sandwich and smiled around it. "This is good."

"Glad you like it."

I wasn't any kind of a cook, but since I'd arrived a little before noon, I figured it didn't hurt to make him some lunch. I'd driven up from Minneapolis to my hometown of Hibbing in northern Minnesota. I planned to stay with Dad that night and the next and then finish my week-long vacation chilling with my friend Rose at the family cabin twenty minutes north of town.

A widower in his late sixties, Ray Marasich remained roguishly handsome. His gray hair was combed back from a deep widow's peak, and he still had a solidly built physique from working as a laborer in the taconite mines all his life.

He finished another bite and washed it down with soda. "So, what's new?"

"Not much. Work's busy but good. I've got an editing project and I started writing another novel. Other than that, just the usual." My reply was noncommittal, but I had learned long ago to avoid mentioning my lesbian friends and gay-related events. Previous confrontations had been between Mom and me. Dad had never once brought up the subject. I always took Dad's silence as agreement with her opinion. My siblings, on the other hand, continued to be vocal in their distaste for my lifestyle.

I asked, "What's been going on around here?"

"Haven't seen much of your brother and sister lately. Bethany called last night. She's good. Her boys are still playing baseball and Stephanie has those dancing classes, so Beth is busy hauling the kids around. Tom hasn't called in a few days."

"Huh. Yeah, I haven't talked to them either." The truth was, the twins and I weren't close and never had been. Other than emergencies or major holidays, we didn't contact each other, and when we did communicate it was in innocuous generalities— their children, the weather, sports or Dad.

"When is your friend Rose coming tomorrow?"

"Early afternoon. I figured the three of us could have dinner before she and I head up to the cabin."

"I brought some pop up for you girls the other day when I went fishing. There's gas in the boathouse for the boat."

"Thanks, Dad."

My best friend Rose and I spent a week up at my parents' cabin every year. Dad and Rose got along well, bantering back and forth about fishing and Minnesota Twins baseball. Mom had been much more reticent. She'd liked Rose until I'd come out, which was when she'd decided she didn't want the two of us at the cabin alone because it didn't "look right." It had taken a while to convince Mom that Rose was straight.

After lunch, Dad settled in to watch the ball game, so I decided to take my bicycle out for a ride. I didn't feel like watching the Twins lose again.

I retreated to the bedroom my sister Bethany and I had once shared. I changed into black spandex bike shorts and a loose, quick-dry T-shirt. A glance in the mirror reflected an average-looking woman with short, spiky brown hair and close-set brown eyes—a stereotypical thirty-something dyke. The shorts and T-shirt fit decently enough. My legs were strong from biking, and there was a slight curve at my hips, mostly hidden by the long T-shirt. My arms showed some definition, and my skin was slightly tanned from hours spent on my bike.

I snatched up my sunglasses, wallet, keys, cell phone and bike shoes. On my way out, I stopped at the kitchen sink to fill two bike bottles.

Sitting down on the cement back stoop, I velcroed up my bike shoes, then click-clacked to the garage to retrieve my mint-green Cannondale road bike from the rear carrier rack on my car. I settled the water bottles in their cages and stuffed everything else into my handlebar bag. A quick check of the tires and the brakes, and I was good to go.

Dad stood in the doorway watching me strap on my helmet and gloves, shaking his head. "All that just to ride a bike?" he asked through the open screen.

"Don't you have a game to watch?" I grinned to take the sting out of the question as I donned my sunglasses.

Dad laughed.

I swung onto the bike, clipped my left shoe and pushed off down the driveway. "Be back in a while!"

"Be careful, Amry!"

I waved as I rolled into the street, then powered north toward the bike trail. I pedaled through an older section of town a couple blocks north of my parents' house and picked up the dirt track at the end of the street that connected to a paved bike trail.

The Mesabi Trail crossed northern Minnesota's Iron Range. About seventy miles long, the paved bike path wound past open-pit mines and through woods and small towns. Beyond the trail, iron-ore tailings dumps rose into the sky like flat-topped red-orange mountains. Two or three hundred feet high, the "dumps" were leftover piles of rock and gravel dug out of the open-pit iron-ore and taconite mines that defined the landscape of the entire Iron Range.

Nature had reclaimed much of the land since the original mines had been dug. Pines, birch and poplars forested all but the steepest drops of rock. The air smelled of dusty grass and weeds, and the early August sun beat down on the asphalt, heating my head and shoulders. Sweat trickled down my back and my legs as I pumped up a short, steep incline. The familiar motions brought a sense of freedom and simplicity that I craved.

I rode past a long-forgotten junkyard and under a divided highway, cruising easily along a relatively straight stretch. I glanced at the watch strapped around my handlebars and decided I'd ride another hour or so before I turned back.

The trail was in great shape other than the occasional weed poking up through miniscule breaks in the tar, and I built up my speed as I pedaled around a wide corner. A few hundred feet ahead, someone leaned over a bike that rested upside down at the edge of the trail. As I closed in, I realized it was a woman bent over the rear wheel. Man or woman, any decent biker would check to make sure all was well. I stopped beside her.

"Hi, need a hand?"

She lifted her head and my heart stuttered.

"Hi," she said. "No, I'm okay. Just a stupid flat." She smiled and held up the wheel she'd removed. Her dark hair hung in a long ponytail, accenting her tanned complexion, deep chocolate eyes, high cheekbones and straight nose. I wondered if she were of Native American heritage. When she straightened, I took in the totality of her lean, solid build. She had to be nearly six feet tall.

I tried not to drool as I said, "I've got CO2 cartridges if you need 'em to pump up the new tube."

"Really? Thanks. They'd be a hell of a lot more effective than my little pump." Her voice poured over me like sweet molasses, slow and low. Christ on a bike, she was hot.

I swung off my road bike. Somehow I even remembered to unclip my shoes from the pedals so I wouldn't fall on my ass.

"Nice ride," she said.

"Thanks. So's yours." *Well, that was lame, Amry.* But she was riding a high-end, fully suspended Specialized mountain bike, with disc brakes. If I weren't already practically drooling over her, I'd be drooling over her bike. Attempting to shake off the idiocy, I fished in my seat bag for the promised CO_2 cartridges and trigger pump.

She very efficiently removed the bad tube from her tire with strong, long-fingered hands. I love those kinds of hands. "I'm Takoda, by the way," she said as she worked. "Takoda Running Bear. Thanks again for stopping."

"Amry Marasich. Nice to meet you." *Really nice, in fact.*

She sat down on the edge of the trail with a new tube and her wheel and started feeding it around the rim. "Are you new around here? I've never seen you on the trail before."

"Not new, really. I grew up here, but I don't get home much."

She shot me a quick grin, and I nearly swooned. It wasn't like me to be attracted to someone so quickly, but seriously, I could have stood there all day watching her fix flats. "You're vacationing, then?" she asked.

I felt my face flush. "Um, yeah. Spending the weekend in town visiting my dad, then a friend and I are going to spend a week up at the cabin."

"What lake?"

"Big Sturgeon. Not too far from the state park. We spend a week every year."

"You picked a great week then. The weather is supposed to stay nice." Takoda worked in silence for a few minutes and finally got her inner tube settled properly. "You have that CO_2?"

"Sure." I handed over a couple cartridges and the trigger.

"Thanks again. Sadly, mine are in my other bike bag. I hadn't been intending to take a long ride today, but when I got going, I kept pedaling."

"How far did you come?"

"Just past Virginia."

"Nice. That's at least, what, twenty miles?"

Takoda nodded and puffed a little air into the tire, checking the seating again to make sure the tube wasn't sticking out anywhere. Then she emptied the cartridge into the tire. "That ought'a do it," she said, checking the tire for hardness.

She handed back the unused cartridge and the trigger. By the time I put the tools away, she had the tire on and was getting the chain reseated. Takoda flipped the bike upright in a smooth motion, then leaned over to scoop up the empty CO_2 cartridge and the flat tube. She stuffed those into her seat pack. "How far are you going?"

"Probably ride for another hour before I turn back. You?"

Takoda flashed me a brilliant smile. I was appropriately dazzled. "I'm not working today, so no real plan. You want some company while you ride?"

And what red-blooded American Lesbian would turn down a woman who looked like Takoda Running Bear? Not me, that was for damned sure. "Sure. Which way?"

She nodded in the direction I was already headed. "I was thinking I should head back anyway, and now I'll have company for a while."

"Works for me," I agreed.

Takoda put on her helmet. She straddled her mountain bike, clipped into one pedal and pushed off. I paced her as we rode side by side. We must have made a slightly comical pair because her mountain bike was about four sizes taller than my road bike.

I asked, "You're from Virginia?"

"Born on the Leech Lake Reservation, but grew up in Alaska. My folks moved us back to Minnesota when I was about nine years old."

"Alaska, huh? I bet you can handle the winter here."

Takoda laughed. "Yeah, this is pretty mild, sometimes. Dad worked for NOAA doing weather research, so we lived way out in the wilderness while he studied glaciers and climate change. When he got laid off, we ended up living outside of Duluth. He was a meteorologist for one of the news stations there before he retired and bought land up here."

We spun up a steep hill and started down again. I caught my breath as we upshifted into another flat stretch.

"What do you do for a living?" I had to admit, I was curious.

"I work for the Forestry Service. We help with the local fisheries, monitoring the health of the lakes and the forests, and then the law enforcement side, monitoring the trails and lakes, hunting and fishing laws, that kind of thing." She glanced at me with a wicked grin. "Do ya have a trail pass?" she asked pointedly.

Huh? I was busy thinking about her in uniform with a gun at her waist. "Uh. No. Should I have?"

Takoda Running Bear laughed and my insides melted. "Yes, you should. I could ticket you, if I were on duty."

Guiltily, I admitted, "It never even crossed my mind."

"Don't worry about it. I can get you one, if we ride again, if you want."

If we ride again? If I want? Like, duh. "Yeah, that'd be great," I managed.

"What about you? What do you do?"

"My day job is editing for an entertainment magazine in Minneapolis, but I also edit novels for a smallish publisher. I write too. Fiction. It's not glamorous like the Forestry Service, but it pays the bills."

"Forestry isn't glamorous. Mostly it's all about mosquitoes, mud and frostbite." She made a face. "I like to read. What kind of fiction do you write?"

Ah, and there's the hundred-dollar question, I thought. What would the reaction be when I told her I wrote lesbian novels? I got a sense that maybe, just maybe, she was family, but that could have just been my own biased reaction to the fact that she was hot as hell. If I were wrong, though, at least we weren't on a tandem, and I could ride away if she took offense. I took the plunge, and the words spilled out in a rush. "Lesbian fiction. Sci-fi, romance, adventure, that kind of thing."

I couldn't bring myself to look at her expression.

"Oh, cool, like Missy Good or Karin Kallmaker?"

My head snapped toward her, and I nearly fell off my damned bike. I quickly turned back to the road. "Uh, not so well known or prolific, but, yeah." I snuck a glance and caught her giving me a once-over.

"Sweet," she said. "So, have you met any of them?"

I grinned. "A lot of them, and I can honestly say they are an amazing group of women, and lesbian writers' conferences are really great hug-fests!"

"Oh my God, I am so jealous!"

We discussed our favorite lesbian authors, touched on gay rights and politics, environmentalism and music, and found we agreed on most topics.

Our discussions took us all the way through to the Kinney trailhead before I decided I'd better head back. It killed me to have to end our ride, but I knew Dad would want to go out for something to eat, and I was going to need a shower.

I turned my bike around, and we stood there, straddling our rides. I wanted to ask for her phone number. I wanted to see her again, even if I was only going to be around for a week.

Takoda cocked her head and gave a sheepish half-grin. "So, do you think maybe you'd want to get together again while you're here?" she asked. "I mean, it's been fun talking to you." She shrugged embarrassedly. It was adorable.

"That would be really great." I was certain I was grinning like an idiot.

After exchanging phone numbers and making tentative plans to meet, I rode home powered by pure adrenaline. My feet barely touched the pedals, and my bike sailed on wings over the asphalt. I had Takoda Running Bear's phone number, and she wanted to see me again.

When I reached my parents' house, a monstrous black SUV clogged up the driveway, forcing me to ride on the grass to get around it. I pulled up in front of the garage, unclipping before I put my foot down on the cracked cement. I didn't recognize the vehicle, but figured it had to belong to either Bethany or Tom. My guess was Bethany because I was pretty sure Tom drove a truck.

The screen door opened and slammed shut as I took off my helmet and gloves. My younger sister strode toward me, flipping her dark blond hair over her shoulder. "About time you got home, Amry."

I wondered if it were possible for Bethany to begin a conversation in a nonconfrontational way. "I was only gone a couple of hours, Bethy." I used the nickname because it pissed her off.

The door opened and slammed shut again.

"Aunt Amry!"

My nine-year-old niece Stephanie jumped off the stoop and rushed past her mother to throw her arms around my waist. Her blond hair bobbed in a ponytail at the top of her head. She wore pink shorts and a matching pink-and-gray T-shirt splashed with sequined hearts. She exclaimed, "Wow, that's a nice bike!"

I gave her a big hug. "Hiya, Stephie, how ya doing?"

"I'm good. We got to go to Target today! Mom said you were staying here this weekend. You wanna go to the park later?"

I had forgotten how fast nine-year-olds talk. "Sure, we can walk to the park if it's okay with your mom." Anything to get away from my scowling sister. "When did you get here?"

Bethany said, "A while ago. I thought you were visiting Dad. Where have you been?"

I leaned down to remove my bike shoes. "We had lunch and then he wanted to watch the game, so I decided to take a ride. I'm visiting, not babysitting. If you're so worried about it, you could probably spend a little more time down here. Dad said he hasn't seen you in a couple weeks."

"Some of us have a life," she snapped and turned back to the house.

"Whatever." Arguing wasn't worth the effort.

Stephanie asked, "Can I ride your bike, Aunt Amry?"

"My bike is way too big for you, hon. But if you brought your bike here, we could go for a ride together."

"Okay. My bike is a girls' bike. Why is yours a boys' bike?"

"Because my bike is for going a long way, and they only make bikes like mine as boys' bikes." I didn't bother to mention that I wouldn't be caught dead on a girl's bike. It had been a major cause for contention when I was Stephanie's age.

Typically, though, my niece just went right past it. "Oh. Okay. Maybe someday I can get a bike that goes real far too. Let's go see Grampa."

"Lead on, kid."

I followed her into the house, carrying my bike shoes, wallet and phone. Stephanie scampered ahead of me and into the living room, while I slipped down the hallway to put my stuff away. I grabbed some clean clothes and headed to the basement for a quick shower. It might have been rude not to join the family right away, but I needed to get cleaned up before I was ready to face them.

When I padded into the living room fifteen minutes later, barefoot and with wet hair, Bethany gave me a disgusted glower from her place on the love seat. I wasn't sure what she was annoyed by, other than my existence, so I ignored her. Dad rested in his recliner with Stephanie sitting on his lap. The Twins' baseball game was still on with the volume turned down. I squinted to see the score. They were losing again. Friggin' Twinkies.

Dad asked, "Did you have a good ride?"

I nodded and settled myself on the sofa. "It was nice. It's a beautiful day for it."

"You're the only person I know that's ever on those damned trails." He teased me with that line every time I visited.

"As it happens, I met a very nice person on the trail today. Helped her with a flat tire and rode with her for a while before I turned back."

"That was nice of you."

I couldn't help smiling at the thought of my new friend. "It worked out okay."

Dad just nodded, oblivious to any undercurrents, and turned his focus back to the ball game.

Bethany sent me a suspicious glance, and I knew she was mentally accusing me of picking up chicks on the bike trail. Or maybe I was reading into her attitude problem.

Stephanie asked, "Mom, can we bring my bike over tomorrow so me and Aunt Amry can go for a bike ride?"

Bethany said to me, "I don't want you on the trail with her. Just around the neighborhood."

"As you wish. I'll be heading up to the lake tomorrow with my friend Rose, so it'll have to be early."

Dad said, "Tom and his wife and the boys are stopping by tomorrow morning too."

I sighed. Wonderful. The whole family together. I hoped Rose would show up early.

CHAPTER TWO

Sunday morning, Dad and I sat at the kitchen table with the local papers scattered between us. I sipped a cup of coffee, splitting my attention between the email on my laptop, chatting with Dad and the vague but titillating memories of last night's dreams of Takoda Running Bear.

"Wonder what time Tom and his family will be here." Dad glanced out the side door, then at the clock.

"I'm sure it won't be too long." I knew Dad was anxious to see his grandkids. I didn't mind seeing them either, but I wasn't so excited about spending time with my siblings. I took a few seconds to consider leaving for the cabin before they arrived but forced myself to relax. Running away was a cop-out.

Still, I'd rather avoid the twins than see them. Was it cowardice or the simple avoidance of confrontation? Was it wrong that I didn't particularly want to deal with my sister examining me as though my soul could never be saved? Was it a sign of weakness that I didn't want my brother to scoff at me?

The old hurts had long ago morphed into anger that sprung up easily and quickly. Most of the time, I squashed it and put on a pleasant face. But I was tired of playing the game and sick of dealing with their crap just to keep peace in the family.

The house rattled as a silver F-350 Super Cab lumbered into the driveway. Dad hurried to the door. I stood off to the side and watched through the picture window overlooking the driveway.

My brother Tom strode around the front of the truck. Tall and muscular, he'd inherited Dad's dark good looks and height. His wife, Darlene, slipped down from the passenger seat and their two boys piled out of the backseat.

Darlene led the way into the kitchen, stopping to give my dad a hug and greet him. She toed off her low cowboy boots. I'd always thought of Darlene as Tom's trophy wife. She had long, wavy blond hair and blue eyes. Narrow-framed and slim, she could have been a model in her tight jeans and neatly tucked-in Western-style blouse. "Hello Amry."

"Hi Darlene. How are you?"

Towheaded and husky, twelve-year-old Joey slipped past her and threw himself at my dad, who wrapped him in a big hug.

Tom came in next, kicking off his sneakers. "Hey Dad, Amry." Tom's glance flicked over me, and there was no warmth in his greeting. I simply nodded an acknowledgment.

Joey yelled, "Hi Aunt Amry!" as he stepped away from Dad, then announced, "I'm goin' outside," and disappeared back out the door.

Tom and Darlene's older son, Nikko, walked into the house as Joey ran out. He greeted Dad, then me and gave me a strong hug, which I returned heartily. I was glad my sixteen-year-old nephew still felt comfortable showing his affection.

"How're you doing, Nikko?" I had to tip my head to meet his gaze.

"I'm okay. It's really cool to see you."

The door opened again, and Bethany, her husband David, and their three kids trooped into the house to another round of hugs for Grandpa. Bethany's kids couldn't have been more different from each other. Stephanie rushed in, bright and happy. Her younger brother Peter greeted Dad quietly, then slipped back outside, presumably to play with Joey. Eleven-year-old Theo sulked into the kitchen and looked over Nikko's shoulder as Nikko flipped through an ad from an electronics store. Stephanie settled happily in my lap when I sat down.

Bethany's husband, David, greeted me with a smile. We did the usual "how are you" routine as he took the empty chair across from me. David wasn't a bad guy; just quiet and unobtrusive.

Bethany got coffee for herself and David and sat at the head of the table farthest from me. Darlene got coffee for herself, topped off Dad's cup and mine and set a soda in front of Tom before sitting down on my left.

Tom grabbed the sports section, already talking baseball with Dad and David as he flipped pages. Darlene gestured to my laptop. "Working on anything new?" she asked.

I was never certain if her interest was real or if she were being polite. "I'm about halfway into the first draft a new novel."

Nikko asked, "This a new laptop?"

"Had it a few months. Take a look if you want. It's not super-high-end, but it's pretty speedy. It's hooked up to my hot spot, so there's Internet, but don't stream any video, okay?"

"Sure. Thanks." He lifted the computer onto his lap.

Darlene cautioned, "Don't break anything, Nikko."

He made a face. I could practically hear the implied "Duh."

"Not much there he can break."

"You kids and your electronic crap," Dad said. His eyes twinkled, softening his words.

Nikko said, "Anytime you want to learn to use one, Grandpa, let me know. I'll set you up."

"You're all gonna ruin your eyes staring at those screens."

Theo leaned over Nikko's shoulder. "Does it got any games?"

"Sorry, Theo, no games, unless you count Mahjong."

His expression told me how boring I was.

"I got a new game for my LeapPad," Steph said. "It's really cool."

"It's a stupid kids' game," Theo muttered.

Darlene steered the conversation in a different direction, and topics bounced around the table, varying from news about the taconite mines to the kids' summer events. I sipped my coffee and decided it was possible I wouldn't be driven insane in the couple of hours before Rose arrived.

Then Nikko asked, "Aunt Amry, is this your new book?"

Aw, crap. The conversation around me stopped. I glanced at the screen. "Yeah, it is."

"Can I read it?"

You could, but I'd likely be tarred and feathered, and you'd probably lose your eyeballs from reading lesbian sex scenes. "It's not finished yet, so I'd rather you didn't."

"Okay."

Over the top of her coffee cup, Bethany narrowed her eyes. "Perhaps you shouldn't let him snoop around on your personal laptop."

I met her gaze. "Nikko is respectful and knows to ask first."

Under his breath, Nikko said, "I'm not stupid."

At that, Darlene smiled. It made me think better of her for not jumping on him.

Conversation picked back up, and I let it go on around me while keeping an eye on Nikko and Theo. For the most part, I mostly chatted with and listened to Stephanie, who rattled on excitedly about her friends and learning tumbling and cartwheels in her dance class.

I jerked in surprise when my cell phone buzzed in my pocket and the message tone sounded a little too loudly over the conversation. I reached around my niece so I could get the phone out of my shorts' cargo pocket. I figured it was Rose letting me know her ETA.

When I glanced at the name on the text message, I couldn't stop the delight that spread across my face. Keeping the phone out of Stephanie's view, I swiped my thumb to unlock the screen.

Takoda: Hey, Amry. I really enjoyed our ride yesterday. Can you do lunch tomorrow?

Oh. My. God. I barely held back an excited cheer as I rapidly texted back.

Me: Absolutely! What time?
Takoda: 12:30?
Me: Perfect. Wanna meet at Riverside? or Bimbo's?
Takoda: Let's do Riverside.
Me: Great!! :)
Takoda: Super! Gotta run—at work. TTYL!
Me: C U tomorrow :)

Un-fucking-believable! I wanted to kiss the phone. Actually, I wanted to kiss Takoda. A wave of giddiness splashed over me.

"Who the hell are you texting?" Tom asked. "You're grinning like an idiot."

Startled out of my ecstatic reverie, I locked the phone. "Just a friend."

Bethany's blue eyes bored into me. "Was the message so important you had to answer it immediately? It's impolite to have your phone ringing off the hook and be texting when you're visiting."

My giddiness drained away in a flash. "Get off your soapbox, Beth. I wasn't part of your conversation so I didn't interrupt anything. And yes, it was an important message."

"If it was so important, who was it?"

Her holier-than-thou tone grated on every nerve in my body. I fought the urge to slap her silly. "Nobody you know."

I thought she was going to push the issue, but instead she turned back to Darlene and picked up their conversation. The guys had already gone back to theirs. I leaned back, relieved to have an end to the inquisition. I asked Stephanie a question about her dance class, and she was off and running.

I did not intend to discuss Takoda Running Bear with my family.

CHAPTER THREE

Rose had arrived at my dad's house early Sunday afternoon and the two of us headed up to the cabin shortly after to begin our annual northland getaway. On Monday morning I relaxed and treated myself to my first idyllic, lazy vacation morning at the cabin. A steaming cup of coffee rested on the faded vinyl tablecloth beside my open writing journal. The morning sun poured into the kitchen, lightening the wood-paneled décor and drawing a bright line up the river-rock fireplace that marked the center of the cabin's main room.

A fresh breeze blew through the open windows, smelling of pine and grass. I gazed out the front picture window that overlooked the lake. The water rippled and glittered under a cloudless blue sky. Stands of birches and a few old pines grew along our property line and down the steep hill to water.

I returned to scribbling in my journal, trying to capture my sense of peace with words. Even if I only spent a week a year up here in the woods, it was a place that spoke to my soul and gave me time to slow down and step back from my life. Not that my life was so horrible or crazy. But it was nice to be able to put work aside, not worry about the world and maybe put things in perspective. Usually, this was the time when I got some good work done on a writing project. Rose and I would spend a few hours hiking and biking or out on the boat, and the in-between times I would write while she read. Rose was one of the few people in my life with whom it was okay to have silences.

Usually, in the serenity of the cabin and nature, my journaling tended toward philosophical meanderings and quiet musings on life in general. Today, visions of Takoda Running Bear and thoughts about our lunch date dominated the pages, and my jumbled stream of consciousness was anything but peaceful. Instead, the scrawling cursive covering the narrow-lined pages was hormonal, anxious, wondering if it was the right thing to meet her, wondering if she felt the same way, and then squashing that last part because I was just too average to be noticed.

"I knew you'd be up early, driving yourself crazy."

Rose shuffled out of the master bedroom that opened into the main room. She wore an oversized T-shirt and shorts, her long hair tousled, and she rubbed her eyes as she wandered into the kitchen area.

"It's almost noon," I pointed out with a teasing smile.

She waved a hand as she got a mug from the cupboard and poured herself a cup of coffee. "Whatever. I'm on vacation." She dropped into the chair across from me.

I held up my pen. "I was journaling."

Rose snorted. "And daydreaming about your hot date."

"Shut up, smartass. You want help getting the boat out before I go?"

"Naw, I got it."

"You going fishing, then?"

Rose sipped on her coffee and stretched. "For a while, anyway. But I'm not in a hurry."

I closed my notebook and pushed it aside. Rose was the receptionist/office manager at the magazine publisher where I worked as an editor. She'd been there all of the ten years I had. Our friendship had started with running out for lunch, then progressed to hiking and biking and annual trips to the cabin. Rose made me laugh. She was so practical about life and relationships and the world. It didn't matter that she was straighter than straight and I very much was not. We got along like sisters.

Rose asked, "So, are you nervous?"

"Yeah."

"She's probably nervous too, you know."

"I don't know. She's a cop. Cops don't get nervous meeting someone for lunch."

Rose laughed. "Most cops spend half their shifts crapping their pants. Don't worry so much. Just pretend you're meeting a friend from high school or something."

"Oh, and that should make me feel so much better." School hadn't been that great an experience. I hadn't been part of the "in" crowd, hadn't dated, and only had a handful of friends who were as geeky as me.

"Maybe you should have spiked your coffee."

"Yeah, well, look who's talking. You were at least this pathetic before you went out with what's-his-name last month."

She shrugged. "I got over it. And hopefully your lunch will go better than my lousy date with what's-his-name."

I glanced at the clock. "Gotta get dressed." I downed the rest of my coffee and retreated to the tiny front bedroom, where I picked through the clothes in my duffel bag. What the hell was I going to wear? I hadn't packed for dating. All I had with me were cargo shorts, spandex bike shorts and T-shirts. With a frustrated sigh I decided on army-green cargo shorts and a black Joan Jett concert T-shirt. If Takoda didn't appreciate my sense of style, then so be it.

When I came back into the kitchen, Rose gave me an assessing once-over and raised her coffee mug in salute. "Well, it isn't preppy chic, but I suppose if you're going for relaxed butch, it'll do."

"I sure as hell hope so." I grabbed my car keys from the fireplace mantel and shoved my wallet into a pocket. "Wish me luck."

"Enjoy your lunch. I'll be waiting to hear all the intimate details." Rose leaned back with her coffee and a book. I wrapped my courage around me and headed out the door.

Fifteen minutes later, I turned into the mostly unpaved parking lot at the Riverside Inn Bar and Restaurant. The weathered one-story building had been here since I was a kid. Cracked paint and missing shakes from the front façade showed its age. The sign at the parking entrance had faded to chipped pastels.

As I stepped out of the car, Takoda rolled up in a black four-door Jeep Wrangler with its top removed. Dark glasses framed high cheekbones and a strong, angular jaw. My heart pounded.

The Wrangler ground to a stop, and Takoda jumped out. "Hi!" She pushed her sunglasses to the crown of her head, smiling widely. "I'm glad you made it." She rocked back on her heels and pushed her hands into her jeans pockets as I joined her.

"Hi. Glad you suggested it." I wondered if we should shake hands or something. I settled for putting my hands in my own pockets. We stood there grinning at each other. I felt like a nervous schoolgirl and got the impression that she did too.

"Shall we?" Takoda nodded toward the building.

"Sure."

We crossed the parking lot and entered the dimness of the bar.

The older man behind the counter raised a hand in greeting. "Hey Running Bear, long time no see."

"How's it going, Leo?"

"Good, good."

I followed her through the bar and into the bright, open restaurant. A wide window at the front of the room overlooked the road, while the picture windows on the side showed a grassy park with a wire-fenced woodsy area and a creek with a small walking bridge.

We claimed a table by the side windows. The frail, stern-looking waitress, who could've been anywhere from sixty to eighty years old, arrived with two glasses of water and single-sheet laminated menus, which she placed before us without smiling. Her nametag said Dora, and I mentally tagged on "The Explorer."

"You girls want something to drink?" Deep wrinkles lined her thin face, and her voice was scratchy and hoarse.

Takoda opted for a Coke. I went with the diet version. As Dora walked away with a slight limp, I asked, "What's good?"

"You're probably safe with a burger. I haven't actually eaten here in years. Been in the bar a few times, though."

"Now you tell me," I said. "I haven't been here since I was a kid. All I remember is feeding the deer out back."

"My grandfather used to take my brother George and me to feed the deer too."

A warm, happy spot grew in my chest, knowing that we had a shared experience. In some way, it suggested that maybe we had more in common than just an accidental bike ride.

When Dora returned with our sodas, we ordered cheeseburgers and fries.

I asked, "Are you off work today?"

"Actually, I'm off for the next week. I was supposed to go camping with my brother, but he broke his ankle. I figure, I'll get some stuff done around the house, maybe do a little fishing."

"Bummer your plans got canceled."

"It happens."

"How'd he break his ankle?"

"Roofing his house. He's lucky he didn't break his neck." She shook her head. "Poor George. He's been working so hard getting his house done, trying to save money doing the work on his own. Best laid plans and all that, right?"

"That so sucks." Just the thought of being up on a steep roof made my insides squirm.

She cocked her head. "You don't come up here much?"

"I try to stop up for a weekend every two or three months to see my dad. My best friend Rose and I are staying at the cabin through the rest of this week. We've made it an annual trip for almost ten years. You should come out and hang with us. Rose

loves to fish. I lounge in the boat with a book or a notebook."
Jesus. I was babbling. I reached for my soda and took a gulp to
shut the hell up.

"I may take you up on that. Tell me about the cabin."

I did, and she told me about the log home she'd built on a
small lake about ten miles outside Hibbing, where she lived with
her two rescued Labrador-mix dogs. Dora brought our lunch,
and we continued to chat, keeping to mostly general subjects.
Takoda was close to her family and spent a lot of time with
them. I spent most of my time with my friends, who were more
like family to me. Her Native American heritage intrigued me.

"Can I ask what the name Takoda means?"

"Sure. My grandmother—my father's mother—wanted
my parents to give me a traditional Ojibwa name. Mom, who's
through and through hotheaded Irish, saw the name Takoda in
some romance novel she was reading. It's Sioux, and it means
'friend to everyone.' Mom liked it, and Grandma could live
with it, even if it wasn't Ojibwa. Then when I arrived, it turned
out I wasn't a boy. Mom still liked the name. She added Lynn
to appease the Irish relatives on her side. So, my full name is
Takoda Lynn Running Bear."

"That's really cool."

"What about Amry? That's a different name too."

"Yeah. They named me Ann Marie. My brother and my
cousins butchered it and called me Amry. It stuck and it fit better
than Ann Marie, so I changed it legally when I was in college.
My mom had a fit. She called me Ann Marie anyway. She was
the only person who ever did."

"I suppose we grow into the names we're given and make
them our own."

We fell into silence and worked on our burgers. Takoda
gazed off into the woods. She wore a pensive expression, and
I wondered what was going through her head. After a few
moments, she asked, "So, how is it that a nice girl like you is still
unattached? I mean, are women in the cities that stupid?"

I nearly choked on a french fry. "Oh, I don't know if I'm that
great a catch. I'm a writer, so I need time and space to create,

and not many women get that. I can't write when someone sucks up all my energy and makes me feel guilty if I have boundaries around my time and space. I can be pretty antisocial if I'm on a roll. And I'm probably too honest for my own good. Sorry." I managed an embarrassed smile. No fucking wonder I didn't have a girlfriend.

Takoda's expression seemed more understanding than put off by my behavior quirks. "I understand the need for alone time. When we moved from Alaska, living in town felt so crowded. It was a big adjustment. It's better now, but I still prefer the quiet. That's why my house is so isolated. It keeps me sane."

Relief made my chest lighter. "Guess we've both done okay for being slightly hermitlike."

A broad, happy smile made Takoda's eyes light up. "I guess so." Takoda laid her hand over mine on the table and gave it a squeeze. My insides turned to goo. Her hand was warm and her dark eyes held mine. When she removed her hand, the thought that flashed through my head was that I didn't want her to let go. "You want dessert? I hear the pie is great."

I had to force myself to respond to the question because I was still thinking about holding her hand. "I'm stuffed. I couldn't eat another bite."

"Me either, actually."

The waitress dropped off the bill, which Takoda claimed before I could get a hand on it. "I got it," she said.

"Are you sure?"

"Positive. Besides, I invited you." She leaned back in her chair. "I really want to see you again."

"Really?" God, I sounded like an idiot.

"Really."

I didn't date much. It was generally a crappy experience, filled with uncomfortable silences or overly clingy, annoying chatterboxes or, in the case of my ex, Susan, manipulative, controlling women who sucked up your life so subtly that you didn't realize you'd lost it until it was already gone. But Takoda wanted to see me again. And there was something about her: she seemed so genuine. Not pretentious. Just straightforward.

I swallowed hard, and the words bubbled out of my mouth before I could stop them. "I want to see you again too. Why don't you come to the cabin tomorrow? Rose will be there, but she's cool. You'll like her. We can go hiking or biking or fishing or something." It wasn't a date. It was safe. She'd probably think it was stupid.

"I'd like that." Takoda touched my hand again. "I know you'll go back to the city, but…" Her eyes focused on her hand. Which rested on my hand. My heart started racing, and my brain turned to mush.

I twined our fingers together. Her darkly tanned skin contrasted against mine. In that tiny moment of time, the air stilled around us. A sense of endless possibility was born and then slipped away in the next second. She was right. I would return to the city and my life there. But while we were here, anything could happen.

Dora returned to take the bill folder. Her gaze went to our clasped hands, and her expression soured into a tight-lipped frown. She grabbed the folder and spun away.

When she returned a couple minutes later with the receipts and Takoda's credit card, we were still holding hands as we chatted. Dora muttered something like "Thanks for stopping in" as she hurried back to the kitchen.

We snickered. I was used to living in the city, where public displays weren't any big thing. People didn't care or didn't pay attention. I wasn't ashamed of my sexuality. It seemed Takoda wasn't either. Takoda signed the charge slip and returned her credit card to her wallet.

Instead of going directly to our cars, we followed the path around the back of the building and into the park, strolling along the chicken-wire fence searching for deer. Takoda took my hand. I looked up at her and smiled. Just like that, the day was perfect.

"There," she whispered, pointing into the brush.

I followed her direction. Two fawns stood at the edge of the brushy tree line. Their soulful black eyes watched us. Dusty brown fur and fading white spots blended into the dappled sunlight of the wooded background. The deer took a couple steps into the sunlight, then at some signal only they knew, their tails stood straight up and they whirled and bounded back into the woods.

We wandered back to the parking lot. I had never felt so comfortable with someone I'd only just met. Holding her hand felt so natural it didn't even occur to me that I was in the homophobic northland. Of course, there wasn't anyone around to see us.

When we reached our vehicles, we stood for another few minutes making small talk, both trying to find a good way to part. Finally, I smiled regretfully. "I should head back."

I wanted to invite Takoda along, but I didn't want to offend Rose. This was her vacation too. "This was wonderful. Thank you for lunch."

"You're more than welcome." Takoda stepped back. "I'll see you tomorrow." She opened my car door for me, then hopped into her Jeep.

I started the engine, and she followed me as I drove out of the parking lot and turned to the left. She turned right, and I watched her Jeep disappear in my rearview mirror.

A warm, tickly feeling fluttered in my chest. I bounced between excited, nervous and slightly nauseated because I had no idea what was going to happen next. Whatever this was between Takoda and me, I knew nothing could come of it. She was here, and I would be returning to the city in a week.

Long-distance relationships didn't work, but maybe we could be friends. A girl could never have too many friends.

CHAPTER FOUR

"Amry, Takoda's here!" Rose called.

My heart raced. I was in the bathroom taking a quick luke-warm bath. I scrubbed the shampoo out of my hair hurriedly. Takoda was early. Or maybe I was running late. Panicking, I used a red plastic cup to pour more water over my head, rinsing the suds down my back and wishing someone would have installed a shower. And a working hot water heater.

I toweled off with a beach towel and pulled on a faded red T-shirt and my black bike shorts. I could hear Rose and Takoda laughing and hoped that was a good thing. Of course, knowing Rose it was likely the laughter was at my expense.

I came out of the bathroom, running my hands through my hair. "Hey."

Takoda turned from the living room window, and my breath stuck in my throat. She wore a tight gray T-shirt over black bike shorts, her long legs ending in worn hiking sandals. She smiled. "Hi."

"Hi." I cleared my throat. "Guess you found the place, huh?"

I saw Rose roll her eyes.

"Guess I did. This cabin is great. Like it's straight out of the nineteen fifties."

"Thanks. Mom was never one for redecorating." I wondered if I were going to be able to come up with more than inane small talk.

Rose jumped in. "Are you ladies ready for me to kick your asses on a bike ride?"

I snorted. "Mine, probably, but I think Takoda's going to kick yours."

"Don't give me too much credit," Takoda said.

I tried not to ogle Takoda's lean, muscular body. "Right," I mumbled.

Rose said, "I'll fill up the water bottles and grab some snacks. We can stop at the park later for a break. You guys get the bikes ready."

As always, Rose took control as lead organizer, and I was perfectly okay with that. Takoda followed me through the back porch and we wheeled my mountain bike and Rose's outside. I checked tires and secured the panniers on my rear cargo rack while Takoda lifted her bike off the carrier on the Jeep and made sure she was road-ready.

Rose locked up the cabin and handed out water bottles, then we headed out, spinning down the packed sand driveway onto the single-lane road.

Rose asked, "Are we going to stick to gravel roads? I'm not sure I'm up for tackling the snowmobile trails."

"That works for me," I said, and Takoda agreed.

"Then follow me, gals. I got this covered."

Takoda sent me questioning glance, and I explained, "Rose is a walking map. She probably knows the back roads up here as well as you do. I think we've been lost on most of them at least once."

"We were never lost. We were exploring. I knew where we were, and I always got us home."

"Yeah." I imitated her voice: "*It's just a little farther, Amry. Just another little bit, and we'll be to the main road.* And two hours later, you were right."

Rose laughed. We pedaled along the worn tarmac, riding side by side unless traffic happened to come by, which wasn't very often. Rose led us on a rollicking tour of gravel logging roads. Hemmed in by trees, the humid air was thick with buzzing insects and the dust we kicked up. Along the way, Rose kept up a running commentary on nature and the ways of the world, and Takoda and I readily joined in the philosophical and comedic discussions. Rose's blunt humor and sarcasm made for entertaining conversation, and Takoda's actual facts about the environment were good-natured counterpoint to some of Rose's and my half-cocked and semilogical theories.

Eventually we picked up a paved road that connected with the single-lane highway back to the state park. I had to work hard to keep up with Rose and Takoda. As much as I loved riding long distances, I was not generally a fast rider, and both my friends had more brute strength than I did.

The sun beat down relentlessly on the black tar, and I could feel the heat of it radiating from the surface. Heat mirages shimmered ahead of us. I gulped more water, hoping my second bottle would get me to the park. My shirt clung damply to my back. The temperature was starting to affect me, and I needed a break. Even so, I pushed on since nobody else was complaining.

After at least forty minutes on the highway, we rolled into the beach side of McCarthy Beach State Park and stopped beside a picnic table. The sudden lack of air movement allowed the August heat to surround me like a suffocating blanket. Suddenly lightheaded and shaky, I dropped my bike, removed my helmet and sat bonelessly on the bench. I fumbled to remove my bike shoes and socks. I felt flushed and my ears started buzzing. I was overheating and my blood sugar had dropped too low. I started to panic.

"Drink." Takoda pushed a water bottle into my shaking hands. I gulped tepid liquid while my vision tunneled gray around the edges. I wanted to say I needed to get to the lake and I needed a candy bar, but I couldn't get the words out. I concentrated on breathing and staying conscious and put my head down toward my knees. Fuck. I so didn't want to do this. I should have known better.

I heard Rose's voice as though from a distance. "One of these days, she'll learn." Water poured over my head and down my back. An unwrapped snack-size candy bar appeared in front of my face. I shoved it into my mouth. Closing my eyes, I chewed and swallowed, still working on breathing and staying conscious.

Somebody finished taking my shoes and socks off.

Takoda asked, "Can you stand?" Her voice was very close to my ear.

I blinked hard, trying to focus on her concerned face as she knelt in front of me. "Yeah."

She and Rose helped me up, and I wavered as the world spun. Takoda caught me firmly around the waist. "I've got you."

I clung weakly to her as we walked, while waves of dizziness challenged my balance. Black smudges blurred my vision. My feet hit the coolness of the lake.

Takoda murmured, "Just a little farther."

When the water reached above my knees, she said, "Gonna sit down, okay? Go easy."

The next thing I knew, I was sitting between her legs. Water lapped up to my chin. She wrapped her arms snugly under my breasts and held me upright against her chest. I breathed some more. The water chilled my skin, but I still saw black spots on the edges of my vision.

I was hyperaware of the heat of Takoda's breasts and body against my back. My head rested against her shoulder. The world spun even with my eyes squeezed shut. It occurred to me, vaguely, that Takoda holding me like this would have my world spinning even if I weren't suffering from heat exhaustion.

Her voice murmured in my ear. "How you doing?"

Breathe. "Okay." *Breathe again. God, I'm a dumbass.* I opened my eyes. "Sorry." My ears buzzed, but at least the grayness had dissipated.

Takoda used one hand to drip water over the top of my head. "Relax."

I nodded and the motion made the world waver again.

Rose floated past on her back. "If ya wanted to go swimming, there are probably better ways to tell us."

Weakly, I raised a hand out of the water to flip her off. "I was doing fine until we stopped."

"It happens to my sister-in-law too," Takoda said.

"Amry's problem is she refuses to admit to needing a break until everyone else has collapsed from exhaustion first. We do this at least once every trip when I kick her sorry ass on a ride."

I managed to glare at her. She laughed and ducked under the water. What sucked is it was true. I did overheat at least once every trip because there was no way I was going to admit that Rose could bike farther or faster than I could. It didn't matter that her bike was bigger than mine or that she was stronger than me. It only made me more stubborn and determined. Besides, I was not going to let a straight girl out-butch me. I muttered, "Whatever."

Takoda laughed and the low timbre of her voice vibrated through me, sending quivers of desire straight between my legs. Visions flashed through my brain of Takoda's hands all over my body. *Oh my God, I can't be all worked up on top of being an idiot!* Feeling completely out of control, I shifted out of her embrace. "I need to dunk my head," I said, and dove under. I did a single breast stroke and came up. As much as I would have liked to return to my spot between Takoda's legs and wrapped in her embrace, I crouched in the water a few feet away, keeping most of my body submerged.

A bunch of grade-school-aged boys dashed across the beach, yelling exuberantly as they splashed into the water.

Rose stood. "I think that's our cue," she said.

Takoda peered at me. "You feeling better?"

"Yeah, much. Thank you."

She held a hand out. I grasped it and let her pull me to my feet. We slogged out of the lake and crossed the sand and grass back to our bikes and the picnic table.

Rose dug through my bike bags. She unpacked two insulated lunch bags, producing three peanut butter-and-jelly sandwiches, a couple bags of trail mix, three apples and a dozen bite-sized candy bars. It reminded me of Mary Poppins and her magic carpetbag.

Takoda raised an eyebrow. "You got all that in those two bags?"

"Rose has the touch."

"Which is good because I'm starved." Takoda claimed one of the sandwiches as she sat down.

I sat beside her, and Rose settled across from us, adding three fresh bottles of water to the middle of the table. I grabbed one and gulped down half of it before unwrapping my own sandwich, pleased to note my hands had stopped shaking.

We lingered over our picnic. Conversation was easy. Takoda playfully traded my Butterfinger for her Snickers. A couple of times, she touched my hand or arm as we talked, sending shivers down my spine. The feeling was as enticing as it was unnerving. I'd never reacted so strongly to anyone. Was it so wrong to enjoy what might be a quick summer fling? Her dark eyes sparkled with happiness, and her smile was wide and genuine. Her wet T-shirt clung to small, firm breasts and strong shoulders. I caught myself staring and forced my gaze to the table, hoping they thought my face was still flushed from overheating.

We relaxed for a while after eating, then took our time biking the couple miles back to the cabin. I was still embarrassed for nearly passing out. Definitely not one of my better moments. On the up side, Takoda hadn't run off screaming. Yet.

At the cabin, we changed into swimsuits. When Takoda strode out of the bathroom in a plain black Speedo, I nearly passed out all over again. Oh. My. God. All I could do was stare. My heart pounded in my chest, and I couldn't breathe. Her legs went on forever. Her arms were well-defined, her tanned skin flawless. Her hair hung loose over her shoulders down to her perfect breasts. She draped a beach towel around her shoulders and gave me a slightly questioning glance.

I swallowed. "Wow," I said, and my voice cracked like a sixteen-year-old boy. The stern voice in the back of my head screamed warnings like "too good to be true" and "you are going back to the city in a week." The voice in the front of my head was too enamored to care.

Takoda laughed, and I wondered if she heard the same voices I did.

Armed with foam floaties from the boathouse on the beach, all three of us hit the lake. The sun blazed overhead. We paddled into the water, floating lazily, sometimes chatting, sometimes half-asleep.

Takoda maneuvered close and took my hand. We smiled conspiratorially. We didn't seem to need to talk. It was one of the most comfortable silences I'd ever experienced.

Rose headed back to shore long before us and settled on a lounge chair in the shade in front of the cabin.

Takoda and I paddled farther out into the lake. I rolled off my float, purposefully dumping Takoda into the water with me and starting a water fight.

She popped up with a laugh and splashed me. We chased and dunked each other until we were both giggling and panting. I clung to my float in the deeper water, but Takoda stood easily on the sandy bottom as we caught our breath. Our eyes met and held for a few silent, heart-pounding moments. She moved closer, pausing a fraction of a second before she snaked her arms around my waist, bringing our bodies together. The heat of her skin seeped into me through the slick material of our swimsuits. I sighed at her touch and draped my arms around her neck. I couldn't turn away from the intensity in her gaze. The muscular solidity of her body took my breath away.

When we came together, her mouth was warm, her lips soft as velvet. Our tongues searched and explored—hot, sweet and absolutely devastating. Desire pulsed through me. I clamped my legs around her hips.

Takoda pulled back, trailed her fingers along my jaw. She was so damned beautiful. She left me speechless. And wanting.

She kissed me again, lightly. "We need to head in before I do more than just kiss you." Her voice rumbled low and sexy. Christ. My whole body ached with wanting her.

She brushed her lips along my collarbone. I reluctantly released my hold on her. The water swirled around me, and I shivered. Takoda pushed my floaty to me then turned and kicked off toward shore. I followed in a daze, still feeling her lips on mine and wishing for more.

As I paddled, I heard the cautioning voice in my head assuring me this was merely the fleeting excitement of a summer fling, and not to expect—or wish for—more.

CHAPTER FIVE

After dusk fell, long after Takoda had left, Rose built a small fire in the cabin's fireplace and settled in the wooden rocking chair beside the hearth to read. I relaxed in the padded wicker chair on the other side of the hearth with my feet resting on an ottoman.

Working on my manuscript, I alternated typing and staring past the screen into the popping and crackling flames. There was something innately comforting about having a fire, even if the windows were open and we didn't need the warmth.

My phone pinged. I grabbed it from the floor to read the text.

"Hey. Think you can get away for a bit tomorrow? Want to meet my dogs?"

I glanced at Rose, feeling a little awkward. This was supposed to be our vacation, not me chasing a date.

My best friend regarded me with a silent question, and I said, "Takoda texted."

Rose smiled slyly. "What'd she say?"

"Asked if I wanted to meet her dogs tomorrow."

"Likely excuse. I saw you two making out in the lake this afternoon."

I hoped the dim light hid the hot blush that had to be covering my face.

Rose laughed. "I love it when you look so guilty."

"Thanks." I stood up. "You want a beer or something?"

"Pour me a glass of wine?"

"Sure." I retreated to the kitchen and retrieved a bottle of wine from the chrome-trimmed refrigerator that was a working relic of the mid nineteen fifties.

Rose asked, "What time are you going?"

I filled two plastic wineglasses and returned to the living room, handing Rose hers before sitting in my chair. "I don't know. I haven't answered her yet. Do you mind if I go? I mean, I came up here to hang out with you."

Rose lifted her glass. "Go for it, Amry. Don't worry about me. I'm a big girl. I'll go fishing." She waved a dismissive hand, but I recognized a flash of resignation—or disappointment—in her expression before she added, "Seriously. Go meet your girl. You both have it bad."

I gave her a grateful smile. I'd make it up to her somehow. "Thanks."

"Besides, even a straight girl can see she's a hot babe." She sipped her wine. "And she seems really down to earth. Good people."

"Are you saying you approve?"

"Yes." With that, she went back to reading.

I texted, *"Would love to meet the dogs. And you. Where and when?"*

* * *

The next morning found me at the kitchen table nursing a second cup of coffee while I worked on my manuscript. Birds singing and the rustle of leaves created my mental soundtrack. The wind chimes hanging on the edge of the back porch tinkled in a breeze that brought the fresh scent of pine and a hint of wood smoke through the open windows.

A car door slammed shut behind the cabin. Curious, I got up and peeked out the window above the sink. My nephew Nikko ducked out of an older model Toyota Camry and stomped toward the back porch.

I met him as he was about to rap on the screen door. "Nikko, what's up?"

An angry frown shadowed his expression. "Can I come in?"

"Sure. What happened?" I stood aside.

He stalked past and threw himself into a chair at the table. "He's a fucking asshole. I can't live with him anymore."

Taking a cleansing breath, I leaned against the counter. I could feel the agitation pouring off my teenaged nephew, and I forced myself to be calm. "You wanna talk about it?"

He glanced around.

I said, "Rose is out fishing."

"My dad is an asshole."

This wasn't a surprise or news to me. I nodded and waited for the rest of the story.

"I was playing catch with Corey Pearson last night at the house. No big deal, right? We were working on his pitching. He's been playing rec league all summer, and he wants to try out for varsity next year with me. He's a good pitcher. Really good.

"After Corey left, Dad started going off about gays, saying fags can't play sports, and Corey's too girly to be any good, and making asshole comments about him." Nikko surged to his feet and paced into the living room area. "Corey's a good guy. I don't care if he's gay or not. Dad says if I hang around people like him everyone'll think I'm gay too. I don't give a fuck what people think. If they wanna think I'm gay, fine. I don't care."

He stood in front of the window with his back to me, his shoulders stiff with tension. I heard the fury in his voice. I was proud of him for standing up for his friend, and I wondered if there was more to it than that. I'd seen pictures and posts from Corey on Nikko's Facebook page. But this didn't feel like a coming-out speech. This felt like Nikko being pissed about Tom's bigoted attitude.

As much as I'd have liked to join in on his Tom-bashing tirade, this wasn't the time. Tom had turned his rude comments on me enough times over the years, and I knew how much it hurt. God forbid anyone should know his sister was a "lezzy," and he always wanted to know "Why can't you act like a normal person?" I wouldn't defend my brother, he sure as hell didn't deserve that, but I wasn't going to badmouth him in front of Nikko. If Nikko needed to, fine.

I asked, "What are you going to do?"

Nikko returned to the kitchen table and sat down again. "I don't want to go home. Maybe I don't want to go home ever."

"You're welcome to spend the day here. But we'd have to talk to your folks if you wanted to stay any longer than that."

He scowled, but I had no intention of getting into a pissing match between him and his parents.

"He's such an asshole."

I couldn't disagree.

"What's the big deal about being gay anyways? So what if Corey likes guys? It's not like he's joining the team to get a date or something. He just wants to play ball."

"Some people are afraid of things they don't understand," I said. "The only way they know how to deal with the things they don't understand, or are afraid of, is to ridicule them."

"That's stupid."

"The world can be a very stupid place."

Nikko huffed and drew patterns on the tablecloth with his finger.

I went to the fridge and got us cans of soda. As I popped the top on mine, I heard the familiar stuttering of an ancient outboard motor on the lake. I squinted out the front window to see Rose glide up to the dock in Dad's fourteen-foot fishing boat.

A few minutes later, she strolled in from the back porch.

"How was fishing?" I asked.

"Not bad. Got a few crappies, a small walleye and some decent sunnies. Enough to add to dinner later." She stopped, did a double take and added, "Hey Nikko, what're you doing here?"

"Hi Rose." He gave her an adorable lopsided grin. "I'm running away from home."

She raised a brow.

"My dad's being a jerk."

"I could have told you that," she said flatly.

My cell chirped.

Rose said, "If that's your girlfriend, tell her to bring the dogs over here. Then Nikko can meet them too."

Suddenly interested, Nikko repeated, "Girlfriend?"

I swiped my phone open to read the message. "Actually, it's Darlene, wondering if Nikko is here because he took the car without asking and he only has a learner's permit." I gave my nephew a disappointed frown. "Seriously, Nikko, that was stupid."

He had the brains to look guilty. I returned Darlene's text, and she asked me to have Nikko call her on her cell. He pushed to his feet and stomped out the back door, dialing his phone. I could hear him talking as the screen door slammed; his tone was angry and petulant, but he moved far enough away from the cabin that the words were lost.

Rose grabbed a soda and stretched out on the sofa. "Ah, youth. Can't live with 'em. Can't kill 'em."

I sighed and texted Takoda. *"Any chance you can bring the dogs over here? My nephew showed up on our doorstep and needs Auntie time."*

Her reply came back ten seconds later. *"We'll be there at two."*

I chewed my lip as I shoved my phone back into my pocket and sat down in the rocking chair by the fireplace. It was going to be an interesting afternoon.

Nikko sulked back into the cabin and threw himself dramatically into the wicker chair across from me.

I asked, "What's the deal?"

He grumbled under his breath then said, "I don't know. She's pissed. I'm sure she's gonna tell Dad."

I waited for more, but nothing was forthcoming. I pressed, "Is she coming to get you or do I need to drive you home?"

"I don't know. I hung up. I don't wanna go home."

I sighed.

Rose said, "In that case, make yourself comfortable, kid."

A while later, Rose and Nikko sunned themselves in low lounge chairs in front of the cabin while I stretched out in the shade with my laptop. Being at the lake was conducive to my muse, and I took advantage of the time to write.

I hadn't heard anything more from Darlene, so I planned on keeping Nikko with us until someone told me differently. I wasn't sure what else to do. I would have loved to scream at my brother for being an asshole, but that wasn't going to happen, nor would it do any good. I settled on waiting it out.

Eventually, I heard the crunch of tires on sand. I glanced at the time on my computer, and it was nearly two. Was it Takoda or Darlene? As I put aside my laptop, I heard a commotion of low barks and Takoda's voice. "Gabby, Xena, sit!"

I scrambled to my feet and jogged around the cabin. Takoda stood beside her Jeep with her two Lab mixes on short leashes at her side. "Hey Amry."

"Hey, yourself."

The dogs panted excitedly. So did I.

Takoda said, "These are my girls. Gabby is the bigger, furrier one. Xena's an excitable love puppy." She patted their heads proudly.

I walked closer and held my hand out for the dogs to sniff before giving each a good scratch behind the ears. Xena whined and pushed as close to me as she could without breaking her sit. I rubbed her head harder. Her sleek, black fur was warm under my fingers, and she studied me with striking bright blue eyes. She fidgeted excitedly when I stopped scratching her ears and pushed her head under my hand again.

Gabby had thick, brindled fur and a fluffy tail. Her wider face was mostly brown, her eyes dark and friendly. She sat patiently as I petted her head.

"They're beautiful," I said. "Come on around front. Rose and Nikko are sunning."

Takoda said "Heel" and the two dogs paced alongside her. Gabby moved in a smooth, measured gait while Xena bounced boisterously on the outside, alternately jumping at Gabby and Takoda.

Nikko hurried over, barely waiting for an introduction to Takoda before kneeling in front of the dogs to coo and rough them up, letting them give him kisses. Takoda kept them on leash until greetings were made. When she let them loose, both dogs raced for the lake and launched themselves off the dock with gigantic splashes.

Nikko returned to his lounge chair and resumed typing furiously on his cell phone, earbuds blasting. Rose looked up from her book to greet Takoda, then returned to reading. I felt a pang of guilt and hoped she wasn't too annoyed at having her vacation time filled with outsiders.

Takoda joined me in the shade. Her lounge chair practically touched mine, and we held hands while we watched the dogs playing in the water.

I asked, "The dogs won't run off, will they?"

"They'll stay within sight of me."

She'd tied her dark hair into a loose tail at the nape of her neck and pushed her dark glasses up onto the crown of her head. When she turned to meet my gaze, I found myself staring into deep chocolate eyes, wondering what thoughts were behind them. What was she thinking and feeling right this moment? I knew I had a surreal sense that I had fallen into a life other than my own. Who'd have thought that I would be sitting here, right now, with this amazing, sweet and intelligent woman who seemed to like me too? It sure hadn't been in my expectations for the week.

"What?" Takoda asked.

"Just happy you're here," I said.

The light of her smile bathed me in warmth. "I'm glad I'm here too." We sat in comfortable silence. After a while, Takoda nodded toward Nikko. "What's up with your nephew?" she asked quietly.

I opened my mouth to reply, but Nikko piped up, "He's royally pissed at his asshole father and hiding out here until the shit hits the fan, which it's about to, because my mother just texted that she and the asshole are on their way to get me and her car."

Well, this wasn't going to be any fun.

Takoda asked, "Should I be leaving?"

I didn't want her to leave, but at the same time, I didn't want to force my family drama on a virtual stranger. "If you'd rather not stay for the fireworks, I wouldn't blame you, and we could maybe get together later. But I'm hoping that they won't make a big scene since Rose and I are here too."

Nikko snorted. "Mom won't. I wouldn't put money on the asshole."

Takoda's expression was serious, her dark eyes studying my nephew. I saw the cop behind that expression, professional but also very concerned. "Nikko, has your dad threatened you or hurt you physically?"

I felt the nausea rise in my throat as Nikko sat up in his chair and twisted to face us. "No. He lets me know how worthless I am without touching me."

"You are not worthless," I snapped. "You are a wonderfully decent, intelligent, loving and talented young man."

"That my father has no use for."

I said, "Please tell me your mom doesn't treat you the same way."

"Mom's okay. At least she tries. They've been fighting like crazy lately."

"About you?" I asked.

"About everything, all the time."

I did not want to get into the middle of my brother's family issues, but I felt a strong urge to defend and protect Nikko from Tom's bigoted attitudes. The problem was I knew my involvement would most likely make things worse.

Takoda said, "If you think you're in danger, we can step in and keep you safe."

"I'm not in danger. He bitches and yells and makes me feel like shit, but he's never hit me. And Mom's on my side. Except for me taking the car today, which I know I shouldn't have done. But I was so pissed. I just wanted to get out of there."

"Are you sure?" I asked.

"Yeah, Aunt Amry, I'm sure."

I sent Nikko and Takoda down to the beach to throw tennis balls for the dogs while Rose and I sat at the picnic table at the side of the cabin, waiting for Tom and Darlene to show up. Nervous energy kept my knee bouncing and my stomach churning. I'd spent my life perfecting the art of avoiding confrontations and dreaded the thought of voices being raised.

Fifteen minutes later, Tom's truck roared up the drive and stopped at the back of the cabin. He jumped out of the cab and slammed the door. "Where is he?"

I stood and called toward the beach, "Nikko! Your folks are here!"

Darlene got out of the truck more slowly.

My brother's brow was furrowed, his expression angry. "I'm gonna kill that little bastard. What the fuck was he thinking?"

"Tom, calm down," Darlene said.

"Fuck that. I am so sick of this shit with him. Nikko!" he bellowed. "Get your ass up here!"

Nikko topped the stairs from the beach and came to face his parents, stopping a few feet away.

Takoda followed a short distance behind him, holding the dogs on leash, and crossed the grass to stand beside Rose at the picnic table. The dogs sat obediently beside her.

Tom immediately got into Nikko's space. "What the hell possessed you to take off in that car? You know how much trouble you could have gotten into? You know what you did was illegal? Jesus Christ! What the fuck were you thinking?"

Nikko dropped his gaze. "I wasn't thinking. I wanted to leave, and I knew Aunt Amry was at the cabin. I know I shouldn't have done that, and I'm sorry."

I cringed as Tom continued his tirade, pushing a finger into Nikko's chest. "You sure as fuck weren't thinking! And sorry ain't gonna cut it. You are grounded. No going out after school, no going out on the weekend. Unless it's practice or school related, you're in your room. For the next goddamn month, Nikko."

Nikko nodded silently.

Tom glanced at me. "And I suppose you don't think anything of this?"

"He already got an earful from me about driving on a learner's permit," I said.

Tom nodded toward Takoda. "Who's she?"

Darlene muttered, "Tom, don't be rude."

He shot her a silencing glare and said to Nikko, "I don't want you hanging around here getting perverted ideas from your dyke aunt or hanging out with that faggot friend of yours either. That little gay boy better stay away from you and my house."

"You are such an ass!" I exploded. "The only perverted ideas Nikko is getting are the twisted, bigoted bullshit ones spewing out of your mouth! It's people like you who ruin the lives of good kids like Nikko. Leave him the fuck alone, Tom!"

"Don't you tell me how to raise my son!"

"I'm not a kid!"

Tom whirled on Nikko. "Yes, you are, and I won't have her and her freak friends turning you into some faggot!"

"She can't turn me into something I've always been!"

Silence.

Panic, fear and horror painted Nikko's wide-eyed face.

Tom stared at him like he was an alien.

Darlene stepped between Nikko and Tom and put an arm around her son's shoulders.

Tom shouted "Fuck!" and stalked off to his truck. The oversized Ford spun its wheels in the loose sand and backed away with a roar, leaving his wife and son behind.

Darlene said gently, "Come on, Nikk, let's go home, okay?" She guided him back toward her car. He went along without a word, staring at the ground. Darlene looked back over her shoulder at me and mouthed, "I'll call you."

As Darlene turned her car around and drove away, Nikko stared forlornly out the window.

I watched with a sick feeling in my stomach. No good was going to come of this. Poor Nikko. Christ. What a horrible way to come out. I wanted to wrap him in my arms and protect him from the shitstorm that was coming. I hoped to hell Darlene would do that when I couldn't. She certainly hadn't seemed surprised by Nikko's words. I hoped she would be as supportive as she appeared to be. Nikko was going to need her more than ever now.

"Well, that was interesting," Rose said.

I sat heavily on the cement stairs leading up to the back door of the cabin. "Fuck."

Takoda released the dogs, sat beside me and wrapped an arm around my shoulders. I leaned into her strength, resting a hand on her thigh. Gabby and Xena snuffled around us, smelling of lake and wet fur.

Takoda said, "He'll be okay."

"I hope so."

Rose said firmly, "Darlene has it under control, and Nikko's with her, not Tom."

That was true. I got the impression Darlene was well aware of what was going on. I sure as hell didn't want to be there to see the fallout, but at least Nikk was able to ride home with his mom, and I trusted Darlene wouldn't let Tom harm him.

Takoda hugged me, and I slipped an arm around her waist and burrowed in, resting my head against her. My imagination raced ahead, seeing scenarios where Tom screamed at Nikko or Darlene or both. I could easily imagine Nikko cornered and cowering. I hoped there would be no physical violence. As far as I knew, Tom wasn't a violent guy. He yelled a lot, but I'd never heard of him hitting. Still, he had been so angry when he'd left. Maybe the drive would calm him down. Give him time to count to ten or twenty. Or a hundred.

The rest of the day remained low-key. Worried thoughts of Nikko stayed close to the surface and colored my mood darker than I'd have liked. Takoda and I took the canoe out for a paddle while the dogs slept in the shade. When we got back to the cabin, Rose had moved into the shade and greeted us.

"Before you get comfy up here, can you bring me a beer?"

I grinned. "Sure. Takoda, pop or beer?"

"Beer. It's still early. Thanks, Amry."

I retreated to the cabin to get our drinks. When I got back, they were discussing the spy novel Rose was reading.

Takoda said, "I didn't like Andrea as a character. He should have killed her off in the beginning."

"I'll give you that, but I think it was kind of the point, to have her as such a contrast to Lee. He's just so controlled."

"I liked that about him."

"I think the author is hiding something about him, though. There's more to his story than he's letting on."

Takoda gave her a sly smile. "Well, since I've already finished the book, I'm not going to say one way or another. But MacKenzie does a great job of tying everything together at the end. You'll be guessing all the way through."

I passed out beers and said, "I want to read that when you're done."

"Sure. Probably tomorrow, at the rate I'm reading. Good thing I brought a couple books with me."

"I read it really fast too," Takoda said.

I muttered, "Too bad us authors can't write as fast as you guys read."

They laughed at me.

We hung out chatting until we got hungry and decided to make some dinner. Rose took over the kitchen, good-naturedly ordering Takoda and I around. She sent us out to heat up the portable grill, then she and Takoda both worked on fileting the fish. I passed. Blech. I'd eat fish, but gutting them and cutting off their fishy little heads and tails? Yeah, not so much.

I put some potato chips in a bowl and put a can of baked beans on the stove, then made sure everyone had a cold beer.

Rose waved a fish head playfully in my direction. "You are such a wuss," she said.

"Keep your fishy bits to yourself or I won't let you have ice cream later."

Takoda snickered. "Should I ask if you make Rose bait your hook when you fish?"

"Et tu, Brutus? And for your information, I put my own worms on the hook."

"She won't kill the minnows."

"No ice cream for you."

Rose and Takoda laughed until tears ran from their eyes, and I joined in. It was funny, and a teasing routine that Rose and I'd had many times over the years.

Rose cooked the fish while Takoda and I put the bratwurst on the grill. Then we had a wonderful dinner, with amicable conversation. After cleaning up, we leashed the dogs and all took a walk down the road to the gas station-slash-bait shop-slash-convenience store for ice cream cones. The three of us got along like we'd been friends for years. It was odd to think I'd only known Takoda for a couple of days as she fit in so comfortably with Rose and I. Beyond that, though, she fascinated me. We had lived different kinds of lives and came from different places, but the similarities far outweighed any differences.

When we went inside for an evening fire, the dogs curled up at our feet and slept. Takoda stayed late, sharing the sofa with me while Rose had her place beside the fireplace. Conversation came and went. Rose spent time flipping through some old magazines. I shared some of my writing with Takoda, who wanted to see what I was working on. I leaned against her as she read the first chapter of my new novel. It made me nervous, but at the same time, I was excited. I wasn't sure what I expected; but I knew I'd likely hear it in her voice or see it in her eyes if she didn't like what I wrote.

"Amry, this is really good. And I'm not just saying that. It may be just a rough draft, but it still flows, and I'm intrigued by the main character. She's dark. Interesting. I sense she's much more troubled than what you're showing, like there is much more to come."

"Yeah. Good. I wasn't sure if I was getting that across. It's always hard at first because I'm trying things out, and I'm not sure exactly where the story is going to go."

She asked, "Do you know what happens in this story?"

"I know how it ends. And I have an idea of how to get there, but this one I haven't mapped out. I'm just kind of seeing where it takes me."

Rose looked up. "I don't know how she does that. I have to outline a letter to my mother."

I shrugged off the compliments.

My phone beeped, and I grabbed it and quickly read the text that came in. "It's Darlene. She said Nikko is okay. Tom's not at home. She thinks he's staying over at Beth's. She'll keep me in the loop." I texted an acknowledgment and told Darlene to tell Nikko that we were all sending hugs and love to him.

Takoda said, "Poor kid. What a crappy way to come out."

Rose leaned over to shift the logs in the fireplace with a cast-iron poker. "At least Tom's not over there. Sorry, Amry, but your brother is a complete ass."

"Don't apologize for the truth. He was a dick when I came out. He was a jerk when we were growing up. I could kill him for what he's doing to Nikko."

"Do you believe he hasn't hit Nikko or threatened him?"

"I'm sure there has been yelling, but I can't see Tom hitting him."

Takoda nodded thoughtfully. "He doesn't act like he's been hit," she said.

"Not to be rude, but how would you know?" Rose asked.

"Domestic abuse training. I've had classes in what to look for. We see so much of that in police work. I'm in forestry, so I'm not out on the street, but I still do all the training. And I'm part of an LGBTQ task force. We step in to help LGBTQ kids and adults in abusive situations. I've fostered a couple kids when they got thrown out of their houses. If Nikko were being hit, he'd likely have shied away from Tom this afternoon, and he didn't." Takoda sat straight, hands on her knees, and I could feel her intensity. She looked at me. "I'm serious when I say I'll make sure Nikko stays safe."

I met her gaze and said the only thing that came to mind. "Thank you."

She smiled. "Anytime."

I wasn't sure how long we sat there staring at each other, but Rose cleared her throat and asked, "Takoda, was it hard for you to come out?"

Takoda leaned back, relaxing into the sofa. I took her hand and said, "You don't have to talk about it if you don't want to."

"No, it's fine. It's actually a pretty bland story. My parents both knew before I did that I was gay, so by the time I came out, it was a nonevent. Mom hugged me. Dad said he hoped I would find a very nice girl. My nookomis—my grandma—told me I was blessed to be a two-spirit, and that she saw in a dream that when I met my mate I would know without a doubt. For me, it was harder to be a Native American in the white man's world than to be a lesbian."

Takoda explained that in traditional Native American culture, a two-spirit was a person who had both a male and a female spirit within them. They were honored and considered to be closer to the spirits and to have special powers. As far as I was concerned, she was a very special person with or without any spiritual powers.

I told an abbreviated version of my own not-so-happy coming-out experience, and Rose related her experiences growing up with a houseful of brothers and sisters in a small farming town. We'd all had our issues and challenges.

As the fire burned down, Takoda decided she needed to get going. Rose made a point of leaving us alone and went to get ready for bed. Takoda and I walked into the back porch with the dogs trailing at our heels and stopped near the door. The inside lights were off. I could hear the soft thud of moths bumping against the window screens around the dim yellow light hanging outside the door. Shadows cast Takoda's face in angular planes as we faced each other.

"I'm really glad you spent the day," I said.

"Thank you for inviting me." She caressed my cheek. I turned my head to kiss her palm. She tipped my face toward her and found my lips with her own.

I sighed, melting into the heat of her kiss, pressing into her body. One of my hands spread across her back, the other behind her neck to twist in her hair. Her tongue moved hot against my own, sending shivers through me.

Her hands slid under my T-shirt and dragged across my heated skin. I plunged my tongue deeper into her mouth as her hand cupped my ass. The pulse between my legs made me want to grind against the thigh she pushed between us.

When we finally parted, gasping for air, Takoda leaned her forehead against mine. God. What I was feeling right now…I was going to explode.

She kissed me lightly and retreated so there was air between us. "I need to go."

I nodded. Either she walked out that door or I was going to fuck her right here in the porch.

"I'll talk to you tomorrow," she said.

"Tomorrow," I repeated.

She turned toward the door, clicking her tongue for the dogs to follow her.

"Drive safely," I said.

"I will." She smiled, and my knees went weak.

I watched until the Jeep disappeared into the darkness, then locked up the porch and shut off the back lights. I could still taste her mouth against mine, still feel her hands on my skin. My racing blood throbbed between my legs and my underwear were soaked. I didn't remember the last time I'd been this turned on just kissing someone. I was in trouble here.

CHAPTER SIX

Rose and I spent a quiet day Thursday. Rose went out fishing, and I spent most of the day working on my manuscript. For dinner, we biked to the new little Italian restaurant about a mile down the road. Takoda was spending the day with her brother George and his wife and daughter at the zoo in Duluth. The day felt strangely quiet and empty without her presence, and I kept wondering if my family drama from the previous day had scared her off. Still, she said she'd return to the cabin Friday, and after our make-out session in the porch, I had to believe she was as interested in seeing me as I was in seeing her.

On the other hand, I reminded myself this was a summer fling. She had a life here, in which she was very invested, and I had my life in the city. I had no intention of chasing a long-distance relationship. Even though I was crazy attracted to her and even though she appeared to be a perfect catch, I couldn't see a future in this vacation crush.

I'd had no word from Nikko. I'd sent him a few short texts to let him know I was thinking about him and was here if he needed to talk. Darlene had texted to let me know he was okay. Tom was still staying with my sister. I was glad he wasn't at home making Nikko's life miserable. Tom and Bethany deserved each other and it was better that he was staying with his twin than with Dad. I was sure Dad wouldn't know what was going on. Tom would never let Dad know if he was having problems, either with his kids or his marriage. That would make him weak, and Tom never wanted to look weak.

Friday dawned sunny and hot. Takoda and the dogs arrived at the cabin in the early afternoon and joined Rose and I on the beach. Rose floated out on the water, sunning herself, while Takoda and I stood thigh-deep in the shallows, playing fetch with Gabby while Xena sprawled on the dock soaking up the sun.

Takoda threw Gabby's neon yellow water toy as far as she could, well past Rose. Gabby took off after her prize. I stared at the way Takoda's black Speedo hugged her water-splashed torso and was startled out of my ogling when Gabby dropped the dummy and soaked us as she shook the water from her thick fur.

"Gabby, good girl! Good job!" Takoda roughed her up and tossed the floating Frisbee she'd been hiding behind her back. Gabby barked happily and splashed after it, and Xena launched herself off the dock to race her pack mate. We laughed as we watched the two dogs wrestling and playing tug.

"Hey Aunt Amry!" I turned to see my nephew Joey barreling down the stairs to the beach, his towel flapping behind him. He grinned and waved. "Wow! Do you have dogs now?"

I opened my mouth to reply, but he was already splashing into the water, having dropped his towel on the edge of the grass along the narrow spit of beach.

"Joey!" Darlene appeared at the top of the stairs with Nikko.

Takoda whistled, bringing the dogs to her.

I said, "Joey, this is my friend Takoda, and they're her dogs. Let her introduce you, okay?"

He splashed to a stop beside me. "Okay, cool."

Nikko and Darlene trotted down the stairs. Nikko's shoulders had a tired slump, and I wrapped him in a tight hug.

It was awkward but heartfelt. It was tough to give Auntie hugs when your nephew was nearly a foot taller than you.

I let him go. "You doing okay?" I asked.

He shrugged. "Sort of."

Darlene laid a hand on his shoulder. Her expression was concerned, gentle, loving, accepting. It was an expression my mother had never used on me after I'd come out. Nikko was lucky Darlene was there for him. She said, "It's going to be okay."

He scowled. "Right. My dad hates my guts. Corey won't talk to me because he's afraid of Dad. By the time school starts, everyone's going to know I'm gay, and it's going to suck. How is any of that going to be okay?"

I had no good response. It sounded pretty sucky to me too.

Darlene said, "Unless you tell everyone at school, they won't know anything. You know Corey isn't going to out you. Your dad certainly isn't going to tell anyone. Corey will come around."

"Someone will find out. They always do, Mom."

Nikko walked away to join Joey, Takoda and the dogs. Takoda gave him a silent one-armed hug and handed him Gabby's training dummy. He took his frustration out on the toy, which Gabby happily brought back for more, while Xena fetched the Frisbee for Joey.

I asked Darlene, "How are you holding up?"

"I'm fine. I'm not the one who came out. Just trying to keep Nikk together."

"Is Tom still at Beth's?"

"Yeah. Not sure how long that will last, though. Do you have any beer? I could really use one."

I patted her arm. I couldn't fix anything with Tom, but I could provide beer. "Come on. We're well stocked." I led Darlene to the cabin and grabbed her a bottle of beer while taking a hard lemonade for myself.

She popped the cap and took a couple long swallows, then leaned against the kitchen counter. "I know we haven't talked a lot, you and I, and I know I haven't defended you from Tom the way I should have. I wanted to apologize for that. I'm sorry I haven't been a better person toward you, Amry."

For a moment, I stood speechless. "Thank you. I appreciate your saying that."

She smiled sadly. "I think I've known about Nikk for a long time. At least, I suspected and wondered and worried. I've tried to be supportive. But I didn't want to cross Tom. I didn't want to set them against each other. It happened anyway. The more I stand up for Nikk, the angrier Tom gets. And Joey is so damned confused. He doesn't understand any of what's going on, other than that Tom is furious with Nikko and me."

"What happens now?"

"I'm not sure, to be honest." She took a couple swallows of her beer and turned the bottle in her fingers. "Nikko and Joe come first. I wish Tom would be reasonable, but I don't know if that's going to happen. Tom's not a bad person. He's just got some twisted ideas about the way things are."

Tom had more than a few twisted ideas. He was a bigoted jerk. I supposed at some level I loved him because he was my brother, but, searching my heart, I found mostly animosity toward him. "Do you think Tom will go back home to you and the boys?" I asked.

"I'm not sure I want him home. I'm tired of the fighting. Nikko and Joey don't need to be around that, and I don't want them hearing his hateful beliefs. I've tried to show the boys there's another point of view, but it's not enough anymore. Nikko's hurting, and I don't want Joe to turn into his father. So maybe it's best if Tom doesn't come home."

"Have you talked to Tom?"

"Last night. We ended up screaming at each other. I told him not to show his face in my house and hung up on him." She downed the rest of her beer. "I think if he walked up to me right now, I'd smack the crap out of him."

"So you're okay with Nikko being gay?"

She opened the fridge for a second beer, twisted the cap off and sipped slowly before slumping back against the counter. "Okay with it? It's a hard thing for a kid to be different than everyone else. You don't choose for your kid to be picked on, you know? But I will love and accept and support him no matter what."

"I'm here for both of you, Darlene." I meant that. A swell of affection for my sister-in-law grew in my chest, and I understood I was seeing the real woman for the first time—not just my brother's wife. It made me wish I'd paid more attention to her before this. I knew I wanted to be friends with this woman who was much stronger and braver than I'd realized.

"Thank you, Amry." She rested her hand on my forearm then took a deep breath and stood straighter. "Let's get back outside and see what they're up to."

I followed her back down to the beach. Rose had joined Nikko and Joey throwing fetch for the dogs.

Takoda met my gaze with a silent question, and I nodded as I sidled up to her. Things were okay. She winked at me and I passed her my bottle of hard lemonade. She took a long swallow and handed it back as Gabby trotted up to drop her ball in front of Joey.

Joey asked, "Doesn't she ever get tired?"

"Gabby will keep chasing that toy until you can't lift your arm to throw and she can't move her legs to swim. So we have to be careful not to tire her out too much," Takoda said.

Nikko said, "This is good for my pitching arm."

"You play ball?" Takoda asked him.

Nikko's smile was blinding. "Rec league this summer, varsity in the spring. We play like two games a week. Most of the time I pitch, but sometimes I play third base. We're playing tonight against the Fridge-Air team. I'm pitching starter."

"Maybe we should come and cheer you on," Takoda said. "You gals up for that?"

I could have kissed her. "Absolutely!"

"I'm totally up for a ball game," Rose agreed.

"Really? Sweet!" Nikko high-fived Takoda. "That'd be really great, you guys!"

Darlene had a smile on her face that could have lit up Canada in the dark.

CHAPTER SEVEN

"Steeeeerike three!"

The batter grimaced and stalked off toward the bench. Takoda, Rose, Darlene, Joey and I whooped and cheered from our vantage point in the metal bleachers on the first base side of home plate. On the pitching mound, Nikko caught the ball from his catcher. He reset his ball cap and stood a little straighter as he waited for his next victim. He was pitching a good game, and his team led three to one.

"Mom, can I get a hot dog?"

Darlene regarded Joey with a shake of her head and heaved an exasperated sigh. "You just had popcorn."

"Yeah, but I'm still hungry." He gave her an endearing, mischievous smirk, reminding me very much of my brother. "I'm a growing boy," he pleaded.

Darlene laughed and handed him a few dollars out of the front pocket of her jean shorts. "Okay, get a hot dog. No candy."

"Thanks!" He took the money and bounded down the bleachers.

"That one is eating me out of house and home and growing like a weed. The jeans I bought him three months ago are already too short."

Takoda said, "My brother and I were both like that. Drove my parents crazy trying to keep us in food and clothes."

I made a point of gazing up at Takoda. "Had to have been a hell of a growth spurt."

She bumped me with her shoulder.

Rose giggled. "Amry, everyone but you had a growth spurt."

"Yeah, yeah, dump on the short person. Thanks, guys."

A snappish voice interrupted with, "I figured I'd find you here."

We all turned. My sister Bethany stood in front of Darlene. She wore a white cap-sleeved blouse, dark blue "mom jeans" and perfectly white canvas sneakers.

Darlene said brightly, "Hi Beth, what brings you here?"

"As if you didn't know."

Someone behind us yelled, "Down in front!"

Bethany sat abruptly next to Darlene. "I talked to Tom."

"Did you?" Darlene appeared unimpressed.

"I would think you'd care more about your marriage than siding with an unruly teenager who doesn't know what he wants."

Darlene's eyes narrowed and hardened, her expression turning coldly furious. When she spoke, her tone was low and even but drenched in barely contained anger. "Nikko is not unruly. He's a good kid, and he knows exactly what he wants and who he is. If Tom is stupid enough not to see it or accept it, then Tom, and you, can go straight to hell, along with everyone else who is too closed minded to have a clue."

"How dare you!"

I bit my lip on about three retorts.

Darlene said, "Shut the fuck up and mind your own business, Beth. I'm tired of your holier-than-thou bullshit, and I'm tired of Tom's bigoted tirades. Stay or leave, but right now I am watching my son play ball." She turned to watch the game, effectively ending the conversation.

I managed not to snicker out loud. I heard Rose laughing under her breath. Takoda muttered, "Good girl, D." She put her arm around my waist, and I leaned into her. *Fuck 'em all*, I thought. *Let 'em think whatever they want.*

After a moment or two, Bethany left in a huff.

From the bench in the dugout, I saw Nikko turn his head in our direction. I flashed him a thumbs-up to indicate all was well. He frowned but nodded and turned back to the game to cheer on a teammate who hit a single and got on base. I noticed he was sitting beside his friend and teammate Corey Pearson, and I hoped they'd worked things out.

Joey returned with a half-eaten hot dog in one hand and a can of Coke in the other. "I just saw Aunt Beth," he said as he sat beside his mom. "I yelled hi, but she didn't say anything back. She was leaving."

Darlene gave him a reassuring smile. "I'm sure she just didn't hear you, Joe."

"Okay." An instant later he was focused on the game, yelling, "All right, Mike! Way to hit it!"

I liked how kids could do that. They took things at face value and went on with their lives. I wished I could be the same way, but anger at my siblings burned in my stomach. I forced myself to settle down and focus on Nikko's game.

Afterward, Takoda, Rose and I piled into Rose's CRV for the trip back to the cabin. I rode shotgun and Takoda sat in the back, leaning between the front seats.

Rose said, "I still cannot believe your bitch sister. What the hell was she thinking?"

"I'm sure Tom's making it sound like it was everyone's fault but his. He's the correct, righteous one, and everyone else is unreasonable. They're twins. They think in tandem. They used to do it all the time when I lived at home, except I was the one who was unreasonable."

Takoda said, "If I heard either of them talk like that about you, I'd slap them both silly. It was all I could to keep my mouth shut."

I patted her hand. "Thank you. I'm really sorry you've had to be in the middle of all this family crap. Both of you."

Rose shrugged it off. "It does make things more interesting. I feel bad for them, though. Darlene's going to have some hard decisions to make about Tom, and Nikko's going to end up feeling like it's all his fault."

"I wish there was more I could do, but it's not my place to get in the middle of their family issues. I feel like all I can do is let Nikko know he can come to me if he needs to talk, or even if he needs a place to stay for a while," I said.

"Please let him know that I'm here too," Takoda put in. "I know I'm not family, and I hardly know all of you, but if Nikko needs a safe place to be, he can always call me."

I turned in my seat. In the shadowed light from the dashboard, her expression was serious. Takoda said, "Sometimes it's easier to talk to someone who's not family."

It made sense and it was so sweet that she offered, though the paranoid little voice in the back of my head still wondered if she was being nice to make a good impression. I'd been badly burned by a woman who started out being sweet and thoughtful, then shifted to angry and manipulative once she'd sucked me in. I wanted to believe Takoda was better than that. I wanted to believe she was the amazing person she appeared to be. If she could be that person for Nikko, it would be a truly wonderful thing.

The late Saturday morning sun smiled down from a clear blue sky, and a breeze teased the lake into gentle ripples. Rose and I paddled the canoe leisurely along the shoreline, a couple hundred feet out, taking advantage of our last full day of vacation. I settled into the relaxing rhythm of the paddle slicing through the water, the wet slap of waves against the thin hull and the occasional *shushing* of weeds as we moved through them.

Rose and I practically had the lake to ourselves. I only saw one other fishing boat, trolling out near the channel into the bay.

We paddled past the state park swimming beach and along the north side of the lake into a shallow bay behind a tiny island.

It was great sunny and crappie fishing, and it was my job to keep us in place, more or less, while Rose fished.

She shifted around so she was facing me and proceeded to set up her rod with bait. The current pushed us toward shore and I was content to occasionally dip my paddle into the water to steady us while I daydreamed and studied the shoreline.

Trees with twisted trunks clung to the low banks, their spidery roots exposed and trapping weeds and leaf detritus among them. Dragonflies hummed over the water and fat bees hovered up and down in confused flight, stopping to feed on the purple, white and yellow flowers dotting the shoreline.

"What time is Takoda picking you up for dinner tonight?"

"She's not picking me up. I'm driving to her place. She's cooking for me."

Rose waggled her brows. "That sounds pretty serious."

I scowled. "Hardly."

"Oh, come on, Am, you like her."

"Well, yeah, I like her. She's really sweet and funny, intelligent, sexy and for some reason, she actually seems to like me. She's like an Amazon goddess and she actually pays attention to me, in all my ordinariness."

"Don't put yourself down. You're a good-looking woman. You're smart and funny and kind and thoughtful. What's not to like?"

I made a face.

Rose said, "If she were a guy, I'd be marrying her tomorrow."

"You're serious."

She played the short fishing rod up and down and let out a little line. "I am. She's good people."

"I barely know her."

"What does your gut say? Hell, what do your hormones say?"

I dipped the paddle in and eased us backward. "We're leaving tomorrow, Rose. I'm going back to my real life. She's staying here, living her real life. We're not a part of each other's lives."

"You could be."

"Be realistic. She's not going to leave this area, and I sure as hell would never live up here."

Rose merely smiled with that all-knowing "I-have-lived-longer-than-you-and-have-more-wisdom" smile that drove me crazy.

I growled, "Give it up, Rose."

"At least get yourself laid tonight."

"I am not having this conversation."

Rose laughed. She was enjoying this way too much. "Troll us along a little bit."

I gave her a pained sigh and paddled. It beat continuing a pointless conversation. Not that I didn't want to get laid. After the heated kisses in the porch at the cabin, all I could think about was what it would be like to be with Takoda, to hold her naked in my arms. But sleeping with someone just for the sex wasn't my thing. I'd never been a player. I always worried too much about what happened the next morning, the next week or the next date. If I wanted someone enough to be that intimate, she needed to mean more to me than getting off for a night. I needed it to have a future.

In the case of Takoda and I, there was no future. Inevitably, we would go our separate ways. I didn't want to let myself get emotionally invested in a relationship that was going to rip me apart when it ended. And yet, there I was, agreeing to have dinner with a woman who made my whole being want more than just a quick summer fuck. What in the hell was I thinking?

Tomorrow my vacation was over and I would return home. Takoda would stay here. I would probably never see her again. But I couldn't bring myself not to see her tonight. I felt like a fly caught in a spiderweb, but it didn't feel wrong or dangerous. I was drawn to her, pulled in her direction from someplace deep inside me, even though the logical part of my brain warned me off.

I had a satisfying life. A good job that I enjoyed. Friends who were practically family. Sure, it was beautiful here in the north woods, and it made a great vacation getaway, but I had left for a reason. I didn't fit here. I didn't want to deal with the closed-minded, ignorant people I'd grown up with. I liked living two hundred and fifty miles away from my siblings and my parents, where their constant disapproval wasn't hanging over me.

Why would I choose to live in a place where I had to hide my sexuality? The city was my sanctuary. I could live in my own skin without having to hide because nobody outside my circle of friends cared. I didn't have to watch my pronouns or worry about saying the wrong thing.

There was no future for me with Takoda Running Bear. But I was going to see her anyway.

Maybe Rose was right. Even if Takoda and I had no future, it didn't mean I couldn't enjoy myself tonight.

CHAPTER EIGHT

I checked Takoda's directions again and took the next right off the county highway. The Forester bumped onto a single-lane road hemmed in by the dense pine and deciduous forest. After about three miles, the cracked and pitted asphalt turned to gravel. I took the final right at a narrow track marked with Takoda's fire-number and a carved wooden sign in the shape of a running bear that said "Spirit Bear Trail."

After a couple of twists, the gravel drive opened into a clearing. Takoda's cabin was a sweeping A-frame log home surrounded by pines and birch trees with a lake glittering behind it. The story-high paned windows in the peak of the A-frame depicted an intricate stained-glass landscape. A deck wrapped around the front and left side of the house and a wide, railed stairway led to the front entry.

As I parked and got out of the car, Gabby and Xena barreled out of the woods, greeting me with excited barks and alternately running circles around me and rubbing against my legs for pets. I ruffled their fur and returned their greetings.

"Hey! Welcome to my humble abode!" Takoda bounced down the front stairs, sexy as hell in faded cargo shorts and a tight black tank. She jogged across the short grass and welcomed me with a hug. "I'm glad you didn't get lost."

I wrapped my arms around her waist, resting my head on her chest for a moment. Her body was solid and warm under my hands, and I reveled in pure bliss.

"The directions were perfect."

We separated, and she took my hand. "Come in and I'll show you around."

It felt completely normal for her to lead me by the hand as we climbed the steps onto the deck and through the front door. I crossed the portal into a bright, open space with darkly polished wood flooring and a two-story ceiling where two fans circled lazily. The main room was sectioned into a dining area, kitchen and a living room and den that opened to a patio overlooking the lake. The décor was rustic and comfortable—lived in but not too cluttered.

I toed my shoes off and added them to the pile by the door. Takoda gestured around. "Make yourself at home."

The aroma of Italian cooking tickled my nose and I sniffed appreciatively. "Smells great."

"I sure hope so, because this is about the only decent meal I can cook. I'll give you the five-cent tour before I have to stir stuff again." She made dramatic arm gestures. "Living room, kitchen, dining room."

"Nice," I said.

To the right of the entryway was a large sitting room with a river-rock fireplace in the front corner. To the left, a dining area with a dining table and four chairs in front of patio doors that opened onto the side deck. The table was set for two, with plain light blue plates and two royal blue tapered candles in crystal holders at the center. A small mudroom opened off the kitchen, which was separated from the main room by a tiled breakfast bar.

Still holding my hand, Takoda led me past the kitchen to the back of the living room and den area. She pointed to two doors behind the kitchen. "First door is the guest bedroom, but the only guest I ever had is my five-year-old niece."

"I bet she loved it," I said.

"She did." Takoda's face lit up. She pointed to the next door. "Most important, that is the downstairs bathroom."

I poked my head into a deceptively roomy space, complete with a Jacuzzi tub big enough for two, a sink in a narrow granite counter and a toilet tucked into the corner. "Love the tub," I said.

"Nothing like a hot Jacuzzi when you've been out in thirty-below weather all day."

Turning back toward the living room, she indicated the railed split-log stairway hugging the side wall. It led to a full-story loft built above the back two-thirds of the living room. "I sleep up in the loft," she said. "There's a small bathroom with a shower too."

I swear I saw the hint of a blush across her high cheekbones. "This is a great place," I said. "Did you build it yourself?"

"I wish. I helped with the design, though." She released my hand and stepped toward the kitchen. "Do you want some wine?"

Takoda poured two glasses of chilled sweet white wine. I swirled mine in the glass while I watched her putter around the kitchen. She checked the rigatoni noodles boiling in a big pot and the garlic cheese bread toasting in the oven. She'd already filled a serving bowl with meatballs and sausage and sauce.

The dogs had been sent to lay down on the cool flagstones in front of the fireplace.

I asked, "Is there anything I can do?"

"I think the cheese bread is done, if you want to grab that while I strain the noodles. And there's salad in the fridge, if you want to take that out and put it on the table. The dressing is in there too."

I set my wineglass on the counter. "Sure. The sauce smells wonderful."

"Thanks. The recipe came from an Italian woman my mom used to work with, so it's authentic." She drained the noodles and put them into another bowl, ladling the remainder of the sauce over them, while I plated the cheese bread, and between us we got everything to the table.

Takoda lit the candles, then held a chair out for me before she rushed back to the counter to get our wineglasses and refill them, finally joining me. I could tell she was nervous, and it was adorable.

The food tasted wonderful. The sauce had a hint of sweetness, the sausage was spicy and the meatballs were moist and tender. "Takoda, this is excellent!"

She beamed. "I'm glad you like it."

"You can cook for me anytime."

We took our time eating and chatting. We got to talking about our jobs, and how sometimes people you worked with made you shake your head.

"Yeah, you really never know, right?" Takoda took time to chew a forkful of rigatoni and sipped her wine before continuing. "A couple weeks ago, we got a call from Mrs. Brecker. Nice woman. Probably in her mid-eighties. She lives by herself now, just a couple miles down the road from here. Her kids are around quite a bit, but I look in on her from time to time, especially when the weather's bad. Anyway, she calls to say there's a bear going through her garbage again, and can we get rid of it."

I raised a brow. "That sounds not so safe."

"It can be interesting. So, I drove over there, and sure enough, there was garbage strewn all over the place, and she was out there, picking it up and putting it back in the cans. I noticed that there were a couple of nice cooked chicken carcasses in the mess. There were no bears around, though, and she invited me in for a glass of pop or a cup of coffee, so I followed her into the house. Fifteen minutes later, we hear all this clanking and banging, and when I look out the window, there are two dogs working together, knocking over the cans and digging through the garbage. And they're my damned dogs!"

I nearly choked on my food as I started laughing.

Sadly, my work stories weren't nearly as interesting, but I shared some of my own "adventures" at local Gay Pride festivities, lesbian writers' conferences, bike rides, and camping follies with Rose.

After dinner, we cleaned up and then took our wine out onto the screened deck at the back of the house. The dogs joined us, sprawled near the lounge chairs we had pulled together so that our thighs and shoulders touched. Heat radiated from her body to mine, through the fabric of our clothes. It made me want to be in her arms instead of lounging beside her, and just that little bit of heat created an aching throb within me.

Our fingers intertwined as we watched the sun set behind the tree-framed view of the lake. The sky shifted from warm oranges and pinks to the deeper blues of dusk. I couldn't help but notice how the shadows played over Takoda's body as the sun disappeared. Birch trees rustled in a quiet symphony over the rhythmic lap of water on the shoreline, accented by the occasional calls of a pair of loons.

Eventually, darkness descended, bringing with it the chatter of cicadas and frogs. Not long after the stars came out, Takoda suggested we go inside. I settled on the sofa while Takoda settled the dogs and arranged a few logs in the fireplace. In no time, a small blaze lit up the corner of the living room.

Takoda joined me and rested an arm around my shoulder. I cuddled against her. It'd been a wonderful evening, spent discussing everything and nothing, and sometimes not talking at all, yet I was nowhere near ready to call an end to the night. I didn't understand what it was about Takoda that made me so comfortable that we could simply sit watching the world, without the need to fill the silence. With most dates, I was always struggling to make small talk and wondering if I was saying the wrong thing or if she was silent because she was bored or uninterested. Tonight felt entirely different.

The flames flickered across the planes of Takoda's face. She was breathtaking—so handsome, but with a feminine softness that drew me like a fly to molasses.

She caught me staring. The next moment we were kissing. I tasted wine on her tongue and savored the soft fullness of her lips. We kissed until we were both panting for breath. My head spun. Foreheads touching, we gazed into each other's eyes. Hers were dark with need. She cradled my face gently in her hands.

"You are so beautiful," she whispered.

No. You're the beautiful one. I wanted to shake my head but was paralyzed by her touch. She kissed me again, almost chastely, before putting a little more distance between us.

She said, "I want you so much, but I don't want this to be a one-night stand. You're too special for that."

I couldn't find any words. My brain had shut down, leaving only raw emotion and sensory input. I swallowed hard, trying to get myself under control. I ran my fingers through her hair, so thick and silky. For a writer, I was totally at a loss. How could I say what I was feeling when I couldn't decipher it myself?

I knew she was right. As hard as it was to put on the brakes, I didn't want to use Takoda for a quick fuck and then walk away. She deserved better than to be treated that way. She deserved someone who was going to stick around. But I wasn't ready for the night to end. I wanted to hold her and not let go.

Me, who didn't want to be involved in a long-distance relationship—I didn't want to be parted from this amazing woman who thought I was special.

All these things went through my head, but, seriously, could I actually say something? I felt like a deer caught in the headlights. I sucked in a breath and hoped whatever came out of my mouth wasn't incredibly inane. I took her hands in mine and held them against my chest. "You're the one who's special. You're an incredible woman, Takoda. Tonight doesn't have to end with us sleeping together, but I sure am enjoying kissing you."

"You're a very good kisser."

"I'm feeling inspired."

"Maybe I can inspire you a little more." The last word dropped off to a low growl as she leaned in and ran her tongue along my lips, teasing. I released her hands and pulled her closer, sucking her tongue into my mouth, savoring the hot, wet feel of her as we practically devoured each other. It was erotic, and I felt completely out of control and I didn't care. My heart was pounding so hard she must have felt it beating against my chest.

She said, "Come to bed with me."

I leaned back, eyes widening.

She gave me a wistful smile, her dark eyes still dilated with lust. "Not like that. I need to hold you. And it's so much more comfortable than the sofa."

I nodded.

Takoda eased away, letting her fingers trace down my back and along my waist as she stood and offered me a hand up. I rose on shaky legs. She led me up the stairs to the loft. When we reached the foot of the bed, she released my hand. "Hang on a sec."

She crossed the room to a low chest of drawers against the side wall and returned with a soft gray T-shirt. "Nightshirt. I think we'd both be more comfortable that way, huh? There's a new toothbrush by the sink for you." She licked her lips. "I hope it's okay?"

"It's great," I said. "I'll just, um, go and change."

"Sure."

I ducked into the bathroom, shut the door and leaned on it with my eyes closed. I concentrated on breathing, trying to slow my pulse. Damn. I was so close to tearing her clothes off and taking her right now. Why were we stopping? She obviously felt the same way.

I took a deep breath and studied my reflection. My face was flushed, lips swollen, eyes too wide, my hair mussed from her fingers running through it. I sat down on the toilet, taking the time to get my head together.

Takoda had set a washcloth, hand towel and bath towel on the side of the vanity, along with a toothbrush still in its packaging. I finished my business, then undressed.

Avoiding the mirror, I brushed my teeth, washed my face and cleaned up, wishing I'd thought to stuff a clean pair of underwear into my pocket. I tugged her shirt on over my Hawaiian-print boxers. The soft, washed-out baseball jersey hung on my shoulders and fell midway down my thighs. I brought the material to my face and breathed in the scent of fresh laundry. It was the perfect sleep shirt.

By the time I'd finished, I felt more in control. When I opened the door into the bedroom, Takoda was sitting on the edge of the bed, wearing a faded state park T-shirt that stretched across her shoulders and clung deliciously to her breasts.

She stood and I stared. Her T-shirt hung loosely around her narrow hips, revealing black silk boxers and legs that went on forever. I swallowed. She may as well have been wearing Victoria's Secret lingerie.

She moved past me, letting her hand brush across my stomach. "I'll be right back."

I thought I nodded. I was speechless. When she disappeared into the bathroom, I stood for a minute, hearing muffled sounds through the door. I thought about sitting on the edge of the bed to wait for her, then shook my head. The covers were already folded back, so I crawled onto the bed, propped up the pillows against the headboard and slid between cool sheets.

I willed myself to calm down. We were not going to fuck each other silly. We were going to hold each other and cuddle. I rested my head against the pillows. The lamp on the nightstand bathed the loft area with soft yellow light. The banked fire glowed from the fireplace below. A gentle draft from the silently spinning ceiling fans cooled my face. In the quiet, I could hear the chirping of crickets and the rustle of trees.

The bathroom door opened and Takoda flipped off the bathroom light before she settled next to me. "Hey," she said.

"Hey, yourself."

"You doing okay?"

"I'm good."

She shimmied down under the sheet and patted the space beside her. "Come and get comfy?"

I scooted down and stretched out beside her, resting my head on her shoulder with one arm draped across her middle. She cuddled me closer with an arm around me and covered my hand with hers. Curiously, as I settled against her, my heart rate slowed, my pulse calming as I lay in her arms. I felt the brush of her lips on my hair, and I kissed the soft material of her nightshirt under my cheek.

Her body felt good. I had never sprawled over a bed partner this way. Lying beside someone, touching, maybe spooning, sure, but this was different in a way I couldn't explain. We fit together and I was content to lie entwined with her, yet aware that the spark of passion wasn't far underneath the calm. "This is nice."

I felt her body relax and settle under me. "It is."

I closed my eyes and breathed in the warm, sunshine scent of her, memorizing it, preserving this moment in my mind and senses. Just in case it never happened again.

* * *

I woke to the sun in my eyes. Colored beams from the stained glass played over the bedding twisted around us. I lay on my side with Takoda's long body spooned against me, one long arm wrapped around my waist, her breath warm on my shoulder.

I felt as though I could stay in her arms forever, warm and safe. It wasn't a sensation I expected. To be honest, there was nothing expected about my time with Takoda. I was floundering in uncharted waters, and it was as scary as it was wonderful. Scary because as perfect as it appeared, I was waiting for the other shoe to drop.

Takoda shifted behind me. "Morning," she murmured into my hair.

I smiled at the husky roughness of her voice. I shifted onto my back, and she leaned over and kissed me softly. I sighed as her tongue teased my lower lip. She nipped gently and I delved into the warmth of her mouth, groaning as desire spiked.

God, I wanted her. But I eased away. We couldn't do this. Not now. I had to leave.

Takoda pressed her lips against my forehead, then lay beside me. We cuddled until the dogs rumbled up the stairs. Xena put her feet up on the mattress and chuffed at us. Gabby jumped up and straddled Takoda, happily licking her face.

"Gabby, off." Takoda pushed the dog away. She sat up, swinging her legs over the side of the bed. "I'd better put them out."

I squinted at the clock on the bed stand. I didn't want to leave, but I had to return to reality. "And I need to get back to the cabin so I can help Rose get our stuff packed up."

She pulled on shorts under her nightshirt. "You can use the shower up here or downstairs. There are towels and washcloths in both bathrooms. I'll get some coffee going."

"Thank you."

She leaned down for a quick, chaste kiss before shooing the dogs downstairs.

I showered and threw on yesterday's clothes before joining Takoda in the kitchen. We had a quick breakfast of toast and coffee. Both of us were quiet, but it was mostly a comfortable silence, filled with shared gazes. I wasn't sure what to say. It felt wrong to talk about the future. This wasn't a real relationship, though it felt like more than a passing fancy. Still, I didn't know if I'd see her again. The logistics weren't positive. It had been a wonderful evening and night, but I felt an uneasiness settling in my chest, like I was saying goodbye when I'd barely said hello.

Takoda walked me out to my car. I put my hand on the door handle, but turned to her before I opened it. She slid a hand behind my neck and kissed me soundly before she stepped back. She stared at me with a serious, earnest expression. "I don't want to lose you, Amry," she said softly. "I know this sounds ridiculous, but I feel like I've finally found you, and I don't want you to walk away and not see you again."

Doubt bubbled up in my mind. In a different circumstance, I would have been certain there was something between us. I didn't want to lose her either. But she was here, and I was going back to the city.

She must have read the uncertainty in my expression. She cupped my cheek. "Please, promise to stay in touch? Text me when you get home so I know you made it?"

I couldn't avoid the intensity of her gaze. I nodded. "I will. I promise."

She kissed me again, the softest, most perfect kiss, full of promise and hope. Then she released me and reached behind me to open the car door. "You'd better get going," she said.

I heard the hitch in her voice and swallowed hard. "Be safe driving home."

"I will." I made myself get into the car, start the engine and roll the window down. "Talk to you soon. Take care, Takoda."

She nodded and patted the top of the car before moving back out of the way.

As I left the drive, I checked the rearview mirror to see Takoda watching solemnly with her hands tucked into her pockets. Turning onto the gravel road, I felt empty inside. I blinked back sudden tears and told myself I was not going to cry.

CHAPTER NINE

Rose had already started packing by the time I arrived. As we worked, Rose asked how the evening had gone. She gave me a hard time when I told her nothing happened, but we were too busy packing for me to get into the reasons why Takoda and I hadn't screwed like bunnies. In any case, I needed to process everything on my own before I was ready to start discussing the "what nexts."

I loaded the cars and cleaned while my brain tried to make sense of the dichotomy between what my overheated libido and my gut were telling me and what my ever-practical-and-realistic-pessimistic head was telling me.

I knew I would be hurt less if I listened to my head, so I clung to that and tried to ignore the crazy butterflies in my stomach every time I envisioned Takoda, and the deep sense of emptiness I felt every time I thought about going back to the city. I settled on convincing myself I was only feeling ambivalence about going back to the daily grind of work after a week of vacation. That was normal. Nobody would rather work than vacation.

I locked up the cabin and said a silent goodbye to my favorite vacation place. Rose followed me into town where we would drop off the cabin keys with my dad and visit for a bit.

When we drove into the driveway, Dad was waiting in his lawn chair, resting in the shade in front of the garage. "Did you girls have a good time this week?" he asked as we joined him. Dad gave me a hug and shook Rose's hand vigorously. He'd set up chairs for us as well, knowing we'd be stopping before we headed for home.

"Thanks again for letting us use the cabin, Mr. M. We had a great week."

"Good to hear it! Sit, have a pop." He eased himself back into his chair and pointed to the lunch cooler by his side. "How was fishing?"

I retrieved Diet Cokes for Rose and I and sipped on mine while Dad and Rose told each other fish stories. I stretched my legs out and crossed my ankles, watching traffic on the highway in front of the house, only half listening to the conversation until Dad commented, "Beth said you girls were at Nikko's ball game Friday night."

Rose said, "He invited us to come and watch. He's a good pitcher."

Nice attempt at a save.

Dad glanced my way. "She said you were there with Darlene."

"We were sitting with her, yes," I said.

"You know Tom isn't living at home?" he asked.

"That's what Darlene said. Bethany came to the game too, for a minute or two. Have you talked to Tom?"

"No. He hasn't called. I talked to Beth though. She said Darlene kicked him out."

"I don't know." I picked my words carefully. "I didn't ask for details. I'm not getting in the middle of their fight."

Dad frowned. "But you have, haven't you? Beth said you sided with Darlene when you were at the ball game."

"Actually, I never said a word. It was all Darlene and Beth arguing. Beth has no business butting into Tom and Darlene's business either. I have no idea what possessed her to show up at Nikko's game just to cause trouble."

"I'm sure she was trying to put in a good word for her twin, which seems to be more than you're willing to do."

I stood abruptly. Anger bubbled up and spilled over. "Do you even know what they're fighting about, Dad? Do you? They're fighting because Nikko told them he's gay and Tom can't handle it. Darlene is supporting Nikk, and all Tom can do is tell him he's a pervert! Poor kid thinks his dad hates him and is scared and heartsick, and all Tom can think about is his own bigoted point of view. So, if I'm taking Darlene's side, so be it. I hope to hell you're going to still be here for Nikko and not abandon him too." Chest heaving, I stalked to the end of the driveway, keeping my back to my father and Rose, trying to get my anger under control. If Dad was going to be like Tom, I was leaving.

I heard the slightly metallic *clunk* of a can being set on the concrete. I watched cars zip past. As my breathing slowed, my anger dissolved and left an uneasy, unsettled tension in my neck and shoulders.

When I finally walked back. I could see Rose was biting her tongue. Dad rubbed his chin with thick fingers, his jaw working.

As I approached, he said, "So, Nikko's like you, huh?"

I searched his face, trying to read his expression to figure out if Nikko being like me was good or bad.

"I don't understand it, but it's part of you. I love you, Amry. I always have and I always will. I love Nikko too. He's a good kid. He's always been a good kid. He's my grandson, and I love him, and that's not going to change." He regarded me with a serious expression before continuing. "If Tom's giving Nikk a hard time, it's not right. Nikk's his kid, and he should love him no matter what and accept him no matter what."

Relief washed over me. Feeling a little weak-kneed, I collapsed into the chair next to Rose. "Thank you." My voice hitched, and I blinked away the tears that suddenly gathered in my eyes.

I'd been out since I was in college, and Dad had never once spoken his mind on my being gay. Mom had been more than willing to berate me and show her disapproval. She had been angry and downright mean at the beginning, worried that people would find out I wasn't *normal*. In her mind, it reflected poorly on the whole family. She had been convinced everyone would be laughing behind her back. My mother and I had barely spoken for the next two years, but had eventually worked our way to an uneasy truce of "don't ask, don't tell" before she died. Dad had never said a word one way or another. We played the same DADT game, but without the animosity.

I'd hoped Mom would finally come around and accept me before she died. But if she had, that secret followed her to her grave. The not knowing still haunted me. I wondered if she was up there watching now, and what she'd think about Nikko, and what she'd think about what Dad had just said.

My father stated firmly, "You tell Nikko he can always come to me if he needs anything, okay?"

I nodded. "I will. He'll be grateful to know that. I love you, Dad."

He smiled, and there was a glistening of tears in his eyes. He glanced down at his watch. "You girls better get going or you're going to be stuck in traffic all the way back."

There were hugs all around, and Dad made us promise to give him a call when we got home. Fifteen minutes later, we were on the road, each with a fresh can of Diet Coke.

I didn't remember much of the drive back to the city. The process of unpacking was as distracted as my driving had been. It took five trips from the underground garage to unload all my crap. As I worked, images from the week scrolled like movie trailers behind my eyes. A thousand confused and contradicting emotions bubbled through me. I couldn't get Takoda out of my head. I remembered the taste of her kisses and I ached.

I saw her laughing and smiling and the sun reflecting in her dark, expressive eyes. I pictured strong, sexy legs pumping bike pedals. Conversations played over in my head. Her voice called to me like a siren's song and I yearned to talk to her again.

I packed away the detritus of my vacation and forced myself to face that my wonderful and surreal week, as amazing as it had been, was over. Takoda didn't belong in the city. There was no place for her here. She belonged to the forests up north.

All my adult life, I'd divided myself between two worlds: my life in the city and my past up home. Every year, I spent a week at the lake in the summer, and then Christmas and Thanksgiving at my parents' house. But my home was here. This little hovel of an apartment was my sanctuary.

When I finished putting away all my stuff, I slumped on my worn secondhand sofa, sipping a Diet Coke. I gazed at the plain white walls with a vaguely sick ache in my chest and stomach. This was my world—familiar and comfortable. But right now, I felt melancholy and alone.

Normally, alone was a good thing. Living on my own came with a sense of independence and contentment. I liked doing what I wanted, when I wanted. I had the quiet time I needed with my thoughts and my writing or reading. I owned my space and my place in the world, and it was enough. I wasn't sure why the silence suddenly seemed deafening and the apartment so empty.

Remembering a promise, I shot a quick text off to Takoda to let her know I had gotten home and all was well. I had a sudden and strong need to hear Takoda's voice, and I debated following the text up with a call.

When the phone suddenly started ringing in my hand, I nearly dropped it. Barely able to breathe, my hands shaking, I swiped to accept the call from Takoda's number.

"Hullo?"

"Amry? Hey." She sounded out of breath and anxious.

I swallowed, my heart pounding in my ears. "Hey. I'm home. I got my stuff unpacked. What are you doing?"

"Waiting for you to call," she said. I could hear the smile in her voice. "Actually, I was killing time beating up my punching bag. I feel so pathetic, but I miss you. I've been thinking about you."

Warmth washed through me, and I settled further into the sofa cushions. The ache in my stomach eased. "I've been thinking about you too."

"I was hoping, maybe, if you were okay with it—I have a weekend off. Not this coming weekend, but the one after. Maybe I could drive down to see you?"

Seriously? Takoda would come to the city? What did that mean? Did it matter? "Yeah, I'd really like that."

"Are you sure it'd be okay? I mean, I know it's kind of fast, but—"

"Yes, come down. It'll be fun." It didn't occur to my mouth to say no, but part of me felt nervous about Takoda coming here. I was about to open a door in the wall between my lives and I didn't know what was going to happen. I hadn't expected her to come here. I expected I would put the past week into a little compartment and hold it there by itself until it faded away.

As we talked, the ease of the past week flowed between us. We chatted well into the night, extending the surreal week a little longer.

* * *

The two weeks before Takoda's visit passed painfully slowly. Takoda and I spoke and texted every day. I alternated between excited, melancholy and anxious, and drove my friends and workmates crazy with my mood swings. I didn't know how to deal with being so conflicted. It was one thing to be with Takoda up at the cabin, but I couldn't quite wrap my head around having her here. I still couldn't see any future in our relationship other than friendship, but I very much wanted to see her.

Our talking and texts had been a little flirty, but mostly just friendly. I didn't know if she wanted more than friendship. Rose rolled her eyes at me when I said that. So did my other friends. The consensus was that Takoda wouldn't waste her time coming down to the city to stay with me if she didn't want to pursue more than friendship.

I wasn't sure what I wanted. Certainly, I recognized the attraction between us, and my libido sure was intrigued by Takoda Running Bear. But the logistics of a long-distance relationship made me want to slam on the brakes. It scared the hell out of me to get emotionally attached and give away my heart, just to have to lose it again when the whole thing blew up in my face. She would hate living in the city. She'd said as much. And I knew I couldn't live up north. Those thoughts left an aching in my heart and a darkness in my soul that I didn't want to consider too closely. But as soon as I got a text or a phone call, the darkness was pushed aside. Scared or not, I couldn't bring myself to stay away.

On the Friday Takoda drove down, I rushed home from work and puttered around my apartment doing last-minute cleaning, hoping Takoda wouldn't be horribly disappointed by my choice of living spaces. I was the first to admit my lack of decorating skills.

What little furniture I had was build-it-yourself from Ikea or Target, except for the secondhand overstuffed sofa I'd inherited from my friends Tashi and Kelly. None of it came close to measuring up to Takoda's cozy home, but I knew she wouldn't run screaming. Takoda was too polite for that. Still, I didn't want to see disappointment in her eyes.

I glanced at the clock for the hundredth time. I kept taking deep breaths to push down both excitement and trepidation.

The apartment intercom finally blared into the silence. Instead of buzzing her up, I took the emergency stairwell and ran down the four flights to let her in.

Takoda stepped through the frosted glass door as I wrenched it open, then dropped her bags and wrapped me in a crushing hug. I buried my face into her shoulder, breathing in the muskiness of her perfume, sinking into the solidity of her body as we held each other.

"I missed you," she murmured into my ear.

I brushed my lips against the warm skin of her neck. "You feel good," I whispered.

I can't explain the feelings rushing through me—relief, warmth, belonging and something so deep inside it hurt. I hugged her hard and then drew away, taking in her smiling face and the intensity of her eyes. Her fingers ran featherlight touches along my cheek and traced the line of my jaw. I couldn't breathe and I couldn't tear my eyes from the depths of hers.

A young man wearing business casual and carrying a backpack pushed through the doors and sidled past us into the emergency stairwell.

I grinned self-consciously as the heavy fire door slammed shut. "Let's go upstairs."

"Yes, let's." Takoda slung her duffel bag and backpack over her shoulder.

I punched the button for the elevators. Takoda wrapped her free arm around my shoulders. I leaned against her, feeling anxious again that my tiny apartment would disappoint her.

Down the hallway, past the enticing aroma of strong curry, past the muffled sound of Mr. McCawley's television, to the far end where I fumbled with the key but got the door open. "Come on in, make yourself at home."

Takoda walked past me and peered around. I gave a rueful shrug. "It's not much, but it's home," I said.

"I like it. It fits you."

I raised a brow. "I'm not sure how to take that."

She blushed. "It's a decent place. It doesn't need to be fancy. You don't hide behind appearances. You are who you are, and you don't pretend to be anyone else. I like that. It makes you real."

I stared at her for a second, then grinned like an idiot. "Well, for better or worse, this is me. Want the tour?"

"Sure."

I swept a hand in front of us. "Living room and kitchen. Balcony." I pointed down the hallway. "Bedroom on the left, bathroom on the right, linen closet at the end."

Takoda chuckled. "Glad I'm not claustrophobic."

I shrugged. "It's just me. It forces me to keep my junk collecting to a minimum." I took her overnight bag. "I'll put this in the bedroom."

Takoda followed me down the very short hallway. "Do you think you'll buy a house at some point?"

"To be honest, I haven't given it much thought. I'd probably do a condo if I decided to buy, but for now, this works."

The bedroom glowed with the late afternoon sun blazing through the single window. There wasn't much to look at—a plain pine dresser, the double bed with a worn navy-blue sleeping bag for a comforter and pressed-wood bookcase headboard piled with books and topped with a clip-on desk lamp.

I set Takoda's bag on the foot of the bed. "I thought we could go and get something to eat, maybe take a walk around the lake. Are you hungry?"

"Yeah, I am. Food sounds good."

"Cool. Come on. I'll drive."

I wanted to take her somewhere quiet where we could talk, but my list of places to eat was along the lines of Perkins or Olive Garden.

Susan, my ex, had dragged me to a couple fancy places. In my opinion, the food had been average, the prices unreasonable, and the dress code uncomfortable. She had considered me an uncultured loser. I never told her I'd stopped at McDonald's after dropping her home.

Takoda and I decided on Olive Garden. We got a booth and sat on the same side, holding hands under the table as we worked our way through dinner and a glass of wine. We conversed and shared our food and lingered over coffee.

After dinner, I drove us over to Lake Harriet. Even though the sun had dropped below the trees, the temperature remained humid and in the eighties. The walking paths were busy with people out for an evening stroll. I noticed a few families, but after eight it was mostly couples or small groups of adults and teens strolling along the wide, tree-lined paths. The lake was quiet. Algae-laden water lapped the shoreline. A handful of bicyclists buzzed past on the bike trail. Occasional bursts of laughter echoed across the water.

Takoda took it all in. "This is pretty nice, for the middle of the city."

"I like it. I like watching people."

Takoda linked our fingers as she fell into step at my side. Considering the difference in our heights, we managed to find a comfortable pace.

I thought about how we appeared together and wondered what I'd done in this world that a beautiful woman like Takoda was spending her weekend with me. What could she possibly see in me? There must have been something, because here we were, rambling hand in hand around Lake Harriet, as though it were the most normal thing in the world.

Nobody paid us much attention; they were all involved in their own business. That was the way of things in the city. It was easy to be alone among so many people. In my more depressed moments, the abject loneliness of anonymity could be a hard thing to deal with. But most of the time I liked that nobody knew my business or cared. It was a big part of why I had left home. In a small town, you were always someone's sister or daughter or cousin. They knew your parents, knew you were an honor roll kid or a party animal or a jock. And if you dared to be a little different, then you were regarded with disdain, distrust or ignorance.

Takoda's low voice jolted me out of my thoughts. "I have a story I forgot to tell you, from yesterday."

"Yeah?"

"Yeah. Olsen and I ended up out on Side Lake Thursday afternoon. We nailed a couple locals well over their walleye limit and drunk off their asses. One of the guys in the group was still on the sober side of the law and being polite, so we'd probably have let them go with a warning and a fine if they'd have turned around quietly and gotten off the lake. But one of the drunks got cocky and started running off at the mouth, so we took the boat keys and towed them back to shore."

I laughed. "They must've been pissed as hell."

Takoda's eyes flickered with a darkness that screamed bad-ass and she grinned, all teeth and dangerous. "Yeah, teach 'em to call me a fucking dyke. We slapped 'em with a hefty fine for fishing over the limit, gave the cocky asshole who was driving the boat a ticket for DUI, then called the sheriff to meet us at the landing so they couldn't get into their trucks and take off driving drunk. I even made sure they cleaned the boat off when we beached them."

We laughed. The thought of good old redneck boys being towed by the law made my day and made me proud of Takoda.

I said, "Hey, not sure if you'd be okay with this, but my friends Tashi and Kelly are having a little birthday gathering for

Kelly tomorrow night. Would you mind if we stopped in, just for a little bit? We wouldn't have to stay long, but I really should stop over, and I would love for you to meet a few of my friends." My words came out in a nervous rush, and I shot her a glance to see her reaction.

She squeezed my hand. "Sure, as long as they don't mind me tagging along?"

I grinned and felt the heat in my face. "Actually, they're all anxious to meet you."

"Been telling tales, have you?" she teased.

"Not at all."

She laughed, and I relaxed. It would be okay.

After our walk, we returned to my apartment, settling on the sofa with a bag of chips and a couple cans of soda to watch the local news and the *Late Show*. It wasn't long before I flipped off the television and we simply cuddled under the fleece throw, content to listen to each other breathe. I rested my head against Takoda's chest. Her skin smelled like outdoors and sunshine. Her arm was a comforting weight around my shoulders. I could have sat that way forever.

We had tonight, tomorrow, and most of the day Sunday. I didn't want to think of the end of the weekend because it made me miss her already. Part of me wondered why I wasn't dragging her back to my bedroom to make the best of the time we had, but for whatever reason, I had no desire to move from this exact spot and this perfect, contented feeling.

Takoda pulled me tighter against her. I buried my face into the crook of her neck, nuzzling her skin. Warm breath puffed on my hair, then against my cheek, and her mouth found mine. I sighed, my lips parting for the warm softness of her tongue. Without breaking our frantic kisses, she lifted me on top of her as she stretched out on the couch. I sprawled over her, sucking her tongue further in. Desire sparked and ignited. She pushed her hands under my T-shirt, fingernails raking up and down my back.

Oh my God. I slid down, licking and nipping down her neck and the pulse point under her warm, salty skin. She arched into me with a groan. I wanted her. I wanted to feel her and touch her, and I wanted her damned clothes off.

"Takoda." Her name came out a hoarse whisper.

She met and held my gaze. Her hand moved to cup my breast. I gasped and moaned as her palm rubbed across my already hard and straining nipple. "Koda, please."

She leaned in to kiss me again, long and deep. When we parted, she whispered, "Yes."

Somehow, we managed to untangle from each other. I grabbed her hand and led the way toward my bedroom, turning toward her as we stopped at the side of the bed. I grasped the hem of her tank top and lifted. "Off."

Of course, I wasn't tall enough to do this properly. Takoda helped by stripping the material off in a single movement, letting it drop to the floor and standing proudly before me, bare chested. Her breasts were small, but pert and rounded. I swallowed hard and reached out, but she shook her head. "Yours next."

She grasped the hem of my T-shirt and gently lifted it over my head. My sports bra came next. I held my breath as her hands caressed my arms, my shoulders and slowly moved down my chest to skim over my breasts.

We kissed and touched and finally divested ourselves of our remaining clothes. We came together, skin against heated skin, and fell onto the bed in a tangle of limbs. The feel of her body against mine was indescribable. Warm, soft, achingly beautiful. Mouths and hands were everywhere, trying to touch and feel every inch of each other. Takoda stretched her long frame over me, one leg between mine. She pushed against my crotch as she nuzzled my neck, tweaking my nipple and sending lightning jolts down to my groin. I was beyond coherent words.

I raked my fingernails down her back and grasped her ass, rubbing myself against the firm muscle of her thigh. My wetness coated her skin as the pressure built.

Her tongue plunged into my mouth as long fingers pushed inside me, matching the rhythm of the kiss. I cried out as I came, way too quickly, and she held me until I stopped shaking.

I took my time memorizing her body then, kissing and caressing every inch of her until she moaned with desire and pleaded for release. Nuzzling the tender skin on the inside of her thighs, I teased my fingers into her hot wetness. The slick heat wrapped around my fingers as I pushed inside, deep and slow, and took her hardened clit into my mouth. She whimpered, writhing against me, and clutched my head to hold me in place. I licked and sucked and thrust until her body went taut. After a few heartbeats, she gasped again, shuddering repeatedly while I kissed my way back up her chest.

I laid my head on her shoulder and we held each other tightly, legs tangled. The rapid pounding of her heart calmed to a slow, steady thump in my ear. I sighed, overwhelmed with a rush of emotion and contentment. It was a feeling I had never known, and I lost myself in it. I'd experienced lust and the pleasure of good sex. But this was different. This was much more, much deeper than just getting off.

Takoda kissed my hair and caressed my back. "You are wonderful," she murmured.

I turned my head to lay my lips on her chest. "And you are perfect," I whispered, not knowing where the words came from, but knowing it was true.

CHAPTER TEN

"I want to see the Mall of America."

I finished pouring our coffee. "What?"

Takoda leaned against the kitchen counter, waving the butter knife in her hand as she waited for the toast. "Let's go to the Mall of America today. I want to see what all the excitement is about."

"Seriously? It's just a big mall." As a local, MOA was anathema. Too big, too overpriced and filled with too many idiot tourists and kids.

"Yeah. Seriously. There's an aquarium, right? And Legoland?" Takoda's almost childlike excitement was adorable.

Laughing, I pointed at the toast that had just popped up, which she had failed to notice. "Sure, we can go," I agreed. Her delighted grin was more than worth the visit.

Takoda and I hit the aquarium first, then wandered the hallowed halls of consumerism. Shopping at places like Brookstone, Legoland and other toy stores was a blast. I sprung for ride tickets at the amusement park in the center of the Mall.

We giggled like teenagers on a sugar rush and screamed through the insane roller coasters and thrill rides, then decided on the Rain Forest Café for a late lunch. Our "tour guide" escorted us to great seats toward the back of the restaurant, where theatrical thunder, lightning and rain rumbled around us. Gorillas hooted and thumped their chests while colorful birds chirped in fake trees.

The food was decent, but I honestly didn't think either of us noticed. We were having too much fun. Takoda made me laugh, and I didn't feel like I had to act like a proper grownup. My ex had hated it when I got giddy and silly. She'd been embarrassed and wanted me to act my age. It was so much better to be with someone who understood and who was as comfortable as I was sitting with a group of kids at Legoland and putting together spaceships.

After lunch, we got coffee and held hands as we wandered past more stores. "So, what do you feel like next?" I asked. "I'm thinking something outside."

"Outside is good. Somewhere we can hang out?"

"Let's go chill at Lake Calhoun. We can walk around or grab a blanket out of the back of the car and claim a piece of grass."

"Sounds fabulous."

"Excellent. Come on."

I drove the scenic route to the string of lakes in the middle of the city and found parking on the south side of Lake Calhoun. We settled on a picnic blanket under an aged silver maple. The volleyball courts near the edge of the lake were filled with exuberant competitors. Frisbees and footballs sailed across the lawns between towering trees. Bicyclists, skaters and pedestrians cruised the paved paths. A couple wind-surfers and a small sailboat skimmed across the water. The not-so-distant backdrop of downtown skyscrapers peeked above the tree line on the north end of the lake, while jetliners thundered across a blue sky spray-painted with wisps of clouds.

Takoda took it all in with a bemused smile as she stretched out on our blanket, leaning back on her elbows with long legs crossed in front of her.

"What do you think?" I asked.

She studied me over the rim of her sunglasses, dark eyes raking up and down over my body. "Mmmmm…I think I like," she said with a wicked grin.

I sat cross-legged beside her. "Flirt."

She laughed. "This is nice. It's hard to believe I'm in the middle of a concrete jungle."

"I'm not going swimming any time soon, but it's a great place to hang out."

"I was going to ask about that," she said. "Kids are having a blast." She nodded toward the beach where a half-dozen youngsters were splashing and frolicking in the shallow water.

"They haven't learned about bacteria yet."

"Don't you miss the lakes up north?"

I chewed my lip for a few seconds and stalled while I opened my bottle of Diet Coke and took a couple sips. "Yes and no," I said. "I miss being on vacation and hanging out at the cabin. Then I think about being that close to my family on a regular basis and dealing with homophobic rednecks, and all the magic goes out the window. I like that I can be myself here, that I can have my anonymity and hold my girlfriend's hand if I want to, and go to the Gay Pride festival and nobody even cares or looks twice."

She shifted so that she was sitting up, leaning against the tree, and patted her lap. "Lay your head here."

I set aside my soda and stretched out on the blanket, using her lap for a pillow and gazing up at her.

She said, "I guess I don't worry much about what other people think. With the guys at work, they know I'm gay, but nobody ever talks about it. It's a non-subject. I've dated, and yeah, it's not like we'd go around holding hands in public. But then again, I've never felt the need to be that way either."

I felt a pang of jealousy at the thought of her dating anyone else.

She ran her fingers through my hair. "It feels different with you, though. I want to hold your hand and I want to be able to hug you or put an arm around you, or sit here with your head in my lap. I can't quite explain it. But there it is."

"Would you feel that way if we were up north, walking around Walmart?"

She lifted a brow. "Would you feel that way walking around Walmart even here?"

I laughed. "Point conceded."

"Honestly, Amry, I just know I'm comfortable with you."

My heart leapt for joy, and I know I had a big grin plastered on my face. "I'm comfortable with you too," I said, even if it sounded dumb as hell.

"I'd miss the woods, though," she admitted. "And the quiet."

I thought about that, realizing how much of the background noise I automatically tuned out. I hardly noticed the planes, or the cars and buses. "Life definitely has a different rhythm here."

"At least there are places like this where you can go to slow down a little bit."

"It helps." In her case, I thought it wouldn't help enough.

Takoda traced her fingers along my cheek. "You're way too serious."

I gave her a reassuring smile and caught her hand, twining our fingers together and bringing them to my lips to kiss her knuckles. Smiling contentedly, eyes half-shut, she said, "I do very much like this."

As I breathed in the warmth of her skin, the slightly musky, outdoorsy essence of her, I could only agree. She sighed, and I felt her body settle under my cheek. A sense of peace and contentment washed over me.

I wasn't sure how long we rested that way. I thought Takoda dozed off with her head against the tree trunk while my mind wandered. Eyes closed, I basked in our closeness. A light breeze skittered across my skin and raised goose bumps in a good way. Takoda's lap was warm, her grip strong, her other hand comforting where it rested on my shoulder. The ground under the blanket was hard and a little lumpy, but I didn't care.

Music blared from a radio by the volleyball courts, and a car stereo boomed as it passed. A multitude of voices laughed, yelled and chattered. Kids' high-pitched giggles and screams echoed over the lake. Birds called and leaves rustled in the tree above us. Under it all was the constant hum of traffic.

I was aware of the rise and fall of Takoda's breathing as I lay against her. It was as though I could feel the pulse of her lifeblood through my body. I had the sensation that where I ended I simply melted into her. I wanted to remain in that heightened awareness as long as I could, to hold these moments in my heart and mind and soul before they slipped away.

After supper, we headed to Kelly's birthday gathering. My friends Tashi and Kelly lived in an older residential neighborhood in South Minneapolis. Takoda had grilled me for names and descriptions as we'd driven to their house. She said it was the cop in her, always looking for information. I thought she was as nervous to meet my friends as I was to have asked her to come along.

I parked on the street a couple doors down from their small two-story home, and we strolled up to the wire-fenced yard. A neat flower garden bordered the wide front porch. Little boys' toys were scattered across the neatly mowed lawn. I toed aside a soccer ball as we walked up to the porch.

I rapped once on the screen door and stepped into the cramped living room. "Hey you guys! Happy birthday, Kelly!"

A multitude of voices greeted us, but the first person to reach us was a five-year-old boy with light chocolate skin and big brown eyes, grinning and signing frantically as he launched himself at my legs. "Trey!" I scooped him up and hugged him. His arms wrapped tightly around my neck. Then he leaned away and signed at me. I set him down so I could sign back, speaking for Takoda's benefit as I made the words, much slower than Trey. "I miss you too. This is my friend Takoda. Takoda, this is Trey."

He grinned up at her, wide-eyed, then looked at me and signed again. I laughed as I translated. "He says you're really tall."

She smiled widely and ruffled his tightly curled hair. "Tell him I drink a lot of milk. And that I'm glad to meet him."

Kelly joined us then. Her fair skin was a contrast to her son's, and her short, spiky hair was bleached white. "Come on in! Everyone is here, and the wine is pouring."

I gave her a hug. "Hey Kell, happy birthday. It's good to see you."

"Thanks. About time you showed your face around here. Now, introduce me to this sexy woman!"

"God. Are you trying to embarrass me?"

"Of course I am!" Kelly giggled. "I'm Kelly. Seriously, thanks for coming over. It's great to meet you."

"Takoda. Thanks for having me."

Kelly wiggled her brows. "Is that an invitation?"

I gave her a playful punch. "Christ, Kelly!"

"Blame it on the wine!"

Takoda smiled and looked brave. I took her hand. "Come on, let's meet the gang."

We moved into the living room. Kelly's wife Tashi strode over. She had deep brown skin and dreads and was nearly as tall as Takoda, lean and lanky and wearing baggy shorts and a tank top. She wrapped a long arm around Kelly's waist and kissed her cheek.

"Hi Amry. Welcome, Takoda. Sorry my wife is already hammered." She grinned and held out a hand, shaking Takoda's firmly. "I'm Tashi. I see you've already met our kid. Feel free to ask any of us for translations. He doesn't always remember that not everyone can sign."

"No problem. It's good to meet you."

The swinging door from the kitchen flung open and a flamboyant voice exclaimed, "Oh my God, Amry, who have you brought me? Lord, get me some air, here!"

Angelina Golden strode from the kitchen, tall and very dark skinned, her hair swept up in an intricate knot, wearing an impeccable, bright and flowery summer dress and heels, and holding a glass of wine that did not spill as she sashayed across the room.

I threw my head back and laughed at Takoda's wide-eyed stare. Angelina always went for the big entrance, and I was certain she'd been timing this one. She held out a long-fingered hand as she stopped in front of Takoda. "You must be Amry's tall, dark and handsome park ranger."

Takoda hesitated for a moment, then the stiffness went out of her shoulders. She very gallantly kissed Angelina's knuckles. "Yes, I'm Takoda. And you must be Angelina Golden. I'm very pleased to meet you."

"Oh my God. This one's a keeper, honey!" Angelina promptly took Takoda by the arm and led us into the living room, introducing everyone to Takoda. I followed, grinning, inordinately pleased that Takoda seemed okay. I'd tried to warn her, but you couldn't quite prepare yourself for the force that was Angelina Golden.

Fortunately, it wasn't a large group. Will and Mike sat together on the sofa, clean cut and relaxed in their polos and khaki shorts, drinking beer from glasses spiked with lime wedges. Derek sprawled in a recliner, tan and muscular. Jackie sat in the other recliner, her partner LeAnn perched beside her on the arm of the chair. Both women sported butch fashion with their short hair, cargo shorts and T-shirts.

Takoda and I pulled up chairs from the dining room. Angelina took the other recliner, folding herself regally into place, and then laughing and hugging Trey when he clambered up into her lap. Kelly brought me a glass of wine and Takoda a bottle of amber beer, then made herself comfortable on Tashi's lap on the sofa.

As expected, Angelina started the conversation, grilling Takoda about her job and her visit to the city, and what we'd been doing all day, imbuing the latter with inappropriate and teasing innuendo. Takoda in turn asked Angelina about her work, and the conversation shot off from there, with everyone participating, covering all manner of topics.

Somebody mentioned a gang-related shooting that had happened not that far from where Derek lived on the north side of Minneapolis. Derek said, "Idiot gangbangers are running wild, and there are too many guns on the street."

"Blame the NRA," Mike commented.

"And the politicians they buy."

Tashi raised her beer. "You got that right, Ang."

LeAnn said, "I really don't like guns."

Angelina turned toward Takoda. "Being in law enforcement, you must have an opinion?"

All eyes went to the woman sitting beside me. Takoda stiffened, her expression turning serious. I felt my own heart stutter. Playful teasing was one thing, but putting my new girlfriend on the spot was not what I had in mind. Not to mention that I realized with a sinking feeling, I had no idea how she felt. We'd never talked about guns. I'd grown up around avid hunters. I'd never shot more than a twenty-two-caliber rifle at empty pop cans, but Dad and Tom had guns in the basement, and I'd never thought anything about it.

Derek scowled. "Every cop I know is an NRA flunky. Shoot first, ask questions later."

I almost groaned out loud. Tashi and Derek had this argument every time Derek was drinking, which, fortunately, wasn't often. He had a chip on his shoulder about law enforcement. I knew he had family who'd had run-ins with the police, but he never gave us details.

"That's not fair, D," Tashi argued. "You're making false assumptions."

Derek ground out, "You show me a cop, and I'll show you a dead black man."

Tashi stood. "You're drunk, and you're overreacting. Ninety-nine percent of the cops are decent."

"Bullshit. How many times have you been pulled over for driving black?"

"Sure, it's happened. Scared the piss out of me. But I'm still saying that most cops are decent."

"Then why do we have to protest in the streets to get justice?"

"I'm not saying there isn't a problem. There is. But the majority of cops are not racist jerks."

Angelina interrupted, "I thought we were talking about guns."

Derek snapped, "We are!"

Takoda spoke quietly into the pause. "I know a lot of responsible gun owners. A lot of hunters. I handle guns all the time. But what you're talking about, with the gangs, that's different. There's no need for automatic and semi-automatic weapons in the general public. In my opinion, those are weapons of war. They were not intended for civilian use. I think most law enforcement officers would agree there are too many guns on the street, and selling more guns, even to the so-called good guys, isn't going to solve that problem."

Derek opened his mouth, started to speak, then stopped and slouched back in his chair with a sullen expression.

Angelina raised her wineglass, "Well said, Takoda! Now, before our little Trey falls asleep in my lap, we should break out the cake and ice cream!"

"Great idea!" Kelly jumped up, grabbing Tashi's hand and dragging her toward the kitchen to get the cake.

I squeezed Takoda's hand and gave her an apologetic look. "Sorry about that," I murmured. *Please, please don't be pissed.*

"It's okay."

I searched her dark eyes. "Are you sure?"

She smiled and kissed my cheek. "I'm sure."

She held my gaze, and I read reassurance in her expression. We were okay. I felt the tension go out of my body. Takoda put an arm around my shoulders, pulling me close, and I leaned into her strength with a sense of relief.

Jackie and LeAnn asked Angelina about how things were going at the Minnesota AIDS Project, where she worked as an assistant to the case managers. That kicked off a new discussion and eased the remaining tension in the room. Takoda and I stayed for cake and ice cream, chatted a while longer and then made our excuses. Kelly and Angelina teased us mercilessly as we left, shooing us off to have some "fun." I was simply anxious to have Takoda to myself for the rest of the night.

Takoda's head rested on my chest as she slept, her long body sprawled beside mine, our legs tangled. I twisted a silky length of her hair around my finger. We'd made love when we'd woken earlier. Takoda had fallen back to sleep. Her breath puffed warmly on my skin in a slow, relaxed rhythm. I was content to hold her and be her body pillow, taking the time to study the gentle muscular curves of her body, defined clearly beneath the sheet draped up to our waists. Even sleeping, Takoda had a sense of strength about her. Not just physical strength, which was obvious, but also a core of mental and emotional strength that I felt I was only beginning to see.

It had been a wonderful weekend, and far more comfortable and fun than I could have hoped. I didn't want our time to end. I enjoyed being with her. I craved her company. We talked. We laughed. We hung out. We made love. And it was amazing.

I hadn't expected this. I expected we would have a pretty good time and we would get along. I expected to be much more uneasy and nervous around her, and to have had more difficulty finding things to do. I expected strained silences where I struggled to find something to say.

Instead, I'd had a phenomenal time, and it seemed Takoda felt the same way. My heart was buoyed with contentment, excitement and happiness. I didn't remember ever feeling this light.

Takoda sighed and shifted against me, her arm tightening around my waist. I caressed her hair. I didn't know what to call the intense and nearly overwhelming emotions flowing through me. I only knew that I had never felt this way before.

But as much as I could have lain there holding her forever, my bladder told me otherwise. I carefully eased from her embrace. She grumbled in her sleep, then curled around her pillow, but didn't wake. I watched her for a few moments. Her dark hair tumbled over the pale blue of the pillowcase and sheet. The line of her shoulders was relaxed. I wanted to run my hands over her soft, perfect skin.

Shaking my head, I grabbed the sweatshirt I'd left on the floor last night, went to the bathroom, then padded into the kitchen and started the coffeepot. I retrieved the Sunday paper from outside my apartment door, separating the news sections from the ads as I waited for my late morning dose of caffeine.

"Hey, you beat me awake."

I turned, grinning as Takoda wandered into the kitchen wearing just a T-shirt. "Morning. Coffee'll be ready in a couple minutes."

She crossed the room to wrap me in a hug, and I leaned up for a kiss. Our mouths came together in a gentle confirmation of passion, tasting each other, tongues teasing with a breathless reminder of the night's lovemaking. I ran my hands up under her shirt, kneading the muscles along her back. God, she felt so good.

We parted to breathe. Takoda nuzzled at my neck and murmured, "So, what's the plan for the day?"

"Keep that up, and we're going back to bed."

She laughed and straightened as the coffeemaker coughed and wheezed behind me. "I could live with that. But I really need some coffee and food first."

"I hope you're okay with Pop Tarts because we forgot to pick up bread yesterday."

She kissed my hair. "You are so not a healthy eater."

"Yeah, yeah. You pour coffee, and I'll get breakfast."

We took our coffee, Pop Tarts and the paper to the living room. After flipping through the paper and the ads, we decided on a shower, then a leisurely walk around the neighborhood. Early dinner was at my favorite pizza place, a seventies throwback with paneled walls and hanging lamps where we dawdled over our food. Neither of us wanted the day to end but the clock ticked toward four and Takoda needed to get on the road, so we reluctantly returned to my apartment.

Takoda collected her backpack and duffel bag while I watched, feeling awkward and sad. We held each other tightly before leaving my apartment, saying goodbye with desperate kisses. I swear time stood still while we devoured each other's mouths. I couldn't get enough of her. I couldn't get close enough. But Takoda had to leave.

We walked out to her Jeep. She put her bags in the back and climbed in, starting the engine and rolling her window down.

I hung onto the closed door. "Call me when you get home. And be safe, okay?"

"I will."

I leaned through the open window to kiss her again.

Her fingers traced lightly along my jaw, her eyes locked on mine. "I'll talk to you soon."

"Yes." Tears burned behind my eyes and my throat was tight.

Takoda bit her lip, putting the Jeep into gear and pulling out. I watched until she was out of sight, then trudged back to my apartment.

The door clicked shut behind me and I automatically set the deadbolt and chain. The apartment was as silent and empty as I felt. I wandered to the living room and dropped onto the sofa, wrapping the fleece blanket around me. It smelled faintly of Takoda's musky perfume.

How could I miss her when she'd only been gone for five minutes?

Tomorrow I would return to work, back to my regularly scheduled life. I wouldn't wake with Takoda sleeping beside me, and I didn't know when I would see her again because we hadn't planned that far ahead.

I didn't want to go to work tomorrow.

I didn't want to get on with my life.

All I wanted was Takoda.

I rubbed the fleece against my cheek and breathed in her scent. The softness reminded me of the touch of her fingers caressing my skin. I savored the memories of our lovemaking—how her body had felt under my hands, the silkiness and heat of her as we had moved together. It was heaven, being with her. I'd never felt so connected to someone both physically and emotionally.

My cell phone rang, and my heart stuttered excitedly.

But when I saw the name on the screen, my stomach sank. Fucking Bethany. I heaved a sigh and thumbed the call to answer it. "Hullo?"

My sister didn't bother with pleasantries before launching into her diatribe. "You had to tell Dad about Nikko, didn't you? I went over there today, and Nikko and Joe were playing catch in the backyard. I asked Dad where Tom and Darlene were, and he said they were at home fighting and Nikko had come over with Joe. Then he said Nikko deserved better than the way Tom was treating him lately. So what have you been telling Dad?"

"Hello, Bethany, I'm fine. How are you?" My voice came out smoother and sweeter than I had expected.

She ignored me. "You have to poison him against Tom and I, don't you?"

I closed my eyes and leaned my head against the back of the couch. I was not in the mood for this crap. "I didn't poison him against anyone. I told him Nikko needed his support and love. That's not poison, that's the simple truth."

"Nikko is a child and he is confused and doesn't know what he wants."

The desire to beat the shit out of my sister rose in my chest. "Bullshit. Nikko is old enough to know if he's gay or not. And so the fuck what if he is? That doesn't make him any less deserving of our love and support and acceptance. Grow up, Bethy."

"He's going to pervert Little Joe!"

"You are so fucked in the head you don't even know what you're saying. Nikko being gay doesn't hurt Joe. It doesn't make Joe gay. It doesn't do anything. I sure as fuck didn't make you and Tom gay. So keep your fucked-up opinions to yourself and learn to love and accept and tolerate differences like a real human being."

"You're a bitch, Amry, and you are going straight to Hell."

"Then I'll see you there." I killed the connection and raised my arm to hurl my cell against the wall, then took a deep breath before dropping the phone onto the coffee table.

The only people in the world who could make me this crazy angry were my siblings. It was like reliving my childhood. Sometimes I truly hated my sister. Everything she said, whether accusing or demeaning, she said to push my buttons.

She and I had never shared our hopes and dreams. We could barely talk about the weather without arguing. The room we had shared growing up had been my half and her half—two rooms where there could have been one.

Bethany and Tom had always been close. I assumed it was the twin thing. They weren't identical, but damned if they weren't two of a kind in most other ways. Our relationships hadn't improved as we'd grown up. If anything, we grew further apart. My moving to the city made a difference too. Out of sight, out of mind.

It went both ways. I gave them as little thought as they gave me. If I needed to know something, Dad would let me know when I talked to him.

I stared at the ceiling and considered calling Takoda but shook off the urge. She didn't need to listen to me whine about my family problems while she was driving.

My anger faded as I thought about the weekend, but now that Bethany had shot my mood to crap, I was unable to shake the dark thoughts that intruded. What would happen if the attraction between Takoda and I developed into a serious relationship? We couldn't continue indefinitely living four hours apart. So who would move where? Could Takoda give up her life to join me here? Could I give up mine to be with her?

Just the thought of living up north made my stomach clench sickly. Could I love her enough to go back to the place I'd run from all those years ago? I really didn't know.

In any case, we weren't there yet. The discussion hadn't happened. Perhaps it never would. Perhaps this intense need and attraction would burn out with time and distance.

The realist in me told me to enjoy the ride and quit worrying it to death. If it were meant to be, it would happen. If not, well, that was life. I wasn't sure I could buy that line of thought, but I clung to the memories of the weekend and knew all I could do was get through to the next day and keep moving forward.

CHAPTER ELEVEN

"It's lunchtime, Amry. Wanna go get something?"

I rubbed my eyes after I finished the corrections to Linda's story copy. Rose rested one arm on the low beige wall of my cubicle. I'd been head down editing and proofing all morning. I frowned, thinking through what I still needed to finish, then shrugged. I said, "If it's pretty fast. I promised Hayley I'd get the rest of Mike's ads proofed by the end of the day."

"Noodles?"

"Sure." I saved my changes and locked the computer screen, then grabbed my wallet from my backpack. "You driving?"

"Of course I'm driving."

I followed Rose out of the office to her silver CRV. She picked up the conversation as soon as we got into the vehicle. "So, tell me more about your weekend."

I clipped my seat belt. "The weekend," I repeated, buying time while I sorted out what to say. "It was good."

"Just good? What did you do? Did you get out of the bedroom?" She leered at me, and I rolled my eyes.

"We walked the lakes and hung out at MOA for a while. We talked a lot, stopped in at Kelly's birthday party."

"Will she be coming back? Are you going up to see her?"

I watched out the window. "Not sure. Probably, but we didn't talk about that, really."

"What did you talk about then, the weather?"

If I weren't so accustomed to Rose's blunt sarcasm, I might have been annoyed. "We talked about a million things. Everything. Just not about when the next visit will be. It depends on her work schedule."

"So you'll see each other again?"

"We'll see each other again." I was certain of that.

Rose maneuvered into the strip mall parking lot and found a spot. We ordered our food, found a table and sat down with our sodas and a number card.

I asked Rose, "What did you do all weekend?"

"Absolutely nothing. I laid around and did chores and cleaned my house. Now let's get back to you. Did you have a good time? Did it go well?"

Rose was like a dog worrying a bone. "It was good. We connected, we laughed, we had a lot of fun. She's not a city girl, though, and I don't think she ever will be."

"Did you ask her?"

"Not in so many words, but we came at it sideways a little. She's tied to the land up there. She can't be a forestry officer in the city."

"You really like her, don't you?"

One of the workers dropped off our food and took our table number. I poked at my mac and cheese with tofu, mixing the cheese into the noodles. "Yeah. I really like her. A lot. And it scares the piss out of me. I mean, she's perfect. The sex is mind-blowing. We can talk about anything. But when does the other shoe drop? When does it all fall apart?"

Rose dug into her Pad Thai before regarding me with a serious expression. "What if she really is that wonderful, Amry? What if there isn't another shoe? Not everyone is like Susan. Not everyone is going to purposely mess with your head."

"Then I'm even more scared, because it can never work with her living up there and me down here. Someone, likely both of us, is going to get hurt."

"You're a pessimist, Amry."

"I'm a pragmatist. Now can we drop it and find a new subject?"

* * *

The next couple weeks fell into a routine of working late at the office and staying up working on my own writing and editing once I got home. Takoda and I chatted every night and texted during the day. I lived in a strange sort of limbo. I was constantly on edge but couldn't put a finger on why. Most of the time I stayed focused on my work and writing, but if I weren't busy, my mind would slip into reliving my time with Takoda and clinging to what felt like a tenuous connection to another life.

The pessimist in me expected Takoda and I would lose touch or lose interest, but it didn't happen. We continued to text and call. Half a dozen times a day, I caught myself wanting to tell her this or that. Every night I desperately missed her warmth, which I found strange because I had never wanted to share my bed. I'd always cherished the space to spread out in the mornings, letting my brain pursue a dream or work out a story while I remained in that half-awake state that produced so many creative thoughts. But I missed waking up with Takoda. I missed the comfort of our physical connection.

I kept telling myself to take it day to day and reminding myself not to have expectations. Takoda was driving down to visit again on Thursday, even though it was a "release week" for the magazine. It would be a hell-week at work, but at least the time would go quickly.

Tuesday morning, I hunkered down with my earbuds in. As I emailed some finished copy over to Michael, my cell phone dinged an incoming text alert over my music.

The text was from Nikko, which set off warning bells because usually we texted in the evenings, while he was supposed to be doing his homework and I was supposed to be working on my writing.

Nikko: Hey, Auntie A

Me: How r u doing?

Nikko: Been better

Me: What happened?

Nikko: Mom kicked Dad out last night. They were screaming again. I don't even know what about. Probably me.

Me: I'm sorry...r u okay?

Nikko: Yeah, okay...don't know what to do...

Me: Not sure there is anything you can do...it's between your mom and dad...they have to work it out...

Nikko: It sucks

Me: I know...You know I love ya, right?

Nikko: Yeah. Wish you were here

Me: I know I'm sorry...

Guilt washed over me. I wanted to be there for him. I just wished it didn't involve the rest of my family.

Nikko: Gotta go...bell gonna ring.

Me: Call if you need to talk, okay?

Nikko: I will...thanks, auntie a

Me: No worries...love ya, kiddo

I set aside the phone and yanked the earbuds from my ears. "Fuck," I muttered.

Michael, who worked in the cube opposite of me, looked up. "Trouble in paradise?" he asked. Michael was the epitome of flaming gay men—perfectly cut sandy hair, smartly styled clothes and always interested in everyone else's business. We got along great.

I shook my head. "My nephew. Darlene kicked Tom out again."

"That's tough."

"I feel bad for Nikko. Coming out is bad enough without all his parents' issues on top of it."

"Keep letting him know you're there for him."

"That's what I've been doing."

"Then keep doing it." He tapped his watch. "You gonna head home on time tonight?"

"Yeah, I think I can. Things are in pretty good shape for this issue."

Of course, just because I'd said that, all hell broke loose when news came out about a local workplace shooting. Four people were killed and ten injured, leaving a whole community stunned and in mourning. I didn't know any of the victims, but it was easy enough to imagine the shock and horror those poor people were dealing with. The gunman was a disgruntled employee with severe mental illness. The situation had the politicos on both sides up in arms. The gun lobby screamed that if everyone had guns, someone could have stopped the man. The anti-gun lobby insisted there were too many guns accessible to people who shouldn't have them.

What it meant for me and the rest of our crew was working late to gather and write last-minute updates and addendums as the story played out. We needed the latest information for the Friday edition, so we pushed the deadlines as far out as we possibly could.

I worked until nearly midnight that night. The following day, Wednesday, I trudged into my apartment at nine thirty p.m. after stopping at the McDonald's drive-through for a late dinner. I watched the news while I munched on fries and a cheeseburger. Takoda was working the overnight, so I didn't expect to hear from her. My plan was to eat, watch TV for fifteen minutes and go to bed.

I wasn't sure what time Takoda would get into town Thursday, but I knew I wouldn't be able to leave work early. I'd been warning her about it since Tuesday. She insisted it was fine; she would meet me at the office and hang out until I was done. She wanted to see where I worked, and Rose would be around for her to visit with while I was doing my editing thing. I sure hoped she wouldn't be bored, since it had the potential to be a long night.

* * *

Very late in the day on Thursday, I was holed up in the conference room with our web designer Devin, Michael and our boss, Hayley. We'd been huddled around the sixty-inch flatscreen on the far wall for the last hour and a half, finalizing the story layouts for the website.

Devin saved our final changes with a flick of fingers over his keyboard.

Michael leaned back in his chair, picking up a notepad and crossing something out. "Okay, we're good here. What's next on the checklist?" He yawned and ran a hand over his hair.

Hayley glanced at her laptop. "We're still waiting on the final updates for the lead story from Linda. She said she'll have them to you in about fifteen minutes, Amry. I'll let Mark know we'll have the final proofs to him for printing in an hour or so." She stood, gathering her laptop. Amazingly, she still looked as fresh and perky as she had this morning, her skirt and jacket neatly pressed and not a hair out of place.

I said, "Okay. I'll watch my email. That's the last copy I was waiting for."

Devin said, "Brent and Josh are cleaning up the last couple pages of the print layout and we're waiting on the final version of Linda's story, but that should just slide in."

Haley nodded and strode out of the room.

I stretched and checked my phone. It was almost six o'clock. A jolt went through me—Takoda should be here! I twisted around in my chair and peered through the glass walls into the office. Takoda leaned casually against the receptionist's desk talking to Rose. My heart pounded in my chest, and it was suddenly hard to breathe. I scooped up my notepad and pen, jumped up and hurried through the cube farm toward the front. "Hey!"

Takoda saw me and smiled widely. Her dark hair hung loose around her shoulders, halfway down her back. She wore a gray plaid flannel over a black T-shirt, tight faded jeans and hiking boots. I grinned like a lovesick teenager.

She opened her arms as I reached her and wrapped me in a tight embrace. We didn't kiss, but I buried my face in her shoulder, breathing in her scent while I held her tightly.

After a few moments, we parted and smiled stupidly at each other.

Rose said, "You guys are too cute."

Ignoring her, I said to Takoda, "How long have you been here?"

"Not long."

"Come sit with me. I'm waiting on a story I need to edit."

She nodded amicably. "Sure."

I took her hand and led her through to my cubicle, grabbing an extra chair from another cube as we passed it.

Michael leaned across the low wall between our desks, extending his hand. "Hi, I'm Michael."

"Takoda. Good to meet you. Amry says you're a lot of fun to work with."

"Amry probably also says I'm a flaming gossip. Welcome to the loony bin. Ignore any yelling, swearing or hissy fits you hear tonight. It's always a challenge at the end."

Takoda laughed. "No worries. I've probably heard worse." She dropped into the chair beside me.

I said quietly, "I'm sorry I have to work late."

"Don't worry about it. It's all good." She pointed toward a photo tacked on my cube wall. It was a selfie of us at the cabin, with wet hair and water dripping down our faces, laughing at the camera. "Nice shot."

"I kinda like it." I moved the mouse to wake up the computer and signed in. When my desktop came up I refreshed my inbox, but there was still nothing from Linda.

Hayley appeared beside my cube, all smiles and holding a cup of coffee. "Well, hello. You must be Takoda. I am so pleased to finally meet you."

I said, "Takoda, this is my boss, Hayley Wilson. Hayley, this is Takoda Running Bear."

Takoda stood and offered her hand. Hayley grasped it firmly, giving Takoda a rather obvious once-over.

"I'm glad to meet the woman who's put such a giddy smile on your face, Amry."

Takoda said, "I'll take that as a compliment. It's nice to meet you as well."

"Well, don't distract my lead editor too much."

"I promise to be quiet as a mouse." Takoda crossed her heart. "And I promise not to be distracted."

"I'll hold you both to that. I have a few things to do before this goes to print, including goading the print guys to finish their pages so I can sign off on them." With that, she whirled away and crossed the room to her office.

I shook my head. Takoda looked a little shell-shocked. I squeezed her hand. "Hayley likes you," I assured her.

Michael snorted. "She sure does, because she didn't kick your beautiful ass out of here."

"Michael, don't be an idiot."

He laughed and turned back to his monitor.

Takoda asked, "Is there anything I can do?"

"Just be here," I said. She scooted her chair next to mine. I took her hand. "How was the drive down?"

"It was pretty quiet until I got into the city. Then it got pretty backed up."

I felt suddenly sick to my stomach. Did she hate having to make the drive to see me? Was she really okay with being here? I must have looked panicked because she squeezed my hand. She said softly, "No matter what, I'm glad to be here."

The sick feeling faded, and I whispered back, "I'm glad you're here too."

Her smile was like sunshine, bathing me in its warmth. I leaned back in my chair. Takoda was on my left, and we held hands while I moused right-handed and refreshed my inbox. Still nothing from Linda. We chatted quietly. Takoda relaxed with her legs stretched out and crossed at the ankles.

I received Linda's email about ten minutes later and turned my focus to work.

Takoda occupied herself reading on her phone. Her presence at my side was comforting. After I finished proofing the copy, we had a final session in the conference room for a complete page-through of the print and web versions of the magazine.

The pizza guy showed up while Michael, Haley, Devin and I were meeting. Takoda and Rose delivered food and soda to the conference room. We signed off on the proofs an hour later. Technically, my work for the night was complete, but I always hung around to make sure some crazy shit didn't hit the fan.

I stood outside my cubicle and stretched, popping my back and shoulders and yawning. Takoda watched with an appreciative eye, and I felt the heat rise in my face. "Time for a bathroom break," I said. "You need to make a stop?"

Takoda nodded, and I led her to the restroom down the hallway.

As the heavy door shut behind us, Takoda pushed me against it. I wrapped my arms around her neck. She teased with her tongue against my lips as her hands glided up my sides. I opened to her, losing myself in the play of her tongue against mine. Her leg pushed between mine, her mouth moving down my jaw to the pulse-point at my neck. I sucked in a breath as she nipped at my skin. My blood rushed downward and I pressed against her thigh.

Oh, God. I am going to get off right here and now if we don't stop.

Takoda gasped and pulled back, not letting go but putting a couple inches between us while we stood panting. Her eyes dilated with lust, her face flushed. She caressed my cheeks with her thumbs. "I've missed you," she murmured.

I moved my hands down to her waist. "Missed you too." I swallowed hard at the wash of emotion that nearly undid me.

For a few minutes, we simply held each other. I rested my head against her and her breath puffed against my hair. Her flannel shirt was soft, and I rubbed my cheek against her like a cat. My heart felt full enough to burst, my brain overwhelmed with the rush of sensory and emotional feedback.

I suddenly remembered why we were here to begin with. "I gotta pee," I whispered. "For real." God, I was such a dork.

Takoda laughed, a low rumble against my ear. "Me too."

She kissed me briefly and ducked into the nearest stall. I sucked in a deep breath to calm my racing heart and took the other stall, hoping like hell we'd be able to leave the office soon.

CHAPTER TWELVE

Takoda had brought her bike with her, and we spent Friday riding the trails and streets in and around Minneapolis before peddling back toward my side of town. It was a leisurely ride, with stops for coffee and ice cream and a walk through the Walker Sculpture Gardens.

It felt good to be able to show off my city and my favorite places to ride. There were always a lot of people out on the bikeways, and lots of things to look at. Eventually, we made our way back toward my apartment, deciding to stop for food before we called it a day. I led the way to the Mexican restaurant just a few blocks from home, where we relaxed in the cramped enclosed patio, sipped margaritas and ate tacos.

We demolished our dinners and lingered, chewing a few chips and having an after-dinner drink, not in a hurry since we had the small patio to ourselves. Takoda leaned her head against the brick wall, eyes half-closed as she sipped her margarita. Her dark hair was pulled back into a long braid draped over her shoulder. She lifted her glass. "This was a great idea. Good call, Amry. To a wonderful day with a wonderful woman."

I slouched back in my own chair across from her and lifted my glass in response. "It really was a good day. And you truly are wonderful."

Her gaze sharpened, studying my face. After a moment, her expression softened, and I saw her swallow. "*Zaagi'idiwin*, love, do you have any idea how special you are? How much you make me feel?" She sat up, setting down her glass and leaning toward me. "And this is not the alcohol talking. This is me." She reached across the table to hold my hand.

I stared at her. I had no idea what to say. Takoda called me 'love' and was telling me that I was special?

There was nothing special about me. I was as ordinary as a person could get. Just your average dyke. I had some skills, sure: I was a published author. I was good at my job. My friends liked me. But what could Takoda Running Bear see in me to make her eyes so warm and caring? To make her say I was special?

She said very softly, "I don't have the words for what's in my heart. But I know it's good."

I swallowed hard, overwhelmed by a wave of emotion rising in my throat. Please, please, let it be good, I thought. I wanted it to be good. I wanted her to be my fairytale Prince Charming, even if I didn't let myself believe in happily ever after.

Sure, I wrote romantic happy endings, but I knew what I wrote was hopeful fantasy because life wasn't like that. My last serious girlfriend had left me pretty messed up. I thought I'd loved Susan, but the only person Susan had loved was herself. I had been a plaything, to be manipulated and toyed with. She'd used my own best traits against me, turned my innate sense of caring into guilty acquiescence and my desire to please into anxious fear of upsetting her. When she was done, I had believed I couldn't do anything right.

I'd sworn to myself I wasn't going to get sucked in ever again.

But right at this moment, I believed Takoda meant what she said. The emotion in her eyes could not have been anything but real.

I clung to her hand, searching for words. What came out, as a breathless whisper, was "Thank you."

She caressed the back of my hand with her thumb. Her smile warmed me to the core, and slowly, I could breathe again. She said, "You're in my heart, always."

"You take my breath away, Koda."

She grinned, breaking the moment with humor. "Just don't stop breathing on my account."

I laughed.

She slowly released my hand and sat back in her seat. After a pause, she cocked her head a little. "Can we talk?" she asked, imitating Joan Rivers' famous line.

"Sure."

"I keep thinking about this. And I'm not sure this is the right time, but..." Takoda licked her lips. I leaned forward, not sure if I should be uneasy. She took a deep breath and rushed on, "Remember, at the cabin, when we were talking with Rose, I told you my grandmother said when I found the right person, that I'd know? And it seems like it's so fast, but I know. My heart knows. It's you. I'm falling in love with you, Amry."

What? My heart skipped about three beats, and all I could do was stare. She was falling in love with me? I wasn't sure I was ready for this. I hadn't let myself consider, in real terms, that Takoda could truly be serious about me. I hadn't let myself think the words out loud, though I knew in my subconscious they'd been there for a long time, and I felt the same way.

When I didn't answer, she swallowed hard, her expression collapsing. "I'm sorry. I—"

I blurted, "Koda, I love you."

The brightness of her smile could have lit a room. I got up and moved around to her as she stood too, and we rushed into each other's arms. Mouths met in a rush of passionate adrenaline, a hard, aching kiss, and for a few moments there was nothing in the world but the two of us. Takoda loved me. I loved her. My heart was full to bursting.

Dishes clinked somewhat loudly off to the side.

Shit.

The kiss ended abruptly as we both pulled back, grinning at each other. Our very sweet amd rather flamboyant waiter, Vincent, cleared his throat, though he was laughing. "Congratulations?" he asked.

"She loves me," Takoda said. "I am the luckiest woman in the world."

"We're both the luckiest."

"I'd say that's worth celebrating," Vincent said, then added conspiratorially, "Don't leave yet. I bet I can find some celebratory fried ice cream." Laughing, he dropped the bill on our table and hurried off.

Takoda and I settled back in our chairs, holding hands across the table. I couldn't stop smiling. Takoda loved me. I didn't know what that meant for us, but I knew that I was happier than I had ever been. I raised my glass with my free hand. "Best. Day. Ever."

When we got back to my apartment and stowed the bikes on the balcony, it was nearly dark. After being in bike clothes all day, we stripped, showered off the road dust and sweat, threw on T-shirts and settled on the sofa. I turned on the TV. We cuddled and exchanged happy, sleepy touches and kisses and nearly fell asleep during the ten o'clock news.

The harsh ring of my cell phone startled us out of our comfortable nest.

I fumbled to grab the phone and swipe open the call. "'Lo?" Takoda stretched and groaned. I cleared my throat and repeated, "Hello?"

My sister's jarring tones cut like a knife. Even Takoda stilled. "Amry, you need to come home. Right now."

"What?"

"You need to come home. Dad had a heart attack and is in the emergency room. It's not good."

I heard both anger and fear in Bethany's voice and was instantly alert. "When did it happen?" Takoda sat up, bringing me with her. I put the call on speaker so we could both hear.

Bethany said, "I don't know. He wasn't answering his phone so I stopped by his house half an hour ago. He was unconscious on the kitchen floor. I'm at the hospital. Tom's on his way."

"Oh, Beth, I'm sorry. God."

"Just get home."

"I will."

I stared at the phone while Takoda rubbed my back. My dad had a heart attack. How could that even be? Dad had always been larger than life to me, my hero and the strong, quiet rock of the family. When I'd talked to him a couple days ago, he had been fine. He was looking forward to meeting his friends for lunch and poker.

I set the phone carefully on the coffee table and closed my eyes. Takoda continued rubbing my back. My dad was in the emergency room. I wondered when the tears would come because right now my eyes were dry and I felt numb.

Takoda murmured, "I'm really sorry, Amry."

I nodded, but couldn't find my voice. I was too busy trying to process. I spoke slowly, as much to myself as to her. "Gonna have to get going. I need to get home."

"I'll help you pack." Her voice was quiet, calm, matter-of-fact. "Are you going to leave tonight or wait until morning?"

"I need to go now. I'll have to take my car." I would much rather have ridden with Takoda, but I needed to have wheels.

"Are you okay to drive?"

I took a long breath and considered. "Yeah, I'm fine. I just need to get there."

Her concerned countenance told me she wasn't quite buying it. "I'll follow you," she said. "We'll take our time."

I nodded.

She asked, "Where are you going to stay? You can stay with me."

I hadn't thought that far ahead yet. "I guess I'll stay at my dad's."

"Okay."

I heard the hint of disappointment in her voice and wondered if I would be better off at her place. No. I'd go home. That was where they'd look for me. It was the easiest answer, and it made sense right now.

I took a step but stalled and stared at nothing. I didn't know where to start.

Takoda wrapped her arms around me, holding me tight, tucking my head under her chin. "It'll all work out," she said softly.

I didn't believe it, but I was too busy freaking out to argue.

* * *

The journey up north was a long, dark, white-knuckled drive. I led the way, and Takoda followed a couple car lengths behind. I didn't turn on the radio or turn on the music from my phone. For comfort, I tried to cling to the warmth and love Takoda and I had been sharing before Bethany's call, but my thoughts ricocheted wildly.

I wondered if my father would recover. I thought about what might happen if he didn't make it. I thought about the last time I'd seen him, and the support he'd shown Nikko and me. I thought about the wasted years, when I could have just asked him what he thought about my being gay. Regrets. Memories. Fears. All those things spun through my head as I drove. But the tears I expected didn't come. Probably I was in shock. Or it was like when my mom had passed away and I'd just dealt with everything, being the strong one, and hadn't allowed myself to break down until after the funeral.

We stopped in Hinkley because I needed coffee and a break from driving in the dark. I got cookies for the sugar rush and called Bethany. Dad was in a coma and in the ICU. The doctors had done what they could. He'd either come out of it or he wouldn't. Additional diagnoses indicated he'd had a stroke as well, so if he did regain consciousness, there was no telling if he would be able to function normally.

When we finally got to the hospital, Takoda followed me into the parking lot and hopped out of her Jeep when I got out of my car. She crossed the space between our vehicles and held me tightly while I clung to her.

"You sure you don't want me to go in with you?" she asked.

I breathed in damp night air and the scent of her flannel, and tightened my arms around her waist. I did want her to be there. I ached to have her support when I walked through those hospital doors. But I knew the resulting tensions with my sibs would push everyone over the edge. Tom and Beth would have a fit that I'd brought my girlfriend, and to be honest, I wasn't up for that fight. Feeling unhappy and overwhelmed, I found myself taking the path of least conflict.

Taking a deep breath, I shook my head against her shoulder. "As much as I'd love to have you with me, it'll cause more problems than it'll solve. I can't deal with that right now."

"I understand." She kissed my hair.

I know she was disappointed, and I hoped she did understand. I didn't want her to think badly of me for wussing out. "I'll text you when I know more."

"Okay. And you're sure you want to stay at your dad's?"

"For now, anyway. Ask me again tomorrow."

She hugged me again and tipped my chin up to kiss me softly. "Anytime you need me, just call."

"Thank you." My voice caught.

She kissed me again, slowly and deeply. I lost myself in her, tasting coffee and sweets on her lips, reveling in the feel of her tongue playing against my own. I felt my blood stirring, desire beginning to flare. She broke the kiss and we gazed at each other for a long time.

Takoda stepped back. "It'll be okay."

I nodded mutely.

She turned me by my shoulders toward the door. "Go on. I'll wait until you get inside before I leave."

I forced myself to plod toward the well-lit emergency entrance when all I wanted was to run back to her. By the time the heavy glass doors closed behind me, I felt very alone.

The security guard at the information desk directed me to the ICU waiting room. It was dim, carpeted, had a tropical fish aquarium and uncomfortable chairs. Bethany and her husband David, Tom, Darlene and Nikko huddled in the far corner.

Tom straightened when he saw me. He stood, his appearance rumpled and tired. "Amry, you got here." He hugged me stiffly.

"How's Dad?"

"They haven't let us see him yet. I think Beth found him just in time." His eyes glittered with tears.

Nikko walked over and threw his arms around me. I squeezed him hard. "Hey buddy."

His blue eyes were bloodshot. What the hell do you say to a kid whose granddad might be dying? I hugged him again and hoped he understood I was there for him and I loved him and somehow, it'd all be okay.

For a writer, sometimes I sucked at words.

Tom asked, "You want coffee or something?"

"No." I was still jittery from the large mocha I'd gotten in Hinkley.

Bethany sat next to David on one of the two-seater chairs. She leaned on him, and he had his arm wrapped around her shoulders. Bethany's blond hair was slightly mussed, her clothes rumpled, a sure sign she wasn't handling things well. She glanced at me through teary eyes and turned away without a word.

David asked, "Long drive?"

"Yeah." I took a chair between David and Nikko. Darlene and Tom sat across from me. Darlene offered me a sad smile. She cradled a Styrofoam coffee cup. I clasped my hands in my lap and half-wished I'd gotten a coffee, if only to have something to hang on to.

Another family clustered in the corner opposite us. I gazed into the fish tank at the center of the room and wondered what the fish thought of this place. Probably, they didn't think much of anything. Lucky fish.

Nikko asked, "How long are you staying?"

I patted his leg. "Not sure. I haven't thought that far ahead yet. You doing okay?"

"Yeah."

I supposed if I were sixteen, I wouldn't admit to not being okay either.

Darlene said, "I told him he didn't need to be here." Her expression, as she considered her son, showed concern.

"I'm not a kid. I want to know how my grandpa's doing."

"I know, honey. Sometimes it's hard for me to think of you as the wonderful young man that you are." Her smile was bittersweet. I gave her a smile and patted Nikko's leg again.

Another two hours passed before anyone came to talk to us about Dad. At nearly four in the morning, I was long past exhausted. The doctor crossing the room with purposeful strides had tired eyes, but she stood tall in her clean blue scrubs. A pair of reading glasses hung on a silver chain around her neck, and she carried a folder and a clipboard. "You're the family of Raymond Marasich?"

Tom pushed to his feet. "Yes, we are."

She held out a hand. "Dr. Angela Hardman. I'm the on-call for the ICU tonight. Mr. Marasich remains in a coma. The machines are breathing for him. His heart is beating on its own for the moment. It stopped a second time after the initial heart attack and we defibrillated him. His heartbeat is irregular, and we're monitoring him closely."

Bethany spoke for the first time since I'd arrived. Her voice sounded weak and hoarse. "What are his chances?"

"I don't want to give you false hope. Between the heart attack and the severity of the stroke, I would say his chances of waking up are less than fifty percent. If he does wake, there's a serious possibility that he's going to have lost a large amount of motor and brain function."

Bethany stared at the floor.

Tom asked, "Are we able to see him?"

"Technically, visiting hours are from eight a.m. to nine p.m., but I can let you see him. No more than two at a time. Family only. I'll send his nurse to bring you back."

"Thank you," Tom said.

Dr. Hardman nodded politely and left the room.

Darlene said, "I'm glad they're going to let us see him tonight."

"Can I go too?" Nikko asked.

"If you want to, yes."

"Can I go with Aunt Amry, so she doesn't have to go alone?"

I blinked. I hadn't seen that coming. I continued to be amazed by how thoughtful and gentle my nephew could be. Even if it were because he didn't want to go alone, it was sweet that he was concerned about me as well. I said, "That's up to your folks, but I'd like that if they're okay with it."

Tom frowned, but Darlene nodded. "That's fine. Just do whatever the nurse or Amry tell you, okay?"

The ICU nurse took Bethany and David back first. When they returned, Bethany clung to David, her face pale. Tom and Darlene went next. I wanted to ask Beth what she thought, but her behavior made it obvious she didn't want to discuss it. She turned into her husband's embrace and avoided eye contact.

Ten minutes later, Nikko and I trailed the nurse into the locked ICU area. She led us to the center room across from the semicircular nurses' station. "You can go in. Feel free to talk to him, but don't expect him to respond. Some people believe patients in a coma can hear their loved ones."

I thanked her and stepped into the room. Nikko followed a half step behind me.

I moved to the far side of the bed, careful to avoid the cables and IV tubes running between my father and the rolling IV stands and monitoring equipment caddies. I rested my hands on the plastic bedrail. Dad's pallor was grayish, and his hair was matted against the pillows. He had a breathing tube down his throat and an oxygen mask covered most of his face. Besides the IV in the back of his hand, there must have been a dozen other lines connected to him—blood pressure, pulse, heart-monitoring wires, sensors attached to his head, maybe tracking brain waves. Four bags of liquid hung on the IV pole, feeding life and medications into his body. I recognized the rhythmic hiss and whoosh of the oxygen machine and the circulation pumps on his lower legs. The heart monitor beeped in time to the green spikes on the tiny screen.

Nikko whispered, "What are we supposed to say?"

Hell if I knew. "Just say whatever you feel. Let him know you're here."

Nikko stood opposite me, gripping the bedrail with white knuckles. He absently shook a lock of hair out of his eyes. "Hey Grandpa. It's me, Nikko, and Amry. I sure hope you'll be okay. It's really scary to see you here. You don't look so good, but you're gonna get better. I love you."

I worked hard to blink away tears. I wasn't going to cry in front of my nephew. I needed to be strong. "Hey, Dad. We're all here for you. Be strong. Be well. Love you."

I gently touched Dad's hand. His skin felt cold and dry. I watched the shallow rise and fall of his chest, knowing the machines were doing the work. The strong, confident man I'd known all my life had been replaced by someone too frail to be my dad. *I don't want to remember you this way because this isn't you.*

The nurse poked her head into the room. "I have to ask you to leave now," she said.

I nodded. I put an arm around Nikko's waist as we left the room.

When we returned to the others, Nikko went to sit beside Darlene. I suddenly felt very alone.

A while later, the nurse came and told us there was nothing more we could do and suggested it would be best if we went home and got some sleep.

David stood, bringing Bethany up with him. "We'll be back at nine."

Bethany stared at the floor and said nothing.

Tom said, "Us too."

David and Beth led the procession out of the waiting room, with Tom and his family following. Darlene had an arm around Nikko's slumped shoulders. I tagged along at the rear.

A wave of exhaustion washed over me as I shuffled behind my sibs to the parking lot. It was still dark, but not for long. As I reached my car, Nikko jogged over and gave me a hug. I squeezed his slim body and dropped a kiss on his cheek, then watched him climb into his dad's truck before I slid behind the wheel of my Subaru. A minute later, I steered onto the familiar streets toward the house where I had grown up.

Parking the car in the driveway, I grabbed my backpack and duffel bag from the backseat. I fumbled to find the right key, got the door unlocked and stepped into the kitchen, assaulted by the essence of "old people," closed-up, and stuffy.

I dropped my bags at the doorway and kicked off my sneakers. The house was silent and empty. There was no sign of where Dad had fallen in the kitchen, or of anyone having taken him out in an ambulance. I wandered through the house, turning on the lights in the bathroom and my bedroom before returning to the kitchen. A few dishes lay in the sink. I washed and dried them and put them away.

My phone rang and I jumped about a foot in the air before scrambling around my pockets trying to find it. Takoda. Thank God. But what was she doing up?

"Hello?"

"Hey. How are you doing?"

"I just got home. It's weird here. I did my dad's dishes."

"How is he?"

"Still in a coma and no change since I texted earlier."

"Damn. Will you go over again right away in the morning?"

"I think so, yeah. Everyone else will be there." I stared at the worn linoleum floor, noting the tiny triangular cuts where Mom had dropped the iron over the years. "I don't know if he'll make it," I said, trying out the words aloud.

"I'm sorry, sweetie."

"I know. Thank you."

"You gonna be okay?"

"Yeah. I'll be fine." Maybe. I signed off after a few minutes, then realized I hadn't asked her how she was doing. I mentally berated myself for the omission.

Sighing, I carried my bags to my bedroom. I sat on the edge of my twin bed, feeling as though I'd walked backward in time. Bethany's bed rested against the wall facing my own. The frilly flowered bedspread on her bed had faded over the decades. I fingered the navy-blue nylon comforter on my own bed. The fabric was soft and cool to the touch.

A cascade of memories formed in my mind. I envisioned Mom and Dad tucking me in when I was little, and later, when we were teenagers, Mom poking her head in the door to say good night and that she loved us. I remembered Dad teasing us about brushing behind our ears and washing our teeth, waking up for school to Mom's sing-song morning greetings and how annoyed I would get. Depending on what shift he was working, Dad would be in the kitchen reading the paper while we got ready for school. He was always more boisterous and awake than any of us kids, and we'd grumble at him over our cereal.

Then I thought of Dad lying in the hospital bed, connected to life by wires and an IV, the deathly pallor of his skin, and the doctor's solemn statement that he may not wake up.

My chest hurt and my throat tightened. I squeezed my eyes shut as tears trickled down my cheeks. Grabbing a handful of my comforter, I buried my face in it, fighting the emotions, pushing them back until I was able to stifle the sobs.

I couldn't stay here. The house was too full of memories, and I wasn't ready to give in to the sadness or the staggering sense of aloneness battering the edge of my consciousness.

I stood up and shouldered my backpack and my duffel. I pulled the comforter off the bed and balled it up in my arms. I shut out the lights as I left, locking up the house with its memories, and threw my stuff into the car.

I dialed Takoda's number as I left the driveway. She answered before the first ring had finished. "Are you okay?" Her voice was anxious, almost breathless.

"I'm on my way to your place. I can't stay here."

"Okay. Do you remember the way?"

"Yeah. I'll be there in half an hour or so."

"Take your time and watch for deer."

"I will."

I dropped the phone on the passenger seat, pulled onto the highway then took the turn onto County 5. The sun had only just started to rise, and low-lying fog drifted across the road. I flipped on my fog lights and slowed down, driving white-knuckled as I searched for the turnoff to the gravel track that led to Takoda. I found it, finally, after half-panicking, thinking I'd missed the turn.

Relief washed over me when I saw the signpost marking Takoda's driveway. I parked in front of the garage and killed the engine. The front screen door opened, and Xena and Gabby bounded toward me with furry exuberance. Takoda trotted down the porch stairs and jogged across the yard as I dragged myself out of the car. She drew me into a tight embrace, and I reveled in the strength of her hold.

"Oh, honey," she murmured. "It'll be okay. Come on, let's get you and your stuff inside."

She grabbed my backpack and duffel while I scooped up my old comforter. I didn't know why I had taken it. It had seemed like the thing to do in the moment. A security blanket, it was something I could hang on to.

Takoda brought my bags up to the loft. I sat on the leather sofa with my comforter. I didn't have the energy or the wherewithal to do anything else. The dogs pushed their noses into my comforter and me. I rubbed their heads. Takoda returned, and with a wave of her hand, the dogs backed off and laid down at our feet. She sat and wrapped her arms around me.

I was physically and emotionally wrung out. None of my scattered thoughts lasted long enough to be coherent or verbalized. I'd learned long ago that it took me a long time to process my emotions, especially when I felt the need to stay in control. I'd held my shit together the whole drive from the cities and while I'd been to see Dad. I'd managed not to completely lose it at my parents' house or getting here. I clutched the comforter balled up in my lap. The tears weren't going to happen yet. I was too overwhelmed.

Takoda either understood what was happening to me or was being ungodly patient with my withdrawn silence. She kissed my hair. We sat for a long time, her holding me and me clutching my childhood comforter.

After a while, she asked, "You want to go to sleep now?"

"I can sleep with you?" I didn't know why I needed to ask and I knew I sounded like a pathetic, frightened child, but I didn't want to be alone.

"I was hoping you would," she said. "Come on." She helped me up and led the way up to the loft.

My duffel rested on the wooden chest at the foot of the bed.

"There's towels and everything on the bathroom counter," she said. "There's a toothbrush there too, if you don't want to dig yours out."

I took a long, deep breath and slowly let it out. "Thank you." I set the comforter on the bed. "I'm sorry. I'm kind of a mess, aren't I?"

She gently brushed the hair from my eyes. "You're fine, *zaagi'idiwin*. This is heavy stuff."

"Yeah." I dug around in my duffel for my toiletries and brought them to the bathroom.

When I'd finished my before-bed tasks and wandered out of the bathroom, Takoda sat on the edge of the bed, wearing boxers and a loose tank top. I dug in my bag for my faded, three-sizes-too-big Pooh-bear sleepshirt.

I didn't bother to turn away when I changed. It wasn't like we hadn't seen each other's bodies. Takoda's hands and mouth had explored every inch of my skin. That thought lightened my heart, but I was too wiped out for anything even approaching romance or desire.

We crawled into bed, and Takoda pulled the covers up over us, also offering to add the comforter I'd brought, but I shook my head. I didn't need it now. I had her.

She spooned against me, enfolding me in her arms. I sighed at the solid reassurance of her body against mine. She kissed my hair. "Sleep, sweetheart."

"Thank you," I whispered. I shut my eyes, safe enough to let my body and my mind rest.

CHAPTER THIRTEEN

I didn't make it to the hospital until about ten thirty Saturday morning. I walked into the ICU waiting room, bolstered by the strong coffee in the State Park travel mug Takoda had pushed into my hands as I'd left. My family had gathered in the far corner nearest the windows. Tom and Darlene sat across from Bethany and David. Bethany huddled against David's side. Tom read the morning paper. Darlene cradled a takeout coffee cup.

For a moment, I felt very alone and angry that I didn't have anyone here to lean on. Screw them for not approving of my lifestyle or accepting Takoda. Damn me for not having the balls to deal with the blowback if she were here.

I shook off the anger and took a centering breath before crossing the room. Tom glanced up. Darlene smiled a little. I greeted them with a quiet "Good morning" and chose the chair next to Darlene.

Bethany lifted her head from David's shoulder. Her blue eyes were tired, shadowed by dark circles. She stared at me. "You didn't answer the phone at Mom and Dad's this morning."

Ouch. Well. To lie, or not to lie? I sipped my coffee. "That's because I wasn't there." I didn't elaborate, hoping she would let it go.

Of course she couldn't. "Where were you, then?"

"I'm staying at Takoda's. I couldn't stay at the house. It's too empty."

Bethany hissed, "Your father is dying and you're shacking up with your girlfriend?"

"No. My father is dying, and I couldn't stand to be in his house alone with all those memories."

"You just have to flaunt your disgusting lifestyle, don't you? You're sick."

I swallowed a dozen angry replies and forced myself not to react. Feigning indifference, I shrugged. "You asked. Have you seen Dad yet?"

"They're doing some tests," Tom said curtly.

I nodded and stretched my legs out, trying to get comfortable in the chair next to Darlene, and as far away from Bethany and Tom as I could get while still being polite. Darlene patted my hand, and I smiled at her.

Bethany glared. If looks could kill, I'd have been a bloody mess on the floor.

I didn't bother to return the hostility. I texted Takoda. *"Here. The sibs r too. B is a bitch. Wish I was with u."*

I sent the text and savored the smooth richness of my coffee, heavy on the cream and sweetener. A few moments later, Takoda answered my text. *"Fuck B. Hugs. Thinking of you. Call if u need anything."*

"I will. Xxxooo"

I settled in to wait, wondering what tests they were doing and if they could determine the damage caused by the heart attack and stroke without Dad's conscious help. As much as I trusted the medical profession, I knew there was a point where all they could do was make their best guess.

When we were allowed to see Dad about an hour later, I took my turn alone.

I entered the cramped room and stood by the bed with my fingers curled around the cold plastic of the safety rails. Dad's normally rugged complexion remained a sickly gray. His left arm lay on top of the blanket with an IV needle taped on the back of his bruised hand.

I laid a tentative hand on his arm. An icy pit formed in my stomach. I squeezed gently to let him know I was there.

"Hey Dad. It's Amry. Keep fighting like the stubborn Bohunk Mom always said you are. It's not the same here without you. I love you."

"I don't know what I'm going to do, Koda." I slumped in the dining room chair nursing a cup of coffee. The morning sunlight slanted through the patio doors and onto the table. "It's been four days. Hayley texted me to see when I was thinking of coming back to work. She said she didn't want to rush me, but I can read between the lines. The doctor said if Dad wakes up, it's not likely he'll be the same man. How long are we supposed to wait? I mean, I don't want to leave. I really want to be here. But I can't stay away from work indefinitely."

Takoda leaned against the kitchen counter, her own coffee mug cradled in her hands. "Is there any hope at all for him to come out of the coma?"

"You know how it is—they won't come out and say anything definite. The doctor says there's very little brain activity. He can't breathe on his own. It seems like he could exist for a long time being kept alive by machines."

"How do you feel about that?"

"Doesn't seem to be much of a life, hooked up to machines in some kind of limbo." I swallowed hard. "When I think about it, all I can think of is what he might be feeling. If he's trapped in his head, if he knows what's going on, if he wants to let go and can't or if he's trying to come back to us. If he wakes up, what kind of life will he have? I don't think he'd be happy if all he could do is lay there, if he can't communicate or do anything. He's always been the kind of guy that that got out and lived his life. I feel like I'm already saying good-bye, and I feel guilty because I should be believing he'll be okay again."

"Don't be guilty, Amry. I think you're being realistic about the situation. Even if you hope for the best, it's normal to mentally prepare for the worst."

My heart ached. I already missed my dad. It was so hard to see him lying there so still, but there was no way I wasn't going to stay here. I had to believe he knew we were there for him. I hoped he could hear me thinking of him and telling him I loved him, and that he knew, no matter what, I wanted what would make him happy.

"What do Tom and Beth think?"

"I don't know. They don't talk to me. Tom sits and broods. Beth prays."

Takoda shook her head. "I think you need to do and believe what's right for you and too bad for what they think."

"I wish I knew what the right thing is for me."

She crossed the kitchen to stand behind me, resting her hands on my shoulders and squeezing gently. "You'll know when the time is right." She kissed the top of my head. "Trust your heart."

I leaned my head into her stomach. "Easier to say than do. But thank you."

She combed her fingers through my hair. "One day at time. See what the day brings and make your decision when the time is right. You know I'm here if you need to talk."

I tipped my head back to meet her gaze. She kissed me lightly, and I put as much love into the soft contact as I could, wanting to let her know how much she meant to me.

As we parted, I reluctantly pushed away from the table. "I'd better get going."

She sent me off to the hospital with a travel mug full of coffee and caring, and another kiss.

* * *

Clutching my coffee mug, I trudged across the parking lot to the hospital. I was not looking forward to another twelve hours of waiting in strained silence with my siblings. I clung to a modicum of hope for my father and wondered if he had improved at all since last night. Maybe he'd wake up today or at least show some sign of coming out of the coma.

When I got upstairs, Tom, Bethany and David stood somberly with Dr. Anderson, Dad's primary doctor. My chest tightened. As I joined them, Dr. Anderson said, "Amry, I'm glad you're here."

Bethany muttered, "Always straggling in at the last minute."

Irritation fired in my chest. Couldn't she be civil for two fucking minutes? I did my best to cling to calm, ignored my sister and focused on the doctor. "What's happening?"

"Not good news, unfortunately," Dr. Anderson said. "I won't beat around the bush. Your father's brain activity has dwindled. I believe what little activity we see is the random firing of neurons. His brain is no longer running his body."

"What does that mean, exactly?" Bethany asked.

"The brain controls the bodily functions—breathing, heart, kidneys, liver, everything. Even with the machines keeping his heart and lungs functioning, his organs are starting to shut down because his brain isn't telling them what to do. To be blunt, it's just a matter of time. I can't say precisely how long. Days, weeks, maybe, if he remains on life support."

"You're saying that if we turn off the machines, we will be killing him," Bethany persisted.

"In most cases, at this point, we would remove all medication and nutrition, disconnect the machines and let him pass on naturally. Even with intervention, his condition is terminal. However, if it is your wish, we will continue the current course of treatment."

"I will not kill my father," Bethany said flatly.

Tom looked at Doctor Anderson. "Are you saying we should turn the machines off?" he asked.

"Medically, there is nothing more we can do for him. We can keep him alive for some time, but his body is shutting down." He took a breath. "I'll leave you to discuss this. Have the nurse page me if you have more questions or if you make a decision. I'm very sorry."

My mind reeled. Before this, I had still held out hope, no matter how small, that Dad might be okay. This news changed everything. If there was no brain activity, Dad was truly lost to us. The man we knew was no longer there. And yet, he was still alive because the life support machines were keeping him breathing, keeping his heart beating. I needed time to process.

I said, "Let's sit down and talk."

Bethany repeated, "I am not going to kill Dad."

Tom said, "What the doctor said makes sense. Why continue his suffering by keeping him all hooked up?"

"No. He is not dead. We need to give him a chance."

David put a hand on Bethany's shoulder, and she shrugged him off impatiently.

"The doctor said he's not going to miraculously come back to us. Maybe we just need to let him go," Tom persisted.

Tears rolled down Bethany's cheeks.

I wanted to reach out to her. I felt her pain; we all did. But I knew she would never accept comfort from me. "Maybe we should all go somewhere we can talk. Go have coffee or something and step away."

Bethany sniffled. "Is that what you do in the city? Go and have coffee and make things all better?"

I sighed. My heart hurt too much to argue with her. "No. It doesn't make things all better. But sometimes it helps to be able to talk things through."

"I have nothing to say." She glared through her tears.

Tom said, "Come on, let's at least go down to the cafeteria and find a quiet corner."

"The cafeteria is not quiet," Bethany snapped. "And I don't want to talk about this."

I tried again because I enjoyed beating my head against a wall. "Beth, I know it sucks. We're all hurting here, but we need to consider what the doctor said. If his brain isn't functioning, he's not Dad anymore. Maybe it's better if we let him go. Let him join Mom."

"You're just saying that so you can go back to your sick life."

I bit my lip and forced myself to breathe when what I wanted to do was lash out. I ground out, "No, Beth. I'm saying that because I want to do what's best for Dad."

Tom said, "I know we're all upset. But I think the doctor is right. They can't bring him back, and he's not really living, laying there all hooked up like that."

"I won't be a party to murder. You want to kill him, fine. Do it. But it's not right. We are not God."

"We're playing God keeping him alive with machines," I said.

I thought she was going to hiss at me; her anger was almost palpable.

Tom asked, "Do you want me to make the call, Beth?"

Tears flowed down her face again. "Do whatever you want." She turned and wrapped her arms around David's waist, sobbing into his shoulder. Her husband held her silently, stroking her blond hair.

Tom said, "I'll see if we can talk to Dr. Anderson."

David said, "Beth needs to go to the chapel. We'll be there a while."

There wasn't anything to say to that. David and Bethany disappeared down the hall, and I returned to my chair in the corner of the room.

My phone vibrated in my pocket. I looked to see Takoda's text. *"Hey, hope you're okay. Meet me for dinner tonight?"*

Was I okay? No. Not really. My dad was dying. I wanted to see her, and I wanted her to hold me until it didn't hurt so much. The thought of food made me feel nauseous. I typed back, *"Not doing so good. Dad not good. I can bring home takeout?"*

A couple seconds later, my phone rang. I stood and walked out of the room as I answered.

Takoda's voice was warm and reassuring. "Amry, I'm sorry. Are you okay? What's happened? What can I do?"

I paced the empty end of the hallway. "I'm okay. Mostly. Dad's brain and body are shutting down. The doctor thinks it would be best to take away life support and let him go."

"Oh, honey, I'm sorry. I know that's so hard."

"We haven't made a decision yet." I wanted to say more, but in the hallway, where others could hear, I bit my lip. Takoda and I could talk tonight. "I really don't think I'll be up for dinner tonight."

"Don't worry about it. I'll make something for us here, okay? Comfort food." Her voice was so gentle, so concerned and caring.

I nodded, knowing she couldn't see me, my throat suddenly tight with tears.

She said, "I'm going to let you go. I just wanted to make sure you were all right. Call if you need anything, or text."

"Thank you. I will."

"Okay. Love you, Am."

"Love you too, Koda."

I hung up and wandered back down the hall. As I reached the ICU's locked door, I stopped and picked up the phone, requesting entrance to see Dad. The door clicked open and I stepped through. The nurse at the desk smiled and nodded at me as I passed. I smiled back automatically, but my attention was already on the cramped room at the end of the hall.

I sat beside my father's bed and rested my hand on his. His skin was cold and I could feel the bones underneath, as though he'd already wasted away, even in the four days that he'd been here.

"What do we do, Dad?" I asked him. "What do you want us to do?" I felt the tears stinging, the sob aching at the back of my throat. "I love you, Dad."

I hoped he heard me. But I knew he couldn't answer. I thought about the man I knew. Ray Marasich loved life. He had friends, and they played cards once a week, they had breakfast at the Sportsman Café and gossiped. He loved his grandchildren. I thought of him out playing catch with Nikko and Joey and, when we were kids, with Tom and me. He wouldn't want to be here, wasting away like this, trapped in his body or in his head. I knew he missed Mom so much. Maybe we should let him go, so he could see her again.

Was it the right thing to do, to take away the machines keeping him alive? I knew that if it were me that was what I'd want. I knew, at the end, that was what Mom wanted. There'd been a Do Not Resuscitate order for her. I thought Dad would feel the same way.

A few minutes later, I patted his hand, told him again that I loved him and returned to the waiting room.

Doctor Anderson stopped to talk to Tom and me not long after I returned, but our discussion with him wasn't exceptionally fruitful. Since Beth was still in the chapel, Tom didn't want to make the call, but we got a little more information. Dr. Anderson let us know we didn't need to give more than a couple hours' notice once we decided to turn off the machines.

I went back to sit with Dad a few more times, talking softly to him about whatever came to mind, telling him about Koda, and how I knew he would love her as much as I did. The longer I watched him lay there, the more certain I was that we needed to let him join Mom.

When Bethany and David finally returned from the chapel a couple hours later, Tom stood and demanded, "How long are we going to wait to make a decision?"

Bethany glared at him.

I said quietly, "I really don't think Dad would want to exist like this."

"How can you both be so heartless?"

"I don't want to lose him either, but it doesn't seem right to force him to be half-alive," Tom said.

"This is our father and you want to let him die!"

I shook my head. "We don't want him to die. We love him. But is this any way for him to live? He can't communicate. His body is shutting down. What if he's in there, and he's suffering and helpless? Isn't it more humane to let him go? Then he can be with Mom. I know I wouldn't want to be where he is right now."

"That's you, Amry. You don't speak for Dad or for us."

"Exactly. That's why we need to talk about it and come to a decision."

Tom rubbed his eyes. Beside him, Darlene, who'd joined us after work, nodded in silent agreement. David stood stoically silent. I couldn't decide if he had an opinion or not. Perhaps he talked to Bethany at home. He certainly wasn't going to argue with her here.

I leaned back in my chair. I had said my piece.

Bethany made her decision by declaring, "I'm going home to pray for guidance." She took David by the arm and marched toward the hallway.

Tom said, "We need to get home and get the boys fed."

Darlene stood with him. "We'll see you tomorrow, Amry."

Tom turned to leave, but Darlene hesitated, then gave me a quick hug. Startled, I automatically returned the gesture. I thought she wanted to say something as she stepped back, but she only nodded and hurried to catch up with Tom. I watched her take his arm, and I wondered if this crisis had brought them together again and made a mental note to check in with Nikko later.

Shaking my head, I slung my backpack over my shoulder and followed them out of the hospital. I was exhausted and my heart ached. All I wanted to do was go back to Takoda's and curl up in the quiet, surrounded by Takoda's warmth.

Later that night, the ten o'clock news droned into the dimness of Takoda's living room. I curled, half-asleep on the sofa, with my head in Takoda's lap and my old comforter thrown over me. Gabby slept in a tight ball of fur at my feet, and Xena stretched out on the floor in front of us. I had almost nodded off when my cell phone rang. I stretched to grab the phone from the coffee table and saw Tom's name on the screen.

My stomach clenched. Tom calling couldn't be a good thing. Tom never called me. I swiped the call to accept it. Takoda muted the television as I put the phone on speaker.

"Hi Tom, what's up?" I grimaced when the words came out a little too forced and bright.

"I talked to Beth. She talked to her pastor. They decided it isn't a sin to let nature take its course. So I called the hospital.

We'll meet tomorrow at nine thirty and turn off life support. The doctor will be there, and I think Beth is calling her pastor to be there too."

I swallowed hard. "Okay."

There was a pause before Tom said, "We'll see you in the morning, then."

"I'll be there."

He hung up. I set the phone down. Tomorrow, we'd pull the plug on the machines keeping my dad alive. Tomorrow, both my parents would have passed on. Tomorrow, everything changed. Xena's ears twitched as I scratched her head.

"Are you okay?" Takoda caressed my cheek with her knuckles.

"I think so. Maybe. No, not really." The pressure of tears made my head hurt, and sadness made my chest feel heavy. I pictured my dad the way I remembered him, strong and healthy and laughing, and tears slid down my nose. I clutched the comforter in my fists. Takoda's fingers combed through my hair, gentle and reassuring.

"What can I do, Am? Let me help. I want to be here for you. You don't have to be alone, *zaagi'idiwin*."

I swallowed. At this very moment, I just wanted her to hold me. I wanted to curl into a ball and be held until it stopped hurting. And I wished she could be at my side tomorrow, so I wouldn't have to be alone. I would have the twins, but they weren't going to comfort me. They would comfort each other and take strength from their spouses.

But was it fair to ask Takoda to be with me? Was it right to ask her to be part of such an intense situation? Was our relationship serious enough that I could ask for her support?

The twins would have fits. There would be a scene. There would be tension and bad feelings, and it would be because of my needs and my decisions. But why should my needs be less valid than theirs? God. I hated this.

Takoda continued to run her fingers through my hair. "Do you want me to be with you tomorrow?" she asked.

Yes. "They're going to hate me for it. They're going to be pissed."

"Let them be pissed. It isn't about them."

"There's going to be arguments and it'll be my fault." I sounded pathetic even to myself.

"Amry, it's not your fault. It's their problem. You're not telling them how to feel."

She said it so matter-of-factly. I wanted desperately to believe the words. I needed to be strong enough to let Tom and Bethany's anger and hatefulness roll off my back, but I didn't know if I could. I dreaded dealing with the confrontation, but I desperately wanted Takoda to be there. I needed her to be with me. I didn't want to be alone when my dad passed on. "I don't know how to do this." My voice cracked on the words, and I couldn't hold back the tears. I was a piece of work—pathetic and weak. What in hell could someone as strong as Takoda want with me?

Takoda lifted me and took me into her arms. "You know how. You just do it."

I wrapped my arms around her and hung on. Was it that simple? Could it be? I wanted it to be. I wanted her to be with me. "You'll come with me?"

"I will."

I buried my face against her neck, sniffling, breathing the comforting scent of her warm skin. "I'm sorry," I whispered. For being such a loser, for being weak and selfish because I needed her.

She kissed my hair. "Nothing to be sorry for, hon. Trust yourself."

I wanted to. I truly did. I settled against her and let her strength and conviction ease away my fear. Someday, I would be as strong as her. Starting tomorrow, I guess I would be trying.

Takoda drove us to the hospital the next morning. I knew it was the right thing to let Dad pass on, and it was right that I should have Takoda at my side for support. But the closer we got to the hospital, the more anxious I felt.

I forced myself to look at my parents' house as we drove past it on the highway. With all the curtains closed and the garage door shut, it looked lifeless and surrounded by sadness. Mom had passed away in the house, in a hospital bed in the living room. I'd been at her side. It'd been about four in the morning. I'd fallen asleep on the recliner beside her hospice bed after a long night of Dad and I doing our best to calm and soothe Mom when she'd been struggling to breathe. She'd been agitated, restless and frightened all night. We'd finally gotten her settled down around three thirty. I remembered jerking suddenly awake and looking toward her bed, knowing she was gone. Dad had been in the kitchen making a pot of coffee.

Maybe it was selfish, but I didn't want to face my father's death alone.

Takoda took my hand as she drove. I twined my fingers with hers and hung on for what felt like dear life.

By the time we arrived, I'd worked myself into a bundle of nerves. I attempted to pull my shit together as we got out of the Jeep and crossed the parking lot, taking deep breaths and trying to calm my mind and my nauseous stomach. I focused on the feel of Takoda's hand in mine. When I hesitated at the doorway, she said softly, "It's going to be fine."

I nodded, straightened my shoulders and strode through the automatic doors. Tom and Darlene were in the ICU waiting room. Tom paced near the windows while Darlene waited near the aquarium. I didn't see Bethany and David, or their pastor.

Tom glowered when we came into the room, his brows lowering into an angry line.

Words tumbled out of my mouth in a rush. "I couldn't do this alone, and you guys have your spouses. I think you remember Takoda."

Takoda said, "I'm so sorry you all have to go through this."

Tom turned away.

"Amry, I'm so sorry." Darlene stepped forward and hugged me, then Takoda. "Thank you for supporting Amry."

"I'm honored to be here for her," Takoda said quietly. She caught my hand again, and I was grateful for the contact.

Darlene said, "Beth and David should be here in a few minutes. Doctor Anderson will be here at nine thirty. The nurse said we'll be able to spend some time with Dad before they turn off life support."

We stood, shifting from foot to foot. It felt wrong to sit down. Nobody attempted to make small talk. For one thing, Tom wouldn't even look at Takoda and me. But even so, what was left to say? Mindless small talk seemed inappropriate. The enormity of what we were about to do hung over us like a dark cloud. Even though I'd justified it logically a hundred times, "pulling the plug" on the machines keeping Dad alive was unsettling and frightening. Were we truly making the right choice? What if we were wrong? The responsibility sat heavily on my heart.

Fifteen endless minutes later, Bethany, David, and their pastor hurried into the waiting room. Bethany wore a black knee-length dress, David a black suit with a white shirt.

I watched Bethany's gaze stop on Takoda. Her eyes narrowed and she hissed, "What is she doing here?"

I said formally, "Bethany, this is Takoda Running Bear. Takoda, this is my sister Bethany, and her husband David."

Beth stepped in front of her husband, effectively keeping him from shaking Takoda's extended hand. "This person is not family, and she does not belong here! How dare you?" Her voice rose in volume as she shook her finger in my face. "How dare you flaunt your sick lifestyle on our father's deathbed?"

The pastor stepped forward, gently putting a hand on Bethany's arm and lowering it as he faced me. He said calmly, "You must be Amry." He shook my hand. "I'm Pastor John." His strong grip surprised me. Releasing my hand, he also shook Takoda's.

Bethany said, "She shouldn't be here. They're living against God's law. It's disgusting."

The pastor shifted uncomfortably. I drew an unsteady breath as I scrambled for something to say.

Takoda rested a hand on my shoulder. "Amry shouldn't have to go through this experience alone. Bethany, you have your husband and your pastor for support. Tom has Darlene. Everyone deserves a shoulder to lean on in times of trouble." She stood strong at my side, my protector and defender.

I saw flickers of varying emotions cross Pastor John's face before he settled on compassionate. "I don't condone your lifestyle," he said. "But that is not why we are here. So for the purposes of this very difficult time, let us simply move forward to the task at hand."

Bethany stared at him for several seconds as though she wanted to argue the point. Finally, she nodded curtly and sent Takoda and me another scathing glare.

Tom wore the dark, barely controlled expression that told me he'd likely have plenty to say later.

Fortunately, Doctor Anderson chose that moment to join us. Another round of introductions ensued before he led us to Dad's room in the ICU. We gathered around the bed. I found myself with David on my left, relieved Bethany wasn't standing next to me. I gripped Takoda's hand with my right. Tom and Darlene stood across from us. Pastor John and Doctor Anderson stood at the foot of the bed.

Doctor Anderson said, "Please, take your time. I'll return in fifteen minutes or so to see if you're ready." He nodded respectfully and left the room.

I released Takoda's hand and clutched the plastic bed railing. I barely recognized the sunken, pale-skinned man under the white sheet and blanket. How could he have become so frail and old in so short a time? My throat tightened painfully; I could feel tears forming and threatening to spill. The man I knew wasn't lying in front of me. We were doing the right thing.

Takoda wrapped her arm around my waist. I leaned into her, grateful for her presence.

Pastor John started to speak. I tuned him out and thought about the days when I was a kid and Dad was my hero. I remembered him playing baseball with us in the backyard. He'd pop the ball up for us and his voice would boom out, "Get under it, get under it! Great job! Good catch!" I remembered him at the cabin, teaching us to swim, holding us up as we'd kicked and dog-paddled in the shallow water.

I smiled at the memory of the time I'd been doing dishes and watching him out the window over the sink while he watered flowers in the backyard. He had come up to the window to tease me, and I'd turned the sink sprayer on him through the open window. He'd laughed and sprayed me back with the garden hose. Mom had yelled at both of us while we'd giggled about our pranks.

All too soon, the doctor and an older nurse entered the cramped room. Suddenly, I was hyperaware of all the noises—the beeping of the monitors, the hiss and whoosh of the oxygen pump.

Dr. Anderson's gaze paused on each of us. "Shall I have life support turned off?"

Tom said firmly, "Yes."

I guessed it was Tom's place as the man in the family to say it. That was fine with me.

The nurse quietly and efficiently turned off the machines, leaving the heart monitor running in silent mode. We backed away as she removed the breathing tube and left the room. In the deafening quiet, Dad's breaths were shallow and hollow, with endless pauses between them.

Time ticked by. I whispered mental prayers to him, telling him I loved him, that we were all here, that it would be okay and he could let go, he could go and meet Mom. I told him I was sorry and I hoped he understood we were doing what we thought was best. And I told him I missed him already.

Dad's final breath released in one long sigh. After a moment, the heart monitor showed a straight green line sliding across the black screen.

The doctor murmured, "Time of death, ten oh three a.m."

Good-bye, Dad. I love you.

I turned into Takoda, and she held me tightly while I cried.

CHAPTER FOURTEEN

The day of Dad's funeral dawned warm and clear. Takoda drove us to the church in her Jeep. I'd hardly said a word all morning. I didn't have any coherent thoughts to share, and Takoda allowed me my brooding silence.

She parked the Jeep in front of the church, behind Tom's truck and Bethany's SUV. I found myself studying Takoda as she slid out, closing her door and walking around the front of the Jeep. She wore a tailored black blazer and skirt with a burgundy silk blouse, black nylons and two-inch black pumps. Her hair fell in soft dark waves over her shoulders. She was stunning.

I opened my door and she gave me a hand down. I straightened my clothes, taking a few seconds to breathe and center myself. I felt uneasy and uncomfortable. I absolutely hated to dress up. An emergency shopping trip had procured a pair of black dress slacks and a black linen jacket over a gray blouse for me. I'd even bought a pair of plain black flats. I hadn't bothered with makeup. I didn't know how to put it on anyway.

Takoda wrapped me in a gentle hug. "You're gonna be okay," she murmured into my hair. I rested my head against her shoulder. She rubbed my back. I breathed in her musky perfume, letting her calming essence suffuse me.

She stepped back, her hands on my upper arms. I met her gaze, drawing on the strength and compassion I found there. "You ready?" she asked.

"I think so."

She cupped my cheek with one hand and kissed me lightly on the lips. "Come on, let's do this."

I let her guide me forward. I hadn't set foot in a Catholic church since Mom's funeral nearly fifteen years ago. We crossed the marbled brown-and-black-hued vestibule and stepped through the carved wood doors into the nave.

I stopped for a moment behind the rows of pews, getting my bearings. I knew this church. I'd grown up being here almost every Saturday or Sunday. It still smelled of wood polish and candle wax. Dark trim framed narrow stained-glass windows with depictions of religious scenes. The wood-beamed ceiling arched two stories above us with plain wrought-iron chandeliers hanging over the rows of oak pews. There was a hushed reverence in the traditional architecture. It made me uncomfortable.

Tom's and Bethany's families stood with the morticians and Father Bennett beside the closed casket in front of the altar. Pulling in a fortifying breath, I took Takoda's hand and strode toward my family.

They turned as we approached. Bethany ran an appraising stare over me. I was sure she was relieved to see me wearing dress clothes rather than jeans and a sweatshirt. Even so, I recognized her disapproval as her gaze flicked over Takoda. For whatever reason, she didn't comment. My youngest nephews sat in the front pew, very subdued. Bethany's daughter Stephanie leaned on her dad, who rested an arm around her shoulders.

Nikko stepped away from his parents, meeting Takoda and I halfway down the center aisle. I embraced him tightly.

"Hey Nikk," I said softly. "You hanging in there?"

"Yeah." He hugged Takoda before we joined the others.

Tom nodded to us but said nothing. Darlene greeted us with a weak smile. She touched my arm as I stopped beside her. "How are you holding up?" she asked.

"I'm okay," I said. "You?"

"I'm fine."

The mortician stepped forward to reiterate the schedule of events, then indicated he would open the coffin if we were ready. After a pause, he and his assistant lifted the lid on the gunmetal-blue military casket.

Bethany's voice broke on a sob. "Oh, Dad!"

I stepped to the side of the casket. I felt Takoda's hand on my back as I gazed down at Dad's body. He seemed smaller than he had been in life, the usual rugged color of his skin pale. A black rosary had been wrapped around his folded hands. I swallowed hard, and tears burned my eyes.

Bethany eased down onto the padded kneeler, her head bowed in prayer. Tom joined her. I remained standing. I didn't want to kneel. I had no prayers. Dad's soul was already where it needed to be, and I believed he was with Mom. I trusted he was in a better, happier place, and in peace. If I prayed for anyone, I would have prayed that Bethany, Tom and I didn't end up hating each other and that we didn't end up destroying what was left of our family. I hoped we'd manage to find some common ground. I didn't want to lose my siblings, as much as they made me crazy. I'd lost enough already.

When the church doors opened to the public, mourners filed in slowly and reverently. I recognized and greeted my parents' friends, our cousins, aunts and uncles, as well as a few of Tom and Bethany's friends and kids with whom we'd all grown up. Takoda stayed by my side, quietly supportive.

I felt horribly guilty as I introduced her as a friend, but we'd talked about it and decided together that it was okay if I downplayed our relationship at the funeral. Given the situation, it would be easier for everyone. We knew we loved each other, and that we were much more than just friends. But I swore it would be the last time I hid who I was and what Takoda meant to me.

After the first hour, faces blurred together. There were many I didn't know. Most I hadn't seen in many years. I managed to participate in small talk and accept their sympathies, but I imagined they all saw me as an outsider. I was the daughter who had left, who lived in the city, out of the loop and rarely seen, standing with a friend they didn't know.

Louder voices and movement drew my attention to the rear doors. I was unable to stop the smile that curled my lips. Relief flowed through me. My friends had arrived.

Rose, Will and Mike, Jackie and LeAnn, Tashi and Kelly with their little boy Trey and Angelina Golden—six feet of ebony beauty in four-inch heels and a flowing black dress and hat, more fashionable than any of the women in the church. I wondered when the church walls would collapse.

Angelina sashayed down the aisle, past the twins, and wrapped me in a long-armed hug and kissed my hair. "Oh, honey, I am so sorry! And don't you look just lovely, all cleaned up so nice."

On the verge of crying, I laughed instead. "Thanks, Ang," I said. "I'm so glad you guys could all be here. You don't know how much it means to me."

Rose patted my arm. "Of course we would be here for you."

They surrounded Takoda and I with love and greetings, throwing me a lifeline as I drowned in a sea of people who had no idea who I had become.

With the exception of Rose, my friends were obviously "family" in the gay sense, and by the few looks I saw aimed at us, other guests had made this assumption. Will and Mike were too perfect to be anything but a happy gay couple. Jackie and LeAnn were as butch as ever with their short hair and swagger. Tashi's dreadlocks hung down past her shoulders, her dark skin contrasting with her wife Kelly's fair skin and short blond hair. That they had their son with them only added to the novelty.

I picked Trey out of Kelly's arms and swung him around. I signed to the wide-eyed five-year-old that I loved him and I was happy to see him. He giggled and signed back and wrapped his pudgy arms around my neck. I squeezed him hard before Kelly took him back, settling him on her hip.

Not surprisingly, neither Bethany nor Tom came over to meet them.

The visitation went more quickly after their arrival, and barely an hour later we were seated for Mass. I was grateful there were no long eulogies. Father Bennett spoke briefly of my father, how he'd known him for so many years, how much he was loved and would be missed. The structured formality of Catholic Mass kept me from completely falling apart. Tears slid down my cheeks, but I clung to Takoda's hand and managed to hold it together.

After Mass, we followed the procession to the cemetery. In dichotomy to the cold sadness in my heart, the sun shone warm and bright as we crossed the grass to stand beside the headstone that already had Mom's name on it. Dad's coffin rested on the cloth-draped contraption holding it over the open grave. Father Bennett asked each of us siblings to take a flower from the spray on top of the casket.

My hand shook as I removed a white rose from the greenery. I put it to my nose and inhaled its sweet scent while the priest recited a couple of prayers. I thought about Dad's careful planting of flowers for Mom's grave every year, how he was out to the cemetery three times a week to water and prune. He made sure to put out her favorite pots on the side of the house, filled with the same red geraniums every year, exactly the way she'd done it. I knew it wasn't because he'd loved flowers. He'd done it for Mom. Now that he was gone, who would take care of the flowers? The thought made me inordinately sad.

There were a few moments of silence as Father Bennett finished speaking, then mourners started returning to their cars. A few stopped to speak with me and express their condolences. I noticed Tom and Beth talking to Father Bennett, Beth's pastor and some of our relatives before they too collected their families and drove away. Takoda and I remained after they'd left.

We stood a few feet from the grave. I gazed at the casket situated over the open hole and wondered if Dad were watching all this, if he were with Mom, and if they were glad to be together again. Two maintenance workers arrived and removed the green cloth covering the metal platform, then used a winch handle to lower the casket into the cement burial vault. The action had a sickening sense of finality to it. My heart ached as though it was being squeezed to a stop inside my chest. A deep, cold aloneness washed over me. I felt completely adrift, both my parents now gone from my life.

I turned into Takoda and cried. She held me, stroking my back as I sobbed into her shoulder. She murmured nonsense words into my ear and kissed my head. I couldn't think of anything but the hole that had opened in my heart, leaving a gaping, bleeding wound.

When I finally managed to stop crying, Takoda produced a handkerchief from somewhere and gently dabbed the tears from my cheeks.

"You going to be okay?"

I sniffled. "Yeah. I'll be all right. Took me a little by surprise."

"Do you feel up to going back to the church?"

I didn't want to, but it was the right thing to do, so I nodded. I'd manage. I'd be okay.

"Come on, then. We don't have to stay too long."

I let her guide me back toward the Jeep. "Sorry I'm such a mess."

She gave me a gentle squeeze. "You're fine, hon."

Takoda and I were the last of the immediate family to arrive at the reception lunch. Walking into the church basement was something of a déjà vu as I flashed back to Mom's funeral. Clusters of friends and relatives filled the rows of white-plastic tables and metal folding chairs. The aroma of casseroles and coffee surrounded us. For a moment, I half-expected to see my dad working the room the way he always did at these kinds of gatherings, then I sniffled again, knowing why we were here.

I clutched Takoda's hand, and she squeezed back. Tom, Bethany and their families were seated at the table closest to the buffet. They'd already started eating. The priest and Bethany's pastor were at the head table as well. There were no empty seats. I was both annoyed at being left out and relieved we wouldn't have to sit with them.

Rose marched up and guided us to the table on the side where all my friends sat. *My true family.*

Rose patted my shoulder. "Let's get some food in you."

"I'm not hungry."

Takoda said, "You should get a little something at least."

"Besides, it gets you out among the people, and they can see you, and that counts as being sociable and appropriate," Rose added.

Sighing, I let Rose lead the way to the buffet line. A handful of relatives and friends of the family stopped me as we made our way to the buffet. I appreciated the words of comfort and reminders of how well-liked Dad had been. It was wonderful so many people had come to remember him. Ray Marasich had a big heart, a friendly smile, and was always willing to help. The fact that I heard a lot of quiet laughter in the room told me his life was being celebrated as well as his loss being mourned. Dad wouldn't have wanted this to be a miserable, solemn occasion. He would have wanted to be remembered for his sense of humor and his positive outlook on life.

As we neared the buffet table, Father Bennett approached us. "Are you all right, Amry?"

Surprised by his concern, I said, "Yes, I'll be fine, thank you."

He smiled at Takoda and held out a hand. "Thank you for being here for Amry," he said.

She shook it. "I'm glad I could be here to support her."

"I've known Amry since she was a little girl. She's grown into a lovely woman."

Takoda smiled broadly. "Yes, she has," she agreed. "She's the most wonderful, giving, beautiful woman I know."

I glanced up and was amazed by the depth of love I saw in her eyes. It took my breath away.

Father Bennett cleared his throat. He smiled and touched my arm. "I see that the two of you will take good care of each other."

Stunned into silence, I didn't answer.

Takoda responded, "Yes, we will."

"I'm truly sorry for your loss, Amry. Ray was a good man and he'll be sorely missed. If there is anything we can do for you, you are always welcome here."

Recovering, I choked out a stumbling thank-you.

As he moved away, I sucked in a long breath. I caught Bethany's disapproving glare from the front table. Ignoring her, I let Takoda guide me to the buffet.

The remainder of the funeral lunch went smoothly. After a while, Nikko and Darlene joined our table and I introduced them to my friends. Stephanie came over for a hug and to see Tashi and Kelly's boy Trey. He giggled at her, and she took his deafness completely in stride. Kelly patiently taught Steph to sign her name and say hello. Trey thought it was great fun. I was tickled to see them make a connection, and their lightness and love permeated the sadness that had settled in my heart.

It wasn't too long before people began to leave, including my own friends who had a long drive back to the city.

Finally, it was Takoda and me, Tom and Beth and their families and the church ladies cleaning up. Takoda and I stopped at the table where my sibs sat. I said, "I guess we're going to head out." I didn't know what else to say.

Tom slouched in his chair. Dark circles stained the skin under his eyes, and his broad shoulders slumped. "We're leaving too," he said.

Bethany set down her coffee cup. She pinned me with her sharp blue gaze. "Your friends made quite a spectacle," she said.

Takoda took a step forward. "It's wonderful that so many of her friends came to support her."

"It's too bad they couldn't be normal people."

I said, "Bethany, you're in a church, for Christ's sake. The least you can do is be civil."

"Your friends are freaks and perverts."

"And you're a bigoted bitch. I hope someday you can find some kind of peace, Beth, because your hatred and fear are going to destroy your soul." I took Takoda's hand and started to leave.

Takoda stopped and turned back to my sister. "I'm very sorry for the loss of your father."

She wrapped her arm around my shoulders, and we left. I was inordinately delighted that my girlfriend had gotten the last word and that she had taken the high road when all I had wanted to do was slug my sister.

We retreated to Takoda's house. The dogs greeted us as we stepped inside. I kicked off my dress shoes and crossed the cool wood flooring and flopped onto the sofa with a heavy sigh.

Takoda stopped to get fresh water for the dogs and let them out. I heard her open the mudroom and unlatch the doggie door so they could come in when they were ready. Then she joined me, propping her feet on the coffee table. I leaned against her. We sat that way until I was nearly asleep and Takoda said, "Come on, love, let's get out of these damned clothes and take a nap."

I barely had the energy to move, but the idea of a nap sounded wonderful. Takoda took my hand and led me up the stairs to the loft. The sun splashed a bright shaft of light across the bed where dappled leaf shadows played in the sunshine. Takoda started undoing the buttons of my blouse.

It was a simple action and shouldn't have been erotic, but that was how it hit me. I was overtired and oversensitive. I stood very still as she gently undressed me and laid my clothes across the trunk at the foot of the bed. With every piece of clothing removed, I could feel the heat building at my core, an aching, pulsing need that had my nipples hard against the material of my bra and my underwear damp between my legs. When she reached around to unhook my bra, I gasped for breath, a choking half-sob. The material dropped to the ground, and she took me into her arms. I clung to her for long minutes, not quite crying, but lost in a haze of indiscriminate emotions as she ran her hands slowly up and down my back.

She undid the button and zipper on my slacks and tugged them and my underwear down over my hips. They dropped to pool around my feet, and I stepped out of them. She eased me under the covers and made quick work of removing her own clothes. In moments, she had slid in beside me and wrapped herself around me, my head to her chest, combing her fingers through my hair. I melted into her warmth and let the tears come.

I didn't know how long we stayed that way, holding each other while I cried, letting go of the overwhelming emotions of loss and anger. I fell asleep using her as a body pillow. When I woke, she was still holding me and smiled when I blinked up at her.

"Hey," she murmured. "You feel a little better?" She rubbed light circles between my shoulder blades.

"Yeah, I do." My voice came out hoarse, and I cleared my throat. "I'm sorry I fell asleep on you."

She smiled. "I nodded off for a while too," she admitted. "Besides I like holding you."

"That's good, because I like being held. Thank you for today. I don't think I could have gotten through it without you. And thank you for not killing my sister."

That got a chuckle. "It wasn't for not wanting to. But it wasn't really the right time for violence."

"True. But I nearly hauled off and slapped her."

"I know. I'm glad you didn't. She doesn't deserve the effort."

I sighed and cuddled closer, kissing her shoulder. Takoda tilted my chin up and kissed me, feathering kisses over my face before running her tongue along my lower lip. I sighed and let her in, pushing my tongue against hers. Desire flashed through me as she deepened the kiss until we parted to breathe each other's air, lips almost touching. She rolled me onto my back. "I want you," she growled, and licked and bit a path down my throat, along my collarbone and down to my breasts.

I writhed under her and scraped my nails down her back to her buttocks, grasping and kneading the soft flesh. I moaned at the feel of her fingers gliding through the soaked heat between my legs. I pushed against her hand, wanting her inside, aching for her, wanting her to be part of me, wanting a closeness that I didn't know if I could reach. "Please. Koda, I need you."

She eased down my body, a rain of kisses and licks and nips, and I thought I would drown in the waves of pleasure. When

I felt her breath between my legs, I forced my eyes open and looked down my body at her.

Our eyes locked, and what I saw in hers was unmistakable want and something far more. Then she dropped her head, her tongue finding where I needed her. Her fingers filled me, thrusting slow and deep. I groaned as the pressure built quickly. My orgasm hit hard and fast, exploding from the inside out, every emotion wrung out of me in those moments of intense pleasure and release. As she crawled up my body, I sobbed like a baby. She cuddled me and rubbed my back and I heard her whisper, "I love you," which only made me cry harder.

I wanted to tell her I loved her too, but the words were lost in my sobs. I held her tight and kissed her and hoped she understood.

CHAPTER FIFTEEN

It was an endless drive back to Minneapolis three days later, and an equally endless week of work. I talked to Takoda every night, fell asleep thinking of her and woke up having wet dreams. Missing her became a constant physical ache in my heart.

Coming home to an empty apartment, which had never bothered me before, made me feel dejected and lonely. I wandered from room to room, completely at loose ends. Exhausted from the long days at work, I couldn't concentrate to finish my own manuscript and was too agitated to make myself sit down and finish the edits I needed to do. Thursday night, Rose dragged me to dinner for margaritas and all-you-can-eat tacos.

We sat in the bar at a high table by the window. Rose was driving, so I slammed my first margarita on the rocks while she sipped hers.

"Talk to me, Amry. You've had your head so buried in your damned computer you haven't said ten words all week." Rose chewed the end of a tortilla chip and raised a brow.

I shrugged and finished my drink. The alcohol warmed me as it went down, settling in my empty stomach. I raised my empty glass to the waitress near the bar then grabbed a couple chips and cracked them into pieces before scooping salsa. "Hayley's been cracking the whip."

"Hayley's always cracking the whip. What's going on with you? You've been more out of sorts than usual."

"I'm tired. I'm lonely. I miss Koda. Beth hasn't called about what we're going to do with Dad's house." I scooped salsa on another chip. "To be honest, I don't even care what they want to do with everything."

"Don't let them screw you out of your part, Amry."

"As much as they're assholes, I don't think they'll cut me out. I don't care if they're in control of the plan. I just want it done."

The waitress came back with another margarita for me, and I smiled my thanks and swallowed a couple big mouthfuls. I deserved to have a night to drink myself into oblivion. I was tired of thinking, tired of feeling and hoped the alcohol would provide numbness for a while.

"When will you see Takoda?"

Thinking of my girlfriend made me smile then frown because I missed her so much. "I'm not sure. She's working all weekend. I really miss her." I heard the crack in my voice. Christ. I was not going to cry over a margarita at Don fucking Pablo's.

"Sounds pretty serious."

"It is serious, but I don't know if it will ever be more than long-distance. I don't see me moving up there—I mean, I have a life here, right? And a good job. And Koda's certainly not going to move to the city." I sucked my drink through the swizzle straw. "We haven't talked about it. There's been so much else going on, you know?"

Rose studied me for a long time. I knew that look. It usually meant she had things to say that I didn't want to hear. "About the only time you've smiled all week is when you're talking about Takoda."

"She's about the only good thing that's happening in my life right now."

"So what's keeping you from making this relationship more permanent?"

I sighed. "I told you. We haven't discussed it. We love each other, that's certain, but it's only been three months. Besides, I've got a life here, she's got a life there. I sure as hell don't want to be any closer to the twins than I already am. I left home for a reason—rednecks and family and lack of job opportunities."

"That's three reasons," Rose pointed out.

I glared at her.

The waitress brought our meals, and Rose ordered a soda for herself and another margarita for me. I sucked the remainder of mine through the straw and felt it go straight to my head.

I know Rose was getting me drunk on purpose because I always talked more when drunk. I concentrated on eating for a few minutes before Rose said, "So other than living two hundred and fifty miles apart, you and Takoda are getting along pretty good?"

I worked through a mouthful of taco. "I've never been so comfortable with anyone. She's amazing. We can talk for hours, or we can just sit quietly, and it's okay. She makes me feel so damned good." I grinned wickedly. "And the sex is mind blowing."

"TMI, Amry, TMI."

I laughed. Takoda made me feel like I was flying, my soul exploding with joy. I'd never felt so cherished, so wanted, so needed or so satisfied. And it was equally as pleasing to make her feel the same way. I grinned and finished my first taco, took a couple good slugs of margarita, and started on the second. Yeah. It was good with Takoda. We made each other smile.

So why the fuck was I down here by myself?

Rose changed the subject. "What are you doing this weekend if you're not going to see your girl?"

"Tashi called. The bike club is doing a final group ride for the season on Saturday, so I'm going with. I think we're peddling about sixty miles. Something like that. Weather is supposed to hold up, so it should be good."

"You're all crazy. But I'm glad you're not going to be moping around your apartment."

I made a face. "Yes, Mom."

"We're on our way to the meeting site," I said into my cell phone. "Somewhere around Northfield or something." I slouched in the front seat of Tashi's super-cab F-250. Our road bikes were safely locked onto the in-floor bike rack in the pickup bed, tucked against the brushed-aluminum tool chest.

Takoda's voice vibrated low in my ear. "Well, have fun and be safe. Tell Tashi hi for me."

"I will. She says to tell you the same."

"Send me a picture of you all geared up."

"Okay. I miss you. Wish you were here."

"I wish I was there too. I miss you."

There was a short silence. Heady emotions flowed across the airwaves between us.

Takoda said, "I'll let you go. Call me when you're done riding?"

"I will."

Another pause.

"Take care, *zaagi'idiwin*," she said. "Love you."

I grinned like an idiot. "Love you too. Talk to you soon."

I hung up and stared out the window for a few seconds. My heart felt so full, it was hard to breathe past the fullness.

Tashi said, "Girl, you got it bad."

"Yeah, I really do." But what was I going to do about it?

Tashi drove into the high school parking lot and drove to the far end where the other members of our bike club had already gathered.

Tall and rail thin, Kevin, a.k.a. Angelina Golden, stood out from the rest of the group. He wasn't in drag, but he proudly wore a rainbow-striped bike jersey and a long-sleeved black undershirt over hot-pink spandex leggings.

Will, on the other hand, could easily have passed as a straight man. Christy and Lisa were both strong athletes and, for the record, were both straight. They'd ridden a couple of MS and AIDs rides with us over the years. Our resident muscle-bound weightlifter, Derek, rounded out the group.

Tashi got our bikes down while I grabbed the air pump being passed around so we could top off our tires. Kevin handed out route maps. It wasn't long before we pedaled out onto the single lane county road and formed a loose peloton. With the wide shoulder, there was room to spread out. Tashi rode up front with Kevin, I slid into the middle with Lisa and Christy and Derek and Will brought up the rear.

It felt good to be on my bike. I set a comfortable rhythm as my body loosened up. The sun blazed high and bright in a cloudless blue sky and warmed my skin through the slight tinge of fall coolness. A light breeze blew out of the northwest, not enough to make a difficult headwind, but enough to keep the air moving when we stopped.

Conversation stayed light and genial. Everyone asked how I was doing without dwelling over the details of my dad's death. They did however dwell on my relationship with the hot park ranger. I kept reminding them she was a law enforcement officer, not a park ranger. Derek and Kevin insisted on calling her Ranger Rick just to annoy me.

The miles rolled under our tires and despite a couple painful uphill climbs, I felt happy and energized to be out with my friends. The only thing missing was Takoda. With her in the peloton, the ride and the day would have been absolutely perfect.

A little past our halfway point we stopped for a break. We relaxed with our snacks around a picnic table in a small park. Chewing contentedly on my peanut butter and banana sandwich, I stood and stretched, groaning as I rolled my shoulders and twisted my neck from side to side.

"Need a massage?" Derek asked me.

"Sure, if you're offering."

"When we're done eating, then."

"Sweet." Derek's neck massages were the best. I'd spent too much time at the computer all week and I was feeling it.

Will swatted Derek's ass. "Sure, offer her a massage, but what about me?"

"Oh, honey, you'll get yours later." Derek leaned over and kissed Will's cheek. We all hooted and hollered.

Kevin crowed, "Your hubby is gonna hear about this, Willy!"

Will's face turned beet red.

"Mike knows Derek's just a tease," Christy said.

I bent over and touched my fingers to the grass to stretch my back.

Tashi said, "Hey Amry, gimme your phone so I can take a picture for Takoda."

"Yeah, Tash, get a picture of that lovely ass."

"Shut up, Kevin," I said as I straightened and went to my bike, fishing my phone out of the handlebar bag and tossing it to Tashi.

"Stand with your bike," she directed.

I picked up my bike, posed and smiled, and she took a couple shots before handing my phone back. I sent the photos to Takoda and sat at the table to finish my sandwich and a candy bar. Derek started working his magic on my neck and shoulders, strong fingers finding the knots and working them hard, slowly relaxing the muscles. "Goddamn, that feels good."

"You're really cranked up, girl."

"It's been a tough couple weeks."

Will said, "I'm really glad you came out with us today. We were worried you weren't going to be up for it."

"Thanks."

Tashi said, "If the weather holds out, we should plan another ride next weekend or the one after."

"I'd be up for that," Christy said. "Even if it's cold, as long as it's not raining."

Kevin said, "We'll figure out logistics over the next few days. If you're free this Saturday or next, let me know."

"You guys ready?" Will asked. "Let's get going."

Lisa gathered the garbage. Kevin and I crossed the grass to the brick restroom building by the parking lot. As we approached, a beat-up blue pickup squealed to a stop beside the restrooms and roared its engine, loud and rough without a muffler. I jumped, not expecting the explosion of noise. The redneck guys sitting in the bed of the pickup truck laughed raucously.

Assholes.

Kevin cursed under his breath.

I forced myself not to react or rush into the bathroom. I didn't want them to think they were intimidating me. Rule one with assholes was never to act like a victim.

The truck was still revving its engine when I finished. Kevin waited for me at the bathrooms' entrance out of sight of the truck. As we stepped into their line of sight someone shouted, "Fucking queers!"

I felt my stomach twist as we returned to our group. Will's lips were drawn into a tight line, his jaw bunching.

Tashi said, "Ignore them, you guys."

Derek said, "Let 'em yell. Stupid fuckers."

"Take the long way around the parking lot. We don't want to encourage them," Christy suggested.

We rode along the outside edge of the parking lot but the engine revving and name-calling continued until we got back out on the street. I glanced back a couple times as we put some distance between us and them, relieved not to see or hear them following. Fucking assholes. I hated feeling so vulnerable.

Kevin led us through town and back onto the highway. I hoped the remaining twenty-five miles of our ride would go quickly. Our easy conversation and laughter had turned to silence and a need to watch over our shoulders.

As we rode, I wondered exactly what it was that had set the rednecks off to begin with. Kevin's hot-pink leggings and rainbow jersey were a definite giveaway. But the rest of us? We just looked like bicyclists. All wearing spandex shorts and colorful jerseys. I suppose to drunken rednecks, any guys wearing spandex were gay. But did it really matter? No matter our sexuality, we didn't deserve to be harassed.

With any luck, the idiots had found something else to do and somewhere else to be.

Derek tried to lighten the mood. "Hey, we're still going for spaghetti when we're done, right?"

"Absolutely," Lisa agreed from behind me. "I'm going to be starved."

"Never turn down pasta."

"Next right is the killer uphill stretch," Tashi announced.

We all groaned and then laughed. We made a right onto the next county road and the final long stretch before we returned to our starting point. I tended to be a slow and steady climber, and fell back to ride with Derek and Will. The climb was steep, but the worst part was that it went on for nearly a mile.

When I crested the hill, my legs were screaming and my lungs burned. I whooped with relief, breathing hard as I clicked up through my gears for the downhill stretch. We grouped up again as we raced down. I kept pedaling, keeping my legs moving without putting much effort into the motion. Even so, my speedometer clocked at almost thirty-three miles an hour. The wind streamed across my face and whistled in my ears. Past the pain of the climb, this was the feeling of freedom I loved, flying triumphantly down the back stretch.

I didn't hear the pickup truck until it came roaring past us doing at least sixty, blaring its horn while the guys sitting in the truck bed shouted obscenities. I jerked reflexively on my handlebars and barely missed running into Will's rear tire. Derek let go a string of curses. My heart hammered painfully in my chest as I got control of my bike, and my hands shook. If I'd have been a less experienced rider, I'd have been slathered all over the road.

Kevin slowed us down, calling back over his shoulder, "Is everyone okay? Do we need to stop?"

Lisa said, "Let's just get back."

Everyone agreed, and we pushed on. The next few cars that passed us made everyone nervous. I glanced at my odometer. We were about ten miles from the high school where we'd started. At the five-mile mark, we labored up another short, steep incline. I pushed myself to stay in the middle of the pack while Derek and Will dropped back. My legs hated me, but I managed to breathe through it and kept pedaling. I hit the top with rubbery legs and coasted a few yards before I started barreling downward. Halfway down the hill, I was in high gear, neck and neck with Tashi and only a couple feet behind Christy and Kevin.

As we came to the bottom of the hill, I heard the unmufflered truck engine behind us.

Will yelled, "Heads up!"

A second later, the old pickup caught up to us. They must have somehow circled around on some back roads.

Someone yelled, "Fuck you, queers! Get off the fuckin' road!"

I kept my attention forward, focused on Christy's and Kevin's rear wheels. We were cruising as a peloton at twenty-eight miles an hour, with scant inches between us. I forced myself to relax. This was not the time to overreact.

Instead of blowing past, this time the truck paced us. I breathed their cigarette smoke and the exhaust fumes from the broken muffler.

"You perverts want a beer? Here!"

Out of the corner of my eye, I saw the bottles fly from the back of the truck as it accelerated ahead with a roar. In slow motion, a bottle hit Kevin in the face and his bike twisted, going down at the same time the other bottle arced into Christy's front wheel.

I heard Tashi yell. Christy screamed. Her back tire popped up in front of me, and the world became a cacophony of sound and motion and I was flying over my handlebars. I got a brief glimpse of fast-moving asphalt and bike parts.

Pain sliced through my side and stars exploded behind my eyes with a jarring concussion before everything went black.

CHAPTER SIXTEEN

Awareness began with sounds. A quiet, steady beeping. The shushing of air in and out. Voices rose and fell, but the words were garbled. After the sounds, I became aware of the pain. It hurt to breathe. I tried to think about why it hurt, but thinking made my head pound and my stomach roil.

A familiar voice broke through the haze. "Come on, *zaagi'idiwin*, open those beautiful eyes and talk to me."

Takoda. Relief passed through me, a momentary break in the pain. I wanted to open my eyes, but I was still trying to figure out how to make my body work. I took a shallow breath and mumbled, "Koda?"

"Amry, I'm here."

I forced my eyes open, blinking against the light as pain lanced through my head. I whimpered and shut my eyes again.

"Go easy."

I tried to breathe, but breathing sent searing knives through my side and chest. Why did I hurt so much? I felt the brush of a hand on my forehead. Takoda's voice washed over me. "Shhhh, you're gonna be okay. Just relax."

I wanted to ask what happened. I managed to squint into the light. Takoda leaned over me, her eyes dark with worry. Featherlight fingertips brushed against my face. I tried to ask what happened, but it hurt to move my jaw, my mouth felt like sandpaper and the words came out slurred and barely audible.

"Don't try to talk. You crashed your bike. You're gonna be okay, but you're really banged up."

Bike crash. Jumbled images assembled themselves in my brain. Riding. A park. Beat-up truck filled with rednecks. A flash of blurry images. Panic. Pain.

I think I slid away for a while. Another voice intruded, male, older. I opened my eyes and light flashed in them. I moaned against the brain-shattering pain and snapped them shut.

The next time I woke up, the room was almost dark and the pain had become more manageable. Though my whole body ached, I wriggled my toes. When that worked, I tried my ankles. I gasped when the movement made my right calf feel like it was going to rip open. When I recovered from the additional chest-splitting pain of gasping, I moved my ankle again, slower, and wondered what I'd done to my leg. On the up side, my legs did move, if painfully and stiffly. So, not paralyzed. This was good.

I took slow, shallow, careful breaths. Anything bigger engendered a shock of pain. Broken ribs? This sucked. My right arm throbbed from my shoulder down. I tried lifting it, but couldn't. I tried to raise my head to see, but that made the room spin, forcing me to lie back until the dizziness passed. I wiggled my fingers. On the right, the movement was hampered by something. A cast? I could move my left arm and hand. Shifting my shoulders produced another wash of pain.

I turned my head very slowly this time. To my right, hospital machines, beeping and monitoring me. My right arm was wrapped in a thick soft cast from my fingers to a few inches above my elbow. I eased my head to the left to take in the most wonderful sight I could imagine.

Takoda slept sprawled in the recliner beside my bed. Her straight black hair draped over the white hospital blanket tucked around her shoulders. My lips lifted into a smile, pulling the tender skin on the right side of my face. I lifted my left hand to feel bandages covering my chin and most of the right half of my face.

My head still throbbed, but my thoughts were a little clearer now. I remembered at least a little of the events before the crash, and had a terrifying snapshot image of flying off my bike.

Suddenly I panicked. Was everyone else okay? My heart pounded and I gasped for breath. A shock of pain jolted through my rib cage. I must have either moved or made a noise, because Takoda jerked awake beside me.

"Amry?"

"Everyone okay?" My voice came out hoarse and breathy. My mouth was dry as a bone.

Takoda retrieved a cup from the table against the wall and put the straw to my lips. "Just take a little."

Cool liquid soothed my throat. I mumbled, "Is everyone all right?"

"Everyone's going to be fine. Kevin is still in the hospital, but everyone else is already out."

"What day is it?"

"Monday night."

I'd lost two days. I closed my eyes, exhaustion dragging me away again.

"I'll be right here." I felt her fingers gently brushing through my hair. I was too out of it to even wonder what she was doing at my bedside in the city.

Someone moving my arm and the compression of the blood pressure cuff woke me. I blinked away the haze to see a tall blond doctor who couldn't have been any older than me. He smiled.

"Hello. I'm Doctor Wilson. How are you feeling?"

I took stock. My leg, my arm and my side throbbed. Sharp pain lanced through my ribs and side with every breath. My head pounded in time with my heartbeat. Shifting my eyes made me dizzy, so I focused on the doctor. I said, "Been better. Dizzy."

He made a note on my chart. "You took quite a fall. You've got a severe concussion. That's why you're dizzy." He put his stethoscope under my gown. "Can you breathe for me?"

I automatically started to take a deep breath, then squeaked when sharp pain flashed through my lower chest. "Ow."

"Take it easy. I want to make sure you're not collecting fluids in there. Try again."

I did my best, and by the time he was done checking me out I wanted to cry. He lifted my arm with the cast on it. "Move your fingers for me," he instructed. When I wriggled the fingers on my right hand, pain shot up my wrist and into my elbow. All I could do was bite my lip and try not to cry like a baby.

Dr. Wilson continued to poke and prod my body. He moved the gown to reveal a ten-inch line of stitches running up my right side, starting a couple inches above my hip. When he pressed around the wound with his fingers, I nearly went through the roof. He told me I'd landed on the pedal of one of the bikes and the sharp edge had ripped a gash in my side. There were more stitches on the inside of my left leg. I had road rash and bandages covering my right shoulder and knees. Two ribs were cracked. Apparently, my helmet had most likely saved my life, but my head had impacted the ground at least twice based on the helmet's damage.

"Do you know what day it is?" he asked.

"It was Monday last time."

"It's Tuesday. Ten in the morning."

"Oh." I thought I remembered Takoda being with me, but since I was alone now, I wondered if I'd dreamed it.

The door opened, and I turned my head. The room spun but I managed to focus on Takoda and Tashi entering the room. Takoda's face lit up with a brilliant smile and she hurried to the side of my bed. "You're awake."

I attempted a smile, but it was more a grimace because my jaw and cheek were stiff with stitches and road rash. Overjoyed that I hadn't been dreaming, I gazed gratefully into her eyes and wished I could wrap my arms around her.

Tashi's voice broke the tableau. "Hey girl. You look like shit."

She stood at the end of the bed with a bandage on her chin and her right elbow wrapped in gauze. She wore loose sweats and a T-shirt.

"So do you," I said.

"At least I don't have any broken bones."

The doctor cleared his throat and held up a light. "Amry, can you look at me?" I did so, and he flashed the light in my eyes. "You're doing better. We'll do another MRI tomorrow on your head. If the dizziness keeps up, we'll get you into a pair of prism glasses and see if that helps. Do you remember what happened? The events before the crash?"

I still had a residual headache if I thought too hard. "There were some rednecks in a truck. They threw a bottle at Kevin and another that I think might have caught Christy. I remember seeing Christy's back wheel clip my front tire, and then I was flying over my handlebars and I don't remember anything after that."

Dr. Wilson typed a bunch of notes into the computer terminal tucked against the back wall. "That's good that you remember it. I think we'll keep you another day or two to make sure the concussion is handled and your breathing stays clear." He finished making notes in the computer terminal, then, after asking if I had any questions, left me to my guests.

Tashi said, "My friend Charlie is a lawyer with the LGBTQ Legal Alliance. She offered to take on all our cases pro-bono, as hate crimes. She'll talk to you later in the week."

"Okay." I wasn't sure what else to say. I hadn't been conscious long enough to consider the legal ramifications of the incident.

"We'll get those assholes," Tashi said.

I started to nod and stopped myself when the room lurched again. I closed my eyes. When the world stilled, I said, "Thanks, Tash."

Takoda said, "You need to sleep."

"I know." I was already slipping away, exhaustion taking over. I met her concerned gaze. "Thank you for being here."

"I'll always be here."

She caressed my hair and I fell asleep replaying her words in my head.

* * *

The rest of the day, at least the parts I was awake for, turned into a revolving door of visitors. Takoda remained by my side through all of it. Two police officers came to take my statement. After they left I dozed off until I was woken by another knock on the door.

"Come in."

A well-dressed thirty-something woman stepped into the room. "Excuse me, Miss Marasich?"

I peered at her, but didn't recognize her.

Takoda asked, "Can we help you?"

"My name is Karin Wheeler, with News Nine. We heard about the incident you were involved in and I hoped I could get an interview this afternoon. I have my film crew with me. It shouldn't take very long. I spoke with Charlie Eton, the lawyer handling your cases, and I have a copy of the police report. Would you be willing to answer some questions about the incident?"

I blinked somewhat blankly at the woman. I was tired and not quite connecting.

Takoda stood. "Have you talked to the others?" she asked.

Karin Wheeler took another step into the room. "I spoke with Kevin Williams this morning. Will Bowmann is meeting me at his house this evening. I believe Tashi Carson and her partner will also be there. My crew will be filming the interview with them." She crossed the room and handed a card to Takoda and to me. I took the card, but the words blurred.

Takoda took her phone from her pocket. "Do you mind if I call Tashi?" she asked me.

"Please, go ahead."

She nodded and turned away. I saw her thumbs moving on the phone, then she put it to her ear. "Hey Tashi...yeah...So what's going on with the News Nine interview? Is it legit?... Yeah, here now... Okay... The lawyer is good with it?...Okay... Thanks. Later." She hung up, and faced me. "It's all on the up-and-up if you want to talk to Ms. Wheeler."

I squinted at the reporter, struggling to get my thoughts in order. "What's the angle on the story?"

"I'm treating the incident as a hate crime to which you and your friends are victims. I want to focus on how it affects each of you personally and how we as a community can better deal with the problem of hate crimes and victimization."

I closed my eyes for a few moments, taking the time to think. I wasn't against being interviewed, though I tried to consider what consequences might come from it. Other than the fact I resembled Frankenstein's monster, I knew if I stuck to telling what I experienced, and didn't make any accusations, there shouldn't be any legal issues. I must have been quiet for a long time, because Takoda asked, "Are you okay, Am?"

I opened my eyes. "Yeah."

Karin Wheeler said, "If you're not up to it, we can schedule for another time."

"No. Let's just do it."

She took a clipboard from her messenger bag. "Would you be willing to do this on camera?" she asked.

"I look like crap."

Her smile was understanding and encouraging. She was a reporter. She wanted this story. "Realistically I don't think anyone expects you to be anything but the victim of a hate crime that put you in the hospital."

Takoda muttered, "Dirty laundry and all that."

Wheeler ignored her and added, "What happened to you and your friends is serious. The public should see how badly you and your friends were hurt. What these young men did was not a foolish drunken prank. It was assault, and it could easily have been fatal."

Karin Wheeler was passionate, and she had a point. I looked toward Takoda who leaned silently against the wall. I couldn't quite read her expression and wondered if she was for or against the interview. I asked Wheeler, "Can you give me a few minutes to maybe wash my face and try to comb my hair?"

"Of course. I need to get my cameraman as well. Shall we say half an hour?"

"Okay."

Wheeler took her leave.

Takoda studied me with concern. "You're sure about this?"

"Yeah. I am."

I wasn't looking for my fifteen minutes of fame. Nor did I want to be a spokesperson for the LGBTQ community. But Wheeler was right; people needed to be aware of the damage that bullying and bigotry could do. I thought of Nikko and wanted to do the right thing. If we let ourselves be attacked and just turned the other cheek, it would continue to happen. We needed to fight back, to press charges, to let the world know we weren't going to take it. And if that meant me being on television looking like crap, well so be it. If it helped just one person, it was a good thing.

Takoda straightened from her position against the wall. "I'll go grab one of the nurses and we can help you get cleaned up a little, okay?"

"I look that bad, huh?"

"Never." She leaned over and kissed me lightly. "But I bet they have that waterless shampoo so your hair isn't sticking up all over."

* * *

The segment with Karin Wheeler aired on the ten o'clock news that same night. The anchor introduced it against a backdrop showing mug shots of the five young men who'd attacked us, and then cut to Karin Wheeler standing on the side of the county road where we'd crashed. She described the incident from the official police report. They showed snippets of the interviews with Kevin, Tashi, Will and me.

The takeaway was that gay bashing and hate crimes were alive and well in the Twin Cities. The five men had been charged with a mix of hate crimes, DUI, reckless vehicular assault and first-degree assault. Wheeler briefly interviewed Charlie Eton, and that was it.

I had, at most, thirty seconds of screen time. I thought I looked awful. Karin had asked what I was thinking when we were attacked.

My voice sounded weak and a little breathless. "I was scared. We didn't know what they were going to do. But when they threw the bottles that was a couple heartbeats of sheer terror, watching Kevin and Christy going down, and feeling myself go over the handlebars." I wasn't eloquent, but I was believable.

I thought the overall effect was exactly what Wheeler hoped for. Each of us had been victimized and frightened, but ultimately not intimidated. We would all go out and ride again, and continue to try to live our lives without fear. But what grabbed my attention was Takoda. The concern and love in her eyes as she stood at my bedside was so apparent even the most clueless person couldn't miss it. She never spoke to the camera, but she didn't need to.

* * *

Takoda brought me home to my apartment two days later. I sported a lovely new pair of prism lensed glasses to help alleviate the ongoing headaches and dizziness from my concussion, which the doctor warned could be a problem for even the next few months. I was favoring my left leg because of the stitches in my calf. My right arm, up to just past my elbow, was newly casted in neon blue and supported with a stylish black sling. I held myself stiffly as I shuffled forward, trying to avoid the jolts of pain from the deep gash in my side and broken ribs.

With Takoda's arm to steady me, I hobbled down the hallway to my door. Takoda unlocked it and followed me in. She said, "I'll put your stuff in your room."

"Thank you."

I wasn't sure why my own apartment felt so alien to me as I watched Takoda walk into the bedroom with the plastic bag containing the few personal odds and ends I had from the hospital. She moved through my space comfortably as though she'd been here forever. It was surreal knowing I'd left here

Saturday morning, and now only five days later, it felt as if I'd been gone a month.

I followed Takoda to my bedroom. Her rolling duffel bag rested against the wall under the air conditioner with a pair of jeans folded over the top.

The bed covers had been hastily straightened, the pillow still indented where she'd slept. She tossed my hospital slipper socks into the dirty clothes hamper.

"Are you okay?" she asked.

"Yeah. Just kind of out of it."

"You look lost."

I shrugged, wincing. "Out of sorts, I guess."

"Still a lot of painkillers in your system. You've been through a lot."

"Yeah."

I wandered out into the living room, pausing to look out the sliding door to the small balcony. My mountain bike, locked and covered with a tarp, leaned against the wood wall between my balcony and the neighbors'. It made me think of my road bike, which made me think of the terror I'd felt flying over the handlebars into Christy's falling bike. Apparently, I'd been propelled onto both Christy's and Kevin's bikes, while they'd been thrown clear. Derek had tried to describe the scene to me, but I'd shut him down. I honestly didn't want to know, as just the thought of it made me want to throw up. There were pictures too, which I had avoided seeing. I shuddered. Will had my wrecked road bike in his garage. I wasn't sure I wanted to see that either.

Takoda came up behind me and wrapped her arms loosely around my waist, careful of my injuries. I leaned gratefully into her warmth. The sun was shining, but I felt cold and gray and vaguely numb, or maybe so overwhelmed it was easier to just shut down.

I had talked with the lawyer, agreeing to press charges against the five men. She had asked me more questions about what had happened, getting more details about what I remembered.

Yesterday Nikko had called. Tom and Darlene were fighting again. The news coverage about me and my friends had made its way up to their local television channels. Tom was furious that Darlene wasn't bothered or upset by the fact that my being gay was flaunted to the world. He blamed me for influencing her and Nikko. He'd threatened Nikko, telling him he'd better not think that my being on television made it okay for Nikko to be gay. So Nikko was hiding out in his room, doing his best to avoid his father. And Darlene was doing her best to keep him out of the line of fire.

I felt terrible knowing my actions had made his situation worse. Takoda kept telling me it wasn't my fault, but I still felt heartsick. And helpless. Nikko sounded so miserable and angry and hurting and depressed, but other than empty platitudes and encouragement, there was nothing I could do right now to help him.

Takoda kissed the top of my head, bringing me out of my dark musings. "How about if I call out for pizza?" she asked. "I'd offer to cook, but you've got nothing in your fridge."

I said, "I've been eating out since I got back after Dad's funeral."

"No, really? Come on, sit down and relax."

She helped me settle on the sofa, and I had to admit it felt good to rest. I leaned back with the fleece throw tucked around me and closed my eyes. I could hear Takoda in the kitchen flipping through my takeout menus. She called back to me, "Pepperoni, onion, green olive?"

"Yes, thank you." It lightened my heart that she remembered my favorite.

A few seconds later, I heard her talking quietly on the phone, and then the cushions shifted as she sat down beside me. She patted my leg. "Doing okay?"

"Doing okay."

"Good. Pizza will be here in forty minutes or so."

"Thanks, Koda."

"You're welcome."

"I'm sorry I'm making you throw away your vacation time."

She kissed the side of my head. "I'm not throwing anything away and you have nothing to be sorry for. I wouldn't be here if I didn't want to be."

My throat tightened and I thought I was going to cry. I cuddled against her, needing the reassurance. She was so good to me, and I hadn't had a chance to return her kindness. What if she got tired of taking care of me? So far our relationship had been wrapped around all my problems and dramas. It wasn't fair to her. "Someday I'll do the same for you."

"I know you will. We'll be there for each other." She squeezed my hand, then put an arm around my shoulders to settle me against her more comfortably. I sighed. I did not deserve this woman. But all I wanted to do was exist in her comforting presence.

Finally relaxing, I felt myself starting to drift off to sleep. How could I be so exhausted when all I'd done in the last five days was lie in a hospital bed?

The shrill ring of my cell phone shattered the quiet and I jerked alert with a gasping whimper. Where the hell was my cell phone?

Takoda sat up and handed me my phone from the coffee table.

I scowled when I saw Bethany's name on the screen but awkwardly swiped open the locked page to answer. I didn't figure she was calling to check on my health. "Hello?" I tapped the speaker icon so I didn't have to hold the phone to my ear.

"Amry?"

"Yes, it's me."

"We need to talk about selling Dad's house. There are papers we all need to sign before it can go on the market, and Tom wants to buy our shares of the cabin."

Her tone was short and curt. I wondered if there would ever be a time when we were more than barely civil with each other. I doubted it. "Sure. Let me know when you want to get together."

"We're meeting at Tom and Darlene's next week Friday at six o'clock. David will have the papers from Dad's lawyers."

"Okay. I'll be there."

"By the way, thanks for putting Tom and I on the spot so the whole world knows our family business." Her sarcasm oozed across the phone line.

"What family business?"

"Your bike accident was all over the news. The whole town knows how you think you're being attacked because you're gay."

Seriously? "Bethany, they called us queers and threw bottles at us. What the fuck else do you call that?"

"You're dragging our family name through the mud!"

Takoda hissed, "Is she on crack?"

I said, "What happened to me has nothing to do with our family name, or you and Tom, for that matter."

"You'd better hope it blows over quickly, Amry."

"I'll be there next Friday to sign papers." I hung up the phone.

Takoda exploded, "What a fucking bitch!"

I closed my eyes against the headache now pounding inside my skull.

"Why do you put up with her crap?"

I didn't open my eyes. I could hear the anger in Takoda's tone and wasn't sure if her ire was aimed at me for being such a wuss or at my sister for being such a bitch. Either way, it was a good question. Why did I put up with their crap? Because it was a habit. Because they were my family and family was supposed to mean something. Because, for some reason, I kept naively hoping that because they were family, they would finally accept and love me for who I am. "I don't know." I was too exhausted to get into it.

"I hate that they hurt you."

I hate it too. "It is what it is. I can't change them."

"No, you can't." She gentled her voice. "But maybe you can stop giving them the power to hurt you." She eased the phone from my hand and set it back on the coffee table, then cuddled me against her and dragged the blanket back up over us. She said no more, and I was relieved to let it go. I didn't have the energy to deal with my screwed-up relationship with my siblings.

* * *

The next morning I struggled to set up my laptop on the kitchen table. One handed, and left-handed at that, it was a frustrating process. I cursed under my breath while I tried to get my programs started. I couldn't use my right hand at all on the keyboard; it hurt too much to hold my cast up or flex my fingers to type. I barely managed a two-handed control-alt-delete to log in. It took me fifteen minutes to write an email to Hayley to let her know I was trying to get online to do some work. I ended up calling her because it was faster.

Hayley's tone was concerned but businesslike and she sounded surprised to hear from me. "Are you sure you're okay to be working? How are you feeling?"

"I'm okay. I'm still sore and I can't type for crap, but I feel too guilty not to at least try to get some stuff done. I've already missed too much time." I did my best to play down the condition I was in, but I didn't sound like my usual chipper self.

"Amry, as much as I'd like to have you jumping back in, we can manage for a few more days. Take some time, let your body heal and then come back to work, okay?"

"But—"

"No buts. I saw you on television. You're in no shape to be doing anything but lying on your couch. Take the rest of this week and next week and get yourself healed or I'll call your girlfriend and make her sit on you until you listen."

I relented. There was no arguing with Hayley when she took that tone, so I thanked her and hung up.

I'd planned on spending the morning working, and now I was at a loss. I sat in my chair, cradling my casted arm in my lap. I wasn't going to admit, even to myself, that I was relieved, but my side already throbbed from sitting up on the hard chair, my headache was starting to come back and I was dog-tired. I felt a little dizzy, but put it down to being exhausted. I pushed the stupid prism glasses back up on my nose.

I heard shuffling on the carpet and turned to see Takoda wandering from the bedroom. She ran her fingers through sleep-tussled hair, temptingly adorable wearing nothing but a T-shirt. It almost made me forget that I was annoyed at my predicament.

"What are you doing?" she asked sleepily.

"Nothing, now. I was trying to log in to work, but Hayley said I need to take time off to heal."

Takoda smiled. "Good."

"Easy for you to say."

"Yup, it is." She laid her hands on my shoulders, lightly massaging the muscles up to my neck.

"But it's not fair you're stuck here babysitting me while your folks are taking care of your dogs."

"I'm not babysitting. I'm helping you out a little. Besides I've got more leave time piled up than I know what to do with."

"I can take care of myself, you know." I felt the anger and frustration building up. I wanted to shut up, but I blurted the words out anyway. "I've managed for years on my own. I'm not helpless."

Takoda's hands stilled on my shoulders for a moment, then resumed. "Well," she said reasonably, "since I'm here, I get to take care of you because I like to, and because you deserve it."

I glared at the table, at the blue cast resting in my lap, and wanted to scream with frustration. Warm hands continued kneading gently and I closed my eyes with an agitated sigh. It felt good. She felt good. I was an emotional basket case. "I'm sorry," I murmured.

She kissed my hair. "You're fine."

The bike club met at Will and Mike's house on Sunday, a week and a day after the crash. Gathered in the living room, we were a battered group. After a week and still dealing with on-going headaches and bouts of dizziness, I had scabs on my jaw and a neat line of stitches on my chin. I wore loose sweats over the road rash up and down my right side. My ribs still jolted painfully if I moved too fast or breathed too hard, and the gash on my right side was generally killing me any time I twisted or bent.

Kevin had a bruise along the side of his face, under his ear where the bottle had hit him, and road rash on the other side. His right arm was in a sling and bound against his chest to keep the strain off his broken collarbone. Christy, Tashi and Lisa were bruised and scarred, though by some miracle they'd managed not to break any bones. Will and Derek had been far enough behind us to avoid adding to the pile of flesh and metal that we'd created.

"Are you going to perform this Friday, Kevin?" Lisa asked from her place on the sofa. "Christoph and I have tickets to the show."

Kevin's relaxed demeanor shifted, and his answer was all Angelina. "The show must go on, so yes, I will. Sling and all. I'm working on an amped up version of the sling to match my outfit. Very glitzy. You'll love it."

"Oh, fun! I'm looking forward to it."

Angelina's expression turned serious. "I was actually going to ask all of you to come out if you can, and tell your friends. I'm working with OutFront Minnesota to use the show to help fund and promote their anti-violence program. I may as well use the situation to do some good."

Tashi said, "Damn, that's a great idea, Ang. I think Kelly and I can be there. If you want to me speak and pound the podium a little, I can do that. Never hurts to add another voice, right?"

"Thanks, Tashi, I'll take you up on that."

I grumbled, "Man, I wish we could go, but I have to be up north that night to sign papers to sell my Dad's house. But it's a great way to fight back against the haters."

Derek scowled, slouched in an armchair. "Why does everything have to be politicized? We got attacked by a bunch of yahoos. It's over. They'll probably get a slap on the wrist. I just want to get on with my life."

I felt Takoda stiffen beside me on the sofa. I rested my good hand on her leg. This was Derek being Derek. He tended to deal with his fears and anger by lashing out. "Not all of us can be as public as Ang is," I said. "I'm certainly not. But I admire anyone who's able to speak for the community and put themselves out there."

Kelly said, "Hey, don't knock yourself. You were brave enough to be on television when you looked like death warmed over."

I managed a self-deprecating grin. "Thanks, Kel. Seriously, I needed to be reminded that my public debut was as Frankenstein's monster."

That got a laugh and broke the undercurrent of friction which was my intent. I settled back against Takoda with a sigh, trying to relax against the pain starting to bleed through my last dose of meds.

"I really hope they get more than a slap on the wrist, though," Christy put in. "I think I've woken up with nightmares almost every night. Every time I close my eyes I see that bottle hitting my front wheel and the blur of the road when I flew into the ditch."

Will had been standing in the doorframe from the kitchen. He said somberly, "They were laughing when they pulled away, the bastards. They saw it all, watched you guys go down, and they were laughing." His sadness was palpable and tears had formed in his eyes. Mike hugged him from behind. Will looked across the room, and his eyes locked on mine. His voice shook. "I've never been so scared in my life. We thought you were dead, Amry. There was so much fucking blood, and you were so still, lying across Christy's bike with your arm all twisted under you, and your helmet was shattered."

I shuddered. I could imagine the scene in my head. I know how I'd have felt if I'd have seen any of them in the same situation. And God, if it had been Takoda? I grasped her hand tightly.

"The others were moving at least," Derek said. "Even Kevin. He was in pain but at least he was conscious. But you were just laid out over the bikes, and you were bleeding all over the road from that pedal stuck in your side. We didn't want to try to move you, but we had to try to stop the bleeding." The color went out of his face and he closed his eyes. He struggled for composure and lost. Tears tracked down his handsome face. "I kept flashing back to when the gangbangers stabbed my brother.

All the blood on my hands trying to keep him from bleeding out. At least we were able to save you."

"D, I'm sorry," I whispered. I knew his brother had been killed. I didn't know he'd been there.

"I'm glad you'll be okay," he said.

I pushed myself painfully to my feet and crossed the room, knelt beside his chair and hugged him as best I could with only one arm. "Thank you. Thank you for being there and for saving my life."

He pulled me into an awkward but heartfelt embrace, and I could feel his silent sobs as we held each other. It wasn't fair that he had lost so much that he had to hurt so badly. I hated that these five ignorant men had caused all of us to be that much more broken.

Takoda joined me in hugging and thanking Derek and Will for what they'd done. Everyone cried and we all held each other. I realized that this was the first time I had stopped to grieve for what had happened on the road that afternoon. I'd been so busy dealing with my own injuries, I hadn't let myself cry for what everyone else had gone through as well. I was inordinately grateful to have such wonderful friends, and that we had this evening to heal and reconnect.

We gathered around the dining room table to share the feast Will and Mike had cooked to make up for the meal we'd missed because of the crash.

Will proposed a toast. "Thanks, all of you, for being here. Tonight, let's celebrate our friendship. Let's celebrate life, and that we will carry on. Love to all of you! Now chow down!"

The emotional tension dissipated over dinner, proving that food and friends were wonderful methods of healing. We laughed and gossiped as we passed around bowls of salad, spaghetti, meatballs, sausage and garlic cheese bread, and celebrated with spumoni ice cream for desert.

After dinner, Will took Takoda and me into the garage to see what was left of my bike. It lay on a large piece of cardboard. The front wheel was twisted around the broken front fork. The handlebars rested at a skewed angle, and one handlebar brake assembly hung limply from its cable.

"Fuck," I uttered. I swallowed hard.

Will said, "I think I can fix it. The frame itself seems okay. I'll have to replace the front fork and the handlebars for sure."

I shook my head slowly. "I wouldn't feel safe riding it again."

"I kinda figured you'd say that. Would you mind if I fixed it up anyway? I'll donate it to one of the bike charities. It'd be fine for a kid, or as a commuter bike."

"Guess next year I'll be bike shopping."

Will patted my arm and headed back into the house, leaving Takoda and I to study the wreckage.

Takoda shuddered. "It scares the piss out of me, knowing how close I came to losing you. I've never been so scared as when I got the call from Kelly saying you were in the hospital and unconscious. I don't even remember the drive down here." She turned me toward her and cupped my face in her hands. "You would have died without that helmet. I saw it, you know. It was fractured into pieces." A single tear rolled down her face. "I don't ever want to lose you. I love you, Amry."

I reached up with my good hand to wipe away the tear. "I love you too."

She captured my lips with the most tender and passionate kiss I'd ever experienced. I melted into her, deepening the connection between us, my good hand fisted in the material of her sweatshirt and my casted arm trapped between us as she held me against her. We kissed until I couldn't breathe, then held each other for a long time, and her embrace took away the pain wrapping around my chest. I rested my head against her and breathed in the clean smell of her sweatshirt, listening to the rapid thump of her heart under my ear. Her hold on me was strong and solid, her hands splayed across my back.

We parted reluctantly to join the others. I would have happily left the gathering right then and taken Takoda back to the apartment to make love all night. Of course, in my condition, that wouldn't have gone too well. Instead, we entered the living room, Takoda's arm around my shoulders, and mine around her waist. We took an open spot on the sofa and settled in to visit until we could take our leave.

CHAPTER SEVENTEEN

Takoda stayed with me the rest of that week. By midweek, I was bored and wanting to get on with my life. I tried bringing up my computer to do some writing, but between the pain pills I was still taking and the headache engendered when I tried to read or look at the computer screen, I couldn't do more than about two hours without an extended break.

On Friday I put aside all the pain pills except Tylenol so I could make the drive up north to sign papers with my sibs. The driving sucked between my ribs and side aching, the awkwardness of driving with my right arm in a cast and a lingering headache. Takoda followed me in her Jeep. We had to stop three times for me to rest. I was not looking forward to driving back to the city on Sunday. I'd be driving alone. Monday I would go back into the office to work, and Takoda was returning to her job as well.

Finally, I pulled into the McDonald's parking lot in my hometown. Takoda parked next to me and came around to my car while I climbed out and leaned stiffly against the door.

"How are you holding up?" she asked.

"I'm managing."

"C'mere."

She held me against her. I wrapped my good arm around her waist and rested my head on her chest. Somehow just being near her gave me strength.

"God, I don't want to do this."

"You don't have to."

"I do. Hopefully it will go quickly."

She kissed the top of my head. "If you don't feel up to driving later, call me so I can pick you up."

"I'll be fine. But thank you. I'll call if I need to." I tilted my head back to meet her gaze, then slid my hand behind her neck. I captured her lips in a kiss, which she returned and then some. My knees were weak when we parted, standing nose to nose.

Her fingers traced featherlight caresses along my stitched jaw, taking away the aching pain. She kissed me lightly. "I'll be waiting for you."

"I'll try to get home as soon as I can," I said, realizing I had referred to her house as home and knowing in my heart that it felt right.

"Love you," she said.

"Love you too."

We parted reluctantly and got into our respective vehicles. She turned toward her house and I continued to my brother's home.

I parked at the end of the driveway where I wouldn't be blocked in case all hell broke loose. The headache I'd been fighting had dissipated for those few minutes in Takoda's arms, but now I was getting achy and tired again. I was sure I looked as bad as I felt. I rang the bell, and Darlene opened the door a few seconds later.

"Oh, Amry, you poor thing, get in here and sit down."

"I'm okay, really."

"And I'm Santa Claus. Tom's running late and Beth and David aren't here yet. How are your friends doing? How's Takoda?"

"Takoda's good. And all my friends are healing, like me." I sat carefully on a chair at the kitchen table while Darlene poured us coffee and put a few cookies on a plate.

She studied me with a frown as she settled across from me. "I hate to jump into ugliness, but I should warn you Tom and Bethany are being assholes."

I sipped my coffee, taking the time to appreciate the warmth of the liquid going down. I wasn't sure I wanted to hear what the twins were pissed about, but I asked, "What's going on?"

"They're still ticked off about the funeral because Takoda was with you and your friends were so 'out.' And now they're angry because you were on television. They've got it in their heads that somehow it's making them look bad and embarrassing them. Seriously, they think nobody in town knew you were gay? It's not like you were keeping it a secret. I mean, you're out on Facebook as a lesbian author. They're such idiots. I've tried to make Tom see sense, but it only makes him angrier."

I turned the mug in my hands. I could see the weariness and the sadness in her eyes. "I'm sorry things have gotten so out of hand with them. I feel so bad for you and Nikko. I've been chatting with him a lot. I know he's struggling. I try to be available for him to talk to, and so does Takoda."

"Every time he hears Tom go off on a rant it hurts him. I try to protect him from it and reassure him, but there's only so much I can do."

You could kick my brother's sorry ass out of the house for good. But I knew that was easier said than done, and I didn't even know if she wanted that. If I were here, I could have him live with me, but bringing him down to the cities, taking him out of school, wasn't going to work. Frustrated sadness washed over me. Poor Nikko. He didn't deserve all the hurt and anger. Being gay wasn't a bad thing, and he shouldn't have to hear those kinds of accusations, especially coming from family. "For what it's worth, Darlene, thank you for being there for Nikk, and for defending me too."

We drank our coffee in silence. I fervently wished I was with Takoda and well away from my family. I pushed the emotions and tiredness away and changed the subject, asking Darlene about her work.

Tom strode through the back door shortly after, giving us a curt nod as he went upstairs to change out of his work overalls. Darlene watched him with a pained frown. Then she blinked, and a bland mask dropped over her hurt expression.

Bethany and David arrived about the same time Tom came back downstairs. My brother grabbed a beer from the refrigerator. The rest of us stuck with coffee.

David set his briefcase on the table and removed a manila folder. "This is all the paperwork for putting the house on the market. You all need to sign. The lines are marked." He pushed the papers and a pen toward Tom, who skimmed over them then scrawled his name where the pages had been highlighted.

Bethany and I signed as well. I glanced at the pages, but didn't bother reading them thoroughly. If David planned to screw us all over, so be it. I just wanted the whole thing done as soon as possible. It probably wasn't wise, but at this point I honestly didn't care. Fumbling awkwardly with the pen in my casted right hand, I signed and dated the papers and pushed them back to David.

I asked, "What about cleaning the house out? I can come on the weekends to help get the house ready."

Bethany said, "We'll let you know. David's going to arrange for a Dumpster. There are a couple options for donations and estate sales for anything we don't want to keep."

Tom announced, "I want to keep the cabin."

I'd been wondering when that was going to come up. I'd given it a lot of thought over the past few weeks. "I'm fine with you buying me out of it."

"Are you sure, Amry?" Darlene asked.

"I'm sure. I can't afford the property taxes and upkeep on my salary."

Tom turned to David. "What about you and Beth? Do you want me to buy out your third too? I'm okay either way."

"We want to keep half," Bethany said.

"Okay. So, between us, we'll buy out Amry's third of the cabin, and we'll split the sale of the house three ways."

David made notes on a legal pad. "I'll make sure the paperwork reflects that and have the lawyer write up the sale of Amry's part of the cabin based on the current market value."

Bethany turned to me. "Since you're in town this weekend, you should go to the house and take anything you want to keep."

I met her gaze and held it for a moment. There was no warmth in her eyes. It was like talking to a complete stranger instead of my own sister. The breath went out of me as the realization hit. I had no family here. Once the legalities were completed, I was on my own. It was a chilling awareness. Even though I'd known, logically, that it was a false assumption, I'd clung to the belief that family was supposed to mean something, despite our differences. In the same way I'd wanted Santa Claus to be real until I was way too old to believe, I'd wanted family ties to be magic. With one cold look, the magic had evaporated.

"There are a few things I'd like to have," I said.

The gathering broke up shortly after that. Awkwardly, I eased my oversized jacket on over my cast as I stood by the back door. Darlene watched with a concerned gaze. "Are you okay?"

I gave her a small smile that strained the stitches on my chin. "Yeah. I'm okay. Been a long day." I fished the keys out of my pocket and held them up left-handed. "And I have a lot to look forward to when I get to Koda's."

Darlene grinned at me. "Yes, you do." She gave me a quick hug. "Drive safe and say hello to her for me."

I returned her hug, feeling my sibs' eyes on me as I hurried on my way to the haven of Takoda's arms.

Half an hour later I parked in front of Takoda's pre-fab three-stall garage. I turned off the car, closing my eyes for a second or two and letting the tension seep out of my body. I probably would have fallen asleep, save for a tapping at the window that made me jerk alert.

My sweet girlfriend stood next to my car wearing a T-shirt even though there was three inches of snow on the ground.

She opened the door as I fumbled to release my seat belt.

"Hey," she said. "You look beat." She held out a hand, and I took it as I eased to my feet. She gathered me into a gentle embrace, which I returned one-handed. Even shivering in the cold, it felt wonderful to be held and to hold her.

Takoda stepped aside, keeping one arm around my shoulders. "Come on, let's get inside."

As we started for the house, it occurred to me that I hadn't been overrun by the dogs. I searched around curiously. "Where are the fur children?" I asked.

"In the house. I got tired of wiping off muddy paws. Did you eat anything over there? How did it go?"

We climbed the porch steps into the house where Takoda gallantly stepped between me and the very excited dogs so they wouldn't jump all over me. I still hurt too much for roughhousing, though I rubbed their furry heads and accepted their sloppy kisses.

I hung my jacket by the door and kicked off my sneakers before padding into the living room. A fire crackled brightly in the fireplace. I paused in front of the metal screen to soak up the warmth for a few moments before carefully easing myself into the corner of the sofa. It felt good to sit and relax. Xena laid her head in my lap, and I scratched behind her soft ears.

Takoda asked, "Can I get you anything? Tea? I have coffee on."

"Coffee would be great."

"Coming right up."

The independent and self-sufficient voice in my head told me I should get up and get my own damned coffee, but I didn't have the energy. Instead I closed my eyes and rested my head against the cool leather. I could hear Takoda puttering in the kitchen, the clink of a stirring spoon in the ceramic mugs and Gabby's toenails on the wood floor as she followed Takoda around. I sucked in a long, careful breath, taking in the scent of the fireplace, pine, coffee and the slight tang of damp dog fur.

"Hey, you sleeping?"

I opened my eyes. "Not yet, no."

Takoda handed me a sealed travel mug and sat beside me. "Are you okay?"

I sighed as the hot liquid warmed me from the inside out. "Ah, that's good. Thank you. And yeah, I'm okay. Glad to have it over with."

"They weren't bastards, were they?"

"No, they were okay. I mean, there was no yelling or anything."

Takoda studied me for a second. "Something happened," she said.

I wanted to laugh. It came out as a choking breath. Was I that transparent? "I think I finally realized that I have no family." Why did it hurt so much? Why did I want to cry? "Bethany was just so cold," I said. "Like she didn't care at all about me. Family isn't supposed to be that way. Dad always believed in family, he tried to show us that. But he was all that held us together. Now he's gone, and I'm alone, Koda."

She wrapped her arms around me. "Amry, you're not alone. You're never alone. You've always had family. You made your own, with your friends, who love you so much. And now you have me too. You're not alone. Please, please believe that."

She lifted me carefully onto her lap and cuddled me against her, pulling a fleece throw over us. I clung to her, my head on her shoulder, soaking in the love and letting go of the hurt and anger. I gazed into the spitting flames and knew, deep in my heart, I had all the family I needed.

Takoda had to work the next morning and was out of the house by five thirty. While she was getting ready, I put the dogs out and started a pot of coffee. I even managed to fix her up a thermos, a travel mug and a sack lunch with a somewhat messy peanut butter-and-jelly sandwich, an apple and some treats.

She tucked me back into bed before she left, kissed me and promised to see me later. She looked sexy as hell in her dark green forestry khakis and pressed shirt, with her hair tied into a thick braid down her back.

I tried to sleep again, but after forty minutes of tossing and turning, I pulled on a pair of sweats and one of Takoda's oversized hoodies and made my way to the kitchen. I started another pot of coffee and sat down at the dining room table. Opening Takoda's iPad, I went to the Star-Trib site to flip through the morning news. The dogs drowsed on their beds by the sliding glass doors to the back deck.

I wasn't in a hurry to go to my parents' house. Truly, I wasn't looking forward to it at all, but better to be there without the twins around. I knew if Beth suggested I go today she wouldn't show up.

It was painfully obvious Bethany didn't want me involved any more than I absolutely needed to be. I couldn't decide if I was glad to be getting out of the work of going through the house, or hurt and angry they didn't want me around. I supposed it was all of the above.

A couple hours later, showered and changed into loose-fitting jeans and an old Metallica T-shirt, I tugged on my jacket and headed into town.

When I let myself in, the house smelled stuffy and stale, so I opened a couple windows to let in some air. The silence was disturbing. I caught myself listening for Dad moving around in the living room. Part of me had expected to hear the television blaring when I came in. But the only sounds were memories.

I toed off my sneakers and walked down the hallway to the bedroom I'd shared with Bethany. The comforter from my twin bed was gone, leaving a light blue blanket over the sheets. On one of the two shelves over my bed, a couple old sci-fi books and classic novels from college were propped between a pair of brass sailboat bookends. The other shelf held a framed photo of me from my freshman year in college, wearing a maroon and gold U of MN hoodie and squinting into the sun.

On my tall white dresser, a couple photos with friends from high school shared space with a wooden treasure box and a pottery bowl from art class that held an array of trinkets. I knew there were a few of my old scrapbooks and photo albums in the closet.

I wondered if I should make a trip to Walmart for plastic bins, then shrugged off the thought. Dad kept a plethora of plastic grocery bags in the hall closet, and those would be easier to carry one-handed anyway.

I left my bedroom and wandered through the rest of the house, taking the time to see what was there. Little knickknacks covered the shelves and end tables in the living room. A few pictures hung on the walls. There wasn't anything in the kitchen I'd want to keep.

I went downstairs. The right side of the basement was a finished rec room. One paneled wall was lined with framed eight-by-ten school photos from kindergarten to our senior photos. Each of us had a row.

Tom's early years showed a mischievous little boy, then a handsome teenager. Bethany was an adorable pixie and then pageant-queen, pretty all the way through her school years. In contrast, after being a cute and bright-eyed child, I had some very awkward years around junior high. It looked like I had been trying to figure out if I should be a girl or a boy. I had settled for plain and ordinary girl, pushed toward "normal" by Mom and not aware enough of my own self to understand why it felt wrong. I decided I'd take the photos of me. Nobody else would want them.

Bookcases lined most of the basement wall that was the front of the house. The smallest bookcase was dark-stained wood with sliding glass doors. It held all of Mom's books—classics like Dickens, and popular novels from the 50s, 60s and 70s.

Other bookcases were filled with board games, books from our childhood, knickknacks and a bright red set of the *Encyclopedia Britannica* from the early 70s. Scary to think the knowledge of the world used to be contained in twenty-six volumes.

A pool table covered by a green plastic tarp claimed the space in the middle of the room. My best friend Tracey and I had spent countless hours playing pool on the weekends, listening to records and dreaming about what life might bring when we got out of here. At the far end of the room, an old sectional couch and a worn La-Z-Boy faced a pre-cable television set that still had a dial to tune the twelve local channels.

I sat on the edge of the tired tweed sofa, resting my casted arm on my lap. I realized my memories of this space barely included my siblings. Early on we'd gone our separate ways. I'd kept to myself, or spent time with a few friends who, like me, were on the edge of being geeks, or just "different." We liked music, we liked sci-fi and reading and were frowned upon by the "in" crowd. We were too smart, not athletic enough and not cool enough.

My siblings had been part of the popular crowd and enjoyed reminding me of that fact. Bethany's disdain for me and my friends had been mostly passive aggressive, but Tom's outright taunting still echoed in my head, "Lezzy!" "Freak!" "Weirdo!"

The words spoken decades ago still hurt.

It's all in the past, I reminded myself. *Once we sell the house, once this is done, I never have to talk to them again.*

It made me sad. Mom and Dad wouldn't have wanted the family to have been so broken. I'm pretty sure they hadn't been aware of the extent of the name-calling and dislike between us kids. It was always done out of their sight, and I never said anything. I could remember the hurt and anger.

Fuck it.

I got to my feet. Time to grab some bags, take what I wanted, and get the hell out. Enough reminiscing and dwelling. I tromped up the stairs, pissed off that tromping made my side hurt.

CHAPTER EIGHTEEN

I pulled off my heavy prism glasses, set them on my desk and rubbed my eyes. My head pounded in time with my heart, adding painful accents when I tried refocus my eyes to clear my vision. I'd already taken my morning dose of painkillers, and they weren't helping all that much.

My first day back at the office was not going well. My inbox was full, deadlines were looming, everyone was glad to see me back in one piece and sitting in my expensive and ergo-dynamic office chair was killing my side after three hours. With my right arm casted and mostly in the sling, the ergo-dynamics were a lost cause, and trying to work only left-handed was frustrating at best. I shifted to using the laptop itself instead of the external keyboard so I could use the touchpad instead of a mouse. If I was careful, I could take my arm out of the sling for a while and prop it so I could use my fingers a little to help with the touchpad.

I had only managed to edit one story before the lines on the monitor were too blurred to read.

I sighed and decided to get up and get some more coffee. I eased to my feet and headed to the back of the office, carrying my empty mug.

Rose appeared at my side as I was pouring. "Hey, how are you holding up?"

I squinted at her, eyes narrowed against my headache. "Managing," I said.

She set her mug down, and I filled it after mine. "Let me know if you need anything. Did you bring lunch?"

"I grabbed a couple frozen burritos out of my freezer."

I could feel her eyes on me. "Sounds tasty," she commented dryly.

I shrugged. "It's food." I finished adding fake sugar and creamer to my coffee. "I need to get back to it. Staff meeting in a few minutes." I knew I was being bitchy, but my head hurt. I picked up my cup and walked stiffly back to my cubicle.

Across from me, Michael said, "I'll take notes at the meeting."

I set my coffee down and folded carefully into my chair. "Thanks." I sent him a grateful smile. "Sorry you guys are having to pick up my crap."

His grin was encouraging. "Hey, you took one for the team. We're here for you."

I took a couple sips of coffee, then woke up my computer screen again. Michael had helped me set it so it wouldn't lock every time I let it sit. Trying to control-alt-delete meant I had to get my right arm out of its sling, so I wanted to only lock the screen manually. It wasn't like we had outsiders in the office to screw with anything.

I flipped to my inbox and tried to ignore my headache as I started going through my email again.

My cell phone rang. The number that came up was Charlie Eton's office, the lawyer handling our hate crime case. Frowning, I swiped the call open and put the phone up to my ear. "Hello?"

"Amry? Charlie Eton here. Just wanted to give you a heads-up. We've got an arraignment date with the first one of the men for this Thursday. We're expecting he'll plead not guilty, and we'll have a trial date set. I'll set up a meeting with all of us as soon as I know more."

I looked at the calendar on my cube wall. "Sure, just let me know. Thanks for calling."

"Good. I'll be in touch."

We hung up after that. I said to Michael, who was watching openly, "The arraignment will be on Thursday. I guess things are moving forward."

"Good. I hope they nail those idiots to the wall."

"Yeah." What I really wanted was for all of it to just be done with and to finish healing. This was affecting my life in ways that I hadn't really thought about. But I knew I needed to follow through. I wanted to be part of the criminal case against these guys, and I wanted to take a stand. It was a moral imperative.

Fifteen minutes later, I was in the conference room. I scribbled one- and two-word notes to myself in barely legible left-handed printing as Hayley, Michael and I, along with a couple of the lead writers and the magazine's owner, Andrew Shelby, sat around the table hashing over stories for the next couple issues.

Hayley said, "Linda wants to do a feature around your hate crime assault, Amry."

I looked up from my yellow lined notepad. "I'm not the only one involved. It should include everyone in the group."

Hayley flashed a couple slides forward in her presentation. Linda's story outline appeared on the video monitor. "It will. She wants to take a look at how the attack is affecting each of you and then move into a series of broader articles on past and present hate crimes in the area, how they are being handled, what law enforcement is doing to curb the crimes, what the State is doing from a political point of view."

"It might be interesting for her to interview and get the point of view of the accused as well," I said. "Maybe explore why they do what they do?"

Michael muttered, "I hope to hell you're just playing devil's advocate here."

I shrugged one shoulder. "Someone is going to want to look at the bad guys. May as well be us."

Hayley tapped her pen on her pad. "It's an interesting thought, but I really don't want to give them a voice."

Personally, I agreed, but my job as an editor was to cover all the bases when we were talking about stories. We talked through the rest of the features on Hayley's list and brainstormed the less developed outlines. Hayley assigned articles to writers and we got a working schedule going for the next edition of the magazine.

By the end of the meeting, I was anxious to get back to my desk to take my next round of pain meds. It was getting hard to think. When I reached my cubicle, I fumbled in my backpack for my meds, swore under my breath at having to use my weakened right hand to hold the bottle while I got the top unscrewed and shook a couple pills out. I took the time to get the bottle closed again and swallowed my pills with the dregs of my coffee. I leaned my head back, eyes closed, and forced myself to breathe through the pain, pushing down the nausea that was starting to rise. Relax, I thought, *and breathe.* I kept my mantra up until the pain eased.

"Amry? Are you all right?"

I jerked alert and gasped at the resulting jolt through my head.

My boss stood beside me, looking down with a concerned frown. I blinked again, clearing my vision. "Yeah. Headache. I'm sorry. I was just trying to get it under control." I pushed my glasses back up on my nose.

Hayley didn't move, and her expression didn't change. "Do you need someone to take you home?" she asked.

There was a note of something other than concern in her tone that set me on edge. Or maybe it was just me. "No," I said. "I'm okay." I forced myself to sit up and woke up my computer. I had to start working.

After a couple moments, Haley moved away.

I groaned inwardly. I hated when the boss was looking over my shoulder, and I hated feeling like I wasn't doing my job. I turned again to my inbox and the next task on my list, trying to ignore the throbbing behind my eyes while I tried to decipher the blurred words on the screen.

Takoda and I both had a crazy couple of weeks. She was working extra shifts because they were short-staffed and it was hunting season. I was working extra because I was still having so much trouble with the computer monitors and the headaches I got from spending too much time with them. It slowed me down at work because I had to take breaks—which meant I ended up either working later or taking work home to finish things up.

Hayley was trying to be flexible and understanding, but I could tell her patience was wearing thin despite her good intentions. I got my work done, but I was pushing deadlines more than she was accustomed to and couldn't jump as soon as she threw something at me.

Two weeks after my return to work, we got the next edition of the magazine out, with the story on my friends and I as the main feature. After a lot of discussion, Linda decided to handle the story by being up front about the fact that I was part of the magazine family. She discussed right away that the story came up because she was seeing, personally, the effect of the assault on a co-worker. And she added that there would be follow-up articles discussing the broader topic of hate crimes.

Linda described the aftermath of the assault, both physically and emotionally. My part of the interview talked a lot about how the concussion and the ongoing pain from my injuries were making it difficult for me to work. Kevin talked about using the incident to create awareness of hate crimes in our communities. Tashi talked about not wanting to live in fear of violence, and broadening her concerns to the vulnerable persons among us: those who were handicapped, like their son, the homeless, racial minorities and women. Will and Christy described their experiences. Derek and Lisa chose not to be involved, and none of us blamed them a bit.

For me, it was unnerving to put so much of my life out into the public realm. Even as an author, other than talking about my books, I didn't tend to put much personal information out on social media. The television spot from the hospital had been twenty seconds of airtime, more about the perpetrators and the whole assault than about me personally. But this story was in print. And there was a lot more information about me in it.

The magazine came out the same week we got a court date for the trial against the first of the five men in the truck. The first trial was set to start January eighth. There was a short splash on the local news networks Thursday night, reintroducing the incident and indictments and allegations in the case. One of the networks did a blurb on LGBTQ hate crimes as an 'in-depth' investigative feature.

I was inordinately glad I wasn't called on for a television interview and that Hayley had decided against a picture of us on the front cover of the magazine. I didn't want to be a poster child, even though I knew our stories needed to be told.

I took a half-day off after the release and drove up to see Takoda for the weekend, even though it would be a quick trip. Takoda only had Saturday and Sunday free. We both had to be back to work on Monday.

It was a bittersweet drive up north knowing I wasn't going to see my dad. It was hard driving past the house on the highway, only letting myself have a quick glimpse as I sped past.

Nikko was going to come to Takoda's for dinner on Saturday. He'd called to say he'd seen the news online, and he'd heard Tom yelling about it. He said he'd had to explain to Joey that I wasn't in trouble, that the bad guys who'd hurt me and my friends were the ones in trouble. Apparently, Joey was confused because Tom seemed to think I was the bad guy.

Parked in Takoda's driveway, before I even had a chance to get out of the car, the dogs were barreling out the dog door from the mudroom on the side of the house. They greeted me as I opened the car door. I eased out, petting their heads, laughing at their excitement. "I missed you guys too."

I got my duffel bag and backpack out of the backseat, put both over my good shoulder and led our little group up the back steps. The dogs were happy to follow me around as I got settled into the house. I put my things away and returned to the kitchen, where I started a pot of coffee.

Gabby padded along beside me, and Xena brought me a battered stuffed animal of unknown species and pushed it into my stomach. She gazed up at me with hopeful eyes, and I laughed and took the toy left-handed and tossed it into the back of the living room. She scrabbled after it with a happy bark.

I leaned against the counter and ran my fingers through the fur on Gabby's head. "You guys are good girls," I said.

Xena returned with her toy and dropped it at my feet, sitting in front of me, waiting. I leaned down to get the toy and tossed it again, then picked my phone from my pocket. I needed to let Takoda know I'd gotten here and all was well. I didn't expect a reply; I knew she was likely out in the woods or driving the back roads.

When I finished tapping out my message, Xena was back with her toy and the coffeepot had made enough for me to pour myself a cup. I chose a sealable mug because that was safest, fixed myself some coffee and tossed Xena's toy again before heading for the living room to relax. There was firewood in the basket by the fireplace, so I made up a small fire.

I should have taken out my computer to work on some writing or done something productive, but I was tired. Takoda wouldn't be home for at least four hours yet. I grabbed the fleece throw from the back of the sofa and pulled it over me as I stretched out. Sipping my coffee, I watched the fire, glad for the peace and quiet. Gabby hopped on the sofa and curled up, making herself a space on my lower legs. Xena stretched out in front of me on the rug.

I swiped open my phone and purposefully set an alarm so I would remember to preheat the oven and start a pizza for when Takoda got home. Just in case I fell asleep.

"Do you feel like taking a walk?" I asked.

Takoda yawned and looked up from reading the news on her iPad as she sat at the breakfast bar sipping her coffee and eating peanut butter-and-banana toast.

I leaned against the counter near the kitchen sink, having just poured a second cup of coffee, and looked out the windows over the sink. The sun was up and bright on the patchy snow. The fall sky was bright and blue.

"Yeah. That's a good idea. You sure you're up for it?"

"I really need to get outside, you know? I'm not going to be running any marathons, but I can take a slow walk."

"Mmmm, and do a few other things." She sent me a wicked grin.

I'd proved that I had skills last night, even down an arm. I felt my face flush and grinned back.

Lucky for me, I had a pair of slip-on calf-high snow boots I could wear for tromping in the woods. This late in the fall I always kept winter gear in the car when I drove up north.

It was a lovely day for an outing, and I was itching just to move a little bit. The air was cool and fresh, and there wasn't much of a wind. I wore an oversized hoodie under a down vest with a scarf wrapped around my neck, and even decided against a mitten on my free hand. Takoda wore a light down jacket and heavy winter hiking boots. It was probably only between forty and fifty degrees, but if we were moving, we were sure to stay warm enough. Takoda helped me secure the sling on my right arm more securely so it wouldn't bounce when I walked.

As we headed out the mudroom door, she stopped and opened the safe up on the top shelf, where she retrieved a small pistol and shoved it into the back of her pants. I gave her a doubtful look and she shrugged, with the simple explanation, "It's hunting season."

"What does that mean?"

She frowned as though she really hadn't thought about it before. "I don't know who or what will be in the woods," she said. She paused, seeming to think about how that sounded. "Maybe it's just habit. I just feel better having a gun handy."

I wasn't quite sure what to do with that, and my unease must have shown on my face. She chewed her lip for a moment, then tried again. "As a forestry officer, I'm always armed when I'm in the woods. I can only think of maybe three times that I've ever needed the gun. Once was because we were attacked by a sick bear, and being armed saved my and Bill's lives. Another time it was a wolf, and we just shot into the air to scare it off. Then there was an incident with some drunken idiots who'd been shooting things up around one of the sandpits. We didn't end up needing the guns, but it definitely made the drunken idiots chill out a lot faster. So I tend to take it with me."

I nodded slowly. I kept forgetting that she was, basically, a cop in the woods. And it made the woods seem just a little less inviting, knowing she automatically took precautions.

She reached out and took my one hand in both of hers. "Honest, I'm not a crazy, gun-toting Republican," she said earnestly. "I'll put it away if it's freaking you out."

I stared into her eyes. I'm not sure what I was searching for. Reassurance? To know that the woman with the gun was just Takoda? She held my gaze, and I felt the warmth of her hands holding mine, and recognized the troubled expression on her face. She was worried that I was freaking out. Maybe worried that I didn't trust her.

"No, it's cool. I'm fine. I just keep forgetting, you know?" I smiled and tried to show her that I trusted her, that she didn't need to be worried. I tugged on her hand. "Come on, Annie Oakley, let's go."

She grinned at me. "Thanks."

I heard the relief in her voice.

We left the house and crossed the yard to a path entrance that would lead us out into the woods around her property. The dogs joined us, made sure we were on the trail and took off into the woods on their own recognizance. The track we followed wound through poplars and birch, pines and a lot of undergrowth. In places, the snow was ankle deep or more, but if I took my time it wasn't a problem.

The sun shone through the empty branches. Only a handful of withered leaves still hung on the trees. Takoda pointed. "Deer tracks."

"There must be a ton of deer out here."

"There are. I've seen wolves too. Not lately, though I'm sure they're around if there are deer."

"Do the dogs ever bring anything home to you?"

She shook her head. "No, but they've come home with rabbit and squirrel on their breath." She laughed.

I saw a No Trespassing sign posted on a steel post. I asked, "How much of this land is yours?"

"I own fifty acres wrapping around this side of the lake."

I blinked. "Wow."

She shrugged. "What else am I going to spend my money on? I got deal on it, though. The owner was anxious to sell. I think it was an estate sale. There was an abandoned farmhouse on the site when I bought it. No barn, no garage or any other structures. I had it demolished and started from scratch."

"I'm pretty impressed," I said. "I think it's pretty cool to have your own forest."

Takoda laughed, then touched my arm. "Hey, careful."

She helped me over a fallen tree, and we continued along the path.

"Did you make the trails through here?" I asked.

"More or less. The dogs running through here helped, and a lot of these were deer tracks. I used to spend more time clearing trails. Now, I just tend to tramp around wherever my nose takes me. Or just follow the dogs if they're walking with me."

I smiled, squinting into the sunlight. "It's really great out here." I took in a deep breath of cool air.

Takoda took my hand and squeezed it. "It's best because you're out here too."

I laughed, my heart soaring. "You sweet talker."

I kept hold of her hand as we walked leisurely along.

In the near distance, the dogs started barking. Takoda slowed to a stop, listening, her head cocked and a frown starting on her face. She said, "Those are warning barks." She shifted our direction. "Come on. Let's see what they've gotten into."

I had to work a little bit to get through the undergrowth as we left the trail and headed in the direction of the dogs barking. Takoda kept a hold of my hand, helping me along, and was careful not to move too quickly. I paid more attention to where I was putting my feet than to where we were going. Moving a little faster, I was glad that we'd tightened the sling, because even the little bounce pulled on my shoulder. The damned cast was heavy.

The barking got closer, a steady *woof-woof-woof* from one of the girls, and a lower, single growling woof from the other.

Takoda slowed. "Hold up," she said softly.

I stopped gratefully. I needed a break. When I looked at Takoda, she was peering ahead into the woods, her expression intense. I followed her gaze. Maybe two hundred yards ahead, I could see the dark silhouette of someone kneeling in the snow. The dogs were standing a distance from the person and barking. She watched for a few moments, then looked around us. She pointed to a wide pine tree with branches spread low to the ground. "This way," she murmured.

We moved back behind the tree. She shifted so that she could look past it, toward the dogs, and watched for another handful of seconds. Then Takoda moved back behind the tree with me, put her fingers in her mouth and gave two sharp whistles. The dogs immediately stopped barking, and I saw them both running away from where they were and back toward what I thought was the direction of the house.

I whispered, "Where are they going?"

"That's a call to home. They'll go back to the house. I doubt they'll stay, since I'm not there, but it gets them away from whoever that is."

She edged around so she could see again. I started to do the same, but she shook her head. "Stay back."

"What are you going to do?" I whispered.

She frowned, seemed to be thinking hard. "Will you stay here?" she asked.

"What are you going to do?" I whispered again.

"Find out what he's doing on my land," she muttered. She straightened, standing tall, her shoulders set. The woman standing beside me was all cop now. "Please, stay put, okay?"

I nodded. I would stay put, but I was going to be watching from behind this lovely pine tree. I could feel the tension coming off her, pumping up my own adrenaline.

She grinned at me, a sudden, confident expression, and ducked down, dropping a kiss on my lips, then striding away, hands at her sides, around the tree and toward the man still kneeling in the snow.

As she moved forward, she picked up speed, moving through the trees with a purpose. She was only maybe twenty feet from the guy when his head swung in her direction. I heard her voice—clear, no-nonsense. "Hey, what are you doing?"

The guy scrambled to his feet, grabbed at the ground for something. When he straightened, he had a rifle in his hand. I saw Takoda's right hand whip behind her, and then she was standing with her pistol in front of her, two-fisted. "Drop it!" she barked.

He froze for a second, then dropped the gun, turned and ran.

I heard Takoda's muffled curse as she took off after him, shoving the pistol back in her pants as she pounded through the snow.

The man may have had a lead on her, but he was at least twice her weight, with a short, stocky build, and wearing bulky boots. She gained on him, taking him down in a tackle when he stumbled over his footing. I had moved from my tree by this point, needing to see what was happening, not taking my eyes off Takoda.

I heard the guy's deep voice, grumbling, swearing at Takoda, and then her voice cutting across the snow. "Just what about No Trespassing don't you understand?" she demanded.

"I didn't see no fuckin' signs," he protested.

She pulled the man to his feet, and keeping a grip on his arm, she pushed him back toward where she'd found him. I kept my distance. Takoda looked my way. "Can I borrow your scarf?" she called to me.

What the hell did she need my scarf for? Shrugging, I started untying it from my neck and moved toward her.

She smiled. "Thanks."

The guy she was holding on to gave me an up-and-down assessment and tried to pull away from Takoda with a grunt. She swung him around so his arm was behind his back, and, while he was getting his footing, grabbed his other arm as well, holding them as though she were going to cuff him.

He jerked again. "What the fuck, bitch?"

She jerked his wrists back and used a knee to collapse him to the ground. He hit the snow with a curse.

She gave me an encouraging smile over her shoulder. "Scarf?" she asked. I swallowed, then hurried to hand her the item in question. She shook her head. "Wrap it tight around his wrists."

I stepped in to do as she asked, twisting it around his crossed wrists as best I could with one hand.

"Good."

She released his hands long enough to pull the scarf tight and tied it securely.

He tried lurching away. This time, she shoved him facedown into the snow and reached around her back to pull her pistol out and aim it at him. His eyes widened. She stared at him. "Settle down."

With her other hand, she reached into her jacket and brought out a wallet, which she flipped open in front of him. "Lieutenant Takoda Running Bear, US Forestry Service," she said flatly. She read him his Miranda rights.

"What the fuck did I do?" he shouted.

She ignored him and pulled out her phone. Without taking her eyes or her gun off the man lying in the snow, she dialed. "Hi Jeannie…Yeah, this is Takoda. Can you send a squad up to my place? I just caught a guy laying illegal traps and trespassing on my land…No need for sirens and all. He's not going anywhere… Thanks."

At this point, I looked past Takoda and toward the copse of trees where we'd first seen the man kneeling. A young deer lay in the snow. Dark stains tarnished the white drift near its feet. Its eyes were open but glazed. I saw its head move, just a little. My heart lurched, and I started toward the wounded deer. I have no idea what I thought I was going to do.

Takoda said, "Am, stay back. There are traps in the snow over there."

I stopped.

"That's what took the deer down. Thank the gods the dogs didn't get caught in them." She turned her attention back to the man lying in the snow. "You, stay put."

Keeping an eye on him, she eased toward the deer. She knelt by the animal's trapped leg, setting her gun to the side with a warning look at the hunter. Leaning over, she did something, and I heard a metallic chink. The deer squealed weakly with pain, and its body quivered. I cringed and felt sick. That poor animal. Takoda retrieved her pistol and moved to the deer's head. She laid a hand on the young animal's fur, closed her eyes and whispered, as though she were praying.

After a moment, she turned her gaze toward me. "You might want to look away."

I nodded but watched anyway. She murmured a few more words, then stood up, stepping back, and fired. I flinched at the sharp crack of sound that echoed into the quiet woods.

The guy muttered, "Fucking Indian mumbo jumbo."

I swallowed.

Takoda stepped in front of him, her eyes cold. She still held the pistol, though it was pointed at the ground. If I were him, I'd have been scared. "How many more trap lines do you have out here?" she demanded.

"Fuck you."

Her jaw tightened. Anger flashed in her eyes as she glared at him. "It'll go better for you if you identify them before I find them. You tell me where they all are and I won't press charges."

"Bitch."

Takoda grabbed his arm. "Get up. I've got a ride coming for you." She pulled him to his feet. She glanced over at me. "Am, can you follow a little behind us? I need you to stay clear."

The guy glowered. "You wouldn't be so tough without that gun."

Takoda gave him a dark look. "Let's go," she barked, helping him ahead with a fist wrapped in the bicep of his jacket. In deference to the gun in her other hand, he went along, and I followed a few yards behind them, my attention moving between his wrists, still tied tightly together behind his back, and Takoda's ass, which looked sexy as hell in her jeans.

This was a side of Takoda I hadn't seen before. Sure, she'd talked about her job, but to see her in action made it all much more real. She was so confident, so commanding, completely in control. She'd never even raised her voice. Watching her now, one hand on the hunter, the other holding her gun at her side, I realized I didn't feel any fear. I trusted that she wouldn't purposefully put me in harm's way.

As we got closer to Takoda's house, the dogs came back up the trail. Xena growled at the man.

Takoda said to me over her shoulder, "Call them to heel to you."

"Gabby, Xena, heel!" I commanded. We'd practiced this a few times, and the dogs knew that they should listen to me. They hesitated, though, both looking to Takoda. I repeated, "Heel!"

Takoda said, "Go."

Both dogs came back to me, falling in on my left. I petted Gabby's head with my good hand as she walked, rubbing against my leg, while Xena pranced around us. Even if I weren't frightened, I felt better with the dogs at my side.

A sheriff's deputy met us when we entered the clearing at Takoda's house. I hung back and watched as he talked to Takoda and the man in her custody. I could hear their voices, but not the words—Takoda and the deputy speaking in measured, even tones, the man's voice, rising above, almost petulant. Takoda shoved her gun back in her pants and untied the scarf from the man's hands. The officer spoke to the man, who seemed to settle down and was nodding and gesturing toward the woods behind me.

The three of them turned and started walking in my direction. I took a step back and watched Takoda for a cue. What was going on?

They paused as they reached me. Takoda waved the two men forward and they headed into the woods. She gave me a hug. "Hey. I'm sorry, Amry. Are you okay?"

I nodded against her shoulder. "Yes."

"I need to go back out with them. Bennett's going to show us where he put the two other trap lines. Orechelli said he'd only write him up a warning for trespassing and illegal trapping as long as he shows us where the other lines are and doesn't do it again."

"Why so lenient? The guy's a jerk."

"Because it's better to give him the benefit of the doubt and keep the peace than start up a feud with him. He's on our radar now. He's the kind of guy who talks big but generally stays in line if you give him boundaries."

I studied her face, seeing so much calm confidence and compassion. And I loved her even more. What an amazing woman. She smiled curiously at me. I said, "You go catch up with them. I'll get some hot coffee on."

"Thanks. This won't take too long." She kissed my cheek, then took off toward the woods at a run with the dogs on her heels. I smiled and shook my head as I headed across the yard to the mudroom door.

* * *

The weekend ended too soon, as always, and Monday started off with a bang. I stepped out of the elevator at work and into a crowd of about a dozen people with signs, pacing in front of the double glass doors to the office.

I stopped in my tracks, trying to comprehend what was going on.

"Hey, it's one of those gays."

The words on the signs registered. "God hates Gays," "No Queers," "Adam and Eve not Adam and Steve." What the fuck?

"What gives you the right to smear the names of those boys? They were just driving by, and you were taking up the whole road!" The man who'd said that stepped forward. He didn't have a sign. He was average height, clean-cut, wearing slacks and a sweater under his thin down jacket. "Those are decent, God-fearing boys."

I stared at him, speechless.

The door to the office opened, and the big boss, Andrew Shelby, stepped out. "Back off," he snapped at the protesters, then strode through them to me. Andrew was a former college football player, and right now, he looked mean and ornery. He gestured and the protesters reluctantly shifted out of our way as he guided me through the doors and into the safety of the office.

"You okay, Amry?" he asked.

I nodded. "Yeah. What's going on?"

Haley nodded toward the conference room. "We're all meeting in the conference room. Looks like Linda's piece on the assault has generated a bit of interest," she said.

"I guess," I muttered, and followed them, pausing at my desk to drop off my bag and my jacket.

In the conference room, about half our staff sat around the table, cradling cups of coffee and looking concerned. Michael stood as I entered and eased up to me. "Hey."

I asked, "How long have they been here?"

"Early enough that I think they beat Andrew in."

I shifted the sling on my shoulder. "I need some coffee."

"Better get some before Andrew starts the meeting."

I glanced at the wall clock. It was just seven now. "I'll be right back." I ducked out the door and to the coffeepots lined up on the back wall. Thank God there was still plenty left. I chose one of the company mugs and fixed myself a cup. I was getting good at working with mostly just my left hand. I could still use my right to help open sugar and creamer packets, but pouring and stirring were all left-handed actions now. By the time I got this damned cast off, I was going to be fully ambidextrous.

I returned to the conference room. Michael had saved me a seat between him and one of the web guys. I asked quietly, "Has anyone given Rose a heads-up?"

"I sent her a text when I got in. I'm sure she's not even awake yet."

"At least she'll know what she's walking into." I sat back, got comfortable in my chair and worked on my coffee.

Andrew stood up at the head of the table. "Okay. This is the deal, folks. These people have the right to protest, as long as they don't harass anyone. It's a public access building, so they have the right to be here. We do not have to let them in our office. If anyone is worried about going in or out, come and get me or if I'm not here, call building security for an escort. If anyone out there gets out of line, call building security." He glanced around the table. "Next thing. There is also some angry mail coming in. Most of it has been to the editorial and opinions account. But some has also gone to staff accounts. If you get any hate mail, any threatening complaints, forward them on to me. Do not reply. We will do a formal press release and say what we need to say. If you happen to get any direct calls, be polite and transfer them to me or Haley."

One of the web guys asked, "So why all of a sudden all this stuff? We've run stories like this before, especially around Pride week, and we've never had protesters. Hell, we had that big spread on the gay marriage amendment and we never had protesters."

Andrew shrugged. "No idea, Gary. They just decided now is the time, I guess."

Michael piped up. "Maybe someone can do a story on them and ask."

Andrew gave him a silencing glance and Michael slouched down in his chair. Andrew brought his hands together. "Okay. That's all I have. Go out, as they say, and do good work. If I have any updates, I'll let you know."

He and Haley left the room.

"Way to stay under the radar," I said to Michael.

He snorted. "Come on, get yourself a warm-up and we'll see what's in our in-boxes."

The protesters returned on Tuesday. I did my best to ignore them. They tried to bait us—at least, they tried with me and Michael and a couple of the others that they thought "looked like gays."

It was the same old stuff, telling us we were going to Hell, and that we were mutants in the eyes of God, and that we were unfairly accusing those "good Christian boys." I could deal with that. It was just crap. But other than the protesters, and being inundated with angry email in our editorial-opinions email account, it was a normal week. I continued to struggle with headaches, and despite the prism lenses, I could only work for limited periods of time without a break. I was frustrated, and I wasn't hiding it well from my workmates.

On the up side, though, Takoda had to be in Minneapolis for a special training class on Thursday. She planned to drive up Wednesday afternoon, attend training on Thursday, and head back Thursday night to be at work Friday morning. It would be a quick trip, but I'd get to see her, even just for a night, which made me a very happy camper.

Wednesday morning I stepped off the elevator and knew almost immediately that something had changed.

"That's her. She's the one."

I looked around, thinking there was someone else in the hallway, but there wasn't. Shaking my head, I hitched my bag further up on my good shoulder, and started walking as purposefully as I could toward the office.

An older woman stepped toward me. "You're going to go to hell for writing the words of Satan."

I tried to get around her, but she moved in front of me, stopping me with a hand connecting with my chest. What the hell? I fought to stay calm. "Excuse me. I need to get to my office."

The woman sneered at me. "You're a pervert and you write smut for perverts. I've seen your books. You're a disgrace before God."

I felt my heartrate ratcheting up. I wasn't sure if I was angry or starting to get frightened, but I knew I wanted to get away from her. "I'm sorry you don't like my books. Now, please, let me past." I used my good hand to try to push her arm out of my way and get by her.

"Don't touch her, you freak!" A younger man grabbed my casted arm by the elbow, pulling me roughly away from her.

I squeaked as pain jolted down to my fingertips. "Ow! My arm is broken, you stupid fuck! What are you doing?"

"That's God's punishment for your perversion!"

I tried to move toward the door, panic rising as they surrounded me.

"All your pornographic books should be burned!"

Someone shoved me from behind, and I stumbled. The sharp movement as I tried to catch my balance shot lancing pain across my side. The torn muscle still hadn't healed. I was spun around. A glaring face too close to mine. "You should be in jail, not them!"

I pushed the person away, but I had nowhere to go, and the door was behind me now. "Leave me alone!" I tried to turn and run, but the protesters had me trapped in a tight circle.

"Hey! What's going on? Leave her alone!"

I recognized Andrew's sharp, deep voice. A moment later, he'd encircled me with a beefy arm. "Come on inside." He led me through the hovering group of protesters, and into the safety of the office.

I was shaking like a leaf. He escorted me back to the break area and pulled out a chair, which I gladly collapsed into. Haley and a couple others rushed up.

"Jesus! Amry, are you all right?"

Andrew knelt beside me. "Did they hurt you? I'm sorry I didn't get there sooner."

My hands were trembling, my breath coming in shallow gasps, and I felt light-headed. I held my casted arm against my middle and tried to slow my breathing. "I'm okay. Just scared the crap out of me."

"Did they hurt you?" Haley asked.

I hesitated, taking stock again. "No, the one guy grabbed my arm, and someone pushed me, but I'm not hurt." I looked at Andrew. "They knew who I was, though. They know I write lesbian fiction. That was what they were yelling about. Yesterday and Monday, they didn't know."

Andrew patted my hand. "Sit here, and take some time, and have some coffee, okay? I'm going to call security and the police and report this incident. Protesting is one thing, but that was assault and harassment, and I won't have that. And please, don't go out there without an escort."

I nodded.

Hayley set a cup of coffee on the table beside me. She said, "I put in creamer and sweetener."

"Thank you."

Andrew patted my shoulder, then stood and headed for his office. Everyone else went back to their desks. Nothing more to see here. Hayley paused. "We'll make sure that there's a security guard, or Andrew, available when you get in tomorrow. Call up here when you get your car parked, and we'll have someone walk you in."

I nodded again. Hayley gave me an encouraging smile and moved away toward her office. I took a few breaths. My hands had mostly stopped shaking so I picked up the cup of coffee, surprised that it was actually sweet enough to drink. The simple action of sipping coffee helped calm my frazzled nerves.

What I really wanted to do was call Takoda, and I wished fervently that it had been her arm around me instead of Andrew's. I wanted a hug. I needed a hug. I clung to the knowledge that she'd be here later that night.

Still wearing my jacket, I got to my feet, feeling only a little bit unsteady from the remains of the adrenaline rush. I shouldered my bag, took the coffee that Hayley had gotten me, and went to my desk. I had just gotten settled when Michael came in.

"Boy, the freaks are agitated this morning," he commented.

I looked up. "Yeah. Tell me about it."

He took a second look at me. I filled him in on what had happened. He shook his head. "Fuck, Amry, that's crazy. You sure you're okay?"

"Yeah. I'm all right. Just shaken up." I shifted in my chair and took a breath. I could feel a headache starting to grow up from my shoulders. Tension. I tried to relax.

"Have you talked to Takoda?"

"Not yet, no. I wanted to get my head together first. She's coming up this evening for training class tomorrow."

"Maybe she'll come early."

I swallowed. I knew, if I asked, that she'd rush up here earlier than she'd planned, but I didn't want to worry her. I was fine. And I needed to get focused and get some work done. I had a few things on my plate, some early stories that weren't time sensitive that needed to be edited. My desktop had come up, and I opened my email to see what was there, and was happy to find nothing other than my existing to-do list.

I opened the first document on my list and started editing. I wouldn't call Takoda. Not just yet. Maybe at lunchtime. I knew she'd worked the overnight last night, and I didn't want to wake her.

The day dragged. Rose brought me some lunch when she ran out. I didn't want to deal with going out through the protesters. But the anxiety I was feeling had given me a pounding headache that even my pain meds couldn't eliminate. By four o'clock, the words on my monitors were doubling and blurring despite the prism lenses, and I still had work I needed to get done.

I leaned back in my chair, taking my glasses off so I could rub my eyes. Michael was packing up his bag to go home. He said, "If you want to head out now, I can walk you out."

The offer was tempting, but I really wanted to finish my work before I went home. Andrew had said he was staying until six, so I planned on leaving with him, and Rose had come in later this morning, and was staying late as well. Either way, I had an escort out of the building. I thanked Michael for the offer, and told him I'd be staying a while yet.

Takoda had called around one to say she was up and would be heading out shortly to drop the dogs off with her parents and get on the road. I didn't tell her what had happened. I didn't want her rushing or driving like an idiot. There was nothing she could do, anyway, and depending on when she actually left, it was possible she'd be able to meet me here before I was done for the day.

I stood to ease the stiffness, stretching my back out and resettling the sling on my shoulder. My neck popped and crackled as I rolled my head. I worked to loosen the muscles around my neck and shoulders, hoping that would ease the throbbing behind my eyes. I was so tired of the headaches.

I felt a little better when I finally sat down.

I focused on the article I was editing, and the print was readable again. Good. I could at least get something done.

My phone beeped with a text at about five thirty, and I grinned when I saw Takoda's message. "I'm here, coming up!"

I texted back a quick acknowledgment and pushed away from my desk to go up front to meet her. Rose was behind the reception counter, working on her computer as I walked up.

"Hey, Amry. Takoda here?"

I grinned. "Yeah. She's on her way up." I looked through the glass doors. The protesters still milled in the hallway around our entrance, and there seemed to be even more of them than there'd been this morning. I frowned, hoping they wouldn't bother Takoda.

Rose said, "A few new faces today. How are you holding up?"

The woman who'd yelled this morning was at the front of the group. She stepped closer to the door, glaring at me, trying to make eye contact, trying to intimidate. I looked away, but felt a shudder go through me. I did not like that woman.

I saw the elevator door open, and Takoda stepped out. She wore civilian clothes, jeans and hiking boots, and a bulky sweatshirt. Her hair was pulled back into a ponytail. I couldn't help but smile at seeing her, and I felt the tension go out of me.

Her expression darkened as she took in the protesters, but she didn't hesitate as she strode through them, and they didn't hamper her as she opened the door to the office and stepped inside. Her smile was breathtaking, and all for me. She opened her arms, and I walked into them.

It felt so good.

I don't know how long we stood holding each other. I know I clung to her like a lifesaver, absorbing her strength and closeness and the feel of her strong hands on my back and holding my head against her chest. I felt her breath against my hair, and the anxiety that I'd been holding all day threatened to come out as relieved sobs.

"*Zaagi'idiwin*, sweetheart, what happened?" she murmured close to my ear.

"I'm okay," I said softly. "We can talk when we get back to my desk."

"Okay." She kissed my head, and we separated, though she kept an arm around my shoulders as she smiled at Rose. "Hi, Rose. Good to see you."

Rose grinned. "Not as good as seeing Amry, I'm sure," she laughed. "How are you doing?"

"I'm good." She looked over her shoulder at the protesters. "Have they been behaving?"

"Up until this morning, yes," I said quietly.

Takoda frowned. I said, "Come on, let's go back to my desk. I'll tell you all about it while I pack my bag, and then you can walk out with me."

She studied my face for a few beats, then nodded, her expression concerned and serious. I stepped away and took her hand in my good one and led her back to my cubicle. She stood at the entrance, and I sat down, starting to shut down my laptop. I'd bring it home, though I doubted I would end up doing any work.

"So what happened?" she prompted.

I spoke slowly, trying to stay low-key, and told her what had happened that morning. I said, "They have my personal email address too. I got a couple of pretty angry emails today, and posts to my Facebook page. I screen-captured those, marked them to be reported, and saved the emails, but I didn't reply back to anything."

Takoda's frown deepened. "I don't like this at all, Am," she said.

I shivered, feeling sick to my stomach. "I have to admit I'm scared. I don't like that they know who I am. And I don't like not knowing how much more they know."

"You said that your boss reported it all to the police?"

"Yes. And I ended up talking to an officer over the phone, giving him my side of it. I talked to Charlie Eton too."

"Good." She moved to kneel beside me, resting a hand on my leg. "I won't lie to you. This makes me uneasy too." She glanced toward the doors, her dark eyes narrowing. "If they so much as look at you the wrong way when we leave I will personally start banging heads."

I muttered, "Then I hope they look the wrong way."

She grinned, dark and dangerous.

I finished packing my computer into my bag. "Ready to head out?"

"Absolutely. I parked just a couple cars down from you. I'll get you to your car and then follow you back to your place. For tonight, you can park in the lot next to me instead of in the underground garage so we can stay together." She took my jacket from where it hung on a hook beside her on the cube wall and held it out for me. I slid my good arm in, and shrugged the other half over my sling. She took my messenger bag from me and shouldered it.

We stopped to say goodbye to Rose.

I mentally braced myself as we stepped out the doors. Takoda's arm was firmly around my shoulders, her expression cold and hard. Most of the protesters moved out of our way. The woman from that morning, hissed, "Perverts, you're going to Hell! God hates gays! You'll get what's coming to you!"

I swallowed and looked down at my feet. I could feel the tension radiating off Takoda, but we walked through the group at a normal pace. The elevator came reasonably quickly, and we made our escape. The parking lot was quiet. Her Jeep was only a space away from my Forester. True to her word, she saw me to my car and put my bag in back for me. "Lock the doors," she cautioned.

By the time I had the car started, she was ready as well. She flashed her lights twice. I lifted a hand and led the way back to my apartment. In the parking lot closest to my building, I found two spots together and pulled in.

We walked across the tarmac together in the early darkness, holding hands. She'd shouldered both my messenger bag and her overnight duffel bag. I said, "I am so glad you're here."

"I know. I am too. It's crazy how much I miss you." She ducked down to drop a kiss on my cheek. I pulled us to a stop and turned my head, capturing her lips, intending a quick kiss, but the passion got away from us. Her tongue slipped between my lips, and I breathed her breath. Intoxicating desire burned in my veins. God, I wanted her. I wanted to feel her heat under my hands, and her body wrapped around mine.

I didn't see the man dart out from between the cars. I wasn't aware of anything until I heard him scream, "Dyke perverts!" I was roughly pushed from behind. I stumbled forward, trying to stop the fall with my left hand and mostly succeeding. I hit the ground on my knees and my left hand and rolled as I fell, coming up on my back, somehow managing not to impact my casted arm or my head.

Stunned with the jolting pain, I fought to get my breath. What the fuck?

I heard the grunts of fighting. *God, Koda!* I pushed myself up to see Takoda blocking a punch from a man in dark clothing. She swung back, connecting with his face, then grabbed him by the front of his jacket and slammed him onto the ground. He yelled, and she flipped him over onto his stomach, jamming her knee into his back, fighting to pin his arms over his head. He struggled, swearing at her, unintelligible. She worked to get her other leg over his, trying to trap him under her.

Groaning, I managed to sit up. I needed to get to her.

"Amry!"

"Here!"

"Call 911!"

I fumbled in my pocket for my phone, dropped it once because I was shaking so badly. Finally, I got it open and dialed 911, frantically describing to the dispatcher what was happening while Takoda struggled with the man under her.

I put the 911 operator on speakerphone, pushed awkwardly to my feet and stepped toward Takoda, letting her know she could talk to the 911 operator.

Takoda barked instructions and information at the dispatch operator. I provided the address and my phone number.

The man heaved himself over, kicking free of Takoda's hold, and started to scramble away. She grabbed at him, throwing herself forward and slamming her fist into the side of his face, bouncing his head off the ground with a sickening thump. She got him down on his stomach again and pulled one arm up behind his back until he screeched in pain.

"Are you all right?" the dispatch person yelled.

Takoda snapped, "Just get someone here."

Adrenaline pounded through my veins, and I felt helpless as hell. "Koda, can I help?"

She shook her head. "No, just stay back, please. Are you hurt?"

"I'm okay. Just got the wind knocked out of me."

Her assessing glance told me she didn't believe a word of it, but she was too busy to make a point of it. My job, for the moment was to remain on the phone with the 911 operator. After a couple endless minutes, sirens sounded, and three squads roared into the parking lot, piercing the darkness with flashing lights and deafening noise.

The officers spilled out with guns drawn. I held my hands up, scared shitless.

Takoda said clearly, "My badge is in my wallet. Back left pocket. None of us are armed. I am Lieutenant Takoda Running Bear, DNR. My friend was thrown to the ground, she may be injured."

One of the officers carefully removed Takoda's wallet from her back pocket. After a tense moment, he relaxed. "Lieutenant. Nice catch. I'm Officer Lee Parker." He gestured with one hand, and two officers stepped in, taking over the attacker from Takoda, who got to her feet in one graceful motion.

"Thanks, Parker."

He started to say something else, and she held up a hand. "Just a second." She walked past him to me. "Amry, I'm so sorry." She wrapped her arms around me. "That should never have happened. I should have known better. I'm sorry."

"Koda, no, it's not your fault." I whispered into the silkiness of her down jacket before tipping my head back to meet her dark, pained gaze. "Sweetheart, I'm all right. It's not your fault. Please." I reached up with my good hand and touched her cheek. "Please, don't blame yourself. I love you."

"I love you too." She held me tightly, tucked my head against her, and I held her back, wanting to reassure her. "Are you sure you're okay?"

As panic began to subside, I could feel the painful stinging in my hand and my knees. "Scraped up my hand and my knees, but I'll be all right."

I felt her lift her head. When she spoke, it was as a law enforcement officer. "I need to get Amry sitting. She took a fall, but she's also recovering from previous injuries and head trauma."

She guided me over to Parker's squad, where he'd opened the back door, and she had me sit down. "You sure you didn't hit your head?" she asked me quietly.

"I'm sure. Just scraped up a little."

She caught my left hand and turned it into the light. The palm was scraped and bleeding. She raised a brow.

Parker cleared his throat. "What happened?"

Takoda released my hand, setting it carefully on my lap, and straightened. "He came from between the cars. We didn't see him until he was on us. He yelled, called us perverts, threw Amry to the ground, then ran. I tackled him and held him until you got here."

"Any idea why he attacked you?" Parker asked.

I said, "He might be tied to the protesters at my office."

"Tell me about that."

I explained the situation at my work, and the incident from that morning, and we gave him our statements.

When we finally made it up to my apartment I was completely exhausted, and I think the adrenaline rush had left Takoda feeling much the same way. I changed out of my clothes, putting my now ripped jeans in the wash pile and pulling on a loose nightshirt. Takoda helped me clean up my hand and scraped knees.

After she finished cleaning and bandaging my palm, I sat on the edge of the bathtub and she knelt beside me with the first aid kit on the floor beside her. I turned on the faucet, adjusting the temperature.

"Are you going in to work tomorrow?" she asked.

I frowned, wincing as she sluiced my scraped and bloody knees with warm water. "I guess I will, yeah. I mean, I don't want them to think they won, you know?"

She sent me a quick grin. "You're a scrappy little thing, aren't you?"

"Not hardly. Just bullheaded like my dad. I'll just call when I get there and make sure there's someone there to walk me up."

"What time do you need to be to work?"

"I usually get there a little before seven. Ouch."

"Sorry."

"No worries." I grimaced as she gently scrubbed away any lingering dirt, knowing it was necessary. She used a plastic cup to pour water over the cuts, rinsing away any leftover soap and debris, then blotted my knees and legs dry with a hand towel.

"Swing around, and I'll put some bacitracin and gauze over those."

I did as asked.

She said, "If you're okay with going in a little early, I can follow you over and walk you up before I go to training."

"I'd like that, if you're all right with it."

She grinned. "It would be my pleasure."

* * *

When Takoda and I stepped off the elevator Friday morning, the hallway in front of my office was empty. I blew out a relieved breath. "Thank God, they're gone."

Takoda squeezed my shoulders. "I agree."

We stopped at the side of the doors. Takoda said, "I'll leave you here, then, and get going."

"Thanks for getting me here safely, and for last night."

"I wish I could stay longer."

I leaned up and kissed her softly. "You go out there and do good training, okay? And be safe driving."

"I will. Love you, Amry."

"Love you too."

She captured my lips in a hard, fast kiss, then stepped away. "Talk to you soon."

I watched until the elevator door shut, then slipped into the office. Looking around, I saw that a couple of the web guys were already there, and Andrew and Hayley. I headed to my desk to crank up my computer, got some coffee and was opening my in-box when Michael arrived.

"I am so glad they are finally freakin' gone," he said as he dropped his bag and hung his jacket over the back of his chair. "How are you doing this morning, Am?"

I looked over from my monitor and decided not to relate last night's events. I would tell Andrew and Hayley, because it could be related to the protesters, and I would tell Rose, but I didn't feel like dealing with everyone else's reactions. I was too wrung out. I said, "Doing all right. Glad it's Friday."

"Got plans for the weekend?"

"Not really, no. Try to catch up on my writing, if I can keep the headaches at bay, though it's usually better at home when I'm not pushing so hard."

His expression switched to concerned. "The headaches really aren't getting better, are they?"

"Some days are better than others. The doc said it could go on for another couple months. He extended my prescription for pain meds and told me to take a vacation." I snorted. "Like I have any extra vacation to take, you know?"

"I hear ya. Hang in there, girl, it's gonna get better."

"It will. I know. I'm being whiny."

His grin was teasing, "Yes, you're being whiny," he agreed.

I sighed but couldn't help smiling. "Thanks," I said. I took a swallow of coffee and turned back to my in-box. I eased my casted arm out of its sling and propped it on the edge of my desk to help reach the touch pad with my finger. I pecked left-handed at the keyboard, shooting off an email to Andrew and Hayley about the incident last night, answering a couple emails, and then opening the next story on my editing list.

A little later that morning Haley instant messaged me on my computer asking me to stop by her office when I had a chance. I told her I was on my way and crossed the room to her window office, rapping lightly on the doorframe. "Hey, what's up?" I asked.

She looked up from some paperwork, a thin smile lifting her lips. "Hi Amry. Come on in. Shut the door?"

I did as she asked, shutting the door gently behind me and sitting down at the worktable across from her desk. A sinking feeling settled in my stomach. Why did she want the door shut? What did I do? Was I just being paranoid? Maybe it was something to do with the protesters or a story she didn't want others to know about yet. I sucked in a slow breath and tried not to act as uneasy as I suddenly felt.

"How are you feeling?" she asked.

"Fine. How are you doing?"

"I'm well, thank you. But I'm concerned about you. I'm concerned about your productivity and how your injuries are affecting your work. I know it's not your fault. I wanted to check in, to see if there's anything I can do to help."

My stomach sunk even lower, and I felt sick. The dull ache behind my eyes started to ratchet up. What was I supposed to say to that? I must have looked as freaked out as I felt. Haley said, "I don't want you to feel attacked here. I just want to talk."

I swallowed. "I'm doing my best to work around things," I said, trying to keep my voice calm and even. What came out sounded defensive and worried. "I know I take a lot of breaks, but I've been staying later to make up for it. I log in from home too to finish up."

Hayley said, "You've been working hard, and I appreciate that. Do you need me to ask Alex if she can take on some additional editing to help cover you?"

All I could think of was that if Alex started taking on more of my work, I was on my way to losing my job. I shook my head. "No, I'm okay. I haven't missed any deadlines that I'm aware of."

She smiled. "No, you haven't. You're fine. Like I said, I just wanted to check in with you because I know you're struggling."

I couldn't help but feel this was a warning as much as concern. "If my work isn't up to expectations, let me know. I'm doing my best to keep up. I'm not as far ahead as I usually would be, but I'm making sure that things are getting done on time."

I met Haley's studied gaze, dark eyes that didn't miss a thing. She managed this company with the power of a general on the field of battle. She could be concerned and sympathetic, but she also had a ruthless business side I didn't want to be on the wrong side of.

She said, "I know you're working hard, Amry. As I said, I just wanted to touch base with you. If you need anything, please let me know, all right?"

"Sure. Thanks, boss." I stood, knowing the conversation was over, and eased out of the office.

"You can leave the door open."

I did, and walked back to my desk. I pushed my left hand into my jeans pocket, knowing it was shaking. Back at my desk, I forced myself to concentrate on my work, which lasted about an hour or so before my vision started blurring and my head started pounding. I took some Tylenol, closed my eyes for a few minutes, and hoped it would help. While I sat there staring at my eyelids and willing myself to relax so my headache would ease, I thought through my task list for the day. It was early enough in our publishing schedule that I wasn't behind in my work. I had some ad copy I needed to clean up, but that wouldn't take long.

After five or ten minutes, I opened my eyes, and the words on my monitor were clear again. I started pecking at the keyboard.

Saturday started with a migraine-sized headache and me staying in bed with the covers over my head until after lunchtime. I thought I slept part of the time. The rest of the time, I just laid there feeling sick and wishing the pounding would stop. When I finally got up, I took a hot shower, pulled on sweats and brought my coffee and a package of graham crackers to the sofa.

I'd wanted to work on writing today, but after a migraine, there was no way I was going to do anything that involved little letters. So I drank coffee and chewed graham crackers and gazed out the balcony window at traffic on the highway. At least it was a gray, sunless day, because I wasn't ready for that much brightness.

I checked my phone for messages, texts and emails. There was nothing I needed to deal with. Most importantly, no texts from Takoda or Nikko or any of my friends. I knew Takoda was working the overnight tonight and figured she was probably napping. I shot her a quick text to say hello, figuring she'd answer back when she woke up. I didn't want to wake her, and I knew that she put her phone on silent when she was working the overnight shifts.

She finally called late in the afternoon, sounding tired and subdued. "Amry, how are you?"

"Good. You sound wiped out, Koda."

"Yeah. Andersson woke me up early this morning. He said they broke up a big party out near the sand pits. Lots of high school kids. Lots of DUIs. One of the kids is having a tough time. They ended up getting a social worker involved, and set up a community service LGBTQ mentorship for them, and then assigned it to me, so that's going to be a lot of extra time for a while."

"What kind of community service will they be doing?" I asked.

"Um. I really can't say. I'm not supposed to talk about it."

Was it just me or had her voice sounded off? She'd never not talked about her kids before. Other than not telling me their full names, she'd told lots of stories about what kinds of issues she'd helped them with and the different community jobs and volunteer work they'd done. Maybe this was a special case for some reason. "No issues. I hope it goes okay."

"Thanks. I mean, eventually I'll be able to talk about it. Just not yet." There was a long pause, then, "Hey, speaking of kids, have you talked to Nikko at all?"

"No, not in a couple days. I was going to give him a call later. Why?"

"No reason, just curious."

We chatted a while longer, then Takoda signed off to get ready for work. I was left feeling out of sorts. Something about the way Takoda had avoided talking about the mentorship struck me as off, though I couldn't put a valid reason to it.

I sent Nikko a text but got no immediate response, so I put my phone aside and decided I would try to write for a while and see how long it took before the words blurred and started giving me a headache again.

* * *

Late Tuesday afternoon, I sat back from my computer with a suppressed groan. The words on the monitor had long since blurred, but I needed to get this feature story edited and back to Amy before the end of the day. I pulled off the prism glasses and rubbed at my eyes. I needed some water and more meds.

I pushed to my feet. The world lurched around me, and I sat back with a thump. My ears buzzed, and I closed my eyes against the dizziness. What the hell? I hadn't had a dizzy spell like this since before I'd come back to work.

"Hey, Am, you okay?"Michael's voice from his cube.

I opened my eyes slowly. "Just dizzy," I said, without raising my head.

When I did raise my head, the room spun around me. I snapped my eyes shut and swallowed down the nausea. Goddammit. I didn't need this. Not now. I had work to do.

I practiced breathing for a couple minutes, hoping the vertigo would settle and willing the pain in my head to subside as well. Then I tried opening my eyes. Gingerly, I raised my head, and the world only shifted a little bit, like I was drunk and light-headed. Okay. This was a little better. Maybe I had just gotten up too fast. I started to stand. My balance shifted wildly before I even straightened up, and I sat down hard and squeezed my eyes shut.

This was not good. I stayed sitting and squinted across at Michael. "Can you get me some water?" I asked quietly. My voice sounded hollow and buzzy in my head.

"Sure. Just sit tight."

"Thanks." What the hell was happening to me? I kept my head down. Michael returned with a coffee mug of water and held it out to me. I took it and sipped, then set it on the desk, all without lifting my head.

"Seriously, Amry, are you all right?"

Was I? "I'm not sure," I murmured. I needed to find my meds. In my bag. I leaned over to get my backpack from under my desk. This worked all right, and I didn't feel dizzy. I found the pill bottle and got it open, then shook two out onto the desk. I got the pills down with a couple swallows of water. I didn't think they'd do anything for the dizziness, but I hoped it would stave off the headache.

I sensed Michael standing beside me, and I thought I should probably say something to him. "I think I just need to sit a while."

"Okay, if you say so. You're looking pretty pale, Am."

I raised my head a little. I still felt light-headed and off, but the vertigo wasn't there. "I'll be okay. It'll pass. Thank you, Michael."

"Sure."

He returned to his desk, but I could feel his eyes on me. I wondered if Hayley was watching from her glass office. When in the hell was I going to get back to normal? I shifted slowly back to where I could see the monitor and try to work. I focused on the words, and they weren't as blurred as they had been. I closed my eyes and took a long, calming breath. I would see how far I could get. Maybe the headache would stay away long enough for me to finish this story.

I pushed through. My headache came back full force after about ten minutes, and I struggled to focus on the words. Looking down to the keyboard to see what I was typing and back to the monitor was making me dizzy in a drunken sort of way, and my stomach was starting to rebel. I worked slowly and took breaks and finally sent the edited piece back to Amy. It was six thirty, well past when I should have left.

A couple of the late-working web and sales guys were still in the office, and Hayley's office light was on. Michael had gone home a couple hours ago. I shut down my laptop and leaned my head back, trying to relax away the pain. I hadn't tried to get up since the incident earlier. But now I needed to get home.

I gripped the chair arm and started to stand. The world went sharply cockeyed, but I managed to sit without falling. Now what? I didn't want to ask Hayley for help. The nearest person I could call was Rose. I tried standing again, very slowly, and this time, though I was dizzy, I didn't feel like I was going to topple over. But I still wasn't in any shape to drive. My seasick pills were at home on the bathroom counter because I hadn't needed them in weeks.

Still standing, I reached for my phone and found Rose's number. She picked up after a couple rings.

"Hey. What's up?"

"I'm really sorry, Rose. I need a ride home. I'm all dizzy, and I'm afraid to drive. Are you able to come and save me? If you're busy, that's okay too. I can try Tashi and Kelly's." I felt like such a loser for having to call for help.

"Are you okay? I can be over there in about fifteen minutes."

"I'm okay. I mean, I'm standing up, which is good. I really, really appreciate this."

"I know you do. Do you need me to come up, or should I just wait down in front?"

"I'll make it down. Thanks, Rose. I owe you."

"Dinner at Don Pablo's, with drinks."

"Deal."

"I'll be there shortly."

I hung up and cautiously reached down for my backpack. The world only moved mildly. I packed my laptop, got my jacket on over my sling, shouldered my bag and started slowly through the office. I felt a little wobbly and off balance, but not to the point that I was in danger of falling. I concentrated on putting one foot in front of the other.

Hayley caught up to me as I reached the reception desk. "Amry, are you all right to drive?" she asked.

I managed a weak smile. "Rose is picking me up," I said.

Her dark eyes scanned me up and down. "If you need to take sick time, take it. You really don't look well."

"It comes and goes," I said.

"Today it was worse than usual." It was a statement of fact. She'd obviously been watching me. I felt my stomach drop, and not because I was dizzy.

I said carefully, "Today was hard, but I had work I needed to get done. I said I would do my work, and I will." I cringed inwardly at my defensive tone.

"If you don't feel a hundred percent tomorrow morning, stay home, Amry. If you need to work from home, that's fine too."

Her tone suggested I'd better not argue. "I have my laptop with me."

"Good. Now get going."

I didn't argue with her. She touched my arm and turned back toward her office. I made my way to the elevator, glad it was a slow one so my stomach wouldn't drop. Rose was already parked in front of the building when I pushed out the main doors. I climbed gratefully into her CRV. "Thanks, Rose."

"You know you can always call," she said. I heard the 'but' in her tone. "I know you don't want to hear it, but we've been worried about you all day."

I frowned. "But the only person I talked to was Michael."

"Who talked to me and probably half a dozen other people. I should have just dragged your stubborn ass home with me when I left."

I opened my mouth to argue with her, then closed it after realizing she was right. I was being stupid and bullheaded. I should have just been smart when I realized the dizziness had come back, and arranged to get a ride home instead of forcing myself to keep going. I sighed and looked down, embarrassed. Sometimes I got so caught up in my own head and my own issues, I didn't consider how it affected other people. "I'm sorry. You're right."

"It's okay, Amry."

"It's not, really."

"I didn't say it so you could beat yourself up. At least, not too much." She patted my leg. "Do you need to stop and pick up something to eat?"

"No, I've got plenty at home."

"Now you're just being a martyr."

"I'm honestly not hungry. My stomach is too twisty, and my head still hurts. I really just want to curl up and sleep for a while."

"Okay."

I said, "I'll probably work from home tomorrow. Hayley read me the riot act before I left."

Rose shook her head. "She has even less tact than I do."

Hayley was the boss. She didn't need to be tactful. "I just don't want to lose my job."

"She can't fire you when you're recovering from a major injury. You're doing as much as you can do."

"I hope it's enough."

"You're being paranoid."

"Probably."

Rose parked at my building and insisted on walking me up to my apartment. I felt a little steadier than I had earlier. She didn't stay once I got in the door. I thanked her again, and with a quick hug, she was on her way.

I left my jacket hanging by the door and my bag by the kitchen table. As I walked through the living room, I set the three-way floor lamp to its dimmest setting. I changed into sweats and thought about just going to bed but went back into the living room and got comfy lying on the sofa, pulling my favorite down throw over me.

My phone said it was a little after seven. I hadn't heard from Takoda all day. I debated calling her. Maybe she didn't want to talk to me. Maybe she was tired of me being injured and pathetic. Maybe she was tired and had gone to bed early. Or had other things to do. She did have a life and family.

I sent a text to Nikko to say hello and check in with him. He hadn't had much to say the last couple days either. I assumed that meant things were okay for him, and he was just busy with school. I knew they'd been doing baseball practice indoors for the fall, just to keep the team working.

Finally, I called Takoda. The call went to voice mail, and I left a brief message and hoped I didn't sound too needy or disappointed. I wasn't in a good space in my head, and it was obvious every time I opened my mouth. I set the phone on the coffee table within easy reach and closed my eyes. I was so damned tired.

"Hey, sorry I missed you earlier. Did I wake you up?" Takoda's voice was a welcome siren's song in my ear when she returned my call an hour or so later.

"Naw, I wasn't sleeping. Just lying around. How are you doing? How was your day?"

"Busy. I slept late, ran a ton of errands and did shopping, then I had my mentoring student. After that, I went up to my folks. Mom made soup and wanted me to come and get some. I haven't been over there in a while, and she needed an excuse to see me." I could hear the smile in her voice. I envied her relationship with her parents. "But enough about me, what about you?"

"Eh. Had a rough day to be honest. I think the dizziness is back again. Rose had to drive me home. I suppose I'll have to go and get my car some time tomorrow. Hayley is being all concerned about my health. But I think she's more worried about getting her money's worth out of me."

There was a pause. "That's a pretty dark interpretation. Maybe she really is just concerned."

"That's pretty much what Rose thinks."

Takoda's laugh was low and gentle and tickled my ear. "Rose is a smart woman. How's the head now?"

"Okay right now, because I'm just laying here on the couch. Did things go okay with your student?"

"Umm, yeah. It was pretty good." She paused, then changed the subject. "Do you have a rough day at work tomorrow? Is Rose driving you in?"

"I'm going to work from home. Maybe I just need a break. If I feel crappy in the morning, maybe I'll call in sick."

"I wish I was there to take care of you."

"I'm okay. Just tired."

"I'd share mom's soup with you. It's chicken noodle."

I laughed. She sounded so earnest. "And I know I'd love it too. You're sweet, Koda."

"Just overprotective when it comes to you."

"Hey, have you talked to Nikko lately? He's been quieter than usual. I haven't heard from him in a couple days." I knew they talked quite a bit. Maybe he was more comfortable talking to her, as a non-family member, if something was bothering him.

"No, he hasn't texted."

"Well, if he does, tell him to at least say hello to his favorite aunt."

She laughed. "Will do."

I called in sick the next day because I woke up with a headache. The dizziness and vertigo were back again too. I stumbled drunkenly to the bathroom, clinging to walls and the bathroom counter. I spent the next while emptying my stomach into the toilet. Definitely not an auspicious start to the day. I took my anti-nausea meds and painkillers and dragged myself back to bed, carrying my garbage can with me just in case.

Bethany texted to tell me Dad's house was going on the market the next day. The message was terse, and there was no reply when I thanked her for the heads-up. Bitch. I closed my eyes and said another silent good-bye to the house I'd known all my life. I'd done the same when I'd taken my things from it, but this seemed so much more final, and it made me sad.

And thinking of family made me remember that Thanksgiving was coming up, and with it the holiday season. And that made me feel even worse. I wouldn't be going to see Dad this year. Takoda had mentioned that I should come with her to her parents', but we really hadn't made any plans.

Nikko texted, but didn't have a lot to say. Just that he'd been "really busy" with "school and stuff." And he missed me. I texted back briefly. My head hurt too much, and I was still too dizzy to want to spend time squinting at words on a screen. I made a call to my doctor to ask if what I was experiencing were normal or if I should go in for an appointment. I hoped they'd call back soon with an answer.

Takoda checked in a few times to see how I was doing. Again, the exchanges were short, and I went back to sleep.

Thursday I worked from home, which let me take a lot of breaks. But I ended up able to get quite a bit of work done. Sitting comfortably on my sofa with my laptop, I didn't feel quite so anxious to make sure that I kept working. I didn't feel watched, and it was easier to sit back and close my eyes, giving myself the breaks I needed more frequently. I got through all my day's tasks before five o'clock, and I decided I would do the same on Friday.

Unfortunately, Friday didn't go as well. Maybe I was trying too hard to be productive and not taking enough breaks. Maybe it was the weather. But I was dizzy again, and my headache was back. I got sick when I got up to go to the bathroom. Weaving my way down the hall with the floor rolling under my feet, I barely made it to the toilet in time to lose my lunch, and huddled on the floor under a bath towel waiting for the anti-nausea pills to kick in.

When I was finally able to safely leave the bathroom, I gave up on work and napped on the sofa instead.

Nikko texted late Friday afternoon. I tried to be bright and upbeat.

Nikko: Hey, Aunti A

Me: Hi! How are you?

Nikko: Pretty good.

Me: How's stuff at home? Things going okay? Haven't heard much from you lately, a little worried…

Nikko: I'm good. Home is okay. I just avoid Dad. And I try not to say anything to piss him off…

Me: That's good.

Nikko: T-Bear said you've been feeling crappy.

Me: Yeah. Headaches and dizzy again.

Nikko: That sucks. Gotta go. My ride is here. TTYL

Me: Love ya, kiddo!

The conversation wasn't exceptional, except that when I talked to her later, Takoda said she hadn't talked to Nikko.

She called me that evening. I was tired and emotional and out of sorts, with a headache that just wouldn't let up. The conversation started out fine but crashed and burned from there.

"Nikko finally texted me today," I said.

"Oh, that's good. How is he?"

"He seemed okay. Did you talk with him?"

"Not lately."

I frowned. "Seriously?"

Her reply was quick and even. "Yeah. I haven't talked to him."

I felt the anger and panic crash over me in a wall of emotion that I couldn't stop or control. Suddenly I couldn't think past the alarms ringing in my head. I could only see that Takoda was hiding something, and all the fears and pain I thought I'd buried with my last relationship crashed over me like a tsunami. "Don't lie to me!" I shouted.

Takoda protested, "I'm not...I can't—"

"He told me he talked to you!"

"I can't discuss it, Amry. I'm sorry."

"He's my nephew! I thought you trusted me!"

"I do trust you—"

"No! You're lying, Takoda! The same way Susan lied to me. Until even the truths were twisted and manipulated, and by the time she was done I didn't know what was real. I can't do this again."

"Amry, please, let me—"

"I can't. I just can't." I ended the call and flung the phone across the room. It bounced off the dining room wall with a heavy *thunk* and landed somewhere behind the kitchen table.

Fat tears rolled down my face, and I fought to breathe past the iron bands of steel constricting my chest. Takoda had lied about Nikko. What else had she lied about?

My old fears twisted around my brain, blocking out everything but the panic. Susan had fucked me over so badly that by the time she was done, I couldn't tell truth from lies. I never knew if I should take her at face value or search for the real meaning behind the words. If I were wrong, I was belittled, maligned and made to feel like it was my fault, again, that she was angry. She'd trapped me into her manipulated world and it took me a long time to see what was happening and longer to find my way out. I couldn't handle Takoda being the same way.

I sobbed until I had no more tears. How had I read this so wrong? How had I read her so wrong? How could this hurt so damned much? It felt like my heart had been ripped from my chest. I curled into a tight ball on the sofa and couldn't bring myself to do anything but sink deeper into sadness.

I didn't turn my phone on all day Saturday. I stayed in bed half the day and on the couch the other half. Most of the time I was either crying or on the verge of tears. I couldn't eat. In my head, I just kept going over and over my disastrous relationship with Susan and all the lies that had broken me. I tried to find the same pattern with Takoda and couldn't. It didn't change the fact that she'd deliberately lied to me about Nikko, but I couldn't break out of the illogical train of thought that convinced me it was Susan all over again.

When Sunday afternoon rolled around, I was tired of being sad and miserable. I made myself shower and drink some coffee and eat some toast, and felt more myself. I didn't feel so fuzzy-headed, and the darkness in my thoughts seemed to lift. It helped that the headache and dizziness had dissipated as well.

I found my phone on the floor where it'd landed. The screen was intact. It wouldn't turn on, so I brought it to the kitchen to plug it in and was relieved when the little charging symbol flashed on the screen. Apparently, sixty bucks for the unbreakable case was worth the money.

I left it to charge and took my coffee to the living room. I needed to think. I played my conversation with Takoda back in my head, but unlike before, it occurred to me that I may have overreacted. She'd tried to explain, but I hadn't let her speak. What if there'd been a valid reason for her behavior? This was Takoda, after all, and not Susan. And Takoda, as far as I had ever been able to tell, was honest to a fault. Yes, she lied. But why?

When I went to check my phone, it had charged at least enough to turn it on. I took the phone and charger back to the sofa with me and stared at it a while. I wasn't sure that I wanted to turn it on. I was still hurt by Takoda's betrayal. But the anger and mind-numbing pain from the day before had eased. I was willing to talk to her, if she'd tried to call. Maybe Nikko had texted as well.

I powered up the phone.

Four voice mails and ten messages.

I went to voice mail first. One from Rose. Three from Takoda. Rose's was short and sweet. *How are you doing? Call me if you need anything.* I'd call her back later. My finger was shaking as I hit play on Takoda's messages.

"Amry, please, call me back. This isn't what you think. Please."

"Amry, I'm really sorry. Can we talk about this? Please. I made a promise to Nikko not to say anything to you. Please, call me back. I love you."

"*Zaagi'idiwin*, it's Sunday morning. I know you must be feeling hurt and angry, but I honestly believe we can talk this out. I didn't mean to hurt you. I totally screwed up. I miss you. Please, call me. I don't want to lose you."

Tears rolled down my cheeks. What the hell had I done? I squeezed my eyes shut.

Shaking, I hit callback.

Takoda picked up after barely half a ring. "Amry?"

Then we were both crying and talking at once. "Koda, I'm so sorry."

"I'm sorry!"

When we'd both calmed down enough to talk, Takoda asked, "Can I go first?"

I agreed, and she took a breath.

"Nikko is the student I've been mentoring. He was at the party last weekend and got charged with underage drinking. While he was being held, he was still really drunk, but he started talking about just wanting to die, and that he'd hoped he could drink himself to death. He was, incidentally, well on his way. Instead of charges, they decided it would be better for him to do some community service, get some help from a mentor and a therapist. He was really upset, and ashamed, and scared, and he didn't want to tell you what had happened. He asked me to promise not to say anything to you, and that's why I lied. I'm really sorry. I shouldn't have made that promise to him. Under the circumstances, it was a bad call on my part."

I closed my eyes with a sigh, letting the tension seep out of me. Takoda was helping Nikko. And she made a promise intended to make him feel safer. I fucked up. God. I was such an emotional basket case lately. And I was in the wrong, not Koda. "I'm sorry too, really I am. I'm sorry I got so freaked out. In the frame of mind I was in, all I could think of was where I'd been, and I couldn't break out of it. And I understand you making that promise to him."

"It scared me that you got so angry. You've never done that before."

Now that I could stand back a little bit and see it, my reaction scared me too, and I wondered how much it had to do with my head injury. "Maybe I need to get in to see the doctor again."

"It couldn't hurt."

"Does Nikko know that I know?"

"I didn't want to say anything to him until I talked to you first. I thought, also, maybe sometime we could talk more about what happened with you and Susan. I want to understand."

"Yeah. We should talk about Susan."

"Another time. Not now."

"What are you going to tell Nikko?"

"I think I'll just tell him the truth and apologize to him for breaking his confidence. I think he'll understand. And I think I can convince him that you don't think any worse of him for what happened."

I swallowed, feeling terrible that Nikko was getting caught between us. "If it would help, you can let him know that I understand his sadness. I never told him that I take meds for depression, and that I've seen a therapist too, over the years. I never shared any of that with my family. But you can share it with him."

"Thank you. That's the kind of information he needs to hear, so he understands he's not alone. Can I tell him you're willing to talk about it with him?"

"You can, sure."

"Are we okay, Amry? Are you okay?"

I closed my eyes. The weight had lifted from my shoulders. "We're okay. And I think I'm okay too. Are you?"

"I am now, yes."

"I miss you."

"I miss you too."

CHAPTER NINETEEN

Life progressed on a more even keel after that. I worked from home at least a couple days a week. A visit to the doctor and another MRI assured me that my head was healing, and that the concussion symptoms I was having, which probably included the bouts of depression and strong emotion, would diminish over time. He reminded me to listen to my body and rest instead of just pushing through the pain. Following those orders, the dizziness subsided a lot, and my headaches seemed to be getting less frequent and less severe as well. Takoda invited me to spend Thanksgiving with her and her family, and despite some anxiety over the official 'meeting the parents', I readily agreed. I couldn't wait to see her again.

On Thanksgiving morning I left the city around seven. By eleven, feeling tired, stiff and nursing a headache, I found myself parked across the street from my parents' home with the car idling.

A red-and-white For Sale sign stuck out of the snow blanketing the front yard. The lower part of the sign bore the realtor's name and swung in the steady north wind. The house crouched silent and dark under the winter sunshine. I felt the pressure of tears behind my eyes.

The car windows started to fog up. I turned up the defrost and rubbed my jacket sleeve over the side window to clear it. I missed my parents. But more than anything, I missed having a family to be part of. And I didn't understand why. Perhaps it was simply the idea of family that was so appealing.

I shook myself. I'd seen what I came to see. Awkwardly, with my cast out of its sling, I jammed the car into gear.

I was fifteen minutes away from my true family. I ached to see Takoda. Even though we talked and texted every day, the nights alone were endless. My apartment was too quiet. I missed her presence. I missed her warmth. I missed her kisses and her hands on my body. I dreamed of making love to her, holding her and touching her. I woke up in the morning reaching out to her, sorely disappointed when she wasn't there.

I maneuvered my car down the rutted, snow-covered back roads to Takoda's house, wishing I could go faster, driving white-knuckled with my left hand and doing my best to support the effort with my casted right one. I had a pounding headache by the time I reached Takoda's place.

The door to the house opened before I even turned off the car. The dogs raced down the stairs from the deck, barking excitedly. Takoda, in a T-shirt, sweats and snow boots, followed them at a jog.

A sense of relief settled over my heart. She drew me out of the car and into a tight embrace. Laughing, I wrapped my good arm around her and we held each other while the wind picked at our hair and clothes. I stepped back, "You're gonna freeze out here!"

She laughed. "Naw." We kissed and she patted my butt. "Get in the house. I'll grab your stuff."

"I can help."

She handed me the lightest of my three bags while she shouldered my backpack and duffel. We hurried into the house, kicking off boots and shoes in the mudroom. While Takoda set my bags at the bottom of the stairs to the loft, I knelt on the kitchen floor to hug and pet the dogs, letting them give me kisses while I ruffled their thick fur.

Takoda returned and held a hand out. "C'mere," she invited. I took her hand and got to my feet with a groan, feeling the dull pull in my side. Eagerly, I leaned up as she bent her head and captured my lips with her own. For several minutes, I drowned in wonderful passion, my good hand twisted in her hair, my casted arm trapped safely between us. She tasted of coffee and when I breathed in her scent, it was the warm, musky, sunlight smell of her skin and the freshness of clean laundry. When we parted, I rested my head against her shoulder.

"I missed you so much," I said.

Her breath ruffled my hair. "I missed you too. I missed this." She rocked us gently as we held each other.

"Me too."

Gabby stood up on her back paws and pushed her cold wet nose between us.

Takoda laughed. "Come on, I'll get us some coffee. Go get comfy on the sofa. We don't have to be over at my parents' for dinner until four."

I crossed into the living room and eased down onto the sofa, leaning my head back on the cushions and hoping to relax away the dull ache behind my eyes and the tension squeezing my shoulders up into my neck.

Xena shambled over and rested her broad head in my lap, gazing at me with clear blue eyes. I scratched her absently.

Takoda handed me a mug with a ceramic cover and sat down beside me. She put her feet up on the coffee table and slipped one arm around my shoulders while she held her coffee mug with her other hand.

"You doing okay?" she asked.

"Just tired." I sipped the coffee, set the mug on the end table, then sighed and closed my eyes. "I stopped at my dad's house. I needed to see the For Sale sign."

Her hand tightened on my shoulder. "That must have been hard."

"Yeah."

She set her coffee aside, then wrapped me in her arms. "Then I'll have to hold you until you feel better."

I cuddled against her. "I feel better already."

A few hours later, we made the drive to Takoda's parents'. Takoda manhandled the big four-door Wrangler as we bounced up the long drive to their house. The tires squeaked on the packed and rutted snow, and the dogs shuffled excitedly in the backseat. She parked in front of a prefab steel barn with blue-gray panels.

A weathered, two-story farmhouse with white-painted shakes and blue-gray trim sat tucked back into the pines. A wide porch ran the length of the front of the house.

Two big white-and-gray dogs raced toward us from behind the house, kicking up snow, barking and howling. From the back seat, Gabby and Xena barked back, Xena scrabbling excitedly at the window.

Takoda growled, "Goddamned crazy huskies," then commanded sharply, "Hey! Xena, Gabby! Quiet! Sit!"

Her dogs settled a bit. Takoda got out of the Jeep and was nearly bowled over by the other dogs' exuberance. "Wheelie, Tiger! Off! Sit!" She grabbed them by their collars, forcing them to stay still.

The two huskies finally settled down but wound excitedly around her legs when she released them. I clambered out of the Jeep, and they turned their slightly downgraded exuberance on me.

"Hey guys." I patted their furry heads, and they jumped on me despite Takoda yanking them down by their collars. They were big and overly excited, but not scary. She finally got them to sit.

She said, "The taller, lighter one is Wheelie. This is Tiger. Dad needs to teach them some damned manners. They're littermates, and only a year and a half old, so they're still nuts." She released them, then reached behind and opened the back door of the Jeep. Gabby and Xena launched themselves at their playmates. The four dogs roughhoused and chased each other gleefully and noisily around the yard.

Takoda took my hand. "Let's go in. They'll be out here burning off energy for a while."

We followed the shoveled path to the mudroom on the side of the house. Three wooden stairs led up to the landing. Takoda opened the screen door, then shouldered open the heavy door into the mudroom. We hung our jackets on two of the many mismatched hooks set at various heights on the wall, and our boots joined those already resting in the plastic boot mats in front of the heater.

Takoda opened the inner door into a brightly lit country-style kitchen that smelled heavenly.

"Takoda! Amry! You made it!"

The petite woman at the stove turned, wiping her hands on an autumn-themed apron. Takoda's mother was nothing like I had expected. Bright green eyes twinkled in a pixie-like face, and her smile lit up the room. Graying reddish-brown hair hung in a thick braid down her narrow back. She held out her arms, and Takoda enveloped her in a hug. My girlfriend towered over her mother by nearly a foot.

"Hi Mom."

"Welcome, girls." She released her daughter and strode over to me, pulling me into a hug as well. "Amry, honey, you must be tired from the drive. How were the roads? There's coffee on. Please have some."

Her warmth and enthusiasm were infectious, and I grinned in return. "Mrs. Running Bear, thank you so much for having me."

"Just Celine, please. No formalities in this house. I am so happy to finally meet you. You're all my Little Bear can talk about."

"Jesus, Mom. Is Dad around?"

"In the living room. I think there's football on already. And George just called. He and Maddie and CJ will be here in about fifteen minutes with your grandparents."

I asked, "Can we help with anything?"

Celine made shooing motions with her hands. "I've got it. You girls get some coffee and sit with John. Or there's pop in the fridge too."

Takoda put an arm around my waist. "Let's go meet my dad, then I'll get us coffee."

We crossed through the kitchen into the living room. The fireplace blazed cheerfully at the far end with two La-Z-Boys facing it. The flat screen television hung just to my left on the wall between the living room and the kitchen and John Running Bear relaxed on the comfortably worn couch facing the TV, his feet propped on a well-used leather ottoman. He had the same bronze complexion and black hair as Takoda, wide cheekbones and piercing dark eyes.

He swung his slippered feet to the floor, standing and smiling broadly. "Hello girls."

"Hey Dad." He hugged Takoda, then turned his attention to me. I held my good hand out.

"Hello, Mr. Running Bear," I said. "It's great to meet you."

He laughed. "Call me John." He clasped my hand with both of his. "It's good to meet you, Amry. Takoda speaks well of you. I'm very sorry for the loss of your father."

"Thank you."

Takoda gave a quick squeeze around my waist. "Go sit down, Am. I'll get us some coffee."

"Thanks." I settled on the love seat.

John used the remote to mute the television as he seated himself. "I'm glad you joined us today," he said.

"Thank you for inviting me. This is really nice." I wasn't sure what else to say, but fortunately Takoda returned with our coffee. She handed one to me and set the other on the end table.

"Dad, do you need a warm-up?"

"No, I'm good."

Takoda nodded toward the TV as she sat down beside me. "Who's playing?"

John shrugged. "It's a college game so I wasn't really paying attention. Green Bay plays tonight. How were the roads, Amry?"

"There were a few icy patches on highway fifty-three, but mostly the roads were clear."

"That's good. Sounds like the weather should hold out all weekend."

"Spoken like a true meteorologist," Takoda teased him. Outside the dogs started barking. "George must be here."

I knew from prior discussions that George was her older brother.

A couple minutes later, we heard a ruckus of doors opening and closing from the kitchen. A small, high voice screeched, "Gwamma! We here!"

Takoda and John jumped up and headed for the kitchen. I eased to my feet, following and stopping to lean against the painted woodwork of the kitchen entry to watch.

Takoda scooped up her four-year-old niece, CJ, who giggled riotously when Koda swung her around in the air. "Hey, kiddo! How's my favorite girl?"

"Hi Aunnie Koda!"

"You're getting so big! You're almost taller than me!"

"Am not! Siwwy!"

Takoda laughed, and I couldn't help but smile to see her in this different role. "Let's get your jacket off, Munchkin." Takoda set CJ on her feet and unzipped her pink down parka, revealing jeans and a purple sweatshirt with pink hearts and a unicorn. The girl's shiny black hair hung past her shoulders, tied into two braids with pink bows. She was absolutely adorable.

Takoda hung the jacket in the mudroom, then picked CJ up and carried her over to me. "CJ, this is my friend Amry. Amry, this is CJ."

"Hi CJ."

Takoda prompted, "Can you say hi to Amry?"

She thought about it a second, then studied me with big brown eyes and said clearly, "Hi Amwy."

Damn, how cute was that? "I'm glad to meet you, CJ."

A man about Takoda's age strode up to us, roughly giving Takoda a one-armed hug. His hair was light brown and on the shaggy side. Wide-set eyes twinkled green. "Hey, little sis."

"Hiya, Georgie. I'd hug ya back, but my hands are kinda full."

He patted her on the back. "Yeah, yeah."

John said, "Where's my granddaughter? I haven't gotten my hug yet!"

CJ giggled. "I'm wight here, Gwampa!" She reached out her arms, and he caught her as she wriggled from Takoda's hold.

Takoda put her arm around my waist. "George, this is Amry Marasich. Amry, my brother George."

I held out my good hand, not sure if this were a handshake thing or a hugging thing. My small hand virtually disappeared in George's firm grip. "Amry, it's good to finally meet you."

"You too, George."

"This is my wife, Maddie Little Wolf," he added as a full-figured woman in jeans and a flannel crossed the kitchen to join us. Her dark shoulder-length hair was tucked behind her ears and her smile was wide and welcoming.

"Hi Maddie."

"Hello Amry." She gave Takoda a quick hug. "You need to visit the Rez once in a while, little sister," she chided with a grin.

"Yeah, yeah, I know. Things have been kind of hectic lately. How've you been?"

"Same as always. Holiday season, so the kids are getting wild."

Takoda explained, "Maddie and George teach at the Rez school."

"No matter what anyone says, teaching has to be the toughest job out there," I said.

"Especially when the kids are bouncing off the walls," Maddie agreed.

Takoda guided me further into the kitchen to meet her grandparents, who stood near the stove speaking with her mother. Slightly stooped with age, her grandfather held himself with a proud bearing. His long, braided hair was mostly white, his complexion ruddy and lined with life. He gave Takoda a hard hug before Takoda wrapped her grandmother in a tight embrace. The solidly built older woman's gray hair fell in a careful tail down her back, and she wore a brightly patterned housedress over jeans. A black knitted shawl covered her shoulders and suede fur-lined house boots warmed her feet.

Releasing her grandmother, Takoda said, "Amry, these are my grandparents, Daniel and Katherine Running Bear."

"Ah, I finally get to meet your Amry." Katherine took both my hands in hers. There was deceptive strength in her arthritic grip. She held my gaze for a long moment, and I wondered if she could see right through to my soul. "You are as beautiful inside as outside, child."

I swallowed and stammered, "Um...thank you. It's a pleasure to meet you."

She patted my hands and turned her gaze up to Takoda. "And you, Little Bear, are more beautiful every time I see you."

Takoda blushed, and I had to bite my lip not to giggle.

Daniel Running Bear had been assessing me with a piercing gaze while I greeted his wife. I said to him, "It's good to meet you, Mr. Running Bear."

He spoke very formally, "Pleased to meet you, Amry. Welcome to my son's home."

I smiled, not quite sure what to make of the greeting. "Thank you, sir, I'm glad to meet you too."

Takoda shook her head and smiled. "Granddad, quit giving her a hard time. He's really an old softy. He just pretends to be an uptight Indian elder."

Katherine chortled. "She knows you too well, Daniel."

His eyes twinkled with a teasing smile.

We loitered in the kitchen until Celine and Katherine shooed us out. Takoda and I returned to our places on the love seat. Maddie and George turned the La-Z-Boys near the fireplace to face the rest of the room while Grandfather sat on the sofa beside his son.

Maddie told us about school and her "kids," and asked Takoda and I about our work. CJ ran upstairs and returned carrying a floppy, care-worn timber wolf. She settled herself on Takoda's lap, clutching the toy and watching me. I smiled at her, and she giggled and ducked her head further into Koda's shoulder.

We all conversed amicably until it was time to set the table for dinner. Everyone helped with either setting the table or carrying out serving plates and bowls, which were simply passed around once we were all seated.

Dinner was casual, and the food tasted phenomenal. It reminded me of Thanksgiving with my own family when I'd been very young, before the relationships between the twins and I had gotten overtly antagonistic, and before I'd come out. After that, I'd always felt a stilted undertone. I had been careful of what I said, what I revealed. With Takoda and her family, even though I hardly knew them, I didn't feel the need to censor my words or opinions. I could be me.

As the mashed sweet potatoes were passed around the table for seconds, Takoda scooped another helping onto my plate. "You doing okay?" she asked softly, for my ears only.

"I'm having fun," I said, realizing there was a ball of happiness warming my chest.

I carefully passed the sweet potatoes to Grandma Katherine on my left. Animated conversations continued through dinner, ranging from sports to state, national and reservation politics, relatives, friends, jobs and CJ's latest antics. I was included in the discussions as though I'd been part of the family for years.

The discussions of Native American politics fascinated me. I'd done some research, trying to get a better understanding of Takoda's ancestry and background, but the websites weren't nearly as informative as listening to Takoda's family discussion.

Toward the end of the meal, conversation was interrupted by a tentative knocking on the front door. The dogs raced, barking, to the entryway.

"Who in the world could that be?" Celine asked.

John got to his feet, quieting the dogs as he unlocked and opened the door. After a few moments, he moved aside, allowing a bundled-up figure to step into the room.

I recognized Nikko almost immediately and jumped to my feet, rushing across the room.

"Nikko, what happened?"

A dark, reddened bruise stained the side of his face. My heart pounded as dreadful thoughts whipped through my brain.

"It's okay, Aunt Amry," he said. His voice sounded rough, and he cleared his throat, seeming embarrassed and uncertain.

I gave him a quick hug. "Are you all right? Nikko, what happened?"

"They're just—Sometimes I really hate them. There was a huge fight. Dad hit me."

"Oh, honey. I am so sorry."

He focused past my shoulder to where Takoda and John stood behind us. "Can I stay here for a while? I didn't know where else to go." His expression was desperately hopeful and sad.

John said, "You're always welcome in our home. Come on, we're still having dinner. Takoda can get you a plate."

Takoda rested a hand on Nikko's arm. "Hey, Little Brother. You sure you're okay?"

His hazel eyes teared. "I'm good, thanks, T-bear. Thanks for letting me stay. It really means a lot."

"Let me introduce you around," she said, leading him with an arm around his shoulders.

I sent John a grateful smile. "Thank you."

"Not a problem. I'll go get another chair."

I followed Takoda and Nikko into the dining room while John went to get another folding chair. Before I took my seat, I sent Darlene a text to let her know where Nikko was and that he was okay. I had no idea how he'd found John and Celine's house. He knew we were going to be with Takoda's family, so he must have looked them up on the web or something. Maybe he'd gotten their address from Takoda at some point. In any case, I was glad he trusted me and Takoda enough to come to us when he needed someone.

Celine filled a plate and set it in front of Nikko, assuring him that he'd feel better if he ate and that there was plenty left for seconds. With no more ado than that, Nikko was welcomed into the fold, and dinner continued with another family member at the table.

As we finished eating, Takoda's father stood up, silencing the conversations. "Every year, we take time on the Thanksgiving holiday to count the good things we have. It's easy to focus on the hardships and our frustrations and anger. But that's not healthy or helpful. So we go around the table, and each of us shares at least one positive thing that's happened in the past year. I'm thankful for my family and that we're able to share this day with Amry and Nikko, whom we welcome with open arms." He sat down.

Across from me, at the edge of the table on John's left, Nikko stood up. "I, um, just wanted to thank you again for letting me be here." His expression faltered, and I thought he was going to cry, but he swallowed hard and added, "You're good people. Thanks for not turning me away."

I felt the pressure of tears behind my eyes and wished I could wrap Nikko in my arms.

George spoke next, and we went around the table. When it was my turn, Takoda rested a hand on my arm, rubbing it softly, almost absently, as she held my gaze with a beseeching intensity. "Let me go first, please?" she asked.

I wondered what she was thinking, but acquiesced, trusting her implicitly. "Sure."

She placed a chaste kiss on my cheek as she stood, squaring her shoulders as she gazed around the table, then focused her dark eyes on me. "I've had a lot to be thankful for this year. But the best, most wonderful thing to come into my life is Amry. She makes me smile, she completes me and I am very grateful and blessed to have her in my life."

I knew I had a silly, love-lost grin pasted on my face. Takoda's smile was blinding, and she laid her hand on my shoulder. I rested my hand on hers, needing to connect. For a few heartbeats, the rest of the room went away as we shared a myriad of emotions between us. I recognized the love in her dark eyes and hoped mine reflected the same.

Someone cleared their throat, and the spell was broken amidst gentle laughter.

I swallowed and stood as Takoda took her seat, taking the time to try to organize my scattered thoughts. "I'm grateful to share this meal with all of you and grateful that we could include Nikko when he needed the comfort of family and friends. It means more than I can say. You've all been so welcoming. And

Takoda. She's the best thing that's ever happened to me, and I don't know how I'd have survived the last few months without her." I looked down because I could feel the tears stinging my eyes. I didn't want to cry like a baby in front of everyone. But my throat ached, and the emotions I'd been holding back all day were starting to break free. I sniffled, and when the tears rolled down my cheeks, Takoda took my hand in hers. "Thank you," I whispered, and dropped weak-kneed into my seat.

"You're family," she murmured into my ear. "I love you."

I couldn't stop crying, but it was okay.

Everyone helped clear the table, including little CJ. Celine and Katherine pushed the men into the living room to watch football. Takoda and I washed and dried dishes while the others dealt with leftovers and put clean implements away. Afterward, we joined the men in the living room with coffee.

I wanted to take Nikko aside and ask what had happened at Bethany's house, but there wasn't an opportunity. I finally decided that it didn't matter as long as he was okay. Darlene had texted that Nikko should come home when he was ready, and that Tom wouldn't be there.

Even though I wasn't with my own family, there was more love and acceptance in Celine and John's house than I'd felt in a very long time. It hurt more than I wanted to admit.

CHAPTER TWENTY

The morning after Thanksgiving, I felt like I'd been run over by a truck. My nose was plugged, my chest was tight, my throat hurt and my head pounded like someone was using a jackhammer on my skull. Lying in bed, I could hear Takoda and the dogs moving around downstairs. I wanted to roll over and go back to sleep, but I had to pee and the sun glaring through the stained-glass windows sent colorful—and painful—patterns of light across the bed. I squinted at the clock. The oversized green numbers read 10:42 a.m.

Groaning, I forced myself out of bed. After a stop in the bathroom, I eased into sweats and a sweatshirt and shoved my feet into fleece booties. I trudged down the stairs, clinging tiredly to the heavy pine railing and grateful that despite the headache and being unable to breathe at least I wasn't dizzy.

Takoda greeted me from the kitchen table where she sat with the morning newspaper. "Morning, sunshine."

"Morning." My voice came out somewhere between a croak and a wheeze.

Takoda was on her feet in a second, her bright smile now a concerned frown. "Honey, you sound awful."

"No, really?" My voice cracked. "I feel awful too."

"Come and sit down. I'll get you some coffee. Or would you rather have tea?"

"Coffee's good." I coughed into the crook of my arm as I crossed to the dining room and sat down.

She put her hand on my forehead. "You don't feel overly warm."

I snuffled. "Thanks, doc."

She patted my shoulder and got my coffee then set it in front of me. "You want some toast or something?"

I shook my head. "No, this is good."

I wrapped my fingers around the warmed mug and sipped the hot liquid, smiling when I realized she'd doctored it up with sweetener and cream the way I liked it.

"I've got some of that cold and flu stuff you add to hot water. It usually works for me."

"Great."

She placed the front page of the *Duluth Tribune* in front of me. "I'll be right back."

The lead picture was of rabid Black Friday shoppers from the previous night. I could not fathom why anyone would want to shop with vicious crowds at midnight on Thanksgiving. I slumped in the chair. All I wanted to do was go back to bed.

Xena nosed my cast with a soft *whuff*. I let my arm rest on her furry back while I scratched her neck and behind her ears.

Takoda returned. "Are you sleeping?"

"Not yet."

"I'll heat up some water."

The hot chamomile-lemon-flavored cold and flu remedy tasted okay, and I hoped it would work. After I made a stop in the main floor bathroom, I joined Takoda in the living room, where she'd built a fire. As I stretched out on the couch, she put a pillow under my head and tucked a pile of blankets around me.

Xena jumped up and stretched out along my legs while Gabby sprawled on the floor in front of the hearth. Takoda settled in her reading chair with her feet up. Within minutes, sleep claimed me.

Sometime later, I jerked awake to the dogs barking wildly, and loud, insistent pounding on the front door.

Takoda was on her feet, stalking toward the entryway. "What the fuck?"

I sat up too quickly and the room spun. I groaned and started coughing.

A muffled voice yelled, "Amry! Get out here! Amry!"

"That's Tom." I rasped. What the hell was he doing here?

Takoda stopped in midstride and turned back toward me, her lips a thin tight line. When the pounding continued, she walked purposefully through the kitchen, grabbed her cell from the counter and crossed to the mudroom.

I frowned as I watched her remove her service pistol from the safe on the shelf. She checked the gun and shoved it into the back of her pants, then grabbed a pair of handcuffs and pushed those into her back pocket.

Another round of pounding started.

Fear twisted my stomach, and I wasn't sure if it was fear of Tom or fear of the gun in the back of Takoda's jeans. "What's that for?" I choked.

Gabby howled.

"I don't trust him." Takoda put a hand in front of the dogs. "Quiet. Enough. Sit."

The dogs sat a half-step behind her. I could see their wary tension in the muscles twitching under their fur. Takoda was a picture of calm.

She unlatched the front door and jerked it open. Standing tall and straight, one hand firmly holding the door, she seemed bigger than life, her solid form mostly blocking Tom from my view. The low, warning tones of her voice rumbled in her chest. "Can I help you with something?"

"Where's Amry?"

"What do you want?"

Tom shifted, and she moved in front of him. "Fucking Indian bitch, get out of my way!"

"I don't think so."

I stood, wavering and light-headed, took a step forward and managed to get the words out loud enough to be heard. "What do you want, Tom?"

"What do I want? Goddamnit! You ruined my kid! You ruined my marriage! Dragged the family name into the mud! Fucking dyke! You ruined my life!" He tried to shoulder his way into the house, and Takoda blocked him with a stiff arm.

I should have been scared. I should have felt something, but I was seeing gray dots in front of my eyes and having a hard time focusing. I mumbled, "I didn't do anything."

He screamed at me, "It's your fault! Yours! You destroyed my family!" He lurched forward. His eyes were wild, his hair uncombed and clothes rumpled.

I stumbled backward onto the sofa as Takoda grabbed him by the shoulders and spun him away from the door. "Enough," she barked. "Time for you to leave."

He tried to fight and she twisted his arm roughly behind his back and pushed him further onto the porch. "Out."

"I'm not done!"

"You can walk away on your own or I can cuff you and call the cops. Your choice."

"Fuck you!" he screamed, struggling.

The glass-paned screen door slammed shut behind them, and I watched Takoda force him down the porch steps.

I could hear their voices as they moved out of my line of sight, Takoda's quietly commanding tones and Tom's nearly hysterical yelling. I sat nervously clutching the blanket that had fallen aside, watching the door.

It finally got quiet and Takoda returned. She knelt in front of me and cupped my cheek. "Are you okay?"

I took a breath and nodded slowly, leaning into the contact. "Yeah."

She handed me a glass of water from the coffee table. "Drink some."

I did as instructed and returned the glass unsteadily. Takoda swung my legs up onto the sofa with an easy movement and readjusted the blankets over me. "I cuffed him, and he's sitting in the truck bed. I need go back out and keep an eye on him. I called the sheriff to send someone to come and get him. I won't file any charges, but I'm pretty sure he's been drinking and I don't want him on the road. They'll likely send someone to get his truck later."

I nodded. I wasn't sure what this meant, but I knew it wasn't likely that Tom would ever speak to me again. "I'm sorry," I whispered.

She ran her fingers through my hair. "Not your fault, sweetheart. It's okay. I love you." She motioned to the dogs. "Come."

They moved to sit beside us, and she motioned them down. "Stay. Watch." She said to me, "I'll be in as soon as I can, okay? Just rest."

She hurried back outside, grabbing a jacket from a hook on the wall before closing the door firmly behind her. I wanted to get up and follow. I wanted to be with her. I didn't want my idiot brother to hurt her. My stomach twisted sickly, and though I knew it was illogical, I felt like it was my fault. The rift between my brother and me had widened immeasurably, and it wasn't likely that it could be bridged. Bethany, surely, would take Tom's side. The complete alienation of my family that I'd feared had surely come to pass, and it saddened me more than I wanted it to.

I tried to tell myself it was just as well, it was meant to be. It wasn't my fault that they were intolerant, angry bigots. I'd tried for so long to keep some semblance of peace between us. I'd held my personal life separate from them for years, hiding my true self in the city and pretending it didn't matter. I'd tried to meet them halfway, silently suffering their disdain because they were my family.

I had to admit now that it had been for nothing. So much wasted energy. It made me want to cry for the foolish hopes I'd held. I swallowed the tears and closed my eyes, listening for voices outside. Eventually, I dozed off, waking again to the sound of tires crunching on gravel and ice and the rumble of a vehicle pulling into the driveway.

Fifteen minutes later the vehicle left and Takoda returned. She hung her jacket, locked away her gun and the handcuffs and came to sit on the edge of the couch beside me.

She rested a hand on my forehead. "I think you're getting a fever."

"Just tired."

She took her cell from her back pocket. "I'm going to call Darlene. I'll put it on speaker. I want to make sure her and the boys are okay."

I heard the tones of her phone dialing and then Darlene picked up. "Hello?"

"Darlene, this is Takoda. Amry's here with me too."

"Hi. What's up?"

"We wanted to see if you guys were all right. Tom came to the door yelling at Amry. He's agitated and has been drinking. I had one of my buddies from the sheriff's department pick him up so he wouldn't be driving. There won't be any charges, but they'll hold him until he's sober enough to leave. And they'll be sending a tow for his truck."

"Hang on." There was a long pause. "Sorry. I didn't want to talk with Joey here. I'm sorry about Tom. We haven't seen him since he took off last night. I'm not sure where he's been staying. Thanks again for taking care of Nikko."

"Not a problem. He's welcome at my place or my parents' any time. You and Joey too, if you need a place to go."

"Again, thank you."

I said hoarsely, "What happened last night?"

"Was that Amry?"

"Yeah. She woke up with no voice, all congested and aching."

"Flu's been going around."

"So you and the boys are okay? Amry asked what happened last night. Nikko didn't say, and we didn't want to push him."

"We're fine. Things got a little ugly. Stephanie asked where Aunt Amry and Aunt Takoda were. Bethany had a fit. Steph would have let it go, I think, but Nikko was in a mood, and he made a snide comment about people not being welcome in a so-called Christian home. So Bethany got on her high horse. I was trying to defuse the whole thing, but Nikko flew off the handle and started yelling and Tom slapped him. Nikk grabbed his jacket and left. Stephanie was hysterical. Bethany threw Tom out of the house for hitting Nikko."

Takoda blew out a breath. "Look, I don't want to alarm you, but have you thought about what might happen when Tom gets home?"

"He's not normally a violent man."

"Unfortunately, this isn't a normal situation. I can't tell you what to do, but my suggestion would be to call a locksmith right now and get the locks on the house changed. I'll text you the number of a guy who will do emergency calls. Tom was threatening and angry when he showed up here, and not likely to be reasonable."

There was a long silence on Darlene's end.

I said, "We want you and the boys to be safe, Dar."

"I know. This has been coming for a long time. I'll call as soon as I get off the phone."

Takoda said, "I'm really sorry."

"I know. Thank you for the heads-up."

"Call or text us and let us know how you're doing or if you need anything, okay?"

"I will. I'll talk to you later."

Darlene rang off, and Takoda rested her elbows on her knees with a sigh.

I said, "This sucks."

"Yeah, it does."

* * *

Even though I slept most of the day, by evening I was running a high fever, had the chills and was coughing up a lung. When I was feeling no better Saturday, Takoda called her mom for advice, and Celine showed up with homemade chicken soup. Sunday, Takoda took me to Urgent Care where they gave me antivirals, a flu shot and a recommendation to rest, rest and rest. With barely enough energy to stay awake for more than a couple hours at a time, there was no way in hell I was going to drive back to the city or go to work on Monday.

Breaking the news to my boss was not a comfortable conversation. For one thing, my voice kept cracking and dropping out while I tried to explain. Hayley's very stilted tones suggested she was less than happy about me being out of work again. I wasn't happy either, but what could I do?

I didn't return to the city and to work until a full week later. I wasn't at one hundred percent, but I was vertical and could function for most of the day before I crashed and burned.

While I slowly recuperated from the latest strain of influenza, the world kept turning and Christmas was around the proverbial corner. In the office, everyone was either excited about the holiday season or bitching about it. I did my best to stay afloat with my work. I was getting things done, but I still tired easily, fighting my headaches—which weren't as bad as they had been—and trying to ignore a lingering cough. Mentally, I shifted between being depressed about my family and the coming holiday and missing Takoda.

I slumped in my desk chair, focused on editing a story, perversely annoyed by this writer's sloppy grammar. I was about to flip to the online style manual to check something when Hayley messaged me through the computer to stop by her office. I saved my updates and groaned as I pushed to my feet.

I crossed the office and leaned on her doorframe. "What's up?"

She gestured me into the small room with its frosted glass interior windows and view of the parking lot. "Grab a chair and shut the door," she said.

Her tone made me blink. Frowning, I closed the door and sat down in one of the two chairs at the worktable in front of her desk. I wondered if this was going to be a rerun of our last closed-door conversation, or if this one would be even worse.

Her dark eyes studied me intently, and I got the sense that whatever she was thinking, it wasn't good. "How are you holding up, Amry?"

"I'm fine. You know. Lots to do, trying to get it done."

"You're struggling," she said flatly.

Anger flashed through me. "Wouldn't you be?"

She raised an annoyed brow.

I took a breath and rubbed my face with my hands. "Sorry. Yes, I'm struggling."

"I know you are, because half the time you're here, your head's somewhere else. You're getting your work done, but you haven't really been with us in almost three months, Amry."

I couldn't argue with that. It was true. I'd been preoccupied and overwrought since my father died in September. Between grief, anger at my sibs, healing from my bike accident and then being sicker than a dog, I was still working on what seemed to be an endless cycle of recovery. "I'm doing my best. Things will settle down after the holidays."

"Will they? When are you going to make the move up there permanently, Amry?"

"What?" That came out of left field.

"Come on, don't bullshit me. You can't tell me you're not planning on moving up north to be with your lady love."

"Hayley, honestly, we have never discussed the possibility. Why would I move up north? My life is here. My job is here."

"And your girlfriend is not."

Well, damn. Fear crawled into my stomach and twisted it into a painful knot. I ran my hand through my hair. I didn't want to say the words, but they tumbled out anyway. "Are you firing me?"

"I'm not firing you. But I'm telling you I need you to focus and get your head back in the game. If you're staying, I need you back full time. If you're not staying, I need you to let me know."

I sat there, blindsided, struggling to process the thinly veiled threat. "I'm not leaving. I'm not going anywhere," I said. I could feel the emotional tsunami rising, the tears at the back of my throat, the darkness starting to close in. "I'm doing my best. I really am." I was not going to cry, goddammit.

Hayley said gently, "I know you're trying. As your friend, I really do understand, and I'm trying to give you time and space. Unfortunately, I also have a magazine to run, and I have to keep that in mind as well. I'm sorry."

I nodded. I couldn't speak. Tears blurred my vision, and I wiped angrily at my eyes with the sleeve of my sweatshirt.

"Take the rest of the day off, Amry. Go think about things. Give yourself some time. We'll start fresh tomorrow."

I bolted out of her office and went to my desk. Michael gave me a worried frown as I grabbed my backpack and my jacket, but I shook my head and rushed out into the hallway.

Rose caught me waiting impatiently at the elevator.

"Amry, what happened?"

"It's okay. I just need to get some air."

"If she fired you, I am going to kick her bony little ass."

"I'm not fired. It's okay, Rose, honest. I'm just having a tough day. Should have taken more happy meds this morning or something."

The elevator pinged and opened. I stepped inside. Rose held the door open. "You'd better call me if you need anything. I'm serious."

"I will."

I glanced up in time to see the very concerned expression on her face as the door closed between us. I wanted to sink down to the floor, curl up and go away. Instead I pulled on my jacket and managed to drive myself back to my apartment.

I fumbled open the apartment door and dumped my things on the floor as I stepped inside. When I reached the sofa, tears were streaming down my cheeks. A dark wall of emotion crashed over me. I hurt. I felt helpless and lost and vulnerable. I curled up on the couch, drew a quilt over my head and huddled beneath it. I wanted to disappear. I knew it wouldn't help me solve anything. I knew this wasn't the end of the world. But it felt like it.

I hid in my cocoon until the need to use the bathroom forced me to move. I glanced at the clock on the bathroom wall. Takoda was likely heading home from work. I picked up my phone and sat on the sofa, trying to decide whether to call her.

It rang in my hand, and I fumbled in surprise before I could answer it.

"Koda?"

"Hi."

Hearing her voice soothed away some of the darkness. "Hey."

"Are you okay?"

"Not really, no." I felt the tears start again.

"Amry, what happened?"

I sniffled and told her about my talk with Hayley. I told her Hayley was pissed about me being so out of it and mentally absent. I didn't mention Hayley thought I would be moving. "I'm trying, really I am. I didn't think things were so bad. I know I've been distracted, but…"

There was a long silence. I wondered if Takoda had finally decided to give up on me. She asked gently, "Do you want to keep working for the magazine?"

"It's my job. I don't want to find something new. I like it there. But I don't know how to get focused. I told her things would be better after the holidays."

"Maybe you just need a break."

The concern in her voice broke my heart. "I don't need a break. Hayley thinks I'm going to quit and move in with you, and that I'm already gone." The words tumbled out before I could think to stop them.

I heard her breathing. I swallowed hard into the silence.

"Is that such a horrible thing, that you'd want to move in with me?" The hurt in her tone made the tears run all the faster down my face.

"It's not horrible. It hurts to be apart from you. But we never talked about it."

"You could, you know. Move in with me. You could even quit your job and just do your writing and editing until you found something here."

"I am not going to freeload off you." My need for independence reared its head. I could take care of myself. I needed to. I'd been doing it since I was eighteen.

"You wouldn't be freeloading. It would be temporary. You need time to recover and grieve, Amry. You haven't done that and it's tearing you apart."

"I can't quit my job. Christ—I have bills to pay. Besides, I left the Iron Range for a reason. My home is here." I stopped short as the statement cut me straight through the heart. I heard her quick intake of breath.

There was another very long silence. Fuck.

"Reasons change, Amry. You can't live in the past."

"I'm not ready yet." I felt out of control, mentally clinging to the rocks in the rapids, terrified of drowning. Everything I'd counted on all my life was in flux or simply gone. And maybe now I would lose Koda too. Oh, God, I couldn't handle that. "Please don't hate me."

"Never that. Never. I'll wait for you. I'm here. I'll always be here. I want you to be happy."

I choked on a sob. "I love you. I love you so much it hurts all the time when we're apart."

"I love you too."

We listened to each other breathing. My head pounded. Reasons change. Did I still have a reason to be here in the city? Was Takoda reason enough to be in northern Minnesota after so many years of staying away? Did this apartment even feel like home anymore?

"It'll be okay," she promised. "We'll work it out."

"We will," I whispered. "We will."

Two days later, I hurried into the office a little before ten a.m., waving my now cast-free right arm at Rose as I passed the reception desk. I ducked through to my cubicle, flipping on my PC before I slipped out of my backpack and jacket. I dropped into my chair and logged in, relishing the ability to type freely again.

Michael said, "Hey, lemme see the hand."

I raised my right arm up. The skin was pasty white and wasted of muscle. "It looks weird, but it feels okay." I opened my email program, letting it load. "Did I miss anything?"

"Not yet. We're meeting this afternoon for a status with the writers. Other than that, just whatever's in your in-box."

"Good. I've got some ad copy that's due tomorrow."

He nodded. "I sent you a feature outline from Missy. Take a look at it and make notes for the meeting. I think she has some good ideas, but it might be a little too broad."

I nodded and turned back to my computer. After the talk with Haley two days ago, things had been low-key. Other than a couple passing greetings and a short planning meeting with the editorial group, I hadn't talked to her, and that was fine with me.

Takoda and I hadn't had any further discussion about me moving in, though I continued ruminating over the possible consequences and options. The more I thought about it, more reasons got populated into my 'why to move' column while fewer stayed in my 'stay where I am' column. Meanwhile, I worked hard to stay focused on work and keep my job, which got easier as we got busier, scrambling to get the pre-Christmas edition completed. We all worked late hours.

I didn't even have time to worry about Christmas shopping until the weekend before Christmas. I had found Takoda a couple cool odds and ends of outdoor gear at REI when I'd been there with Rose, but that wasn't going to cut it.

I found myself wandering through stores at Southdale Mall late on Saturday night when a bracelet caught my eye. It was a men's bracelet, but when I saw it, I immediately thought of Takoda. The chain was comprised of heavy, brushed silver rings, flat and utilitarian, with a narrow bar that could be engraved. She didn't wear jewelry often, but she had another heavy chain bracelet I'd seen her wear off and on. I had her name engraved on the front and on the inside I had them write "Love You Forever, Amry."

I wandered the mall until I'd found a couple more presents for Takoda, and something for all my nieces and nephews and for Takoda's family. It was hard not buying anything for my dad. I would see things as I wandered through the stores, thinking, "Dad would really like that." Each time, it slapped me in the face, and I'd stand there for a few seconds, letting the sadness wash through me.

I didn't buy presents for the twins, but I found a pretty wool scarf I knew Darlene would like. It was odd how she'd become more my sister than Bethany ever had been. Takoda and I had made tentative plans to get together with her and Nikko and Joey over the holiday.

The Christmas edition of the magazine went out late on December twenty-second, and Hayley kicked us all out of the office at noon on the twenty-third. I was relieved and excited to get out of town early and head up to Takoda's.

Since my sweet forestry officer was working, I decided to stop at Bethany's with presents for Stephanie and the boys. I wasn't sure what kind of reception I'd get, but I knew, no matter what, it was important that the kids—especially Stephanie—understood I hadn't forgotten them.

I parked in front of Bethany's house about four thirty. Festive red-and-green Christmas lights outlined each window, the front door and the eaves. A lighted, life-sized manger took center stage on the front lawn, complete with Joseph, Mary, Baby Jesus, two lambs and a donkey. The front bay window framed a Christmas tree adorned in a sea of white lights.

I retrieved the red plastic bag filled with brightly wrapped gifts from the back of my car, plodded up the driveway to the side door, and rang the bell.

Theo answered the door. "Hi Aunt Amry." He moved back and I stepped into the entryway.

Bethany came through the kitchen. "Who's—" she stopped as she saw me, and her expression shifted from curious and smiling to angry. "Amry."

"I have presents for the kids. I just wanted to drop them off."

"You didn't need to buy them anything."

Theo glanced from his mom to me, clearly not sure what to do or say. I handed him the sack full of gifts. "These are for you and Peter and Stephanie, from me," I said. It was probably wrong of me to bypass Bethany and give the gifts to him, but I didn't care.

"Thanks, Aunt Amry! Mom, can I put them under the tree?"

She frowned but nodded. "Yes, you may."

He rushed off. I shuffled my feet. "Well, I guess I'll get going."

"Auntie Amry!" Stephanie barreled through the kitchen and threw herself at me, wrapping her arms around my waist. "Merry Christmas, Auntie Amry!"

I hugged her. "Merry Christmas, sweetie."

"I made cookies! Do you want some? They're frosted! And you can come and see the tree!" She took my hand, but I didn't move.

"I'm sorry, honey, I can't stay. I have to go, okay?"

"But why?" She frowned. "Mom, can Amry stay for cookies?" Bethany's expression was stern and angry.

I said, "I have to meet Takoda for dinner, Steph, so I can't stay." I gave my niece another tight hug. "Merry Christmas, kiddo. Remember, I love you no matter what, okay?"

She hugged me back. "I love you too," she said.

I patted her on the head, then turned and let myself out. When I reached my car, tears were freezing on my cheeks. When I drove away, I could see Theo and Stephanie in the window by the tree. I hoped they would like their presents. And I hoped someday my niece would understand why she wasn't going to see much of her Auntie Amry any time soon.

Takoda was still at work when I got to her place. The dogs greeted me jubilantly at the mudroom door and I let them out while I unloaded my car, making a few trips to bring everything into the utility space. Once I had everything, including Xena and Gabby, inside, I toed off my boots, hung my jacket and locked the outer door behind me.

Walking into the kitchen, what hit me first was the smell of fresh pine. A towering seven-foot spruce stood proudly to the side of the fireplace, naked and undecorated. The dogs moved around me, nudging me for attention. I doled out pets while I brought my backpack into the dining room area and then carried my duffel upstairs. While I was up there, I changed into fleece lounge pants, one of Takoda's sweatshirts and a pair of slipper socks.

Then I went to the kitchen and cranked up the coffeepot. I was chilled, and caffeine was never a bad thing. I moved the bags of presents out of the mudroom and set them aside in the dining room, and was pouring my coffee when Takoda arrived.

"Honey, I'm home!" she called from the front entry.

"Good timing! Coffee's on!"

She rushed into the kitchen, skidding across the tile in her socks, and wrapped her arms around me. "Hi," she said.

I tugged her down for a kiss. "Hi," I said, when we'd caught our breath.

We held each other for a few more minutes, then she reached behind me and picked up my coffee cup, taking a slurping sip. "Mmm, good."

"Get your own."

"Hey, did ya see the tree? D'ya like it?"

"It's perfect."

She grinned like a schoolkid. "I found it in the woods near Mom and Dad's. I don't have anything to put on it, though. I've never had a tree here before. I thought we could run into town. Walmart's open twenty-four-seven. We can pick up some decorations, then come back here and put on a pizza. We can even watch Christmas videos."

I clapped my hands, feeling lighter than I had in months. A breath of Christmas spirit touched me.

She exclaimed, "Look! You have two arms again!" She took both my hands and kissed both sets of knuckles.

I wrapped both arms around her tightly and squeezed.

"That's much better for hanging ornaments," she decided. "Come on, let's go shopping!"

I laughed. "I need to change clothes," I protested.

She gestured down at her own uniform. "Me too."

Takoda grabbed my hand and led me upstairs. Changing clothes involved a lot of kissing and touching and escalated into both of us getting naked and me pushing Koda onto the bed. Straddling her body, I leaned over her, attempting to kiss her senseless. I ran my hands up and down her sides, teased at her breasts. It was so much better having both hands available. She felt so good.

The next thing I knew she'd reversed our positions, pinning me down with her weight, her hair falling over us, brushing my face. I could feel the liquid heat of her against my skin, igniting desire that flared through my blood. I leaned up to catch a hard nipple in my mouth and suckled it, loving the way she gasped and moaned.

She slid down my stomach, leaving a wet trail, and I had to release her breast. She kissed me hard and deep. Her hands were everywhere, touching and teasing until every nerve in my body was so hypersensitive I thought I might burst. She settled over me, her fingers finally going where I wanted her most. "Koda, please."

She kissed me again, moving her tongue against mine in rhythm with her fingers as she thrust inside. I moaned against her lips and fumbled to get my hand between her legs, to feel her heat. She drew back, gasping as I entered her. Hot, slick, swollen walls clamped around my fingers. I reveled in the feel of her as we thrust and moved against each other. My orgasm rose quickly and screamed through me as she rubbed her thumb hard against my clit.

I returned the favor, bringing her with me. We collapsed into each other, gasping and panting in a tangle of limbs.

"God, Amry, that was amazing."

I could only nod against her chest.

We held each other for a long time. I think we'd both needed the connection badly. Needed to reconfirm what we shared.

Downstairs, one of the dogs scratched at the back door and barked.

Takoda sighed and rolled onto her back. "There's a mood-killer," she muttered.

I laughed. "Guess it's a good thing the store's open all night, huh?"

"We'd better get dressed, then. We have a tree to decorate." She sat up and swung her legs over the side of the bed. I ogled her nakedness for a few moments before I huffed and sat up as well. We dressed and headed downstairs where the dogs were waiting to go out.

Takoda and I had great fun picking out a mismatched selection of shiny glass ornaments and more multicolored LED lights than we probably needed. Fortunately, Takoda felt about lights the way I did—the more the merrier. We got tinsel, a lighted star for the top and a red tree skirt.

When we returned to Takoda's I put a frozen pizza in the oven while she started a fire in the fireplace. We decorated our tree, and I lost myself in the excitement, simply enjoying the moment. We ate pizza as we put the finishing touches on our gaudy, well-lit masterpiece, then settled on the sofa, basking in the Christmas lights.

Takoda stretched out on the couch, and I mostly lay on top of her. She had one arm wrapped around me, rubbing slow patterns on my back. "You doing okay?" she asked.

"Yeah. This is perfect. Thank you for getting the tree."

"I wanted to have something special for us."

"It's very special." I leaned up and kissed her lightly on the jaw.

She smiled. "You're very special."

"So are you."

She leered wickedly. "You ready to go up to bed? I think we could pick up where we left off earlier."

Despite my exhaustion, a wave of desire washed over me. "Absolutely," I agreed.

CHAPTER TWENTY-ONE

Christmas Eve greeted us with low-hanging clouds threatening snow later in the day. We slept in late and lounged around with breakfast and coffee. We planned to head over to Takoda's folks' house around lunchtime and visit for a while, then have the evening for ourselves. At midnight, we would exchange our presents to each other.

We left the dogs safe and warm at home when we went to Takoda's parents'. Celine got us settled in the living room and brought coffee spiked with chocolate shavings and a plate of Christmas cookies. John sat in his recliner reading the morning paper. Takoda grabbed a couple sections and brought them to where we sat on the sofa. I curled into the far corner nearest the fireplace where a fire already blazed strongly.

I wasn't sure if it was the dark, dreary weather or knowing it was the first Christmas without my dad and the rest of my family, but as I sipped my coffee, I felt a bout of the Christmas blues settle over me.

My heart still ached at the loss of my dad. His jovial laughter and teasing echoed in my mind. He always said Christmas was for the children and he spoiled us, and then his grandchildren, with toys and love and attention. I missed how he'd always seemed so pleased that I stayed with him at the house, sleeping in my old room over the holidays. I missed his smiles and the way the skin around his eyes had crinkled when he was joking around. I missed Mom too, despite our issues. She'd loved me, in her way, even if she'd never approved of my life. And it saddened me that I wouldn't see Stephanie's joy as she opened her gifts.

I studied the varied array of ornaments on the Christmas tree in the corner of the Running Bears' living room, and recognized the pall of depression dulling the sparkle I should have felt on Christmas Eve.

I'd been fine waking up this morning with Takoda, but my mood had shifted and now I felt the pressure of tears behind my eyes and the tightness of sobs trapped in my chest. Movement at the entry to the living room caught my eye. Celine watched me with her hands in the pockets of her fleece vest. Her expression was kind and sympathetic, and I blinked back tears.

She crossed the room and rested a hand on my shoulder. "It will get easier," she said.

I glanced up. "I hope so. Doesn't feel like it right now, though."

"It never does. Is my Little Bear taking good care of you?"

I smiled then. I couldn't help it. "Yes, she is. She takes very good care of me."

Celine patted my leg. "Good. You're good for each other. She won't ever admit it, but she needs you as much as you need her."

Takoda lowered the paper and gave her mother a warning look. "Mom, honestly."

Celine laughed and shrugged innocently.

John said, "You should hear her and your grandmother talk about the two of you. Your ears would be red."

I stifled a half-hysterical giggle.

Takoda said, "I think my elders should mind their own business."

John snorted. "Since when is your life not our business? Turn on the TV, I think the Vikings game is starting."

"Football? On Christmas Eve?" Takoda complained, but she grabbed the remote to turn on the TV, then tossed it to her father. "You can find the channel yourself."

Celine shook her head. "I need to call your grandmother." She disappeared into the kitchen, and I heard her talking quietly on the phone while she puttered about.

Takoda laid a hand on my knee and set the paper aside. Our legs touched, and I leaned against her. It didn't even occur to me not to. She kissed the side of my head and asked, "You doing okay?"

"Yeah. Mostly. Comes and goes, you know?"

"I know."

We sat quietly. Takoda had half an eye on the football game as she continued to flip through the paper. John turned the recliner so he could see the television. Celine joined us, settling on the other recliner with a basket of knitting to work on something bright pink and purple. When she caught me watching, she said, "It's going to be a sweater for CJ. She picked out the colors."

"CJ's a lucky kid," I said.

Celine smiled and went back to her knitting. Takoda and I hung out for a while longer and had chicken and wild rice casserole for lunch. The snow started coming down shortly after, and we decided to get home before it started in earnest.

When we got back to Takoda's everything was covered in fat, wet flakes and accumulating fast. The highway had been slick, and I was relieved to be off the treacherous single lane. At least we had the back roads to ourselves, and the gravel under the snow gave the Jeep some traction.

We let the dogs out when we got home, and they decided to continue chasing each other into the woods while we headed inside. Takoda left the doggie door into the mudroom open.

I rekindled the fire we'd banked while Takoda turned the tree lights on.

"Still up for movies?" she asked.

"Sure." I hoped the familiar Christmas shows would help me retrieve my Christmas spirit, though my mood had improved over the course of the afternoon.

"I'm going to make some hot chocolate," Takoda said. "You want that or coffee or tea?"

"Hot chocolate sounds great. I'll change into my jammies and get comfortable."

"I'll be right behind you."

We called the dogs back in, dried them off and got comfortable, cuddling on the sofa with steaming hot chocolate and marshmallows. I threw my old comforter over us because I can't watch movies without a blanket. Sighing contentedly, I felt most of my tension and sadness melt away. *I could get used to this.* The best place in the world was curled up at Takoda's side.

Takoda checked the television schedule, and we figured if we timed it right, we could watch *White Christmas* after our videos, which would take us to midnight when we would do our gift exchange.

As the final credits rolled on Bing Crosby and company, we put the dogs out one more time and shut off the television. I turned out the lights, leaving only the cheerful flickering of the fire and the glow of the Christmas tree.

We sat cross-legged, facing each other in front of the tree with our presents between us.

Takoda said, "I get to give you one first."

I never argued about presents. She reached for a shirt-sized box covered with bright cartoon teddy bears wearing winter hats and mittens. I studied it, checking for weight, shaking it to see if it rattled or made any noise.

Takoda blew out an impatient breath. "Just open it!"

I gleefully tore off the paper and opened the box to reveal a pair of thick red slipper socks with leather soles. "Perfect!"

"Your feet are always cold."

"Thank you! Okay, your turn." I passed her a palm-sized box wrapped in gold foil.

She ripped into it without bothering to try to figure out what it was. "Oh, cool!"

I'd gotten her a new Swiss Army knife because she'd lost her good one in the woods somewhere. I'd even had it engraved, so the animals could return it if she lost it again.

We did a couple more fun, small presents—a sweatshirt for me that said "Up North" across the front, a new pair of flannel-lined jeans for her.

Finally, there were only two small boxes left between us. Takoda said, "I want to save yours for last, okay?"

"Sure." I handed her the box from me.

She attacked this box more slowly, carefully removing the paper and opening the flat rectangular box. The stainless-steel bracelet gleamed in the light of the tree, flashing color. Takoda beamed. She picked it up, running her fingers over the shiny links and her engraved name. "It's beautiful."

"Flip it over."

She was silent as she read the words, but her smile widened into a joyous expression. "Amry, it's wonderful. It's perfect, just like you. Help me put it on."

I wrapped the cool metal around her right wrist. It fit nicely, tight enough not to be a bother but loose enough to move. "I'm never going to take it off." She leaned forward and kissed me. "Thank you."

"You're welcome."

She put a small box in my hands, then held my fingers closed over it for a second before letting go and sitting back.

I eased the metallic-green paper off the box and opened the cover. Inside was another box. A red velvet ring box. My hands shook as I opened it to reveal a thin silver band tied into a complicated Celtic knot with a small blue stone at the center. "Koda, it's beautiful."

I took it carefully from its pillow, turning it in my fingers. The inside was engraved, and I held it close to a tree light to read it. "My heart, T."

Tears welled in my eyes. Takoda took my left hand and slid it on my ring finger. "It's a promise," she said. "I know I'm probably rushing things. I know that this probably isn't the best timing. But I love you. I love being with you. I love everything about you. And I feel so empty when you leave. So I wanted you to have this, to have me with you always. And I wanted to ask if you would marry me and be with me forever. And you don't have to answer right now. Or tomorrow. Just, when you're ready. If you're ready. But I have to ask."

Her earnestness and anxiousness was written in her expression. Love sparkled in her eyes, and I threw my arms around her. My heart knew my answer, even if my head didn't. "Yes," I whispered. "Yes, I want to be with you and marry you, and somehow I know we can make it work. I love you too, Takoda Running Bear, and I always will."

There wasn't a lot to say after that, and honestly, words weren't necessary. I shut down the clamoring part of my brain that didn't know how in the hell I was going to make this work and let my heart lead me forward. We made love on the comforter in front of the Christmas tree, by the light of the fire and the twinkle of tiny glass bulbs.

The howl of wind and the slap of snow whipping against the house brought me out my dreams and into the heat of Takoda's sleeping embrace. I lay curled on my side with Takoda spooned around me, one arm wrapped possessively around my hips. Her breath puffed lightly against my hair. I thought of last night's loving and shivered at the tingling passion that shot up and down my body. God, what she did to me. And what I could do to her. I felt the pulse of desire and wondered at how easily it came.

I blinked in the dim morning light and squinted toward the stained-glass windows at the front of the A-frame. Through the muted colors, I could see the gray and white of clouds and the swirling snow of a stormy Christmas morning. I smiled, knowing that the best Christmas present ever slept beside me. I snuggled further under the blankets and closer to Takoda. She murmured and slid a leg over mine, wrapping her arm tighter. Sighing, I closed my eyes and slipped back into sleep.

It was still early when we woke again. Takoda quickly put the dogs out and fed them before returning to bed. We spent the rest of the morning cuddling and slowly making love. The snow stopped, though the wind still gusted against the house. If we didn't need to snow-blow and shovel our way out of the house and down the driveway, we'd likely have stayed in bed well into the afternoon.

After a very late breakfast, we bundled up and tackled the drifting snow. I shoveled off the deck and attacked the narrow front walk while Takoda cleared the driveway and the back walk using a four-wheeler with a plow attachment. Two hours later, we came in and warmed up with coffee and Christmas cookies. Takoda started a fresh fire, and we got comfortable on the sofa with our feet up on the coffee table, watching the flames and relaxing. We talked a little, but mostly cuddled in comfortable silence.

I kept touching my new ring, twisting it around my finger, feeling the texture of the finely looped Celtic knot under my fingertips. The ring changed everything. It gave me a future I'd never believed could be a possibility. For today, I didn't want to think past how wonderful I felt right at this moment. I didn't want to think about the logistics or the decisions I needed to make to move in with Takoda and to marry her. I simply wanted to live in the moment and bask in the love and joy. I loved Takoda, Takoda loved me and we were going to be together forever.

As the flames flickered, I thought of my parents. I wondered if they were watching their children. Were they disappointed in us? Angry? Hurt? Part of me felt like I'd failed them. Tom, Bethany and I were no longer a family. I could have stopped it from happening. I could have hidden my relationship with Takoda. I could have done what I always do and continued to live two lives. But I didn't. Was that a failure or a victory for me? How could it be a victory when it put an end to being a family?

But had we been a real family? We had played our roles. I had played the good, normal daughter. But had I been happy? No, not really.

Was I happy now?

Yes. I was over-the-moon in love, and my heart sang with the thought of her.

Even so, I grieved the loss of my parents. I grieved the loss of family, though it hadn't been perfect.

The dichotomy of the situation had me reeling from one end of the emotional spectrum to the other. I cuddled closer to

Takoda, where her strength and love could help me push away the darker thoughts.

Around three o'clock, we got the dogs in the Jeep with us and started the slow trek to Takoda's parents for Christmas dinner. The gravel roads weren't fully plowed, but in the thickly forested areas, the snow hadn't drifted as much and we could four-wheel our way through to the main road. When we arrived at John and Celine's, Gabby and Xena took off into the woods with the huskies. Takoda and I gathered the two bags of presents from the back hatch and headed into the house.

As we opened the mudroom door and stepped into the kitchen, the wonderful aromas of roasting turkey, fresh-baked bread and coffee assailed me. Celine greeted us with hugs.

"Merry Christmas, girls! Come in, come in!"

"Merry Christmas, Mom."

"Merry Christmas! Wow, it smells great in here!" I returned Celine's hug. She was such an easy person to love.

The thought stopped me for a moment. I loved Takoda's folks. They made me feel welcome without judgment or expectations. I felt like part of the family even though I'd only known them a very short time.

I wondered if it would have been the same way had it been Takoda coming to my parents' house for Christmas. Would my parents have been even half as accepting of Takoda as her parents were of me? A flash of sadness ran through me.

John strode into the kitchen. "Merry Christmas!" He gave me a quick, hard "dad hug" which was much less involved than a "mom hug."

"Merry Christmas, John."

"How were the roads?" he asked.

Takoda said, "Passable. Hope they plan on coming out again tomorrow and widening it out."

"George is going to have a time of it."

"I imagine the double-lane highways are in better shape."

Celine opened the oven to baste the turkey. I joined her. "Can I help with anything?"

She smiled and shook her head. "Not yet. Probably later, but thank you, dear. Why don't you grab some coffee and keep me company, though?"

"Sure." I started to turn toward the cupboard to my right.

A warm hand on my left wrist stopped me abruptly. Celine cleared her throat. "Do you girls have something to tell us?" she asked as she studied the silver ring on my finger.

I opened my mouth but couldn't come up with any useful words.

Takoda said, "Uh. We're sort of engaged."

"Yup, we are," I agreed happily.

Takoda stepped behind me and wrapped her arms loosely around my waist. I leaned into her.

John whooped happily and clapped his daughter on the shoulder. "About damned time! Congratulations, both of you!"

Celine hurriedly set aside the baster and wrapped us both in another embrace. "Oh, this is wonderful! I'm so happy for you both!"

I couldn't stop the smile that settled on my face as we thanked her parents for their blessing. John wore a smug grin. "I knew you were special," he said to me. He glanced at Celine. "Didn't I say that? She's the one, I said."

"Yes, you did, dear."

"You two are scary," Takoda said flatly, then laughed. "I hate to think about what you're saying behind my back."

"Oh, the usual parental discussions."

"Right."

Celine retrieved the baster she'd set aside and returned to finishing with the turkey, which was already a nice golden brown. My mouth watered at the aroma of turkey and stuffing.

Takoda kissed the side of my head. "Love you," she murmured in my ear.

"Love you back," I whispered. I stepped away to get a coffee cup. I missed the contact immediately as her arms dropped away.

"Can you grab me a mug too?" she asked, "I'll pour for us both."

"Sure." I crossed the room, retrieving two mugs from the cupboard.

Celine said, "There's Bailey's in the 'fridge."

I did a double take, and Takoda asked, "Are you trying to get us drunk?"

Celine swatted her on the backside. "It's a celebration. So celebrate."

CHAPTER TWENTY-TWO

Christmas had landed on a Friday, and Takoda had to work Saturday. I had to be back at work on Monday. Knowing the holiday was over and our time together was running short made me sad, but I put on a positive face. I wanted to make the most of the time I had with Takoda.

We woke up late, so while Takoda showered and dressed, I made scrambled eggs and toast for breakfast. She ate quickly, repeatedly thanking me for cooking and apologized about eating and running. I poured most of the pot of coffee into her thermos as well as filling her favorite travel mug while she tied up her work boots and threw on her jacket.

"Be safe, love," I cautioned, setting the coffee on the little table to the right of the front door and then squeezing her tightly.

Her arms wound around me and she kissed the top of my head. "I will. Have a good day, *zaagi'idiwin*. I'll text or call if I can."

I tipped my head up and she teased my lips with her tongue. Desire blossomed as the kiss deepened between us until we parted to breathe. She leaned her forehead against mine. "Love you," she whispered.

"Love you back."

For a few moments, we stood breathing each other's air until I reluctantly stepped back. "You'd better get going."

"Yeah. I'd better." She zipped her jacket up, gathered the thermos and her mug and removed her keys from her pocket. "I'll see you soon." I opened the door for her. She dropped a last quick kiss on my cheek and slipped out into the cold.

I watched out the door's rectangular window until her Jeep disappeared down the driveway. The house was too quiet and empty without her presence. She hadn't been gone for five minutes, and I missed her already.

Shaking my head, I put on a second pot of coffee and let it brew while I put a couple more logs on the fire. The dogs ambled over and curled up on the rug in front of the hearth. I waited for the coffee to finish before I filled a travel mug and returned to the living room. I settled in the corner of the sofa, facing the fireplace, stretched my legs out and pulled a down throw over me.

More and more, over the past few months, I'd come to think of this house, and Takoda, as home. She made me feel warm inside. I'd never been in a relationship that felt so right or even had a friend I wanted to be with so constantly.

I never tired of Takoda's company. When I was with her, I never thought about wanting to get away. We could talk for hours. Or we could sit quietly and not talk at all. The thought of a life without Takoda made my stomach roil and my chest ache.

I loved her. I loved being able to make her lunch pail and send her out the door with a thermos full of coffee. I wanted to make her smile. I loved how she felt in my arms and how she reacted to my touch. I loved knowing I could generate the flame of desire in her eyes.

I thought about her proposal. She'd asked me to live with her, to marry her and be with her forever. I wanted to. I really did.

But what about all the reasons I'd left this area to begin with? I had gone away to school and never looked back. I'd created a life in the city because the small-minded people and the cliques in high school angered and frustrated me. It drove me crazy that everyone had expectations and judged me by my friends, my parents or my grades. When I'd gotten to the city, nobody had known who I was or who my friends were. I could be myself.

The disastrous relationship with my siblings also spun through my thoughts. They were yet another reason I'd left. I had no desire to be around them, putting up with their belittling teasing or button-pushing arguments. Living with Takoda meant I'd be closer to them than I'd been in many years. On the upside, Takoda and I would be available to support Nikko, and Darlene too. But could I keep my distance from Bethany and Tom?

Realistically, if I didn't seek them out, it was unlikely they'd come looking for me. And why should I allow them to dictate my actions? Wouldn't it be stronger of me to do what made me happy, regardless of their approval or disapproval? I'd been letting my family affect my decisions all my life. It was time for me to make my choices based on what I wanted, on what was best for me, and me alone.

I thought about my job. Would I perhaps be able to continue to work remotely, even in a lesser capacity? What if I had to quit? Would Takoda really be okay with that? I still had a fairly steady, if small, income from my fiction writing and editing, and I could easily branch out into doing more freelance editing while I was searching for something full time. There had to be companies in the area that could use a writer. Hell, I'd be willing to do secretarial work if it came to that so long as I had a job.

Depending on when Mom and Dad's house sold, there would be money from that, as well as what the twins owed me for my part of the cabin. No matter what, I wasn't going to be a kept woman. I could do my share.

As much as I had doubts, what I wanted—and what I needed—was to be here with the love of my life.

I started trying to build a mental list. What did I need to do to move here?

I had the apartment. I'd need to move all my stuff, maybe sell some of it or donate it, rent a U-Haul. My lease wasn't up until June, but maybe I could negotiate something to get out early.

I'd talk to Takoda when she got home and try to talk with Hayley on Monday. I wasn't sure what my options were or what Hayley's reaction would be, other than to say "I told you so." The thought of talking to her made feel a little anxious. Okay, a lot anxious. It was a big deal to change jobs after almost ten years in the same place.

I liked the security of sameness. I had never been the kind of person who moved from job to job, either to try new things or to make more money. I liked the people with whom I worked and I liked what I did. Until now, I had seen no reason to make a change.

I sipped my coffee. Gabby left her spot in front of the fireplace and jumped up to sit with me on the couch, stretching out along my legs to lay her head on my lap. I ran my fingers into her thick brindled fur. Xena still slept, sprawled in front of the hearth. The fire crackled quietly. I loved the coziness of it and I felt calmer watching the flames.

It was going to be so hard to leave tomorrow.

A cold chill moved through me as I imagined the silent starkness of my apartment. It would be like returning to a different world. But, really, wasn't that what I'd been doing for half my life? I lived in two separate worlds, the one that I fit into, being out and living my life the way I wanted to, and the other, where I pretended to be the person they thought I should be.

Marrying Takoda, living with her, I would finally be living one life, how I wanted to, with the woman I loved. I wouldn't have to hide any more. I didn't have to protect my parents and my siblings from my "differentness."

What Bethany and Tom thought no longer mattered.

So what did I have to worry about?

It was still a big step.

But was it any bigger than any other giant steps I'd made? I left home after high school to go to college in the city, not knowing anyone. I took a chance on a writing career instead of something staid and certain like teaching, which was what my parents preferred.

Takoda and I needed to talk. We needed to discuss logistics, and I needed to know, for sure, that we were thinking the same things and had the same expectations. In my heart, I'd made my decision, and my decision was to be here with Takoda for the rest of our days. Now I—no, we—had to figure out how to make it happen.

EPILOGUE

The fire blazing in the fireplace and the glow of the television provided the only light in the house. A late-February snowstorm howled furiously, rattling the windows and pelting the house with icy pellets. Takoda and I cuddled on the sofa with our feet up on the coffee table and a down blanket over our laps. She wrapped her arm around my shoulders, and I leaned into her side. The dogs slept near the hearth and a hockey game played on the flat screen.

Takoda yawned. "I'm wiped out, but I'm glad we got the last of your stuff moved before the weather hit."

"We got a lot done. I'll run to Goodwill with what's left in the garage when the roads are clear. It's good to finally be settled."

She kissed the side of my head. "I'm happy you're here."

"I am too. I'm tired of the commute."

In the end, there were only a few odds and ends of furniture that we kept from my apartment. We'd set up my writing desk in the back of the living room, with a view out the patio doors facing the lake. We'd also kept two bookcases and the framed posters of my book covers, proudly displayed near my desk.

I ended up quitting my job. Hayley had been less than accommodating about the possibility of working remotely. On the upside, I had a couple of freelance editing jobs lined up and was planning on enjoying a little time to get a lot of my own writing done while I hunted for a job locally. I'd still be spending time in the city because of the ongoing trials for the men who'd attacked us on our bikes. The initial trial ended up in a plea deal; the man got three years in jail. We all felt it should have been more, but at least it was something. There were two more trials pending next month. I wasn't stressed about it though. I had Takoda at my side, and no matter what, things would be all right.

"You're thinking awfully hard, *zaagi'idiwin*. I can almost hear your brain overheating."

I shifted closer. "Just thinking how lucky I am to have you."

She gave me a squeeze. "Not as lucky as me."

"Hmmm…" I worked a hand under her T-shirt, tracing my fingers up warm, soft skin while I placed teasing kisses along her neck. "Are you really watching that game?"

Takoda laughed and the television turned off with a click. "What game?"

Bella Books, Inc.

Women. Books. Even Better Together.

P.O. Box 10543
Tallahassee, FL 32302

Phone: 800-729-4992
www.bellabooks.com